THE
FORTUNE
SELLER

ALSO BY RACHEL KAPELKE-DALE

The Ingenue
The Ballerinas
Graduates in Wonderland (with Jessica Pan)

THE
FORTUNE
SELLER

A Novel

Rachel Kapelke-Dale

ST. MARTIN'S PRESS
NEW YORK

First published in the United States by St. Martin's Press, an imprint of St. Martin's Publishing Group

THE FORTUNE SELLER. Copyright © 2024 by Rachel Kapelke-Dale. All rights reserved. Printed in the United States of America. For information, address St. Martin's Publishing Group, 120 Broadway, New York, NY 10271.

www.stmartins.com

Library of Congress Cataloging-in-Publication Data

Names: Kapelke-Dale, Rachel, author.
Title: The fortune seller : a novel / Rachel Kapelke-Dale.
Description: First edition. | New York : St. Martin's Press, 2024.
Identifiers: LCCN 2023036061 | ISBN 9781250286130 (hardcover) |
    ISBN 9781250286147 (ebook)
Subjects: LCGFT: Novels.
Classification: LCC PS3611.A64 F67 2024 | DDC 813/.6—dc23/eng/20230825
LC record available at https://lccn.loc.gov/2023036061

Our books may be purchased in bulk for promotional, educational, or business use. Please contact your local bookseller or the Macmillan Corporate and Premium Sales Department at 1-800-221-7945, extension 5442, or by email at MacmillanSpecialMarkets@macmillan.com.

First Edition: 2024

10 9 8 7 6 5 4 3 2 1

For all of us who were young together

Let me tell you about the very rich. They are different from you and me. They possess and enjoy early, and it does something to them, makes them soft where we are hard, and cynical where we are trustful, in a way that, unless you were born rich, it is very difficult to understand. They think, deep in their hearts, that they are better than we are because we had to discover the compensations and refuges of life for ourselves. Even when they enter deep into our world or sink below us, they still think that they are better than we are. They are different.

—F. Scott Fitzgerald

I do not believe in a fate that will fall on us no matter what we do. I do believe in a fate that will fall on us if we do nothing.

—Ronald Reagan

There are a million ways to predict the future. Read the stars, shuffle tarot cards, study your palm; I'm sure it wouldn't take long on the internet to find people searching for answers in yarrow sticks or Nordic runes or chicken entrails. Ask your angels, pull a message from the oracle, and then just wait for it. The answer you're looking for.

You almost never get it, of course. Instead, you get a card that's about your current mental state, telling you to chill out. Or you get a card that answers the question you should have been asking but didn't. Or you get a card that seems utterly meaningless.

I can hear Annelise's voice now: *That's because nobody ever asks the one right question.*

BOOK 1

2005

1
THE FOOL

The thing about the Fool? He's excited. But he's also scared. It's like . . . he knows there's an adventure in front of him. But he doesn't know what it will bring. And he doesn't know if he's ready.

IN LATE AUGUST BEFORE senior year, I returned to Yale to find that my best friends had locked me out of our house.

If it were one of them, they would have simply gone to a boyfriend's apartment or the suite of a prep school friend—or, fuck, into the city for a night at the St. Regis, faster than you could say *Amex Black.* But I didn't have a boyfriend. I hated asking favors from anyone, let alone mere acquaintances. And though there was $3,000 in my bank account (enough for about three nights at the St. Regis), it was the most money I'd ever had at once, by a lot—and it had to last me until the following May.

I wasn't like them.

They didn't know it.

But I'm getting ahead of myself.

You cannot believe the beauty of Yale until you bathe in it yourself. And unlike some of my friends, who wrinkled their noses at the run-down city, the broken-glassed sidewalks and empty lots surrounding us, I found New Haven necessary to actually enjoying Yale. When we'd visited colleges the summer before my senior year of high school (driving through the night, my father grim-facedly adding up the costs of tuition), I'd found Princeton too precious, Harvard its own colonial world, Cornell and Dartmouth so impossibly remote they might as well have been in Western Plains. But to watch Yale's Gothic greenness arching up out of the jagged city around it—it was like plunging into a pool on a baking hot day.

And I was so ready for it. After two weeks in my southern Illinois hometown, a layover after a year in Buenos Aires, I felt dried out, like my skin was cracking from within.

I had craved the green of Yale before August even began. By the time I left for school, I could almost feel it in my hands, juicy as an aloe leaf. I thought about its trees, its grass, its stones, and its gates the whole eleven-hour trip: car to plane to subway to train.

Almost there. Almost back. Almost quenched.

I'd already realized that Cressida had forgotten to send me the keys to our shared house, of course. But these were the things my friends were particularly bad at. I always astonished them a little when I offered to return their overdue library books or to pay back the twenty dollars I'd borrowed. They looked at me like I was a stranger.

It took spending my junior year abroad—working at Miguel and Ana's polo stables, studying at the *universidad*—for me to realize the power of what I could do on my own. I didn't need my friends' approval. I didn't need to keep proving myself to them.

I was one of them, wasn't I? I'd been one of them for years.

As I stood outside the train station in the late-summer heat, I was already sweating through my white tank, wishing I'd worn my denim cutoffs instead of sweatpants. There was no sign of a taxi, and the walk toward campus offered little shade and *total danger,* as older girls had warned us our first year.

Then again, that had only made it more appealing to me, not less. I was brave. I'd always been the one grabbing the wildest horse for a trail ride, the one confronting a bitchy rider who was not being a *team player.* Besides, it couldn't have been more than two miles, and it was good to move my legs after all that sitting. Still, I could feel the grime of eleven hours of travel coating my damp skin as I walked, could feel my curly red hair frizzing out from its ponytail. The whole time, my mom's voice echoing in my head: *There's a fine line between brave and stupid, babycakes.*

But then, there it was: Whitney Avenue. My new home.

I saw the tower before I saw the house as a whole. From a spacious, grassy corner lot, that garret was visible before I'd even turned onto the street. Most off-campus housing was in run-down three-story houses with ancient vinyl siding kept by slumlords, as we called them, specifically to be rented out to a never-ending cycle of students one year at a time. The rest were college-owned, glossy modern apartments that *lacked character* and that none of my friends had any interest in.

No, Cress had written to me the previous spring when I'd mentioned getting one of those suites. She was the only one of our little equestrian group left on campus, training through junior year so she could go pro after graduation. *Just no.*

I'd trusted her. And I'd been right to. Our new home was a tasteful white Victorian with a wide wraparound porch, bay windows poking out from every side, and an enormous stained-glass panel framing the door in purple and red and gold.

I trotted up the front steps and rang the bell.

I could hear the little melody ringing out inside; around me, bees buzzed, everything smelled like summer and grass. I held myself back from ringing again too soon, but there were no thumping footsteps on what had to be hardwood floors.

I flipped my phone open. No calls, no messages. Cress's number went to voicemail after two rings, while Lila's was off. I didn't bother calling Andra; she never picked up.

I texted all three of them: Here! Anybody home?

Nothing.

The four of us had kept in touch throughout junior year, through expensive texts that wouldn't always send from the farm and what Lila called *Skypey* when the internet connection would allow for it, but I'd only had a few random emails from Lila and Andra over the summer, once they were back in the States. I was in Argentina through July, and they had quickly dropped into their summer routines of family travel and hometown parties without a backward glance.

Cress, on the other hand, sent rambling, almost manic emails with surprising regularity throughout the school year and summer—about her horses, the shows, the team, but most of all, about her new BFF, whom she was clearly waving in my face, trying to make me jealous.

Cress was my best friend, but was I still hers? Then again—who else would be? The other girls on the team had always treated her with a respect that bordered on awe. The kids she'd gone to Dalton with had always told her whatever she'd wanted to hear. It was one of the things she loved about me, she'd said many times—that I couldn't lie, not without a splotchy red blush spreading from my cheeks down to my neck and chest.

But could Annabelle, the new girl on the team, have taken my place? *Annabelle's such a great rider, Annabelle has this crazy style. Annabelle's like this beautiful witch, she's so floaty and ethereal and calm.* I'd never acknowledged any of it. Cressida was just mad that I'd gone abroad, mad because *You know I have to stay here, Rosie, if I'm ever going to win a thing after college. You're going to leave me all alone?*

But I think, deep down, she also respected that I'd stuck to my choice.

What she didn't know was that Argentina hadn't entirely been my choice. It had just been the cheapest program on offer—plus I had guaranteed free housing and even a job through a friend of our coach's.

I'd spent my whole childhood just outside doorways beyond which my parents whispered furiously about paying suppliers, about this month's gas bill, about new shoes. Eighteen years of that made being among my Yale friends a revelation. The idea that if you needed something, you could just buy it, pay for it, and forget about it. The idea that if you were stuck in a bad situation, you could just leave, pay to transport yourself somewhere else.

The idea that all of life was open to you, not just a little sliver of it—that all you had to do was go around pointing at things, experiences, people. Saying *mine, mine, mine.*

The ability to choose?

That was my idea of heaven.

I MET CRESSIDA TATE EARLY IN OUR FIRST year at Yale. It's so easy now to say, yes, she had an aura; yes, everyone knew her name, knew about her father's money. But there are actual Kennedys at Yale, princesses and heiresses and stars; there are models and actresses; there's every kind of person you never thought you'd meet in real life, gathered all around you. The daughter of a hedge-fund manager wasn't all that notable.

But in a place where nobody stared at the famous people, they stared at her because she was just so beautiful. She was like an Old Master painting; she glowed in a way you couldn't name but you couldn't tear your eyes from. And she dressed so perfectly, every detail so exactly right that you felt if you studied her hard enough, you could learn how to do it, too.

That's why the straight girls stared at her, at least. The straight boys stared at her for a different reason; she was voted *hottest new meat* by the frats our first year.

Tate. I hadn't put it together yet. At that point, assuming she was related to Grayson would have been like meeting a Becky McDonald and assuming she was related to Ronald. What were the odds? I still hadn't realized that, at Yale, when you met a DuPont—yes, they were one of *those* DuPonts. If you met a Rockefeller—yes, they were one of *those* Rockefellers. And if they weren't, you could bet they'd tell you, if somewhat abashedly, in your first or second conversation.

From the first equestrian recruitment meeting, I heard the other girls whispering about her. She didn't come—why would she? From what everyone had said, Cress was basically already guaranteed a spot. She was that good. By the end of that session, as senior captains Mallory and Beth explained the logistics of tryouts and the season's schedule, the sound of Cressida's whispered name had already started to get my back up. Cressida Tate. What kind of girl had that kind of name?

And I got even pricklier when I saw her riding an incredible thoroughbred around the outside paddock during the tryouts themselves. While I was trapped in the inner ring, walking and trotting and basically proving that, yes, I did know what a horse was, I caught glimpses of that horse's coat gleaming in the sun every time I passed the open door.

"If I make it, what are the chances I get to ride *her*?" I asked Mallory on the way back to the barn.

She followed my gaze to Cress's horse.

"Bambi?" she said, and snorted. "She's Cressida's. A present from his holiness. She pays a fucking fortune to board her here, but what do you expect from a first-year with a Range Rover? Good luck getting her to share. The horses *we* ride are mostly rescues."

But I was still looking at Cress, soaring over the jumps in creamy leggings. The kind you could only wear once or twice before staining irrevocably. "His holiness?" I said absently.

"Grayson Tate." Mallory and Chips, the school's gray gelding, had gone up ahead, and she threw an impatient look over her shoulder. "Billionaire developer. Hedge-fund founder. Sponsor of the team? Also, Cressida's dad."

Sponsor of our 4-H club, too, back in Western Plains. Once a fort for wagon trails going farther west, to somewhere fortune could still be found, the town now had a main street of whitewashed storefronts, displaying only what *used to be*: a Woolworth's, a Gimbels, an A&P. Outside of town, there were fields of monocrops where farmers took their government subsidies or sold out to corporations, whichever devil they found easier to live with. And then there was my parents' little veterinary practice, still chugging along out of our ramshackle Victorian *mansion*, as the locals called it with no trace of irony. One hundred fifty years in the Macalister family, even though the neighboring dairy had sold out to Nestlé (with their in-house vets) the year before. We were proud of that.

"Oh," I muttered. "Of course."

I didn't meet Cressida that day. She was yards ahead of me in ability, miles ahead socially. Anyway, she was always with two other girls, sleek brunettes: pleasant-faced Lila and sly-eyed Andra, never *Alexandra*. The three of them reminded me of a gang of cats that had once taken up residence in our back shed. Thin as anything but glossy, as though they'd been taken care of; looking sweet as pie but hissing like devils whenever you'd come near them.

My social life at the time focused exclusively on the first people I'd met in my own college. Plain, serious girls who planned to major in science, nice but awkward boys whose jeans came from Hollister. It was discomfiting that they were at Yale, too—kids like the ones I'd grown up with. The bland ones I thought I'd gotten away from. Mostly, they were just people I hung out with during orientation so I wouldn't have to go to things alone—the ice cream socials, the welcome dances, the safe-sex talks.

Cressida Tate didn't do ice cream socials.

No, I didn't meet her until a week after making the equestrian team.

Did I know, as I looked around the classroom of EQ girls during our first official meeting, that they would end up being my only college friends? Of course I knew. And I was vibrating like a rung bell with the joy of it. These girls weren't wearing anything you could get at the mall.

And Cressida Tate, with her perfectly waved pale beach hair, her tan from a summer in Greece still dark. Her earrings (Chanel but without the interlocking Cs; she found anything with a logo on it *tacky as fuck,* she would *never*) were slick mother-of-pearl disks that winked in the light. She looked like a tall Olsen twin—at the time, the absolute paradigm of cool. Heart-shaped face, pointy chin, huge eyes. At her side, Andra Cooper, shiny and self-satisfied, and Lila Farrow, an apple-cheeked girl with glossy chestnut hair who seemed by far the nicest of the group.

My future friends, the only other first-years. But I couldn't bring myself to talk to them yet; not even Lila. They already knew some of the upperclassmen from their time competing on the junior circuit, and were chatting languidly with any who stopped in front of them.

Mallory, the captain, explained how it would work. We were divided into levels based on our competition history. As I'd never done an official show (did 4-H count? I certainly wasn't going to ask), they were placing me in Walk-Trot-Canter, the second-lowest level, stacking the deck. I'd have lessons with Kelly, Lacy, and Anna: two sophomores and a senior who'd never managed to make her way up the ranks. Andra was Novice; Lila, Intermediate; and Cressida was placed in the highest level, Open.

Without lessons together, we'd only ever see each other at shows. Yet, I was still on the team. I still had a place where I belonged; and as far as Yale went, it was a good one. It wasn't Skull and Bones, but it still said: I am an athlete. I have talent.

I have money.

I wore my gear to meet the rest of my level for our first lesson of the season. I didn't know yet that I could change at the barn. At the library, I'd printed out MapQuest directions to the place where Anna had said to meet—a couple miles off campus. Could that be right? But she was a senior, she must live in a house with friends. And so I trudged through the already-turning leaves in the stiff Ariat show boots my parents had gotten me for graduation (should have worn paddock boots and half chaps, like

I did back home—but these girls were fancy, surely they'd be wearing show gear?), blisters already grating on my heels.

The Gothic arches fell away, replaced by town houses. The town houses fell away, replaced by row houses. There were a hundred trees per block—then fifty—then ten. Stained glass gave way to double glazing gave way to chipboard and flapping plastic and duct tape.

I stopped in front of a boarded-up house, one side of it sunk into the ground at almost a forty-five-degree angle, planks from its small porch plucked out like missing teeth.

This couldn't be right.

I double-checked the directions. My feet throbbed; the Ariats were so stiff they could have been made of cement.

Behind me, the faint sound of male voices sent my heart stuttering. I was wildly out of place in my shiny black boots, my skintight beige leggings, the J.Crew outlet purse that looked so much more expensive than it was and that held the flip phone I'd begged for as well as all the cash I had for the rest of the month (what if we went out to lunch afterward? Better to look flush, surely?).

The voices hooted and hollered. I squinted into the windows surrounding me, but I couldn't see anyone. They sounded closer. They sounded like they were talking about me. They sounded—

And then a black Jeep. No, a Range Rover, a car I hadn't even realized existed in America until I saw Cressida Tate cruising around campus in it. The team assumed that enough girls would bring cars that they didn't organize public transport from campus to the stables. Instead, they left it to each group to figure out who would drive the rest.

Cressida, as usual, was one step ahead.

The car rolled up in front of me. As I stared at its tinted windows, it suddenly occurred to me that it wasn't necessarily Cressida inside; it could be anyone. But then the driver's window rolled down.

Cressida, three-quarters of her face covered by Jackie O sunglasses, 50 Cent blaring from her radio.

"Get in," she said.

"What—"

She pushed her sunglasses up into her hair. And then, she made the strangest face I'd ever seen. An index finger on either side of her mouth, her middle fingers pulling her eyes down. It was a grotesque mask of a face, a ridiculous, disgusting expression—and I never would have thought such a beautiful girl would stoop to making it.

"Get. In," she said again through her stretched lips. Then she let them go and giggled.

I didn't know it yet, but Cress had a deeply silly streak. The kind of silliness an uglier girl, even an average-looking girl, would have hidden. Later, during sophomore year, she had a horrible allergic reaction to aspirin. Her whole face swelled up until she looked like a cross between a purple balloon and a red chipmunk. But she just stood in front of the mirror, laughing and laughing. She wouldn't let us take her to health services until we got a photo of it.

I scampered into the car, where calm washed over me and I took a breath so deep I could feel the bottom of my lungs. It took me a minute to figure out why. It was the cool of the air conditioning. The scent of the black leather seats. The thrum of the bass in tune, it seemed, with the powerful engine.

"Thank you so much," I gasped. "But how did you—"

"They did it to me yesterday," she said, bumping up over the curb as she made the most egregious U-turn I'd ever seen.

"But Anna's not in your group . . . ?" I said.

She paused so long I could practically hear her eyes roll.

"It's hazing," she said, an unspoken *you idiot* hanging between us. "Did you really think Anna lived here?"

The empty beer cans on the porch, one of them turned on its side and rolling back and forth in the wind. The hoots and hollers that might have followed us, that I could no longer hear from inside the car. The pair of ancient sneakers tied together and hung over a telephone wire.

"Somebody does," I said softly.

"I know," she said, and wrinkled her nose beneath her sunglasses. "Ew."

THE MORE I THOUGHT ABOUT my friends, the more I suspected I already knew exactly how to get into the house. I followed the porch around back, and sure enough, the screen door swung open at my touch.

I stepped into the kitchen, which definitely wasn't designed for students. Had the house been left by some professor on sabbatical? The floor was wonderful, blue and white Portuguese tile that was echoed in the backsplash over the sink. A huge slab of a driftwood table surrounded by chairs with a distinct designer feel to them took up the center of the room. Already there were water rings on its unfinished surface; already there were piles of dishes overflowing from the sink onto almost every inch of counter space. Flies buzzed over a pan *left to soak,* rainbow grease shining on its surface; and yet, all I could think was, one of them *cooked* something?

It made me smile.

Sophomore year, the common areas of the suite we'd all shared after ditching our randomly assigned first-year roommates had been disgusting. It was only my perfunctory attempts at tidying up that had kept it from slipping into a full-on biohazard. I hadn't minded because my own single room was clean. The other girls hadn't seemed to notice the squalor of their own rooms. After all, we were almost never there.

I slipped into the main hallway, lit from the sun filtering through heavily curtained windows. A double-depth living room featured a suite of elegant white couches that, though pristine, made me wince. All I saw was nine months' worth of dabbing away red wine stains in the faint hope that I'd get my six-hundred-dollar security deposit back.

An image of me in the Argentinian paddock, finally breaking Perdita, the wild horse nobody'd been able to get near, flickered briefly in my memory. Would that girl have cleaned up somebody else's wine stains? No. And she wouldn't have cared about a piddling security deposit either.

Up the wide wooden staircase, my sneakers squeaked the whole way. Cress must have done some number on the owners. Really, who in their right mind would have rented this place to a bunch of students? I stopped at the top, pausing for a moment to watch the light dance through the golden stained-glass scroll above the window seat at the end of the long hall. To smell the warm wood, the beeswax and polish, to imagine the family that must have vacated the place just months before. It made me ache.

The first door, the same gleaming walnut wood as the floorboards, had a tarot card taped on it: the Queen of Swords. *Andra,* somebody'd scrawled beneath it in handwriting I didn't recognize. The next had the

Queen of Wands with *Lila* below. Then a tiled bathroom, already in disarray.

On the other side of the hall, the Empress: *Cressida*. I couldn't help it; I twisted the doorknob to peek at the room she'd chosen for herself. The tower room, the garret that I'd seen from outside. Two levels with a spiral staircase connecting them; the second level was just a wrought-iron walkway, its walls lined with bookshelves, empty now except for a few crumpled, quilted handbags here and there. Cress was never much of a reader. Below, a white wicker bed with a silk quilt twisted up with a sheet, clothes on the floor mixed in with bootjacks, lotions, magazines.

The last, then. A blank door, the one that had to be mine. But it took me a minute to open it, the metal knob sticking in the heat.

The room overflowed with color and life.

Eggplant velvet curtains hung at the windows. There was a blue, purple, and red mandala tapestry on the long wall, a photo of a bare-breasted Janis Joplin. Half a dozen plants, scattered on side tables, an antique bureau, the windowsills. Overlapping rugs of various colors and patterns.

Cressida had promised to furnish my room, but this?

That was when I noticed that the far half of the room was empty.

I flung open the closet door. There, overstuffing exactly half of the small space, was a jumbled collection of bohemian garb. Patterned cotton scarves that would wrap around a neck six or seven times. Chandelier earrings. And mixed in with them, the kinds of attire my friends always defaulted to: tall polished boots, pea coats, cashmere.

Whoever lived here, she had style.

But she wasn't me.

I was supposed to share my room, and no one had told me? I'd been gone for a year, but so had Lila and Andra. And just because I was poorer than they were, I'd been demoted to coach?

I took a deep breath, smoothing my palms down the front of my jeans. It could be a mistake; there must be another room that I'd missed. I went back into the hallway. But the only doors were the ones I'd already seen.

There had to be an explanation. Cress would tell me why.

2
THE THREE OF CUPS

*People always say that the Three of Cups is about sisterhood,
about celebration. And that's true, to some extent. I mean, look
at these chicks. They're raising their glasses, they've got flowers
in their hair. It's girl power squared. But you have to remember
that the movement from two to ace in each suit is a journey. And
here, we're only on three. So it's not the overflowing, unconditional
love you get from, say, the Ace of Cups. It's a little juvenile. It's a
little . . . shallow, almost.*

But that doesn't mean it's not nice.

I POKED AROUND DOWNSTAIRS while I waited. A library—okay, we were
definitely in a professor's domain here—with a stained-glass bay window.
A half bath with a toilet and sink; at least we wouldn't have to deal with
the crew team vomiting in our upstairs bathroom during parties. A
wood-paneled room with a huge flat-screen TV and framed Audubon
prints dotting the walls. A dining room where, I was relieved to see, the
glass display cabinets had been cleared of the china that they must normally have housed. The one pragmatic decision these professors made
before renting their beautiful house to messy college girls (*Smart people*,
my mother always says, *are dumb*).

But anyone would have trusted Cressida, I realized. With her jaunty,
pointy little chin and her wide, guileless eyes. With that clear aura of
money radiating from her designer clothes, expensive highlights, car. If
anything got damaged, they must have known she'd pay for it.

Slightly reassured, I sank into the leather couch in the den. It couldn't have been more than five minutes before I was sound asleep.

I DREAMED OF EMILY, my best friend from back home. The only friend I'd kept in touch with since I'd gotten out of there. She was arguing with me about why the car wash was an acceptable post-graduation employment choice for me, and she wouldn't listen to any of my arguments, not a single one. In the dream, I was so frustrated I began to cry.

But then their voices, bright and laughing, woke me.

I sat up quickly, my face yanking away from the leather couch like I was removing a Band-Aid.

"And then she pulled the Page of—" Cress was saying, but she must have heard my footsteps because she came whirling around the corner at full speed. The scent of verbena enveloping me, the reality of her hard, warm body barreling into me. It was overwhelming in the best possible way.

"Rosie-Rose!" she cried, pulling back, hands on my shoulders. Her eyes danced over my face, stopping as she frowned at the red mark on my cheek. Long fingers darted up and she was palming my face, as if I were a little kid and she were my mother. "Where *were* you?"

I blinked at her. "Argentina?"

She laughed. "No, just now! Were you here all along?"

"I got here this afternoon. I texted . . ."

She waved a hand. "I can't find my stupid phone. I can't believe you're back! I missed you so much, it was total hell here without you. Come in, say hi!"

I followed her into the kitchen. Lit bright by the hanging lamp against the night-mirrored windows, it dazzled me. The first thing I saw were Andra's legs, long and tan. She'd spent last year in Bologna, trotting down cobblestoned streets in expensive heels. Of the four of us, she was the absolute worst about keeping in touch, and that was saying something. I'd seen her pixelated face over Skype just a handful of times, always for only a few broken-up minutes as I held my computer closer to the window in the vague hopes of a better connection, as she sat on her balcony and laughed a chopped-up version of her laugh.

Andra and her high cheekbones and tilted eyes; everything about her was carved like an Art Deco figurehead. She was terrifying. I'd found her too scary to talk to at first. Until one evening—at a party at the end of first year—when I was drunk and heartbroken over Davy, a fuck buddy who'd never turned into anything more, I'd found myself confiding in her.

She'd listened unblinking, then turned to the room.

"Hey, Davy!" she called out.

"Yo," a voice came back, muffled by the crowd. She elbowed her way toward him, dragging me in her wake.

"Let me see your phone."

Davy looked at her for a second, nearly swaying, and then his soft face melted more as he grinned.

"What—"

But she'd already grabbed it out of his hand and dropped it into his red Solo cup.

From that point on, Andra was terrifying *for* me.

"Get over here, bitch," she called, wagging two fingers and a cigarette at me. I ran to her, kissing either cheek. She grinned. "Now go away," she said, fluttering her hand to the countertop where Lila sat, cross-legged, drinking what smelled like gin out of a stoneware mug.

Lila was so much like Annie Hall in appearance and voice that I actually thought of her as Annie for the first six months we knew each other. Annie Hall if Annie Hall wore Marc Jacobs, all black leggings and studs and rips. But she had the same face, full-cheeked and open; the same chestnut hair, though she straightened it until it hung in sleek curtains; the same lilting voice and funny, antiquated expressions.

"For heaven's sake," she'd mutter when she stubbed her toe.

For a long time, I thought the weird good-girl act was a by-product of her all-girls high school called, of all things, Miss Porter's. But when I said as much to Cress, she'd just rolled her eyes.

"I don't know what rom-com you think Lila came out of," she said, "but that place is *twisted*. Some of the girls who come out of there . . . fuck." She raised a shoulder. "Just twisted."

I was working with a sample size of one. How was I to know?

She'd spent last year in Prague, surrounded by writers in smoky basement bars. I would have given almost anything to overhear just one of their conversations. In contrast to Andra, Lila was the one who'd emailed us all about Skype; Lila was the one who called most often. My heart had sped up when I first saw her username, Lilaly83, pop up on my screen. What did the two of us have to talk about? I couldn't remember ever having hung out one-on-one before.

But the thing about Lila was that she could ramble on forever without any reply. I wondered sometimes if she felt a different version of the same nervousness I did with the other girls. You know those moments where you zoom out from the conversation and it's like you're observing from the ceiling? I'd always think, I've ended up in a room full of rich girls.

Lila's parents were lawyers and far richer than anybody in Western Plains, of course. But they worked for their money, unlike Andra's chocolate-bar-heir father and socialite mother. And they probably topped out around seven figures a year, unlike Cress's father's ten (though during one very good year, *Forbes* had estimated *eleven* figures; I'd been through the library archives).

I'd come to like Lila's nervous babbling. It brought us closer together. And, I hoped, my *calm unflappability* (another trait Cress had annoyingly attributed to *Annabelle,* as it was a trait I prided myself on) had finally struck her as valuable, too.

"Lila-Ly!" I called, and threw myself into her arms. She always smelled like daisies, and she kissed the top of my head.

"Oh my gosh, you got taller!" she said. "You guys, didn't Rosie get taller?"

"I'm twenty-one," I said. "I don't think that happens anymore."

She widened her eyes. "But it did. Or maybe you just got strong? Look how strong you are!"

Cress had gone over to the stove, which was something I'd never seen before. I went up behind her and wrapped my arms around her waist.

"It's so good to be back," I muttered into her shoulder. Then I pulled away, staring at the boiling pot of water on the burner in front of her. "Cress, are you—are you making *pasta?*"

She blew out her lips. "Yeah, right. I tried once last year. Did you know if you forget to set a timer, the pasta just disappears? It just *goes away*." Her eyes were huge, half her face.

"Yeah," I said, trying not to laugh too hard. "It dissolves."

"They should put that on the box! Anyway, I'm making tea."

I glanced at the tea kettle on the back burner, then looked over at Andra, who shook her head. I decided not to ask the obvious question and tried another instead.

"Cress, how did you *get* this place, even?"

"It's the dean's!" her voice bounced back, chirpy.

"The . . ."

She twisted around. "The dean of finance? The bursar or something? The guy was friends with my dad back in the day."

"And he just . . . left?"

She giggled, turning back to the stove. "He had a sabbatical year, or his wife was sick or something? Maybe both. I think they're in England? Anyway, we have to keep it nice. That's why we've been so clean."

My eyes darted to the greasy sink pots.

"So last year was good? You're a total Olympic superstar now?"

That had been Cress's excuse for not going abroad. Personally, I'd always thought that her on-again, off-again boyfriend Blake finally asking her to be his *girlfriend-girlfriend* at the end of sophomore year had something to do with it as well—but I'd never have dared say so. Cress liked to believe she was completely independent. That she, and she alone, was responsible for what happened to her, for how she moved through the world. The idea that a boy could have changed the course of her life? Unthinkable.

We never challenged her on it. Because there was the underlying question, the question you could really never ask: If she weren't independent, if she weren't the source of all of her good fortune . . . well, who was?

"Um, *yes*, basically," she said with a giggle. "Shannon went so fucking hard on us, she was like a totally different person. But with Annelise on board, she really thinks we can win Ivies this year, so it makes sense she'd go hard."

Annelise. Not Annabelle. I'd remembered it wrong.

To tell the truth, I hadn't thought she'd be worth remembering, once Cress had her actual friends back.

I also hadn't been entirely convinced she was real.

"Annelise?" I said.

"Oh my God," Andra said, black eyes boring into Cress. "You said you'd *tell* her."

"I forgot! Annelise," Cress continued, "she's the best. The absolute best. She's like this crazy fortune-teller, if the fortune-teller were also Mark Todd."

The Kiwi eventer who'd won every competition he'd ever entered. As good at dressage as he was at show jumping and cross-country. Rider of the twentieth century, Mark Todd?

I tried to put the pieces together. "She's an eventer?"

We didn't event in college equestrian. We did equitation: showing off our riding skills on horses we'd never ridden before.

It's about how pretty you look on a horse, Mallory had explained three years earlier. *While still maintaining control.*

"She's an eventer, she's a jumper, and before she got here, she'd *never competed before*," Lila cut in, "not even once! So she's still in the low levels and we win, like, every single time."

"And," Cress said, sipping her tea with a wince at the heat, "she wants to go pro next year. Like me."

"Wow," I said. "She sounds great."

But the point of senior year had not been to make new friends. The point of senior year had been to get the same confidence my old ones had.

"Anyway, she'll be back tonight, so you'll meet her soon enough," Lila finished.

Suddenly, it fell into place. She wasn't just on the team—she lived here, too. With me.

"Can't wait," I said stiffly. "But why am I the one sharing a room with her when I haven't even met her?"

All three of them looked down simultaneously. They couldn't have timed it better if they'd rehearsed, dark lashes sweeping against full cheeks. That practiced innocence.

Cress spoke up first.

"You're going to *love* her," she said. "Seriously, the two of you? Total soul mates." She held up crossed fingers. "And last year was just so messy. But then it all turned out so well! I got so close to Annelise, and I couldn't let her live in the dorms, Rosie. I just couldn't. And anyway, you said you wanted the smallest room. And Annelise said the same thing. But there were only four, so if we divided one up—"

"But you didn't even ask," I said.

Cress sat up straight, her eyes kitten round.

"I really didn't think you would mind. Seriously. Oh my God, if I did, I would have asked in a heartbeat! But you're always so laid-back, and Annelise is *amazing*. I think when you meet her, you'll be excited. You'll love her, you really will."

"You think?"

She ignored my tone. "It was so lonely last year without you guys. But then I got to know her from the team—she transferred from Stanford. And like Lila said, we got to put her in Walk-Trot-Canter, and she swept it. Blue at every show." On college equestrian teams, Walk-Trot was the lowest group, the beginner's group.

"She's amazing," Lila echoed, her voice rising to a chipper, flutey pitch that she used before shows to pump the team up. *C'mon, girls! We got this.*

"Okay," I said, unable to keep the chill out of my voice, frozen between fear and anger. I'd never been mad at Cress before, not to her face; how would she react? "But if she's so *amazing*, why isn't one of you living with her? Why me?"

A second of silence rose up between us.

"Come on," Andra said to Lila, who unfolded her legs and pushed off of the counter. They were right—this wasn't about them. But how quickly they left me alone with Cress made my blood run cold.

I wasn't scared of her. She was my friend, she loved me.

Besides, I was the girl who'd tamed Perdita.

"Cress, this is messed up."

Her pale arched brows drew together.

"But you're going to love her. Everyone does."

"That's not really the point. I don't even know her, Cress. And—"

"But nobody knows her. And *someone* had to share."

"*You* know her, Cress! *You* do."

"Yeah, okay. But I'd already signed the lease for us and taken the corner room, and I'm paying nine hundred—way more than anyone else. And I can, so it seemed like the people who wanted to pay less should be the ones to get to pay less, you know? And"—she grimaced—"can you *imagine* putting that poor girl in with one of the others? They'd eat her alive."

I blinked away.

"Look," she said, and she grabbed my wrists with her warm, strong hands. "I knew you'd be nice to her. I knew you'd be *kind*. And I knew you'd love her as much as I do."

"I don't know. I mean, maybe I can look into getting a dorm room—"

Like I ever would have. But Cress's eyes flared.

"No! No, Rosie. Fuck, I'm sorry, I didn't know you'd take it like this. It is way cheaper, after all. And I thought that's what you wanted when you said *small*. Don't be like that, come on."

Confidence. This is what confidence could do. Beyond which—

"Cheaper?"

"Well, since you're splitting it, it's three hundred instead of six hundred." She searched my face. "But seriously, if it's that big a deal, we could talk to the other girls and see if either of them want to share. Just don't go back to the dorms. Seriously, Rosie. Come on."

But the acid-sour anger in me was already being swept away in the wave of relief.

Three hundred dollars.

Three hundred dollars a month to me was a fortune. I had three thousand saved from the summer when I'd been able to work on the farm full-time, but that wouldn't last me long. Not with the way we lived.

Three hundred a month would make all the difference.

Cress, with her endless allowance, with her unlimited supply of everything, couldn't possibly know that.

But Cress also divided restaurant bills to the penny. Cress was the one who made sure I never had to pay more than my fair share.

"Yeah," I said. "Yeah, no. You're right. It'll be fine."

Her face softened. "Good. By the way, there's an IKEA bed for you in the linen closet upstairs. The house was furnished, but there was only one bed in that room. See, I didn't forget! I remembered!"

"Great," I said weakly.

Cress grabbed my hand and squeezed. "You're back. I'm so glad you're back," she said. "And I can't wait for you to meet Annelise. She's like this mystical—guru—genius, I don't know. You have to meet her to understand." I tried to remember the first time Cress had mentioned Annelise, but I all I could remember was my own bitterness. "She's this amazing rider, she's funny as fuck, she's the coolest. She's like nobody I've ever met before. At first, I thought she was this total hippie freak show, I'll be honest. But once she actually starts reading the tarot cards for you, it's . . . I mean, you get this feeling that everything makes sense. The world makes sense, and it's like it's the first time you ever saw it? Like everything always has been and always will be all right, and you just needed her to tell you about it to understand." She stopped, seeing my face. "I can't explain it. But five minutes with her and I swear—" She let off with a sigh. "You're going to love her."

All I could think was: She's going to smell like patchouli, isn't she?

"Guys, come *back*," Cress called. And suspiciously fast, both Andra and Lila returned to the room.

"I was just saying how great Annelise is," Cress said.

"*So* great," Lila said with huge eyes, pouring herself more wine.

"The greatest," Andra said, less sarcasm than usual in her low voice.

Perfect, I thought. I'm rooming with a cult leader.

3

THE MOON

It looks like the moon's constantly changing, but it's always the same, really. You know? It's not actually getting bigger and smaller. It's always the whole sphere, even though we can't see it. It's only our perception of it that changes.

And that's kind of how the Moon card works. It's saying you have to cut through all the bullshit that your subconscious is telling you, all those childhood fears and anxieties and insecurities. Only then can you see what's actually there.

You have to want it, though. You have to really, really want it.

BUT THE CULT LEADER DIDN'T come back, even after I'd assembled the IKEA bed the girls had left for me and fallen hard asleep. And she was already gone when I woke up in the morning. I got that she wanted to be a future Olympian or whatever, but who needed to ride *that* much?

"Where is she this time?" I asked Lila out on the porch late the next afternoon. She rolled over in the hammock to look at me.

"Cress? At the stables, I think."

"No, Annelise." Hard to keep the sarcasm out of my voice.

"Oh." She sat up. "Probably at the stables, too. She rides, like, a crazy amount. Like, *crazy* crazy," she said, and I wondered, not for the first time, how a Yale student could have such a limited vocabulary. "But you're right, it's weird, Andra and I were talking about it." She leaned forward, her voice dropping, and I fell into the chair across from her. "She disappears for, like, hours and hours at a time. And she never tells us where she's going."

"Did you ask?"

"I mean, I'm *sure* someone did. It's got to be some guy, that's what Andra said."

"Why wouldn't she tell you if it was?"

"Yeah," Lila said, flopping onto her back, the hammock swinging wildly to and fro. "That's what *we* want to know."

IN THE GLISTENING DARK OF THAT second night back, our original group—Cress, Andra, Lila, and me—piled into Cress's Range Rover and drove over to Olivia's loft. Annelise, it turned out, had gone into the city for the day (the city being New York City, the only city that any of us really believed mattered). But even Cress didn't know why.

"Shopping?" she'd said with a raised shoulder. "She's there all the time, but she gets weird if you ask her too much. Anyway, she said she'd meet us at the party."

So that was that. And anyway, I was happy for it to be just us again. As we rode through the old New England streets, Coldplay blasting as loud as the stereo would go, too loud for talking, we started to meld again into a unified whole in my mind. Just like we were before: except this time, I would prove that I was their equal.

The bubble lasted until Cress killed the motor and we had to get out of the car. In the August night, my white silk minidress, intentionally loose, shivered around me, my chandelier earrings chiming in the wind. I'd saved the outfit from too-muchness with my Grecian sandals—I'd thought. But now, as we filed into the loft, I felt ridiculous beside the designer jeans and simple tank tops the others wore. Conspicuous. A feeling I'd known from my first two years at Yale and yet somehow had forgotten existed. I was part of my friends' group, yes. I was a key part of it, though I still didn't fully understand how. But I wasn't at all part of their *scene.*

Olivia was a Dalton girl right out of a Ralph Lauren ad: shiny brown hair that swung from side to side as she walked, every seam and corner and edge of her perfectly polished. I'd never liked her; she spoke so slowly that by the time she finished a sentence, I couldn't remember how it had started. But her loft fit her like a pair of broken-in boots: dark velvet couches, a gallery wall of framed pictures, a blue-and-white-striped love seat. She'd had the exposed bricks painted over, matte white. (Of course she had.) It was an adult's apartment; "SexyBack" and "Mr. Brightside" screaming from a top-notch sound system only made the strangeness of this space belonging to a college girl even more glaring.

Cress actually hated Olivia. The feeling was mutual, for some unremembered or unspoken slight back at Dalton. But *you have to go to parties or you stop getting invited to parties,* Cress had told me earnestly our first year. And Oliva's mother sat on almost every charity board in New York City, while Anthea, Cressida's mother, was famous for her generous checks and the number of events of all stripes that she managed to fit into a season.

So Cress and Olivia pretended to be friends in front of each other. But one of Cress's more infamous first-year pranks was capturing the mouse that had been haunting her suite for weeks, gift-wrapping it (she put holes in the box, she wasn't a total monster), and leaving it outside Olivia's room. Lila loved that one. I always worried about the mouse. No version of the story ever revealed what had happened to it.

For the first hour or so, we clustered together by the door, whispering about the crowd. This was my favorite part of every party: the part where we were together. Us against the world for a brief moment before the world began to absorb us, to take us one-by-one into the masses. No Solo cups here; after grabbing some cut-crystal glasses and a bottle from the kitchen, Cress poured our wine as she filled us in on the people we hadn't seen in over a year, the people I hadn't missed. Davy, the guy who'd broken my heart first year, was now rumored to have herpes. Fawn, a girl who'd tried out for the equestrian team all three years, was pointedly avoiding us.

"Cressy," a voice boomed, and I knew that our bubble had been popped. Blake towered over us, swooping down to kiss her. He was enormous, a rower, and apparently a pretty good one at that. Though I never really knew how anyone could tell, because weren't there a bunch of boys in the boat all at once? We didn't have crew in Western Plains. Where would they have practiced—the high school pool?

But I knew the score. Dark-haired Blake would appear with his *Zoolander* quotes and his absolute lack of anything resembling a personality or style except, in summer, a penchant for seersucker. And then the other crew boys would amble up around him, all as tall, all as muscular, all utterly interchangeable to me. I'd had to work hard to memorize Blake, particularly during those first weeks of their relationship three years earlier when he'd seemed like just another Ken-doll jock. The rest were still indistinguishable.

That type wasn't for me. I wanted someone gentle. A musician, maybe. Someone quiet. Someone who listened more than they spoke, thought more than they listened. They must have existed at Yale. But I'd never met one, though I suspected that the group of boys smoking outside of the arts building day and night had potential. Anyway, those types of guys probably went somewhere else. Bennington. Maybe Brown.

I knew the drill, and I nodded at Lila and Andra. Together, we inched slightly away from Cress and Blake until we'd formed a closed-off circle a few feet away. Just in time, too; a roar at the door told us the other crew members had arrived.

Which meant that for me, the best part of the night was basically over. Once Cress left the group, the others would start to scatter. Sure enough, it was only minutes before Andra drifted away with Milo, a boy she'd been occasionally hooking up with since September of first year, casting an apologetic look over her shoulder. Then it was just Lila and me, blinking at each other.

"Do you think it'd be kind of hot if I started dating girls?" she asked absentmindedly. As I stared at her, trying to work out a response, the thinnest blonde I'd ever seen came up and threw her arms around Lila with a shriek. Someone from Miss Porter's, I divined from their chattering. I guess they'd gone skiing together a few times.

I slipped away.

But then I was just alone at their party. And it was *their* party. Each one of them had friends and boyfriends and acquaintances that went back years, surrounding them by the dozen.

After three years here, I still only had them.

I felt the solitude shiver over me. Not the solitude of an Argentinian farm; the solitude of a Pampas deer surrounded by pumas who just hadn't noticed her yet. Muting the wild panic beneath my skin, I scanned the room for someone, anyone, to talk to.

Off to the right, Cress had parted from Blake to gather with a group of kids she knew from New York. More Dalton kids, the kids she'd partied with during the school year in the city when she wasn't out chilling in Greenwich for weekends, holidays, summers. My parents thought it bizarre that she'd wanted to go into the city and live *in some shoebox,* as my mother had put it (it was a Classic Six at the Pierre), when she could have gone to schools just as good in Greenwich. But then, it had been a long time since my mother had been a teenage girl, and she'd never been to New York City.

I think the truth of it was this: Cress adored her father. Hero-worshipped him—which, fair enough, he was a bona fide hero, given everything he'd done both for the economy and for charity. And since he spent most of his time in the city, so did she.

I made myself stride up to the Dalton kids. Even after all this time, I didn't know them that well, but my feigned confidence let me force my way into the circle, nudging my way to my friend's side. The group opened up to make room for me, but fell silent. Cress's hand snaked out and grabbed my wrist. I'd forgotten that about Cress: that gesture. How, as she held on to me, it felt like I was wearing her like jewelry.

"Rosie just got back from Argentina," she said.

"Oooh," one of the girls—I think her name was Bianca—said. "Was it all, like, hot Spanish boys?"

She was looking at me with bland, wide eyes. *You go to an* Ivy, I wanted to scream.

"No," I said, and something struck in my chest: the pride of the semester I'd spent laboring. "I was actually working on a farm."

Silence, emptier than before.

"Cool," Bianca said, finally.

"Hey, beautiful." Blake's voice made me jump; why did it have to *boom* like that? He set his chin on Cress's head. "Know if anyone's got some weed?"

She twisted around to smack him on the chest.

"You're an *athlete*," she said with mock disdain.

He tilted his head.

"Ugh, come on," she said, taking his hand and disappearing into the crowd.

I turned, unwilling, back to the group.

". . . disgusting. I mean, you'd think she was a *princess,* but her father just runs some *hedge—*" Bianca caught me looking at her and stopped short. The girl she'd been muttering to had the grace to blush, but Bianca just rolled her eyes.

"I mean, *you* know what I mean," she said.

That was when I felt it. Felt the power surge through me, that confidence I'd been searching for since I first arrived on campus. I didn't care if I burned every bridge I had in this apartment to the ground. After a year away, I knew those bridges were all made of straw anyway.

"Grayson Tate," I said in a measured voice, "is *the* financial genius of his generation. You know how many funds don't outperform the market? Eighty-five percent. His has every single year since it was founded. By an average of *eleven* percent. And that's just Tate Associates. Tate Foundation? *Forbes* gives them credit for preventing total economic collapse in the plains states after the nine-eleven recession." I held her gaze for just a second too long for her comfort, then rolled my eyes. "But you don't even know enough to know what that means."

She made a face. "Why do *you*? You fucking him or something?"

"Nope," I said lightly, and tilted my head. "I know because *I'm* the financial genius of *our* generation. See you later, going to make the rounds."

Oh my God. Oh my *God.*

The looks on their faces: the frozen stares. The looks of people who had never seen anyone like me before.

The kind of girl who knows her own power.

The kind of girl who'd wear pointy heels. The kind of girl who'd buy and sell billions of stocks with a single keystroke and never once question whether she'd accidentally hit *delete* instead of *enter*. The kind of girl who could save her family, maybe even the world.

That girl could make herself into whatever she wanted to be.

The high lasted approximately five seconds, until I realized that I'd walked myself literally into a corner and would have to cut back through the Dalton kids to get to the rest of the party. I took a deep breath, pretending to study the framed album covers of Top 40 bands on the wall, sipping whatever had been poured into my crystal wineglass.

"Oh my God," Cress's voice bounced off the walls as she emerged from behind some curtains. I frowned, trying to figure the space out. I'd thought the back of the loft dead-ended, but I'd been wrong. Just to the left, hidden from the view of the rest of the party, was an alcove. Long white curtains billowed on either side of it, obscuring it further. She clutched my wrist. "There you are! I've been looking everywhere for you!"

She'd been off seeking weed about thirty seconds ago, but I let that go.

"Annelise finally got here and you *have* to meet her. And I convinced her to do readings!"

I stared at Cress's flushed face. She looked pretty when she was flushed, which was annoying.

She stopped just outside the curtains.

"I'm *coming!*" she called to someone I hadn't heard yell for her. And then she was gone, leaving me alone again.

I stepped through.

Cross-legged and sideways on a velvet couch, running a deck of tarot cards from hand to hand, there was Annelise.

She wore a sleeveless purple dress that cascaded around her body, sitting with a straight back and square shoulders—as though inside her chest there were a single unflickering candle, lighting her from within. Thick amber hair fell halfway down her back, a halo of frizz around it, like she'd gone at it halfheartedly with a straightener.

She turned like an owl, swiveling her head without moving her body an inch.

And she smiled.

"Hey!" she said. "You must be the Marcia to my Jan!"

"I don't . . . sorry, what?"

She giggled, so like Cress it was startling. Little fizzy bubbles of contagious joy.

"Like, we're the Brady Bunch. Bunk beds, sharing . . . I don't know, it made sense in my head. Anyway, I'm Annelise. You're Rosie?"

I gave a startled laugh.

"Yes," I said. "How did you . . ." I glanced down at the tarot cards. She smiled, then shook her head.

"Oh my God, no, they're never that specific. Cress, of course. Anyway, I saw you this morning before I left for the barn. But I didn't want to wake you up . . ."

"It would have been okay. I was worr—" I cut myself off. "Honestly, I wasn't sure how you'd feel about having a roommate."

"It's no big deal," she said. "I'm used to—having a lot of people around."

"Oh." A pause went on just a beat too long. "Well, that's good."

Her head twisted as she bit her lip.

"Do you want a reading?"

The only *reading* I could think of was an open mic I'd been to first year, before I'd made the team: the horrible, paralyzing awkwardness of being a member of the small audience in front of all that earnestness.

She must have sensed my confusion. "Like . . . do you want me to read the cards for you? A tarot reading."

Something about her eyes sent a shiver straight through me, despite the warmth of the apartment. In the dim light, in the candles, they weren't really one color or another: blue, gray, nearly translucent. Like water. I'd never seen eyes like that before.

"Maybe later?" I said, turning away.

"Just one card, then?" That voice seeped over to me, soft. I didn't know when it had happened, but she'd slipped into a different persona than the one cracking *Brady Bunch* jokes just seconds earlier: she'd become a priestess before my very eyes. "Everyone wants to know something. What do you want to know more than anything?"

I raised a tentative shoulder. "I probably want to know what everyone else does."

"And what's that?"

"I mean, we're seniors. Don't we all wonder the same thing?" Annelise still hadn't dropped my gaze, and my skin was starting to goosebump in the warm August night. "What's going to happen to us next? Are we good enough for what we want?"

But she was silent as she placed the deck of cards in my hand.

"Isn't that what everyone wants to know?" I pressed.

The cards were worn, soft, their purple diamond-patterned backs almost like cloth.

"Shuffle," she said.

"This seems like a bad idea," I said with a short laugh. "I mean, what if it tells me I'm *not* good enough? That I won't get what I want? What happens then?"

She shrugged.

"Maybe you'll think of something that would be better for you in the long run. The cards don't really predict, you know. They just describe." I could feel her eyes on me even as I stared at the cards, which had begun to move between my fingers. "Focus on your question."

Would I be able to get a job that got me on the right track? Would I be able to make enough money so that I never felt trapped again?

I handed the cards back.

She sat them in front of her with a determined hand. "Cut," she said, and I took off the top half of the deck, then watched as she flipped over the next card.

The Moon. Beneath it, two wolves howling; a scorpion emerging from the water. Her eyes crinkled.

"Are you a Scorpio?"

I shook my head. "Capricorn."

"Scorpio moon, I bet. I'm Scorpio. Born the same week as Cressida. Do you know what the others are, by the way?"

"Andra's a week after me. Aquarius. And Lila . . ." I squinted, trying to remember. "Summer sometime. We're always gone by then. I think it kind of pisses her off, not getting a party like the rest of us do."

I waited for a reaction, but Annelise was staring at the card, at the moonlight pouring down.

"Sorry," she said absently. "It's just this card. It always gives me trouble."

That didn't seem like an entirely promising thing to say during a reading. "Why?"

"The Moon is all about illusion," she said. "About things happening behind the scenes." Another beat, and she bent forward, fingertips brushing the top of her deck.

"And . . ."

She held my gaze, her eyes half closed. *"Why can't people have what they want?"* she said, and it was a different voice altogether: dreamy, veiled. *"The things were all there to content everybody; yet everybody has the wrong thing."*

Her eyelids snapped open.

"Ford Madox Ford," she said.

My lips were open, but my throat had closed. I couldn't make a sound.

"I think," she said gently, "that you're asking the wrong question."

"What?" I said, hoarse.

"I think you might want the wrong things." She shifted, then, and her face animated, twitching back into life. "I mean, maybe, I don't know," she shrugged. "There are a million ways of interpreting this stuff. Maybe we should pull another card, just to clarify?"

I cleared my throat. "Um. No."

"You're sure?"

I shook my head. "I don't . . . I don't want to know. I don't believe that the knowing of things changes them. I don't . . . think this is helpful."

And, with slow hands—she was like a statue that had come, unwillingly, to life—she reached out for the Moon and slid it back into her deck.

But it seemed rude to just get up and go.

"So why are you doing this, anyway?" I asked. "Here, at the party. I guess I get why in general, but, you know . . ."

She nodded. "Most people have questions. I like having answers."

"Yeah," I said. "Everyone says you're good at it. Your reputation precedes you."

"I'm sorry you didn't get the answer you wanted," she said. "But really—the cards can mean a million different things, and it's not like I know you or anything—I'll be so much better at reading after I know you—"

I shook my head. I slid my purse from my shoulder, opened it. "I should pay you something. What do I owe you?"

And those opal eyes, those water eyes, closed.

"Nothing," she said, and shook her head so hard her hair, that crinkled halo, shivered and fell back into place.

She opened her eyes.

"Nothing," said Annelise, again.

4
THE QUEEN OF PENTACLES

The Queen of Pentacles is the lady of the manor. She's everything you'd want her to be: rich, generous, warm, practical. She's kind of mom-ish. If you get into some kind of crazy trouble, the Queen of Pentacles is definitely who you'd want by your side. At least, she's who I'd want by mine.

OKAY, I THOUGHT, as we lay silent and drunk in the dark of our room a few hours later. I liked Annelise enough to live with her. It wasn't a particularly high bar. First year, I'd learned approximately three things about my roommate Melanie: she went to the gym at 7 A.M., she made her bed up with her floral comforter perfectly before she did, and she was asleep by nine every evening.

Annelise was totally doable, by comparison.

And that would allow me to focus on the things that mattered.

"Financial genius of our generation?" Cress had whispered to me with a giggle as we left the party. I'd laughed—of course that had already gotten back to her, and of course I wasn't. But I was good at econ. Or rather, I'd *made* myself good at econ. And that meant more to me than coasting through the biology and chemistry that came so much easier.

You might want the wrong things. Anneliese's words hung heavy in the quiet room. Yeah, no shit. I hadn't needed her to tell me that; I'd known from the start that I'd chosen a hard path.

The problem was: it wasn't enough to be good in econ classes. The problem was: I needed a job after graduation. The problem was: unlike most of my classmates, I'd never had an internship.

But I couldn't do anything about any of those problems right now.

Annelise's heavy breathing was metronomic, from her throat, verging on a snore. So, she wasn't perfect. I let the even, jagged sounds lull me to sleep.

I HADN'T CONSIDERED HOW she'd change the group.

I woke alone the next morning to the smell of cinnamon and apples. None of us could cook, so it had to be Annelise. Making breakfast for everyone, being that perfect friend, the one who made everyone else's lives just that little bit better.

I had always been the helpful one—the one with real-world skills and common sense. We already had a scary guard dog in Andra. We had a sweet space cadet in Lila. And we had a cool-as-fuck It girl in Cress. If Annelise overtook me as the helpful one, I'd be left with the identity I'd brought to Yale.

Nerdy mouse.

That wasn't who I was anymore. I'd sworn I'd never be her again.

When I padded into the kitchen, Annelise was at the stove, face pink from the heat, as the other girls lounged around the table. She had on a red Stanford T-shirt with the neck cut out, red pajama bottoms. Not too different from my own outfit of plaid pajama pants and one of my dad's T-shirts. Except that above it all, she wore a crazed, multicolored patch-work kimono with huge, open sleeves that hovered precariously above the steaming griddle.

"Oh, good, you're up!" she said, smiling over her shoulder. "How do apple-cinnamon pancakes sound?"

"How can I help?"

She waved a spatula at me. "Sit down! Relax. I've got this."

I clocked the apples turning into compote in a saucepan, a pile of plates on the counter beside her.

"What about some whipped cream?"

Behind me, Lila squealed and clapped her hands together.

"If you want some," Annelise said. "But I don't think we have any ready-made. There's some heavy cream for a dinner I was going to make later this week—"

I'd seen my grandmother do this a few times when I was little. Mixing bowl, sugar, whisk—I poured the ingredients in and started whipping.

"There's some vanilla in the top cabinet," Annelise called over to me, loud enough so that I could hear her over the low murmurs of the others' hungover conversations.

"I prefer it without."

She shrugged and turned back to the stove.

Like I really had a preference. I should have been competent in the kitchen. *Farm girl,* right? But my mother had found cooking impossibly tedious, though growing up in 1960s Missouri had turned her into what she called a *good plain cook.* Our dinners had been full of steamed green beans, meatloaf without enough seasoning, mashed potatoes made from a box. She wasn't interested, and neither was I. Even if I had been, where would I have found the time? Between riding and test prep and studying, getting my math grades high enough to show that I *could* do the work at an Ivy, I really *could,* learning to cook felt about as urgent as learning to play the harpsichord.

But I was a fast study. I—was getting really tired already from whipping the cream. My grandmother must have had monster forearms. I'd thought mine were strong, but it hadn't even been five minutes and I was *dying.*

The *whipped cream* was still a bowl of sweet liquid by the time Annelise started spooning the compote over the pancakes, sprinkling cinnamon on them. I tried to speed up, but my arms barked in protest.

Five plates laid out on the counter, then she turned to me.

"Here," she said gently, taking the bowl from my hands. "Just relax. Have some coffee."

And then she put the bowl under what I now saw was an electric mixer. Less than five minutes, it took her.

I glowered over my coffee as the others ran through details from the party. How Andra and Milo had had sex in the bathroom. How Blake and his crew buddies had gotten disgustingly (predictably) wasted. How ditzy the Dalton girls were, how ugly the Dalton boys had gotten, how we hated anybody and everybody who wasn't us.

Annelise started handing out plates.

And she did it with such ease. All of it. The cooking, the serving. Like someone who'd helped at family dinner for years. Somebody who'd actually *made* family dinners while her parents were off at work.

Somebody without staff.

She slid my plate in front of me, and I looked up to see her smiling, one dimple showing.

I realized: she wasn't sucking up. She was doing this because she was used to doing this. She was doing this because she'd wanted apple-cinnamon pancakes and she knew how to make them; and it had never occurred to her not to make them for everyone else, too.

"Thank you," I said, and meant it.

"Of course," she said, her dimple deepening.

The pancakes were light and fluffy and autumnal and perfect. We ate every last bite, listening as Cress and Annelise filled us in on what we'd missed last year. A lot of horse shows, a fair amount of gossip. Also, one muffin recipe that Annelise had gotten from Gwyneth Paltrow's assistant that turned out *absolutely inedible!* Cress cried. *Like papier-mâché props!*

After all, I thought as I scraped the last of the whipped cream from my plate, maybe it would be nice to have someone helping *me* for a change.

"Okay," cress said, shoving her plate away and turning to me. "Magic, right? Annelise. Total magician."

Annelise, a smudge of apple mush on her cheek, laughed. "Only you would think that mixing together, like, six different ingredients was alchemy."

From her wide eyes, I could see Cress about to overflow with praise.

"It is when you get this kind of result," I said quickly.

"But can we do *real* magic, too?" Cress wheedled, so close to a whine that I blinked in surprise.

"For fuck's sake, you made her read all last night," Andra said, stubbing a cigarette out on her plate.

"No, she didn't." Annelise was soft but firm.

"She *wanted* to. And I have questions."

"Just let me clean up first?" Annelise said.

"I can do it," I said.

"Okay, princess," Annelise said to Cress. "Looks like you'll get your wish. But just three cards today, yeah?"

Cress clasped her hands together like a little kid. "Yay!" Turning to Lila and Andra: "Okay, scat."

I lifted up a single plate and took it to the sink as Andra and Lila left. How long did a reading take, anyway? If I was canny about my pacing, I could make the cleanup last for the whole thing.

At the table, Annelise shoved the plates and cutlery away from the corner between her and Cress. She pulled a block of purple silk out from what looked like her sleeve but must have been a pocket.

Silence as I rinsed the stickiness off of the first plate. Then, the sound of shuffling cards as I opened the dishwasher and put it in. They must have had their routine down; they didn't even need to talk.

Then:

"Focus," Annelise said in her melodious fortune-teller tone.

"I am focusing."

"Tell me about your question."

"Am I going to win my shows?"

"More specific."

"What's my future as a rider?"

"Better."

"What's my future as a competitive rider?"

"Yes. Keep shuffling."

I went back for the second plate just as Cress stopped.

Annelise nodded.

"Cut."

Cress split the deck in two, then put the bottom half on top. As easily as she tied her shoes; as easily as she tossed her hair. This was far from their first reading.

Annelise took the deck as I went back to the sink. By the time I risked a glance over my shoulder, she'd laid three cards facedown between them.

"Past," Annelise said, and turned the first card over. "The Empress."

Going back for another plate gave me the opportunity to glance at the card. A blond woman on a throne, a crown of stars atop her head. She bore a passing resemblance to Cressida. Other than that Roman nose; Cress's was small and pert.

"Ugh, who cares about the past? It already happened."

"It's useful context for me. And this tells me you've been the queen of your domain. It's about feminine power, about abundance."

"I mean, I guess." I couldn't see her face, but I could practically hear Cress's eye roll.

"Here's your present and near future, then. The Six of Wands."

"That's winning, right?"

"Definitely. It's one of the winningest cards in the minor arcana."

"There's a better one?"

"It's good. It's really good. It's winning prizes. Success. Having the advantage. Being praised, looked up to. Being the victor."

Cress laughed with a kind of relief I'd never heard from her before.

"Yeah, great. But that's still just college. After . . ."

They were almost done. I grabbed the last dishes as Annelise flipped the last card over. But she didn't speak. The Roman numeral ten above a man dragging a huge bundle of sticks toward some village.

"Is it bad?"

"The Ten of Wands isn't bad." But Annelise's voice had turned prosaic, harder. "It's about hard work. Effort."

"Well, yeah. I mean, it's not easy on the circuit. Dad always says—"

"Does he tell stories about it?" Annelise interrupted.

"Ugh, always. But what does it mean? Am I going to do well?"

"Well . . ."

I felt it then, whatever I'd been missing the night before. The desire to know. The belief that the answers were there. The faith that if you had someone wise enough, loving enough, smart enough at your side—that you could know them, too.

Tell us, I thought silently to her. *Tell us.*

"So. Well. The Ten of Wands can be about a burden. So, what I'm wondering here is if you'll do so well that it starts to weigh on you. Like, you feel the pressure to succeed no matter what. Or maybe the press starts following you around—"

Cress blew out her lips with a laugh.

"The press starts following a *show* jumper?"

"You never know. But I think you're going to get what you deserve," she said, and there she was again: the mystic. "You're going to work hard, you're going to put in the effort, but never forget: success is its own kind of power, and it's its own kind of burden, too."

"I mean, I'll take it." Cress hopped up. "You're amazing! That's such a crazy relief. Thank you so much, I swear, you're the best—"

She was still spewing praise as she left the kitchen.

But it was no wonder, I thought, as I closed the dishwasher and started it. As Annelise gently lifted her cards and placed them back in the deck, wrapped it reverently in its worn purple silk. There was something special about Annelise. Even I couldn't deny it.

What's more: I wasn't even sure I wanted to anymore.

5
THE HIGH PRIESTESS

*The High Priestess looks like an outer figure, but she's actually
an inner one. Okay, less woo-woo? She looks like someone else,
but she's actually part of you. She's the part that links your inner
and your outer worlds. She goes back and forth between them
like a mystic traveler. She's the part that knows, deep down, when
something's off. She's the part that tells you who you can trust and
who you should fear.*

She's the guardian of the places we keep only for ourselves.

THE DISHES WERE DONE, the table clean, and Annelise stood to go
upstairs. It felt too weird just to follow her, too much like I'd been spying
on them, so I wiped down the countertops for another minute before
heading up.

I didn't have to be intimidated, though, I reminded myself as I climbed
the stairs. She wasn't one of them. No matter how much money she
had now, whatever money she'd used to buy all those gorgeous clothes.
Somehow, I knew she'd been raised like me.

She'd even made her bed. She was sitting cross-legged on it, cards in
hand, when I came in.

"That's not what the Ten of Wands really means, is it?" I said.

Annelise blinked up at me, that smear of compote still on her cheek.
Feigned innocence didn't suit her. She looked too knowing for that.

"It's not *not* what it means," she said.

"I get it," I said, sitting at the foot of her bed. "Someone like Cress . . ."

Her gaze fixed sharp on me.

"What do you mean?"

I shrugged. "You don't want to tell her bad news. She's not equipped for it. Country house in Greenwich, going to the fanciest New York schools. You grow up under Grayson Tate's wing, and it . . . it protects you from things." My words faded out guiltily. I hadn't said anything bad, so why did I feel so disloyal?

"What's Grayson like, anyway?" Annelise asked, staring at the cards as she shifted them from hand to hand.

"You've never met him?"

She shook her head. "Cress didn't go home much last year. Just for a few family things. And always by herself."

I felt my heart soar. So, they weren't as close as Cress and I were. I'd been to that house ten, fifteen, twenty times.

"He's the literal best," I said, with a smidge of cloying enthusiasm. "He's this amazing finance guy, but his foundation? It's not like other foundations that rich guys set up for tax breaks. He actually runs it like a business, but he focuses on good things. Things that don't get attention from other places. It's actually through the foundation that I learned how to ride in the first place."

I swallowed again; how had my mouth gotten so dry? You don't know anything about her, I reminded myself. You don't know if you can trust her. I'd never even revealed that to Andra or Lila, let alone Cress. I wasn't sure what had come over me. "How'd you learn to ride? Where are you from, anyway?"

"California," she said, her eyes not moving from the cards. "Outside the Bay Area. Then LA for a bit to do Crossroads, that whole hippie-dippie scene. I learned on my mom's horses."

Her mother had horses. Plural. And yet she could cook; and yet she was helpful; and yet she was unlike any of the other extraordinarily wealthy people I'd ever met.

And Cressida loved her.

Maybe she *was* an heiress after all.

Maybe California was just different.

"And what about all this?" I said, gesturing at the cards.

"A friend of Mom's."

"And you just like to . . . tell people what they want to hear?"

She looked up. In the morning light, her eyes were bright clear blue; almost as bright as Cress's, but with a ring of gold around the center.

"You want the truth?" she said.

"Of course."

She raised a shoulder as she smiled. "I like to read the cards because I'm good at it. I'm the best reader I know. And when you grow up with as many hippies as I did, that's saying something."

I frowned. "But the Ten of Wands . . ."

Her face went hard. "I'm not a scammer, if that's what you're thinking. It's not as easy as you think it is. You can read the cards in a million different ways. You can tell someone the worst-case scenario or the best. Or something in between. It's all about what they can handle. What they're equipped for. It's as much about them as the cards."

The Moon. Illusion. Asking the wrong questions. She'd been confusing me, and the whole time it had been to feel me out. To see what kind of person I was, to see what I could handle.

I respected that.

"Can you teach me to read?" I blurted out.

"You want me to read for you?"

"I mean, tell me how while you're doing the reading. Like, teach me how to do it for myself."

"I'll read for you whenever you want, you know. But it's a long road to actually understanding all of this stuff."

I scrunched up my face, trying to find the words. "I'm sure, but . . . just asking for readings all the time. It doesn't seem fair. I mean, I could pay you?"

She burst into laughter. "Why do you keep offering to pay me?"

I shrugged. "Because it's a service."

"It's a pleasure. Doing anything you're good at—it's a pleasure. And a privilege. Most people don't have anything they're good at."

"Still. I feel bad. I mean, you're not some automaton, you must get sick of it sometimes."

She shook her head, golden hair flopping everywhere. "You'd be surprised."

Already she was starting to align the cards.

"It's just . . . I wish there was something I could do for you in return. But unless you want a mini-lecture on economic elasticity—"

"You're good at math?"

"Good enough. I could, like, do your taxes," I said with a laugh.

"For real? Oh my god, *please,*" she said. "I can't add two numbers together, it's a total nightmare."

But I'd been joking. Were we supposed to be filing taxes as college students? Someone would have told me about that, surely.

That was all I needed, some kind of tax misdemeanor on my record as I started looking for jobs in *finance.*

"Uh, yeah," I said. "Sure."

I'd never done taxes before. But how hard could it be compared to multivariable calculus?

"Deal," I said.

She held the cards in her palms. "So what kind of reading *do* you want, then? The worst-case scenario? The best?"

"I want to know what you actually think," I said.

After a second, she nodded and put the cards between us.

"For real readings," she said, "I do a prayer first." She must have seen the hesitation on my face. "Because it's something to be taken seriously. It's something to respect. To be grateful for. Knowledge," she said, her eyes lasering into mine. "It's a privilege, you know? Put your hands on the cards."

My arms goosebumped. But if Cressida could do it, I could.

Cress hadn't prayed, though.

I put my hands down. She set hers atop mine.

"God, Goddess, all that is. Please guide—" She stopped. "What's your full name?" she said in an undertone.

"Rosemary Jane Macalister."

"Rosemary Jane Macalister with clarity, truth, love, and light. For the good of all, and according to the free will of all. So mote it be."

She stared at me, her hands still covering mine.

"So mote it be," I mumbled after her, though I wasn't sure what the words meant.

Her hands lifted, leaving mine suddenly cold.

"Shuffle," she said, and I picked them up. "It's important that you imbue the cards with your energy, with the energy surrounding your question. And you have to get the question right. Shuffle," she said again, nodding at the cards, and I started to. They were worn, soft; almost like cloth in my hands. "And think about what you want to know. What kind of information you want."

"Isn't there just the one kind?"

Annelise's brows drew together. "Of course not. You can ask for a description of a situation. For the outcome of a situation. For advice about a situation. There are a million—"

"Description," I said. It seemed the least scary, the least occult. Although of course everything we were doing was both.

"Okay. Now phrase it. Specific, but not so specific that you limit what you can see."

Whatever that meant.

"Will I make a lot of money?" I asked. So engrossed, so interested in her reaction, that I didn't even realize at first what asking that admitted about my family.

Disappointment flickered across her face.

So, no.

"Will I get what I want?" I asked.

But her face had taken on a new gaze: looking at me while also looking beyond me.

"So, the tarot," she said, and she pronounced it differently than she had before: tar*ot*, like a foreign word. "The tarot, it's not good at yes/no. Mostly life isn't yes/no, you know. It's a bunch of other things."

I kept shuffling, mulling over each word.

"What's my financial future?" I paused. "How about that?"

She nodded. "Good enough for now."

"When can I stop shuffling?"

"When it feels right. Keep thinking about your question."

In the silence, the shuffling became hypnotic. I don't know how long I did it for. Just over and over again: What's my financial future. Future. Financial. Financial future.

And then I stopped.

"Cut," she said.

I cut the deck and handed it to her.

"There are a ton of ways to arrange the cards," she said, laying three facedown between us. "And I'll teach them to you later if you still want to learn. Right now, I'd ideally do a more complicated arrangement with a bunch of different cards, but since I'm teaching, let's keep it simple. Past," she said, pointing to the card on her left. "Present." The middle. "Future." The right.

The same as she'd done for Cressida. Was I really going to get the truth?

"The past," she said, flipping over the first card. "Okay, so you've got the Eight of Swords here. First things first: this is minor arcana. A tarot deck is split up into two groups of cards: the major arcana, the huge, life-changing cards that tell you just how important something is. There are twenty-two of those. And then there's the minor arcana, which are the rest of them. Those are divided up almost like playing cards, into four suits: cups, wands, pentacles, and swords. We'll get into each of those later. For the moment, the eight. What do you see?"

In the picture, a woman stood blindfolded and bound in a circle of swords.

"Being trapped," I said slowly. "Being alone."

"Good," Annelise said, too brightly. "Yes. Imprisonment and isolation are two of the meanings of this card. What else?"

"The circle's incomplete," I said. "She could get free."

"Yeah. She just can't see how. And see this water at her feet? It's like, if she used her intuition, she could figure out her situation. But she's too encumbered to do anything about it. So there's a little bit of victim mentality in here, too."

I glared at her.

She raised an eyebrow, and I sighed. Every time I'd felt poor. Every time I'd felt like there was nothing I could do to make money, save money, stop money from pouring away from my family like we were a sieve. It had all been in my mind?

"So that's the past. Present . . ." And she flipped over the Nine of Swords. "What do you see?"

A woman crying in bed. Nine swords on the wall above her.

"Grief?" I said.

Annelise bit the inside of her cheek. "It's not that any interpretation's wrong. But look at her closer. See that stress, just along the curve of her back? It's more like anguish. More like she's torturing herself."

"Oh, like a two A.M., can't-stop-thinking kind of thing?"

"Exactly. There might be some blocked emotions at play, some guilt . . ."

The amount of the parental contribution to my financial aid package. The enormity of what failing to get a good job would mean. My future as a burden rather than a savior of the family business.

Everything I was feeling, had been feeling, hadn't allowed myself to feel.

I think that was the moment I actually began to believe.

"It's all about the individual situation, what the anguishing emotions are. Fear. Stress. Overwhelm. Sometimes it just means you can't sleep, but I don't think . . ." I shook my head. "Right. But anyway, this card's all about mental torture."

"Great," I muttered.

She gave a gentle smirk. "You're doing it to yourself, you know. Which means you can stop doing it, too."

Before I could tell her how wrong she was, she'd flipped over the third card.

"Oh, the *Sun*," she said.

And there was worship in her voice, there was joy. It almost seemed to warm the room, just slightly, just for a second.

It was kind of a silly card, to be honest. A baby waving a flag and riding a horse. A sun that looked like a child had drawn it, all squiggly lines and round face.

The horse seemed like good news, though.

"It's abundance," she said. "It's abundance of all kinds. Peace. Success. It's major arcana, so it's important. So that's your future."

"Financial future."

She nodded, but she was far away.

"How do I know that you're telling me what it really means?"

And her eyes narrowed; and Annelise the twenty-one-year-old was back in the room with me. She sighed.

"I mean, you can't believe just the bad things and not believe the good. You don't get to pick and choose that way. You either decide to trust the messages or you don't. And anyway," she said, her arched brows higher than I'd ever seen them, "I don't have any reason to lie to you."

But why, then, would she have lied to Cress? To make Cress like her?

"But Cress—" I started.

"I told you," she said, and her words were swords themselves. "That wasn't lying."

"Sugarcoating her fate, then."

"Fate's . . . not a word I like to use," she said as she swept the cards together, then back into the deck.

"I'd think it would be one of your favorites."

She twisted the silk cloth around the deck. "Nope. Fate, for me . . . it's about events you can't control. It's about a path some higher power has put you on. Like you're a knight on a chessboard that can only go zigzag. Or, like . . . like you're a bowling ball that's rolled into the gutter. There's only one way to go."

"But that's what we just found out, isn't it? The one way I'm going to go?"

Her eyes got big. "Oh no. No, that's not what the cards are at all. That's not what they tell you, because the cards describe potentials, possibilities. They tell you what will happen if you continue down your current path, sure. But they'll also tell you what will happen if you decide to take a different one, too. You see the difference? *Decision.*" She let the word resonate for a second, then dimpled. "The cards don't believe in fate, either. They only believe in you." But before I could let that sink in, she leaned over and grabbed my wrist. "Do you know what time it is?"

I was still in my pajamas, so I twisted over to look at my bedside clock. "Eleven thirty."

"Fuck!" She hopped up, but not so fast that she didn't set the cards carefully on her bedside table first. "I've got to get down to the stables by noon. Fuck, fuck, fuck!"

I went over to my own bed and picked up a book, pretending to read as I watched her grab her leggings, her sports bra, her perfectly packed bag. If she was rich, she was the first tidy rich person I'd ever met.

It wasn't until she was gone that I realized I still didn't know what she wanted from Cress.

It took me even longer to realize. If Annelise was running a cult? I was all in.

I'd even asked how to mix the Kool-Aid myself.

6

THE LOVERS

Everyone thinks the Lovers card is about love. Wrong. The Lovers is really about choice. About saying, this is who I am, and this is the path that's right for me. It's about vulnerability, and it's about boundaries.

I guess it is about love, in some ways. Just not in the ways that most people think.

AND SO I LIKED ANNELISE, despite myself. Not because of the free tarot readings, though they helped. But because of her sheer weirdness, the weirdness combined with her gentleness. The music and the fashion and the esoteric cultural references, nothing I'd ever come across before. New worlds being born every time she opened her mouth.

Yet deep down, in a place I almost couldn't admit even to myself, it also made me wonder. If Cress found Annelise so fascinating—and of course she did, of course she had—why would she bother to keep someone like me around? Annelise had all of my good qualities, from her even temper to her practicality, and a whole lot more that I didn't possess at all.

"Well, it's decided. *You're* the Mary," she said one morning as I pulled on a polo shirt.

"Mary . . ."

"Mary and Rhoda. It's okay. I've always identified more with Rhoda, anyway. All those scarves!"

And it's true that she had an impressive collection of scarves. All of them vintage, some of them fancy. Fendi, Prada, Hermès.

"I'm sure I'd agree with you," I said, "if I had any clue what you were talking about."

Big eyes. "Mary Tyler Moore, of course! You're the clean-cut girl next door, I'm the bohemian mess upstairs. And anyway, I've never been the good girl in my life."

"Don't be ridiculous," I said. "We live in the same room."

She giggled. "We watched a lot of TV when we were kids."

"I did, too, just different things."

She raised an eyebrow.

I laughed. "Oh God, absolute trash. My parents told me I could only watch the Nature Channel or PBS, but they were always out working and I got obsessed with *Lifestyles of the Rich and Famous*."

She joined my laughter. "A taste for gilded cherubs?"

"Oh yeah. But I think the thing that really got me was how they always called everyone *self-made*. Like, *self-made millionaire*. I had no idea what it meant, but it seemed like these men had just wanted money so much, for so long, that it just started—*flowing*—into their lives. It felt like magic."

Annelise tilted her head. "Maybe they did. Magic can work like that, you know."

"What?"

"Focusing on things in the right way." She shrugged.

"Yeah, well. Anyway, that show practically raised me. Two veterinarians and Robin Leach."

She smiled. "Same. Mom was always off with the horses. So, you know. Mary and Rhoda, the Brady kids, Laverne and Shirley. All that jazz."

"Off with the horses? All the strings and strings of them?"

She laughed, low.

"Must be some equestrian dynasty you come from," I prompted. But she said nothing, so I knew I was right. I didn't know how or why she'd learned to make her own bed. To cook. To like and trust people. But I knew I was right.

At least, I thought I was.

LATER THAT WEEK, STILL A few days before classes started, Cress and I sped out to the stables together. Annelise was already at the barn; I hadn't seen her come in the night before or leave that morning. Getting practice in before her Open lesson that afternoon, the girls said. She practiced more than anyone I'd ever seen.

I studied Cress in the driver's seat, Gwen Stefani blaring from the speakers. It was good to have some time alone with her. We'd hardly been without the others for more than a few minutes since I'd come back. And the times that we were alone—she didn't seem entirely the same to me. Maybe it had been a year with only Annelise and Blake for company. But Annelise, at least, was funny; Annelise had an actual personality. That should have kept Cress in practice, at least. But she seemed more subdued, almost turned inward on herself, when we were alone.

Blake, maybe. The two of them seemed more serious than ever, with him at our house or her at his almost every single night. His DC background, his congressman father, his varsity crew spot—on paper, everything about him seemed perfectly designed not to offend. Except for those *Zoolander* quotes, which he couldn't seem to help. But besides that, he was pleasant and clean-cut and uninteresting; he seemed like a black hole to me, a place where personality went to die.

Maybe it was him, I thought, watching Cressida's hair whip around her head in the breeze from the open window. Maybe she's on track to become a politician's wife.

And then she turned to check her blind spot and saw me watching her. She stuck out her tongue.

"I'm so glad I'm back," I said, laughing. "I missed this."

"Missed . . ."

"You! All of it." I'd said it lightly, but it felt like a confession pulled from my chest.

"It's not like before, though, is it?" To her credit, Cressida was always good at cutting through bullshit.

"Well," I said carefully. "Annelise is here."

"Okay, then, it's not like I thought it would be. I thought it would be the three of us."

It didn't seem fair: to have opened up, however little, and get hit in the stomach with accusations. "It's the five of us."

"You know what I mean," she said.

"I don't. Three of us?"

"You, me, and Annelise," she said, the frustration rising from the back of her throat. "Annelise being all . . . wise, and mystical, and funny. And you so practical and honest and . . . I don't know, *real*."

It was a relief at the same time it was an indictment.

"But then what's changed?"

"It's—you make me feel like I can't come to you for advice anymore. Like I can't be silly with you anymore. With either of you."

I felt the heat rise to my cheeks. "You can, Cress! You just don't." My words made her turn her head, sharp, to me; beneath her sunglasses, her eyes must have been flashing. "You're with Blake all the time. And I get it, it's our last year here, who knows what happens after? But it's not that we don't want you with us. We *always* want you with us."

"*We*," she muttered. "*Us*. Do you remember the time in the library?"

I laughed, and for just a second, the tension dissipated. Of course I remembered. Sophomore year, she'd seen the list of books and call numbers I needed for an econ paper, prepared carefully in advance. She'd found it so funny that I'd do that much preparation before even going to the library. Knowing Cress, she probably found it funny that I was going to the library in the first place.

And when I got into the stacks a few days later, every single book I needed was gone. Instead, when I went to where each should be, I found a new book in its place:

Toilet Paper Origami.

Real Men Don't Eat Quiche.

Knitting with Dog Hair.

Outwitting Squirrels.

And my favorite: *Don't Get Mad, Get Even.*

After my initial suppressed laughter, I'd texted her, asking where the actual books were. Finally, she'd written back: she'd put them all on hold for me behind the main counter.

"One of the best all-time pranks."

And she smiled.

"Does Annelise get your pranks?"

She bit her lip. "You know, I've never pranked her. It seemed mean to do it when we just met. And then of course it was just the two of us, and . . . I don't know. She's funny, but she's not that kind of funny. I didn't want to hurt her feelings."

"She is a different kind of funny," I agreed. "What made you like her in the first place?"

"It wasn't the tarot cards," Cress said, exiting the highway. "It was despite that, actually. I thought it was so weird. No, it was seeing her with the horses. She was so, like, gentle and kind and natural with them, but she was always in control. And usually it's one or the other, you know?"

I did know. Andra ruled her horses with an iron fist. Lila darted away whenever a horse would so much as flick its tail.

"I guess," Cressida said, "she reminded me of you."

"Oh," I said, so quietly I'm not sure if she heard me.

We pulled onto the country road that would take us to the stables.

"Anyway. Now you know and it'll all be better. So let's talk about something more fun."

"Like . . ."

"So obviously, next year, I'll be the darling of the circuit, while you'll be becoming *the financial genius of our generation*. But what do you think the others will do?"

I knew that Lila had been emailing every acquaintance's godfather's hairdresser's son that she could track down out in Hollywood, hoping to turn her cinema degree into something tangible, to make actual things that existed in the real world. I knew, too, that Andra's father was stomping his foot, insisting she take a chocolate-world job to learn the ropes of their company from the bottom up.

But pretending was more fun.

"I think Lila will become the first wife of a Greek shipping heir and get really into yachts for a while," I said slowly. "And Andra will be one of those businessy businesswomen who clacks around in pointy heels and yells at everyone."

"Oh," she said with a chuckle. "I was thinking more like innocent pole dancer and mean pole dancer's boss."

"Cress!" A really sweet girl from my high school, Amethyst, had started pole dancing right after high school. Emily had gone to see her once and said she was actually kind of amazing. Athletic, she'd said. And the money wasn't bad, not for Western Plains.

But it wasn't the kind of thing you could tell Cress.

"What about Annelise?" I said.

"Huh. I can't see Annelise's future," she said slowly. Did she know that Annelise wanted to join the circuit, too, and was just playing dumb? Or was she actually unsure?

Hadn't *she* been the one to tell me that Annelise wanted to go pro?

"Funny," I said. "She probably could."

We were laughing together as we pulled up to the stables. Just like we'd used to.

THE YALE STABLES WERE, as a therapist would later explain to me, *my happy place.* The place where everything I loved—animals, biology, the outdoors, my friends—came together. Where the work you put in had a direct impact on the results you got. To a point, of course; I was never going to be a world-class show jumper. But the more I worked, the better I became. It was beautiful and golden and in the fall, the trees surrounding the valley colored so vividly, it looked like they were on fire.

A year in another barn hadn't erased my love for our stables. If anything, the similarities, the same things that every barn has—the stalls, the feed, the horses—only sharpened my nostalgia.

We approached the barn door. Hanging bridles, snorts and whinnies, the wholesome golden smell of hay.

I was home.

I stood for a second at the entrance and breathed it all in. And then started to make my way down the center, running back and forth to greet all of the horses I'd known, all of the horses I'd loved. All of the horses I'd missed.

They were the main reason I'd come that day. Honey, Lady, Bambi, nickering and nuzzling my shoulder, stomping in anticipation, demanding that I come see them. And Cress, following behind me with a low giggle at each silly animal.

It wasn't technically my lesson—I was in Intermediate, a level below Cress, and I'd have my own lesson group—but beyond my need to be in the one place that felt like home at Yale, I had to see Annelise. She'd taken a taxi out on her own at the crack of dawn. The promise of seeing her ride was too appealing: she couldn't possibly live up to the rumors of her greatness. If she was that good, I wanted to see it. And if she wasn't, I wanted to see it, too.

And then there was Thumper. Cress had had Bambi with her since first year, and now she had a second horse, a Dutch warmblood. Nobody but Cress would be allowed to ride Thumper, just like no one else was allowed to ride Bambi.

Not even you, she'd written me over the summer. *You need more than bravery to ride that guy.*

At the very end of the dusty row, peeking over his gate with large, curious eyes, there he was.

Even in the dark, Thumper glittered. Curious, perked ears; a white streak down his nose. And an awareness to his gaze that you couldn't train in—they had to be born with it.

"Cress, he's *gorgeous.*" I reached out a hand to stroke him, but—

"Careful!" she shrieked, just as his teeth snapped down, sharp, on my hand. For a second, I couldn't figure out what had happened; horses just like me, they always have, and it had been ages since I'd been bitten. It felt like getting my hand caught in something heavy, and I yanked it back, staring in a daze at the blood welling up from the places where he'd broken the skin.

Cress grabbed his halter, pulled his head toward her. He let her stroke his nose, all right. "Fuck, sorry. Yeah, he's gorgeous, but he's mean as a snake. Dad says Queen of Sheba was the same."

Queen of Sheba. The first time I met Grayson, it had been at Cressida's birthday party in Greenwich, October of first year. The night we arrived, Cress had been showing Lila and Andra and me the stables they kept on the property, where her childhood ponies, the lesser jumpers, and Grayson's own horses still lived.

All of a sudden, a long shadow stretched over the pristine floorboards and Cressida had squealed.

"Daddy!" she'd called. "You have to meet my friends."

Grayson was tall, six-three according to his old athletic records online. At forty-nine, he'd still had a full head of sandy hair, though his tanned skin showed smile lines around his clear blue eyes. He'd approached us with an open grin so like Cress's and yet so much more in so many ways: more confident, more assured, more charming.

And he'd turned to me first.

"With that red hair," he said, "you must be Rosie." And he'd winked.

"Daddy," Cress cried, but all I could do was crane my neck up at him and stare.

"Queen of Sheba!" I'd blurted out.

Grayson Tate had begun his career as a rider. His own father had been a real estate guy. Not a fancy one, but a New York one, and from what I'd picked up over the years from Cress's offhand comments about her grandfather, they were their own breed. A little bit sketchy, a little bit slumlordy. But he'd had enough money to get Grayson horses that were good enough for the professional circuit. Had enough money to get Grayson trained to ride at that level in the first place, which wasn't insignificant.

Grayson, though. He'd had a genius for finding bargain-basement horses that he turned into stars, for seeking out those diamonds in the rough. The kind of horse every poorer rider dreams of finding but almost never seems to. And year after year, he won. Not always at first, he wasn't a superstar, but he and his string were good enough to get him on the team for the 1980 Olympics. Which, as they were being held in Moscow, the US boycotted.

The first stroke of bad luck in a life full of good. But he'd decided to turn it into an opportunity and used the time to work intensively with one of his more problematic horses, Queenie (official name: Queen of Sheba). Her bloodlines were impeccable, her conformation ideal: amazing hindquarters, with a long hip-bone-to-buttock point. She had jumping power built into her body. And she could have made a fabulous hunter with those gorgeous sloped shoulders that would allow her to just fly. Her temperament was *almost* right, too: she had that fierce yet lighthearted competitiveness that you want to find in top animals.

But the thing about Queenie was that she just didn't want to please. She didn't give a damn about people. She didn't *want* to be trained; she didn't *want* to be led. A bad fall off of her one day screwed up Grayson's knee, and the continued attempts at training just made it worse. He was suffering, and she was suffering, too.

Because what she wanted to do was run.

During his month in the hospital for knee surgeries, Grayson made the decision to train her as a racehorse. And the second he got the experts in, the second she was free to bolt as fast as she wanted to—Queenie came *alive.*

He'd sold her for more than a million dollars. And, too injured for the circuit, he'd used that money to found Tate Associates and never got on a horse again. It was an origin story I'd known by heart.

But in that moment he'd just laughed.

"What, my daughter here?" And he rubbed Cress's hair until she shrieked and ducked out from under his grip. "She may *think* she's the Queen of Sheba, but let me tell you—"

"The horse," I'd said, still wide-eyed. "She was amazing."

And he'd stepped back, sliding his hands into his pockets as he took a wide-legged stance. Still smiling.

"Yup," he'd said. "She was really something."

A phrase I'd hear him say a hundred, a thousand times to others over the coming years, though I didn't know that yet.

"Really something," I'd echoed.

Now, standing in front of Thumper, I wondered if he'd secretly hated her all along. A horse like that reminded you that even though you thought you were in charge—even though you'd paid for the land and the stables and the lessons and the animal itself—she was still a two-thousand-pound wild thing. And she didn't care about money.

"Yeah, I've heard that about Queenie's temper," I said to Cress now, laughing shakily as I stared at my hand. The area around the toothmarks was flushed bright red; it would bruise. I was lucky he hadn't taken off a finger. After all, I knew animals: I grew up with cats, dogs, rabbits, an unfortunate hamster, and a gerbil with a nasty temperament.

"Come on, let's get you a Band-Aid," she said, steering me to Shannon's office at the end of the row. I held my hand up in front of her. "Or, like, one of those wraparound bandages," she said, looking at the size of the bite. "Fuck."

The first-aid kit was ancient but had an Ace bandage, and Cress obligingly dabbed me with rubbing alcohol, despite my hiss, and wrapped it up for me.

"I don't think I want to fuck with this today," I said weakly. "Maybe I'll just watch."

She looked at my gauzy hand, opened her mouth. Paused as the blood seeped through to the outer layer.

"Good idea," she said, finally. "And hey, you'll get to see Annelise ride."

"You guys were saying she's only in Novice?"

"Yeah, she sweeps it. You'll see."

"But why's she in Novice if she's so good?" Novice was the dividing line between the non-jumping classes (Walk-Trot and Walk-Trot-Canter) and the jumping ones (Novice, Intermediate, Open). When you won or placed in your class, you got a certain number of points; after hitting a point threshold, you *pointed up* to the next level.

Cress giggled. "Because she didn't compete before. We already had Walk-Trot stacked, so we put her in Walk-Trot-Canter. But she pointed up too quickly, the bitch. She'll be Intermediate any day now."

"Is she good enough for that? Like, is she as good as me and Andra?"

"She's better," Cress said, and made an exaggerated wince. "Sorry. But, that's why she takes Open classes. She's one of the best riders on the team, full stop."

"Why didn't she compete at Stanford, then?"

"Something about the captain and the coach. They had it in for her, I guess? She says she did two weeks first year but couldn't take the vibes. So she just trained private after that."

"Is she okay on a team, then? Not too competitive?"

Cress smirked. "Just . . . you just have to see, okay? But, I mean, yeah, she still has stuff to learn. Like, she asked to ride Thumper the second she saw him."

Nobody rode Cress's horses.

"Oh shit," I said.

"Right? And then, when I said no"—Cress leaned in toward me, lowering her voice—"she offered to *pay* me to let her ride him." She widened her eyes.

I snorted, despite the disloyalty of it all. Then the laughter came, rolling out of me. The one thing Cress had no use for at all was extra money.

Cress, though, wasn't laughing.

"I mean, I guess it's funny," she said. "But it's also just . . . *weird*. There are some things you can't buy, you know? Who doesn't know that?"

Besides that: An untested rider on a temperamental horse? It wasn't a combination that would lead you anywhere good. And only Cress herself would be to blame.

"I can't wait to see what Thumper can do," I said as Cress yanked a beautiful, rich brown saddle from the wall—brand-new, barely broken in—and a fluffy saddle pad.

"Will you grab his bridle?" she asked.

"If you think I'm getting anywhere near his mouth again . . ." I called as I headed to the corner where it hung, shiny and new among the worn school bridles. At the stall, I handed it to her and stepped back. "So, why'd you bring him?"

For most of us seniors, this was the last time in our lives we'd ride seriously. For most of us, it was the last time we'd ride, period. And we competed on whatever horses the host school provided; that was what we were judged on, after all. How well we adapted. Bringing your own horse to train on seemed, at best, pointless. At worst, a total waste of money, with the fees it cost to stable them.

But Cressida had always been different.

"Dad says I have to get better, fast, if I'm going to make it on the circuit," she said as she slid the bridle on, then reached for the saddle pad. "He thinks I can only do it with the right horses, though. He said it's like learning another language. And the only time to do it is when you're young."

"That makes a lot of sense."

She paused, cradling the beautiful new saddle in her arms.

"Rosie," she said. "Do you really think I can make it?"

I swallowed. "Again," I said. "Another question for Annelise."

"I've asked her. What do *you* think?"

The thing was, I hadn't seen more than a handful of professional shows. They weren't televised, except on the premium cable channels that my parents had canceled after the expenses of my grandfather's funeral when I was six. And the ones I'd seen in person had all been with Cress first year, when the riders and the horses had seemed so far from anything I'd ever experienced in person before that they might as well have been in a movie.

"Nobody can tell you that," I said firmly. "You decide for yourself. You decide every day through the way that you work and the time you put in. You have everything you need to do it, if it's what you really want. But you're not going to get there if your only desire is to outdo your father. Fear's not going to get you there. Only love."

I stopped short, amazed that I'd had the balls to bring up Grayson, her favorite person in the world, in even remotely negative terms. I braced myself for her reply, but she just nodded slowly as she plopped the saddle on Thumper's back. He flinched.

"See, there," she said. "There's the old Rosie."

I cocked my head, questioningly.

"You never tell me what I want to hear," she clarified. "Not ever. And so I always want to hear it."

"Oh," I stammered. "Well, good."

I watched her finish tacking Thumper with a weird ache in my throat. Imagining her days on the circuit, I couldn't help thinking that in the *best*-case scenario, my life next year would consist of fourteen-hour days behind a desk. No matter how glamorous the setting, how plush the benefits. How good the title.

And hers would be—what? Speeding the Range Rover to misty early-morning practices, pushing her body to its limits, working in sync with this beautiful, vicious creature before us—

I clenched my fist, letting the sting of the bite pull me back into my body.

It was ridiculous. You couldn't miss something while you were still living it.

Thumper pranced down to the paddock with his new tack; I stayed carefully on the other side of Cress. It was still summery in the valley where the stables were. The paddock was on perfectly flat land, but the hills rose up around it, thick and green and so leafy you felt like you could run a comb through them. The afternoon sun was slanting down sideways, gilding us all, getting in my eyes as we turned into the ring, where a single figure rode a punishingly difficult course. It wasn't high—the highest fences were about three feet—but it had a few rollback turns, in which the horse landed from a jump and had to immediately take its thousand-plus pounds and heave them in the opposite direction.

It was fiendish; Shannon had never set anything nearly as difficult for Cress, even. Also, Annelise was on Jazz, a real bitch of a mare. Jazz hated everybody and everything. She was fast as you like—or rather, fast as *she* liked, because she had two speeds, stop and go, and changed them to suit her whims. Beyond that, Jazz was small, only just over fourteen hands, and even from across the ring I could see that Annelise made her look even smaller. She was solid, Annelise: tall, with muscle to her. Like an Amazon.

More than anything, she made me think of the video we'd had to watch every year at the beginning of the TFRA camps: the Tate Foundation Riding Academy, with its summer riding intensives offered for free to *deserving* (read: *working-class*) children ages five to eighteen in every state. I'd watched it for thirteen years on the first day of each four-week program, and I knew it by heart. Once I'd even dreamed about it.

The sound of cantering hoofbeats on a black screen. Then, emerging from the dark: Grayson. Broad-shouldered, his muscles visible through his perfectly tailored black jacket as he and Anne of Cleaves, his champion mare, cleared a water jump by more than a foot.

I could hear his voice, watching Annelise now.

Hi, I'm Grayson Tate. You don't know me, but I know you. At least, I feel like I do. Because I was once just like you—just a kid who wanted to learn how to ride.

It had felt like listening to Willy Wonka as he described the different lessons we'd have over the coming weeks. The foundations for the newer riders; explorations of different disciplines, from dressage to eventing, for the more experienced.

And the whole time, that footage of him on Anne of Cleaves, on Katherine Parr, on Jane Seymour. So perfectly smooth, so perfectly in control. So perfect.

Annelise? She was exactly the same.

I looked around for Shannon, ready to share my excitement with someone who wasn't Cress. Cress had sung Annelise's praises, sure, but I'd had no idea. *This* was a winning rider. *This* was a champion.

I didn't know what Cress was. Had I given her false hope?

But Shannon was nowhere to be found. Running a stable isn't easy, and she was always darting from one place to another, hard to pin down as a mosquito.

Still, though. Who would give a young rider a course like *that* to do and then just walk away? Annelise was more than capable of riding it. Of dominating it, even. But better riders than her have fallen on easier courses. There's just an inherent danger to the sport, and I couldn't believe she was allowed out there alone.

But she was only alone for another second. Annelise started the course again just as Cress and Thumper entered and began walking around the outside of the ring.

College riders don't ride for speed. We rode for equitation: the apparent effortlessness with which we effectively communicated with our horses. In other words, how much we could make it look like we weren't doing anything at all.

And Annelise, on Jazz? They looked like one being. They looked like a fucking centaur.

Jazz was fast, but I'd never seen her as fast as she was going that golden afternoon, cantering so quickly that I had to listen for the hoofbeats for a moment, make sure it wasn't a gallop. And the way she pinged over the jumps, it was like she was a different animal altogether—a rabbit, or a kangaroo, something with springs in her legs and a desire to please.

Up, down. Pivot, around. Two strides and over, and a turn I'd have had a hard time making on my own two feet.

She was like nothing I'd ever seen. I think she just loved to move.

She was so wonderful that I didn't even notice Thumper's magnificence until Cress trotted by at the end, pulling her new animal sharply out of the way of the temperamental mare. Then his shine caught my eye—

And all I could think was, Annelise should be riding *him*.

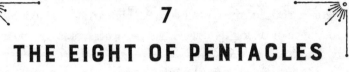

7
THE EIGHT OF PENTACLES

In children's books, kids are always trying something new and immediately being the best, the master, the chosen one the world has been waiting for. But that's not how real life works. Learning new skills requires a focused patience, an applied curiosity. It's not glamorous and it's not always exciting—definitely not like pulling a sword out of a stone or holding a wand for the first time would be. But I'm starting to believe that true learning is worth more.

Maybe I have to believe that, though. Because what other route is open to us mere mortals?

I COULD HAVE STOOD THERE all day, but I had my own business at the barn. It was lucky, in a way, that I wasn't riding, because I didn't want my friends to overhear what I had to say.

My friends. Funny how quickly Annelise had slipped into that category, I thought as I climbed the hill back to the stables. Despite my friends' view of me as *the nicest*, I actually didn't like most people very much. I'd meet someone and instantly get a gut feeling: *self-absorbed*, or *boring*, or *cruel*. And time after time after time, I was proven right.

Annelise wasn't like that.

Annelise was the kind of person I'd hoped I'd meet at Yale and never had. Someone I couldn't make sense of right away. Someone whose initial mystery only grew, until the overall effect was that I adored her and I couldn't have said why. *She's an enigma*, I once heard a younger rider say; *she's an old soul*, said another. But those were just shorthands to describe the ineffable. They never captured the essence of her. Not the way you just wanted to be around her all the time, not the way she always surprised you. In most of the conversations I had at Yale, I could predict the exact sequence of dialogue, written out like a screenplay, by the time we were two or three sentences in.

But I never knew what Annelise was going to say.

I finally found Shannon checking Honey's feet in her stall. Honey was a gorgeous palomino that Shannon had bought at a steep discount when the tween who'd owned her had aged into faster, harder, more expensive horses.

Shannon had an eye for bargains like that. Most people in the equestrian world fall into one of two camps: the wealthy who ride, and the workers for whom horses are such a vocation that they're willing to accept the piss-poor salary and wild hours that go with that life. Shannon was in the latter camp, as most stable owners are. But unlike most of them, she had a true talent for working with the rich. They weren't just part of the job that she tolerated; she could cajole and soothe them to the exact right degree that they felt they deserved whatever she was offering them—and, what's more, that they were lucky to have it.

"Rosie!" she said, letting Honey's foot drop, and holding her arms out. "Get over here!"

I hugged her. For the first time, I didn't feel like a doughy sack in her hard arms. We were the same now: work-hardened and strong.

"How are Miguel and Ana?" she asked, pulling back.

"Oh my God," I said. "They were amazing. I can't—I don't have the words, Shan. You changed my life."

Miguel and Ana had spent a summer as teenagers working at Shannon's mom's stable down in Florida. Even after returning to Argentina to start their own polo stable, they'd kept in touch. A few of our horses—Paloma, Tia, Fidel—had come from them, potential polo ponies who didn't have the nerve to plunge into a field full of flying balls and humans swinging sticks. Few horses do. But they made great training rides for some of our shorter riders. (Polo ponies aren't really ponies; they're just small horses.)

Shannon's freckled face split into a huge grin.

"I knew it," she said. "If there was ever a match made in heaven . . ."

"Let me know if you ever want to stick-and-ball," I said. "I got pretty good."

"I bet you did. Just make sure we don't lose you to the polo team," she said with a crooked eyebrow.

I laughed. "I'd never. Which, speaking of . . . are we okay for work-study this year?"

Work-study was a necessary part of my financial aid package. It paid for the extras beyond tuition and housing that my grants and parental contribution didn't cover: books, transport, the niggly little fees that Yale seemed to tack onto each bill with increasing boldness. And it made up the difference between the small activities grant I got each year and the actual cost of riding on the team.

When I'd approached Shannon tentatively first year to ask how other girls managed it, she thought for a second.

"I'm not sure we've ever had a rider on financial aid before," she said. "But what about helping out around the stable? Say, five hours a week. You could come during two other lessons to help me out. And it would just look like you were being a supportive team member."

She was amazing, Shannon. I knew she could barely afford it; she did everything around the stables herself already. After all, she owned them, not Yale. I'd accepted, and it did look exactly as she said. And so I'd developed a reputation among the team as sweet. Nice. Helpful. It didn't occur to a single one of them that I was getting paid $7.15 an hour for mucking out stalls while they rode.

"Of course," Shannon said. "What am I going to do next year without Rosie?"

"The thing is," I said, "I want to actually help this year. I mean, I can still do the grunt work for sure. But I learned so much last year. I can help you train the horses. I could even help you scout the new ones. I . . ."

But I trailed off at the barely contained amusement on her face.

"So you've decided to use your hundred-and-fifty-thousand-dollar degree to become a stable hand, then?" she said, and laughed, short and low.

"Well, no. Of course not."

The thing is, I would have made a great stable hand. I *did* make a great stable hand. I loved the animals, I had basic veterinary knowledge, I didn't mind early hours, and, above all, I had it: the calling. But I'd been fighting that calling my whole life, ever since I'd told my mother that I wanted to be a vet like her when I was six years old and she'd looked—sad, almost. *It's a hard life, Rosie.*

"Just keep helping me out here. That's all I need, really. And senior year, with the job apps and the classes and the shows and the parties . . . it's not the right time for you to pivot to training."

"No, of course. I'm sure you're right."

"Could you give me a hand with Honey, actually? One of the girls went out on the trails this morning and just kind of . . ." she trailed off.

She didn't want to tell me which girl had been remiss in her duties. But she also hadn't made sure that the girl had taken care of Honey before putting her away.

Because that was the thing about Shannon. What Shannon wasn't great at was coaching. Her unique brand of deference to the wealthy breeders and owners made it impossible for her to yell the way coaches needed to yell at young girls riding enormous animals that have only barely been tamed. She was best with the girls who wanted it, the girls who were hungry already: Cress and Annelise and even me, on my good days. Not the mediocre masses.

I slid past her into the stall, hand on Honey's still-warm, thick, rough coat, as Shannon slipped out. She handed me the hoof-pick, and the actual fact of working made me remember my conversation with Annelise.

"Oh, Shan? Do you know if I should have been filing taxes on the money I earned here the past few years?"

She looked wary. "Yeah, of course. It's a job."

"But I always put it towards school fees. Like, health insurance and the activity fee and stuff . . ." I trailed off. The seventy-five-dollar activity fee was such a small price to pay for all of the riding we got to do, and it didn't nearly cover Shannon's expenses.

"I wouldn't risk it. We're not like the families of the girls here with their fancy accountants who could keep the IRS tied up for years. We're the ones who are easy to go after." She shook her head, curls bouncing in ironic joviality. "You've got to be careful about that kind of stuff."

I swallowed. "Okay."

"And careful with her, too," she said, nodding at Honey as she shut the gate. "There's inches of gunk clogging up those poor hooves."

"Poor baby," I said, gently shoving my shoulder into the horse's side so she was forced to lift her hoof. Shannon wasn't wrong: all four hooves were covered with mud and moldering leaves and things I didn't even want to know about. I couldn't believe that any of our riders had left her in that state.

I got to work.

WE DROVE BACK TOGETHER, Cress and Annelise and me. It was a relief, the way we filed naturally into our seats: me in the front, Annelise in the back behind Cress. She hadn't replaced me. She was someone new and different. Entirely her own.

I'd thought that we'd be bouncing around the car in celebration of Annelise's amazing ride. But of course, Cress had spent a year watching her ride like that. And Annelise was so much better than I was that it was possible I didn't know what I didn't know; possible that she was currently castigating herself for mistakes I hadn't even noticed.

It took me a minute to realize that Cress hadn't turned on the radio. None of her blaring Top 40, just a ringing silence. Not even chatter to fill the empty spaces.

I'd never heard the car so quiet.

"Should we put on some music?" Annelise asked tentatively.

Cress snorted. "Some of your golden oldies? No thanks. You know she's secretly a sixty-year-old lady," she said to me.

"No sixty-year-old could ride like that," I said. Maybe nobody else in the world, period. "Fuck, Annelise. You were amazing. I'd love to see you on Thumper."

"I mean, Thumper's the *dream*," she said, and I could hear it in her voice: the yearning. "I meant it earlier, Cress. I'd give anything to ride him. And I would, I could even pay—"

Cress's snort this time sounded almost equine, it was so loud and intense. I looked over at her, and her eyebrows were so high, I could see them arching over her enormous sunglasses.

"Nobody else rides Thumper," she said sharply, making a left turn so tight we tilted with the car. "*Pay* for it? Who do you think I *am*?"

The silence bounced around the chilled leather interior.

"Nobody rides Thumper," she said again, quieter. "Just me."

I FELL INTO A DEEP SLEEP, sleep like I was stoned, when we got back.

I dreamed of my parents. Alone without me, poring over a pile of bills so high, it looked like they were in an illustration of a lawyer's office in a Charles Dickens book.

I just don't see how we're going to make ends meet this year, my dad said finally, clutching papers in each fist.

This might be the year we finally have to do it, Mom said. *Sell the business.*

It's only a few more months! I called to them. *Hang on just a few more months, can't you? Can you?*

But they couldn't hear me.

I woke up sweating. Alone. I would have thought that Annelise would want a nap after the session she'd had; I always did when I rode half that hard. But her bed was perfectly made as always. No sign of her.

"You know where Annelise is?" I called groggily to Lila as I passed her on the stairs.

"Out *gardening,*" she said with a giggle. "Can you imagine?"

I could, actually. Easily. The house was bordered by a rich, thick overflow of flowers that nearly hid the fence separating it from the neighbors. It was easy, too easy, to picture Annelise with a tiger lily tucked behind an ear, arms full of blooms.

And that was where she was, though somewhat more prosaic than I'd imagined. She had on the ugliest, dirtiest pair of gardening gloves I'd ever seen. A pair of flower clippy things in the other hand. The flowers were spread out a few feet away, on a black velvet blanket featuring an overblown version of the Fleetwood Mac *Rumors* cover.

She turned to me, face pink and sweaty.

"I thought I'd do the owners a favor and do a bit of pruning," she said, then grinned. "And if we get a few bouquets in the process, well . . ." She shrugged.

"That's so nice," I said. "Hey, I wanted to grab you because I've been researching this tax stuff, and I'm not sure I know—"

"Oh," she said, and turned back to the rose bushes, away from me. "I've been meaning to talk to you about that, too. Don't worry about it, okay? It's so ridiculously complicated, all this family stuff, and anyway. I'll figure it out."

I shifted my weight between feet. "Are you sure? I'm sorry, it's just that I figured out I've been making mistakes on my *own*, and I don't want to risk—"

She turned back to me. "I'm sure. But that doesn't mean we can't read."

It was exactly what I'd hoped she'd say. But it burrowed a hole deep into my stomach. I didn't want to owe her.

"We could even read now," she said, yanking off her gloves and pulling that purple-wrapped bundle from her pocket.

"Can I ask the same question as before?"

"You can," she said slowly. "If the situation has changed. Think about it like a story. If something's happened to change the story, the cards can tell you what story you're in now."

But nothing had changed. I still didn't have a job for next year, and if my dream were any indication, my subconscious was still consumed by my parents' tenuous financial situation.

Annelise watched me.

"Tell you what," she said. "We'll do a fuller spread this time. A Celtic cross. That'll give more information, even if it's the same story. And it'll help me explain the different positions to you at the same time."

"Double trouble." But the expression didn't sound right.

"Double duty," she modified. "Yes. Here, shuffle. Think about the same question."

But now that the cards were in my hands, a different question came to me.

Will I have an abundant life? Will I have all the choices that I could want? Will I be like Grayson Tate?

Her voice broke my light trance.

"You're not asking the same question as before," she said.

I stopped.

"Keep shuffling."

"How can you tell?"

"Your face. What are you asking?"

"It's . . . embarrassing."

"Trust me. I've heard it all."

"Will I be like Grayson Tate?" I muttered.

"Grayson Tate," she said sharply. Then, coming back to herself, she took the cards gently from me and began laying them out in a complex pattern, still facedown. "Why would you want to be like him?"

"Why wouldn't I? The companies that he invests in, the projects that the Foundation takes on—"

"Are they good?" she asked, no judgment in her voice, just curiosity. I had to love her for that. "Ethical?"

"It's not like a socially responsible fund per se," I said. "But that has a specific definition, you know. I think he's ethical *enough*. And what he does with the Tate Foundation—I mean, it changed my life. The stables near me ran the Tate Foundation camp every summer, bringing instructors from around the country . . ." I stopped myself, aware of how limited I was making his work sound. "But beyond equestrian stuff, they fund job retraining, housing for the homeless, vaccination programs, not to mention their investment in agricultural infrastructure . . . It's like he sees everything that's wrong in the country and he's trying to fix it."

Annelise put the last card into place.

"He sounds amazing," she said.

"He is. And he's also just a really nice guy."

"Okay, so the Celtic cross." She ran through the ten cards quickly, explaining each one's position as she pointed at it. "That's you"—in the center—"and the challenges you face"—the card over the center. "The root of the issue. The recent past. The present. The near future. Advice. Other people involved. Your hopes and fears. And the ultimate outcome."

I was the Fool. No big surprise there. Crossing me, my challenge: the Hierophant.

"That indicates a structural issue," Annelise explained. "Maybe because you're a woman. Something to meditate on."

There were so many cards, we must have sat there for hours. The ones I remembered best were the near future, the King of Pentacles, and the outcome.

"Oh, the King," she said, smiling softly. "He's always Grayson Tate when he comes up in my readings."

"Wait, what? Why does Grayson Tate come up in your readings?"

She flinched, just slightly.

"Because. Well, I guess because I want to ride as well as he did. You know. Olympics and all that." She waved her hand. "But the King of Pentacles. He's like the faithful ruler, full of abundance and success. It's good, no matter who you see him as. You could even see him as yourself."

And then the outcome: the Seven of Cups.

"Choices," Annelise said. "There are gifts in each of the cups. Some are jewels and flowers, some are snakes and curses. It's about diving deeper, understanding what's beneath the surface. Not building castles in the air, but instead choosing what is right for you."

But I'd barely heard her beyond *choices*.

"It's like when I came to Yale," I said. "It was the first time I felt like I had any choice in my life."

"Really?" Annelise had started to clear the cards and I stared at the spread, trying to memorize it.

"Oh yeah. I mean, it was a choice between U of I and Yale, so it was really no choice at all, but it was the first consequential choice about my life I ever got to make. It felt . . ." But I didn't have the words for how good it felt. "You must know about that, though. I mean, you transferred. That's such a deliberate choice."

She just smiled slightly and began to wrap the cards in their silk.

"Why did you transfer, anyway?"

"Family stuff," she said quickly. "And riding. I wasn't on the team there—the captain freshman year had this grudge against me, I don't know what. And even with the new captains, I just couldn't seem to make it on. The upper levels were always full."

"And it was important to you to ride on a team?"

She stood up, brushing a few stray leaves from her jeans. "It was crucial. Before deciding to go pro. I had to know what it was like, what it would be like. To ride for America, all that patriotic sentimental whatever. *You* know."

I actually had no idea. But the trust in her voice made me nod.

"So you chose Yale?"

She shrugged. "It was something I felt like I had to do."

"I know what you mean. For me . . . it was that I wanted the best. I wanted that branding on me. That idea that no matter what else happened in my life, I could never just be sent back to Western Plains like a package being returned to its sender. I'd have this invisible logo. Anyway." I hopped to my feet. "All that's to say, I get it. Yale was our destiny."

But Annelise frowned.

"Of course not," she said. "Yale was a decision that we made. We picked it, every bit as much as it picked us."

"And look what happened," I said, spreading my arms wide.

"Because of *our* decisions. Destiny—it's something that's meant to be, something that will definitely happen in the future. It implies that there's some higher power with a plan for us."

"But how can you read the cards without believing in that?"

She was silent for a moment, then sighed. She looked almost sad. "Because the cards, for me . . . I told you. They don't predict. They only describe. I've never had luck with predictions. I'm sorry, Rosie. I wish I could say that this was perfect and accurate and would turn out exactly like I'm telling you," she said. "But the only thing I'm really good at is reading current situations. Telling the story of what's happening now."

"But someone, some*thing*, must be giving you access to that. Don't you think?"

She closed her eyes for a second. "Maybe there's an invisible force guiding my hand. Maybe there are patterns in the universe that the cards have to follow. The thing is, it doesn't really matter to me. I only know that there's some power out there that shows me what *is*."

Fate, fortune, destiny. Choices, patterns, possibilities. I didn't know if I believed in a higher power, but the realization hit me in my chest: I believed in Annelise.

8
THE ACE OF CUPS

The Ace can be the first card of a suit or the last: beginning or ending, fresh start or culmination. For a long time, I thought about it as the ending, as the most intense version of a particular suit—so the Ace of Cups was all about absolute love to me. Unconditional, unfailing love. Like a fairy-tale happy ending, a love that you've earned. But the way I see it now, it's about the different kinds of soul mates that come in and out of our lives. We don't all just have one soul mate, you know, and not all soul mates are romantic. They can be friends, parents, animals. The Ace of Cups points them out to us.

But it makes no promises about how long they'll stay.

For the last two weeks of August, the campus had felt like our own private playground. The only other people around were fellow athletes, back to start training early, and the seniors who were determined to stretch their final year to the fullest. Even the first-years arriving for orientation a few days ago hadn't changed the vibes. They only cemented our feeling of ownership: this was our campus, and their presence was a necessary evil.

But when September came, when everyone else started trickling and flooding back, the reality of classes started to loom over me. I'd almost forgotten—in the delight of getting to know Annelise, in the reunion with my friends, in my return to the stables—that we'd be taking classes at all.

So though our days continued much like before in the brief period before official learning would begin, I finalized my plan for the semester.

Reviewing the courses I'd selected while still in Argentina, targeting professors for independent studies that would, I hoped, make up for my lack
of internships. Putting recruiting events on my calendar. Bracing myself
for the workload to come.

Cress and Lila and Andra kept partying and riding like nothing was
changing, like nothing would ever change, like we weren't about to be
catapulted into the real world. It was one of the reasons I was so grateful
for Annelise.

By that point, she'd read for me a dozen times. I was starting to prefer
reading on my own, pulling a card in the morning that would give me
advice for the day and then looking up its meaning in a little yellow-paged
booklet from the seventies that she kept in her bedside drawer.

You don't have to do that! she'd cry if she saw me. *I'm happy to read for*
you!

I tried turning her down as much as I could, but I was finding that
refusing a gift was something you could only do so many times before
it got awkward. And that was how she read: like a gift. Like an offering.

Not that the readings always made sense to me. We had different
kinds of minds. But I let her read, and she told me beautiful things that
always seemed slightly more than half true. *The Page of Cups just wants*
to play, but he's bound here by the Hierophant, by the representative of the in-
stitution. You see?

But beyond the readings, I think I liked it best when she danced. One
of the first things I learned as an EQ girl is that we didn't dance well, on
the whole. Our training made our postures too stiff; we were too tightly
coiled to ever really let loose. At clubs, we'd instead light cigarettes, sway
a little, sip our drinks. But Annelise danced with every part of her body,
like the music itself was running through her bones, her sinews, her muscles. I only ever watched her out of the corner of my eye; it would have
been too weird to stare. But while I was at my desk making my plans,
she'd be spinning through the room with a book in her hand. Her music
was all screaming or floating, Janis Joplin and Neutral Milk Hotel or Co-
coRosie and Modest Mouse.

Then, one day, she broke out Jim Croce.

Jim Croce wasn't new to me. A folksy seventies guy with a wild mop of hair and wilder mustache. *Jim Croce: His Greatest Hits* had been part of my dad's regular CD rotation. I thought I knew them all: "Time in a Bottle," "Operator," "Bad, Bad Leroy Brown." So when his voice came out of Annelise's stereo, I waited to recognize the song. But it wasn't anything I'd ever heard before.

> *Hello Mama and Dad, I had to call collect*
> *'Cause I ain't got a cent to my name*

Croce's songs? They're stories. But none of them had ever felt this resonant to me. The southern Illinois boy who just gets whomped by the big city, who has to call back home for help. Not once, just over and over again.

Annelise was doing a funny, floaty square-dance mix to it, and I was facing my desk. So it took her a minute after the song ended to see the tears running down my cheeks.

"I'm sorry," I stammered. "I don't know *why*, it's so—but it's—"

She sat down at the foot of my bed with a nod.

"I get it," she said. "The idea that you're at the absolute bottom, you've fallen down. And there's someone out there who wants to save you."

"And someone who can," I murmured.

She nodded. "Right? It's sad and sweet. The idea that someone will help."

"But all those things . . . they're not even his fault. It's like, he didn't even fuck up, he was just trying . . ." I was being ridiculous. This imaginary character in this song from forty years ago was making me cry because he was just a hick in the city and people kept stealing his money.

But Annelise kept nodding.

"That's true for most people; it's not their fault either. It's just the cost of living. The cost of life. People mostly aren't going around buying Dolce and Gabbana they can't afford. Mostly they're charging their groceries on one credit card and paying it off with another and just praying the due dates don't ever fall on the same day."

I wiped my eyes. "Maybe that's it. I'm just tired of being poor."

"Poor," she said, and she pulled her knees to her chest, sticking them

under the huge silky garment she called her *study kimono*. "Poor. I fucking
hate that word. People never use it right. There's a big difference between
broke and poor. Broke, you got yourself into. Broke is temporary, broke
is fixable. Broke is having to skip a gala because you didn't budget for the
ticket." She closed her eyes. "Poor is—poor is being stuck at the bottom
of a well. And everyone's forgotten about you and there's not even a
bucket. So if you get out of it, you did it because you clawed your way
up with broken fingernails and scraped knees. You did it because you had
to see the sky. And the idea that everybody—or even most people—are
capable of that climb? It's ridiculous," she said, opening her eyes, fierce
as I'd ever seen her. "Broken bodies, water rising up around their necks,
a sky too far up to see. It's not possible for most people and it's *supposed*
to be that way."

"Supposed to?" I wasn't sure I understood what she meant.

"Built to," she said after a long moment. "It was built to be that way."

She rolled over, hopped to her feet. "Enough of that. And now, for
something completely different."

It was still Croce—"Working at the Carwash Blues"—but it was different enough. Enough to remind us that we weren't washing cars, after
all. We were at Yale, at the beginning of our senior year, and the sun was
so warm that it still felt like summer, even though it was September. And
for this moment, at least, we were protected. Safe.

It wasn't until she left for the stables that I started to wonder: How
did she know about being poor? With her designer clothes and lavish
equestrian wardrobe, with her mother's string of horses and her years
of training?

Her family had made their money when she was older, I decided.
Probably when she was a teenager. Or maybe she'd had a deadbeat father
and her mother had remarried into money.

Whatever it was, she'd tell me when she was ready.

THAT SEMESTER, I HAD enrolled in Accelerated Multivariable Calculus,
Advanced Microeconomic Applications, International Financial Institu-
tions, and an advanced section in Statistics and Econometrics. And then
I'd added on Animal Psychology, just for fun. I'd drop it if I could get

one of the professors to take me on for an independent study, which I'd sketched out already: macroeconomic risk and how it came into play for hedge funds, particularly regarding their decisions and their returns. Part of me hoped that I'd get to do it; the other part really wanted to know what squirrels thought about.

Cress, with her Art History major, didn't have classes in any of the same buildings that I did. Andra's English major and Lila's Film Studies were the same. Annelise, though—

"What are you studying?" I asked her late one night. Religious Studies, I had her pegged for. Or Anthropology; something Californian like that.

We'd taken to chatting long into the dark, after we'd shut our Mac-Books (mine shining new, bought in August with a too-large portion of my savings to replace the battered HP I'd had since high school). For the first few nights, we'd laid in awkward silence until we finally fell asleep. Annelise always dropped off first, snoring lightly.

"I'm doing Evolutionary Biology," Annelise replied.

"Oh my God, you're so fucking lucky," I blurted out. I could only dream of having the freedom to take those classes. Learning about the sinews and tissues and muscles I'd seen my whole life; studying the strange underwater creatures and invertebrates I'd never seen. But my major was a tough one, and I didn't have room for too many electives. Especially not as an athlete, especially not having taken a year abroad.

She snorted, a very un-Annelise sound. "Hardly. I *was* doing Equine Studies, but obviously, that's not a thing here. So, it's been two years of just getting through prerequisites for the major. Orgo and physics and statistics."

"Stanford has Equine *Studies*?" If I'd known that, would I have applied?

"What are you doing?" she asked.

"Econometrics and qualitative economics," I said.

"Fuck, you must be smart."

"Um. Thanks."

I had a lot of secrets from my friends, I was realizing. Secrets I'd never thought of as secrets. They didn't know that I was on financial aid, for one thing. They didn't know what my hometown was really like. I'm not sure they even knew it was called Western Plains.

But there was one secret that nobody at Yale knew: I wasn't that smart.

At least not when it came to econ, my chosen major.

Math did not make intuitive sense to me. But I liked it all the more for that. Biochem and physiology—those were different. The science was in my soul, my blood. I could have anesthetized the sheep they had us dissect in sophomore-year lab and brought it back to consciousness again, even after having removed this organ or that one. It just made sense to me.

"Why?" Annelise asked, and there was genuine curiosity in her voice.

"Because I want to go into finance. It seemed the best way."

"Oh," she said after a minute. "Why?"

Was it her voice that made me want to reveal more than I usually did? There was something so soothing about the timbre of it, something so calming. But it takes more than that to say: *Because I want to save the people who save animals; I want to help the people who don't see a way out; and I want to never, ever have to make choices based on what I can afford. I want to never, ever be trapped like my parents. I'm afraid of getting stuck at the bottom of that well.*

"Because I'm good with numbers," I said.

"Well, I'm not, but I'm taking five classes, too," she said, her voice getting wispier with sleep. "Because next year I'll be going pro and I won't have time for learning anything else."

If I were going pro next year, I'd be taking as little as I could, like Cress, with her Impressionist seminar that met once a week. Show jumping didn't care about your grades. Show jumping cared about your muscles and your grit and your horses.

"I guess you'll have to stop going into the city all the time, if you're taking that many classes?"

It was so long before she responded that I thought she'd fallen asleep.

"No," she said, then paused, a long silence that stretched and seemed to take on a life of its own.

"So Andra and Lila were right, then," I said, teasingly. "There *is* some boy."

"A boyfriend?" She laughed. "I'll deal with that once I get the important things sorted out."

"The important things like . . ."

"Like my career."

"So you're working in the city, then?"

But did she even need the money? If she did, I definitely understood why she'd chosen New York. If I hadn't had the work at the stables, I might have gone into the city, too. Better than having to make lattes and cappuccinos for my friends at a local café; better than serving them at the library or the gym or the cafeteria. Go somewhere where you could be anonymous, where you could slip in and out and cash your paycheck.

"Grayson Tate worked throughout college, you know," I said, after a long moment of silence in which Annelise didn't answer me.

"For real?"

"Yeah. He trained polo ponies at one of the yards near here. He was the founder of Yale Polo. But he started off by training the smaller horses to play. Probably only an hour a week. Still. Makes a nice story, though."

I could hear her swallowing from across the room, her mouth was so dry. "Yeah."

"There's nothing shameful about working," I tried again. "I work at the stables, you know."

But she hadn't known. Of course she hadn't. Nobody did.

"Your parents don't give you money?" Her voice was almost eager, and I didn't like it. That delight in my situation.

"They would if they could," I said, not bothering to hide my irritation. "But having a job . . . it's fine."

"I didn't say I have a job."

"Then why are you in the city so much?"

Another of those long silences.

"You know the High Priestess?" she said finally.

"You taped it up on our door."

"But do you know what it means?"

"No."

"It means, you'll know if you need to know. When you need to know. Or you already know, deep down. It means, accept the mystery into your life."

I thought maybe she was mad at me, that this was her Annelise way of saying it.

But when I showed up in the first Animal Psychology section the next day, Annelise was there. She'd even saved me a seat.

9

THE FIVE OF WANDS

I mean . . . in its best form, the Five of Wands is all about sportsmanship. But let's be honest, it's a five. Those aren't usually great. So it's more about conflict and competition. I guess the good part is that it can also mean diversity, bringing in new ideas, new kinds of people, that kind of thing. But generally, people don't tend to like that, either.

I DECIDED TO MIX IT UP that morning with my questions. The cards still weren't speaking to me in the way that they seemed to speak to Annelise. She was probably right: I was asking the wrong questions.

What hidden truth do I need to know about today?

"Oh, the Five of Wands?" she said, glancing over at me as I plucked it from the deck, wrinkling her nose. "Bleh." And then she explained.

I didn't love her interpretation, but I liked the pamphlet's even less: *pain. Conflict. Strife.*

Not a good day for it, as I had to go into the econ department for an interview. Apparently, I'd been late in approaching professors for an independent study. Only a handful even bothered to reply to my emails, mostly just telling me that they'd taken on all the students they had time for last spring. Why had nobody told me to apply back then?

But that was just an excuse, I scolded myself. Why hadn't I looked it up myself from one of the computer banks at the *universidad*? Distraction. Laziness. I had only myself to blame.

But Marta Nussbaum, cochair of the econ department, was willing to meet with me. I'd had her for a low-level macro class first year, and

I couldn't believe that she'd remembered me. *Normally, I don't take on students this late. But I understand you were abroad last year,* she'd written to me, *and the project's fascinating. Let's talk.*

An independent study with Marta Nussbaum would be huge, as good as an internship for sure. Other possibilities were arising, too: Goldman Sachs and J. P. Morgan announced their on-campus recruitment dates. Yet another came from my mother, of all people, that morning: a link to a *New York Times* article about a pilot program of financial fellows at Columbia University in partnership with a group of investment banks.

It had to be a fraction of what a job as an actual analyst would pay. But a guarantee of something to do after senior year, something prestigious; a bargaining chip, perhaps? It took me all of an hour to get my application together. I already had letters of recommendation on file. I modified the essay I'd used to apply to the study-abroad program about the necessity of international understanding in nonprofits (the job that I only realized I'd wanted once I wrote about it—making enough money to run my own foundation for animals someday) to the necessity of financial education in nonprofits.

And then suddenly: "Rosie, get *down here!*" Cress called.

As the only seniors on the team, Cress and Lila and Andra and even Annelise had been running tryouts all month. And they resented my absence. Not that they needed me; of the group, I was by far the least likely to actually give a critical opinion—or an overly positive one, for that matter.

Cress was waiting for me at the bottom of the stairs.

"Look, Rosie. With Annelise on the team, we could win Ivies this year."

But what did it matter? For anyone who wasn't Annelise or Cressida, it would just mean an extension of the season through second semester; more money, more travel, more time. And then it would be over, and what would you have to show for it?

"But I need a strong string behind us," Cress went on. "I need team unity. And I need you there. Shannon can't come, she's going to be with the vet; Honey's sick. I need your opinions. I need you there with me."

I was almost sure we weren't allowed to ride without Shannon on the premises. But anyway: "Cress, I've got—"

"Skip it," she said, and then grinned to lighten the harshness of her tone. "Come on. There's always going to be another class or problem set or whatever. There's only going to be one more day of tryouts, and it's going to determine *everything*. Besides, I miss you. I thought it would be just like before, but you're always with Anne*lise* now. We haven't hung out even *once*."

You were the one who put me in a room with her. You're the one who's always with her boyfriend. But wasn't I glad of that now? And even gladder for the extra cash?

I sighed. Emailing Professor Nussbaum was going to be a fucking nightmare, after all she'd been willing to do for me. But she'd been willing to meet with me today; surely tomorrow would be just as good?

"Can I bring my homework?"

She giggled, putting her hands on my shoulders and squeezing.

"I mean, you could," she said, turning and heading toward her room. "But why would you want to?"

LATER, SMASHED IN THE CAR again with the others, I wished I had. They couldn't stop talking about the candidates as "Gold Digger" blasted in the background, and I couldn't keep any of their names straight, not without meeting them first. Chloe Bianca Maddie Skylar—they were all the same person to me.

They were all the same person until Tiffany.

"All those fucking *questions*," Andra groaned. *"Do your boots have to be Ariats? I saw that you all have Ariats,"* she went on in a squeaky, infantile voice. "I mean, who even pays *attention* to that?"

People without Ariat boots, I thought.

"Did you *see* the holes in her leggings?" Lila said, giggling.

"It's like, where does she even think we are," Andra said.

"You guys, come on," Cress said in her team-captain voice. And then, breaking: "She said she learned to ride at 4-H, like I was supposed to even know what that was. My *dad* probably paid for her lessons, for fuck's sake."

Just like he'd done for mine.

"Was she any good?" I asked.

"Good enough," Cress said finally.

"She was amazing on Timothy," Annelise said. "And she hasn't competed before. She'd sweep Walk-Trot."

"But we also have to think about culture fit," Cress said, her captain voice back on.

"I mean, she can borrow stuff for shows," I said. Half the girls did; we weren't the types to lay out all of our gear neatly the night before, and the moments before each class were full of muffled shrieks and rustling through bags searching for a replacement whatever—crop, glove, helmet, even.

"Timothy's basically a *couch*," Andra said, turning back to face front. "I mean, fuck, put her on someone actually hard."

"Put her on Jazz," Lila said with a giggle.

Only the riders in the upper classes, Intermediate and Open, ever rode Jazz. She spooked at her own shadow; she'd even given Mallory, a strong rider, a concussion our first year when she'd reared going past a barn door some idiot had chosen to close at that moment. Pranks were one thing. The seniors had continued to strand the new riders in the inner city systematically since our first year, warning Cressida not to go pick them up. But that was just stupid. This was dangerous.

"I mean, you could just give her an easy ride and then tell her no," I said.

Cressida's gaze flicked back to me.

"We could," she said. "*We* could tell her no."

TEN GIRLS LEFT AT THE tryouts: two for each class. I didn't know why four of them had even come; Intermediate was already full, what with me and Andra and Georgia, a talented junior. And Open was full, too.

"It's not democratic otherwise," Cress said vaguely when I asked. "Come on, help tack."

Normally, each rider tacked their own horse. But you couldn't trust these new girls, girls we didn't even know, to do it correctly: not until we'd trained them. So my friends and I tacked five horses, Annelise finishing with Jazz first.

"Here," I said, taking the reins. "I'll take her down." No way were they giving her to Tiffany.

Down at the barn, the girls were all waiting, ten gazes pounding into Jazz and me the second we rounded the corner, so intense I could feel the horse stiffen beside me. I walked her in at an angle, then stopped and stroked her on her withers, just where her mother would have nibbled her.

"Who's here for Open?" I called, as softly as I could while still being heard. Two girls raised their hands, and I gave her to the taller one to warm up. I wasn't taking any chances here.

I couldn't tell who Tiffany was just from looking at them. Not at first. It wasn't until the other girls in the first group were mounted that the small differences became clearer. The weird stiffness of her paddock boots when she shifted from foot to foot: synthetic, not real leather. The French braid she wore her hair in: trying way too hard, we would never. And her teeth, when she smiled nervously over at us: stained, the top ones overlapping.

Yeah, it was visible. Even from across the barn. And it was confirmed when I crossed in front of them and noticed one of the shiny blondes nodding toward Cress.

"Her dad's *Grayson Tate*," she whispered to Tiffany. Even across the stable, it seemed to me that Annelise went stiff and alert. But I must have been imagining it. Nobody could have heard that whisper from that far away.

"Who?" Tiffany said.

"The *Olympian*? The . . . never mind," said the blonde, just barely suppressing a disgusted sound at the back of her throat.

The girls were good. They were all good at this point in the tryouts. Cress watched with a blank face, Lila took loopy notes. As though she had to. I'd put good money on Cress having already made up her mind before we'd even come to the barn. The potential Open rider—though not *potential,* actually, no chance in hell we'd bench Cress or Lila—handled Jazz well and safely. But she wasn't anywhere near as good as Annelise. She wasn't even as good as Cress, I saw with relief.

"Thank fuck," I whispered to Lila, who'd just written *no no no.* "We don't need another Open rider. It just goes to show you, training can only get you so far. There's got to be natural talent, too."

"Totally." She put a bunch of question marks next to a rider's name.

"It's kind of crazy that Annelise has never competed before," I said. "As good as she is."

Lila scribbled away.

"I mean, maybe she couldn't afford it? Like, show gear's expensive. What do her parents even do?"

"I think they're in horses," she said vaguely, then glanced straight at me. "Why do you even care?"

I cared because of Tiffany. I cared because if I could show them that Annelise had come from nothing and won so much for us, that Tiffany could, too. I cared—but I didn't want to tell them anything more about myself. I was a total fucking hypocrite.

"Thanks, ladies," Cress called, after a few spins around the ring. "Okay, then. Switchovers. Andra?"

Andra glanced down at a Post-it Note.

"Chloe on Timothy," she called out. "Bianca on Pip. Julia, Titus. Emily, Lorenzo. And Tiffany," she said, her same bored tone barely audible over the shuffling of horses and riders, "on Jazz."

"Wait," I said, stepping forward and grabbing the reins from the Open rider. "Wait, let me see that—"

"Rosie," Cress said, rolling her eyes. "We already decided."

"Cress. Jazz is—"

Cress clapped her hands together, Jazz flinching at the noise. "Come on, ladies."

I looked at the girl approaching me. She was tiny. I'm small, particularly for a rider, but she couldn't have been more than five feet, maybe ninety pounds.

"She's a lot of horse," I said. Half to Tiffany, half to my friends. To myself, maybe. I didn't know. Beside me, Annelise pressed her lips together.

"Maybe—" she said, turning to Cress, but Cress cut her off, wrenching the reins from my hands and shoving them in Tiffany's.

"Let's go, we're late. Tiffany, we want to see what you can do. You're a good rider, but we don't know how you'll do on tricky horses. You made a good list," she said to Andra as Tiffany headed to the mounting block. "And you," she said to me, her voice dropping. "You are barely. Even. Here," she said between her teeth.

My heart fell in a vertiginous swoop. Was I going to be kicked off the team? Was that why they were auditioning Intermediate riders?

With Annelise beside Cress, they looked like a pair for once, Art Nouveau bookends, a matched set. For a second, it was too easy to imagine what they'd been like last year. Two kinds of power: the seen and the unseen. The master of the material world and the master of the spiritual. Both of them their own kinds of smart, their own kinds of funny.

Had I grown too close to Annelise? Spent too much time with her? Or spent too little with Cress?

But then Cress turned to me as the riders filed into the ring, and winked.

She just wanted her prank.

Still, I couldn't take my eyes off Tiffany. She was doing well on Jazz, though the horse kept slipping away from her control, just a split second at a time: a little jig when another mare got too close, a tossing of her head when Tiffany squeezed her legs a little too hard.

That is, until the barn door smacked shut with a bang.

Jazz lost it. She reared, she bucked, she went back and forth in a crazed, asymmetrical rocking-horse dance. Tiffany, to her credit, held on well. She clung to the mane, she shifted in the saddle with an easy grace. It wasn't until Jazz went galloping, then stopped suddenly before Annelise, who'd run out to grab her flying reins, that Tiffany fell.

"Oh shit," Lila muttered.

Annelise held Jazz still while Cress and Andra and I sprinted to the rider's side. She was on her back, which I didn't like.

"Don't move," I said sharply as she pressed her hands into the ground. "Lila, call an amb—"

"Oh, she's *fine*," Cress said, grabbing her hand and pulling her up. You could hear the collective intake of breath as we waited for a scream, a shriek, from Tiffany.

But Tiffany just smiled shakily.

"I'm fine," she said to me. "I'm fine," she repeated to the rest of the girls.

"Good. Grab a water, go get cleaned up," Cress said. "Rosie, take Jazz out to the pasture, will you? Ladies, let's keep going."

I took the reins from Annelise, who wouldn't meet my eyes. As the other riders began their tentative walks around the ring again, I stopped in front of Cress.

"I assume she's made it?" I said softly.

Cress didn't look away from the ring.

"Are you kidding?" she said. "We need a rider who can actually handle a horse. Did you *see* that fall?"

10

THE STAR

The Star, to me, is the most beautiful card in the deck. It's the card without which all the other cards are useless. Because the Star is about hope.

It's not like the Sun, which tells you about abundance and joy right here and now. And it's not like the Wheel of Fortune, which can inspire hope but can also erase it. The Star is inspiration. The Star says: keep going. The Star says: you have power, you are held by the Universe, you are blessed. And all of this will show up in time, no matter what you feel like in this moment.

The Star says: you've got this. And I've got your back.

A<small>NNELISE WAS QUIET ALL</small> the way home. When we got to the driveway, she jumped out of the car before it had even pulled to a full stop. By the time I got to the door of the house, I could hear her running up the stairs, two at a time.

I found her in our bedroom.

"I'm going to do a reading now," she said, not looking at me, already getting into her cross-legged position, already unwrapping and stroking the cards, whispering to them in words I couldn't hear. I knew the respect she had for the cards, the respect she felt she owed the cards. But it still was a strange sight.

I put my headphones on. Van Morrison, *Astral Weeks*. I pretended to lie there listening, eyes half closed. But the whole time I was watching.

Annelise shuffled for a few seconds, then she laid the cards out in a Celtic cross faster than I'd ever seen her. Normally, she would bend over them like she was studying some rare specimen at the Beinecke. But this time, she took a single glance at the spread and swept the cards back together with her hands.

Another short shuffle, and she laid them out again. A frustrated sound at the back of her throat, and she'd swept them back together again.

By the third shuffle, I couldn't help it.

"What's going on?"

She didn't look at me as she set out the ten cards.

"I'm doing a reading," she said absently. Then, with a glimpse at the cards, "Fuck!"

Conflict resolution is not a natural strength of mine. But three years of knowing Cress and Andra and Lila had schooled me. "You were going to tell me about the suits, remember?"

Cards gathered together in her hands again, she took a deep breath, close to a sigh. And then she smiled sadly.

"I'm not a good teacher today," she said. "Just look at me. Trying to read until the cards come out right. You should *never* do that."

"What does that mean?"

Her almond eyes drooped at the edges, even as she smiled.

"I'm trying to read about what's happening with us. With the group. With Cress. About what's going to happen. But in this mood . . . nothing's coming out right."

I moved tentatively across the room to her bed, but she didn't stop me.

"What does it mean? For a spread to come out right?"

She gnawed her lip. "For it to make sense to me. For it to tell me about the current state of things."

"But you said that if it doesn't make sense, keep studying it until it does," I said gently. "To take notes, to take a picture."

"Well, I'm impatient today."

"About Tiffany?"

"About Cress, too. And all of us who were there and just stood by, watching." She paused. "Why was Cress like that? I didn't know she could be like that. It just felt like . . . I don't know. Bad vibes. Bad fortune."

I understood. I understood her sadness and her fear and her disgust.

But I also understood why Cress had done it.

Because she wasn't entirely wrong. You *did* have to be able to ride any horse to be on the team. At shows, the whole point was to get on a totally new horse and ride it well from the very start.

I'd never seen a horse like Jazz in the lower classes, though.

The thing that crawled under my skin and stayed there, shooting tiny needles of dread through my blood, was that I hadn't seen Cress like that before, either. Never with me. I'd seen her turn cold and terrifying when a waiter in the city had refused to serve our nineteen-year-old selves wine with dinner (*It's a hundred-dollar bottle. Don't you live on tips?*) or when the registrar's office had put a minus behind her *B* in Intro to Impressionist Art (*Isn't that, like, your one job?*). It took the office less than a day to confirm that it was not, as Cress had been convinced, an administrative error.

"I thought you said there's no such thing as fortune."

She rolled her eyes.

"I said there's no such thing as destiny or fate. There's for sure such a thing as *fortune*. I mean, come on! Why else would I be doing this?"

I shook my head. "I don't understand the difference. If there's no higher power—"

"I never said that either. Pay attention, Rosie! Words have meaning. Fortune is different. Fortune *exists*. It's chance. It's luck. It feels random; it can knock us onto our asses in half a second with no notice. But there's a pattern in there. We're just creating the pattern fresh every time we make a choice."

Self-made.

"Fortune," she went on, "it's not clean and clear like destiny or fate. Which makes it messy; which makes it true. It's serendipity and it's accidents and it's the business of daily life. And it's readable," she said, tossing her treasured cards with a muffled thump on the velvet bedspread between us, "if you have the talent and the knowledge to read it."

"And the focus," I said, picking the cards up gently.

She smirked.

"Yeah. And that."

"Would it work if we read together?" I asked. "We're both part of the group. We were both there. Maybe somehow the combination of energies . . ." But I didn't know how to finish that sentence.

"Worth a try, I guess. Shuffle first? Then pass them over to me."

Our reading really didn't make much sense. At least, not to me. Maybe you really couldn't do a four-handed reading. But it seemed to soothe Annelise a bit.

"What do you notice about the patterns?" she asked after we'd gone over each card and its placement individually.

"Um. Lots of wands," I said. "Lots of swords."

"Right. So the wands, they're creativity. Spontaneity. They can be thoughtless, but they can also be . . . funny, sometimes. Whenever the universe wants to tease me a little, I end up pulling lots of wands. That might just be me, though. It can also be ambition, but that tends to come up more with pentacles."

"O-kay," I said, trying to apply what she was saying to the spread.

"The wands are fire, basically," she said. "So think about fire. It's wild. You can't predict what it will do. It can be helpful or harmful. It's . . . it's wild," she said again.

"And the swords?"

"Well, cups are emotions, love. And pentacles are money, the material world. So what does that leave us with?"

I stared at her.

"Swords are air," she said. "Intellect."

"Intellect?" I said. Tricking a poor girl into falling off of a horse?

"But sometimes they're more literal than that. Because they're swords, not knives. You know?"

I thought for a minute, but came up short.

"They're double-edged," she said. "They can hurt anyone, even the person holding them."

I nodded.

"So altogether . . ."

"A spontaneous decision to inflict pain," she said absently. "What really interests me, though, is this." She pointed to the outcome card: Temperance.

"Major arcana," I said.

"Right. It's important. It's a key moment in—if not Cress's life, then the team's. It's reassuring us here, that things will balance out. That life is all about cause and effect; that karma comes into play." She glanced up, relief over her features. "It's saying that we're going to find the middle way."

"Couldn't . . . couldn't it be saying that Cress and the others will get what's coming to them?"

Annelise looked me directly in the eyes.

"Right." She smiled. "That's what I said."

ANNELISE'S INTERPRETATION didn't make much sense to me—what, so Cress and Andra and Lila were each going to take bad falls in their own time? I didn't want that either. I didn't want to live in a universe where that kind of literal karma existed.

But also, a fall didn't seem like adequate repayment for what they'd done. Taking away all their money, making *them* into Tiffanys, was the only thing I could think of. And not only did I have no way of doing that, but I wouldn't have, even if I could.

Annelise was as genuinely mad as I was. But in the closed air of our room, there were so many other emotions circulating. Embarrassment that we hadn't stopped it. Desire to make things right. Shame that we knew we wouldn't, that we couldn't.

And, more than anything else, fear that the other girls were going to be mad at us. Fear that we'd cave in the face of whatever crumb of forgiveness they offered us, if they were in the crumb-offering mood, and immediately apologize for being sticks in the mud, the ones ruining all the fun.

Although that last one might just have been me.

But as I approached the kitchen, I saw the beat-up old weekender bag Cress had inherited from her mother, complete with her initials: *AGT,* Anthea George Tate, burned into the leather.

Shouldn't it be ATG? I'd asked naively the first time I saw it, thrilled with my knowledge of the way things should be done.

Cress had made a face. *Not when they're all in caps like that.*

She was chugging a coffee when I came in. Not looking at me, so I didn't look at her. Was this it now? Was this what the rest of the year was going to be like?

No.

"Going over to Blake's?"

She tipped her mug back and swallowed the dregs before setting it on the counter just a little too hard. "Yeah."

I was trembling, scared in a way that I'd never been before with Cress. Had I known that Cress had this side to her? The side that could risk a life just because she didn't like the person who was living it?

"Tell him I say hi."

"Tell the same to your Siamese twin," she spat. "Annelise."

I recoiled at her tone.

"Cress, you were the one who found her. You were the one who brought her into the group, who said how similar we were. And you were the one who put us in the same fucking room, for fuck's sake!"

I think it was the rare appearance of my swearing, more than anything else, that momentarily silenced her.

"And look at you now. Thick as thieves. But not thieves, you're like . . . *nuns* or something. The two of you like to pretend you're so righteous. Like you're better than the rest of us."

"Well, for fuck's sake, Cress, we didn't just try to kill a first-year!"

"Neither did I! It was just a joke. You've gotten so . . . dour lately. It's really a fucking drag."

"And you've gotten . . ." *evil,* I wanted to say. But it was the kind of thing you could never take back.

Her eyes flared at me.

"What, Rosie? What have I gotten?"

I swallowed. Time to reel it in.

"It's like . . . your silliness is turning dark. It used to be just . . . goofy. It was amazing. And I miss that Cress."

And for a second, every trace of artifice fell off of her face. All that was left was a kind of stunned hurt.

"So who am I, then? Who am I now?"

"That's the point!" I cried. "I don't know. I don't know, and it scares me."

We stood for a moment in silence. Never in my life had I said such true things to her.

Never in my life had I not known what was coming next.

"When did you stop being fun?" she asked. "I miss *that* Rosie."

This, I hadn't expected. My throat choked with anger. Because the truth was, I stopped being fun the second I realized that my choices for next year were limited in a way that nobody else's in the house were. I stopped being fun the second I'd had to start separating my money for the week into envelopes so I didn't go over my budget. I'd stopped being fun the first time I had to use an ATM like I was playing a slot machine, unsure of whether any money would come out.

I stopped being fun the second I realized that Tiffany was me.

"I'm right here," I said instead.

She rolled her eyes and headed to the doorway, grabbing her bag. "Back in a few days. I need to get the fuck away from . . ." She waved her hand around the house, and she was off.

Fun Rosie. She was still here, I'd said.

But I wasn't sure I was.

And Marta Nussbaum never did email me back.

11

THE SEVEN OF SWORDS

Cheater, cheater, pumpkin eater. Okay, maybe it's not cheating, per se. But maybe it is. Maybe there's a cheater in your midst, a thief or, like, a . . . a bandit. Don't laugh, it's serious. There's definitely deception somewhere. That's not to say that the cheater's going to get caught, so, you know, take a deep breath. It can also just be as simple as acting strategically. Or maybe you're fooling yourself. Cheating yourself. Deceiving yourself. It could just be you, in the end.

But it almost never is.

B<small>UT CRESS CAME BACK</small> the next day. I heard the door and went down the stairs tentatively. She came over and threw her arms around me.

"Ugh, *so* dumb," she said into my hair. "It's our last year, and here I am, going all just batshit. Look, let's not fight, okay?"

"Um, yeah, of course," I said, pulling back. It was the closest to an apology that I'd ever heard from her. "But what made you—"

"That time of the month," she said, stepping back toward her bag still at the door and rolling her eyes. "You know."

Fine. I didn't have the time or the energy for a fight. So far, September had been a blur of classes and long practices. I hadn't had time to go to any of the recruiting events I'd marked in my calendar, but October would be my month, I knew it.

A few days later, I came home from a late stats seminar with a warm glow in my chest. The house was lit up bright, like a Victorian mansion in a Christmas village. Impossible from the street to see the dishes overflowing from the sink onto the counters, the fine layer of dust that coated the bottoms of your feet if you ever forgot and walked around barefoot. It felt, I thought as I opened the heavy front door (unlocked; the others always left it unlocked, even though I kept reminding them that it was *New Haven*, you couldn't *do* that), like home would feel, one day when I was an actual adult. A nip in the air, autumn settling in steady, and a warm golden haven to return to.

It was warm inside, too, against the falling day; the girls had already started cranking the heat up to seventy, leaving every light in the place on. I walked around turning them all off, punching the thermostat down, but it wasn't much use: there were three of them and one of me. And Annelise, of course, but I don't think she noticed or cared. I could hear her voice, wafting from the den.

"What it's saying in this context is that you *deserve* those things. That you shouldn't doubt yourself, because they'll be the result of your hard work towards your goals. And when—" She cut off, card in hand, as she saw me in the doorway. Beside her, Andra's glossy head twisted to look.

"Oh, hey," she said. "Annelise is just doing a reading. You want one next?"

I shook my head. "No thanks. I've got a ton of work. It just sounded interesting, that's all."

Andra's full mouth broke into a grin.

"Sounds like it's good," I added.

"It's *hopeful*," Annelise said, as though it were a correction.

"Well. I'll leave you to it."

"You're a kind person," Annelise continued as I went up the stairs, her voice echoing along the wooden halls. "And it's important to take care of yourself, as well as those around you—" I was still fixated on Annelise's voice when someone flew out of Cress's room and directly into me. Lila.

"Fuck," I wheezed. "I didn't see you, Li—"

I followed her stricken gaze to the piece of paper that had fallen between us.

A check. To cash. For ten grand.

From Cressida's account.

Lila grabbed at it quickly. Cramming the check into the pocket of her jeans, she scrambled to her feet, scanning my face.

Wondering what I'd seen.

"Sorry," I said. "Sorry, I—I thought Cress was at Blake's tonight?"

Her blue eyes darted back and forth.

"She is." Lila shoved her hands in her pockets. "Don't worry about it, she just loans me some money when I'm a little short. You know Cress, she's so generous—" She must have seen the doubt on my face, and her cheeks flushed as she set a hand on my arm. "You know she won't miss it. Come on. She's not like us, she doesn't even check her bank statements."

"But it's—hers," I said. I would have said something better, but that *like us* was still ringing, tinny, between my ears. "Aren't you okay? Money-wise?"

Lila looked up at the ceiling. It took me a second to realize she was trying not to cry. And then, hand still on my arm, she yanked me into her room.

She shut the door, flipping around with her back to it, both hands twisted behind her on the knob.

"I'm not *like* them," she said, hoarse, not meeting my eyes. "I'm not. My parents—"

". . . are lawyers."

"Yeah, but they're, like, self-made lawyers. They don't have the money for this," she said, waving a hand around at I don't know what. "They pay for school, but they both worked in college, and they wanted me to get a job." She let go of the doorknob. "But you know I can't do that with the team. The team is its own job! You know I can't. But then the boots—and I have to *wear* something—and I have to *eat*—"

She stopped then.

"What?" she said. "You don't believe me?"

"No, I do. It's just—ten *grand*, Lila." Enough to cover my parents' expenses for a few months. Enough to keep me in luxury for the rest of the year, to get me a good apartment in the city, to pay the security and first and last month's rent and even a broker's fee, too. Barely enough. But enough.

"But that's it," she said, starting to pace. Her hands gesticulated wildly as she spoke. "It's enough to get me through the year. I can't interview in New York like the rest of you—I'm going to have to fly out to LA at least a few times to actually get *any* kind of on-set work for next year—and it's just this once, I didn't want to have to do it again—and do you *know* how much is in there? Over a *hundred*," she said, stopping with wide eyes. "I'll put it back," she said, and a little sob escaped. "I will. I'll figure something out. Just—don't tell her, Rosie? Please?"

"Fuck. Lila, I—" I wanted to sit down somewhere, but where? Her bed was too intimate. And anyway, it was covered in clothes. "What will you do?"

"I'll tear it up," she said. "I will. Really, I will. Just don't tell her? Please don't. Rosie, you're, like, my best friend."

"No, I'm not." The words were out automatically and we both stood for a moment, hearing them again.

"Don't tell her?" she repeated, lips trembling. "She's not like us. She doesn't understand."

I'd have to tell Cress, of course. If Lila didn't cash the check, all the better.

But then the rest of the year, living with both of them. The rest of the year, with Cress looking over her shoulder at every turn.

The rest of the year, with Lila hating me.

I shook my head, and she thrust her arms around me.

"Thank you," she whispered. "I promise. Thank you."

So I didn't say anything. Maybe I should have.

But the thing was? Cressida hadn't earned that money any more than Lila had.

12

THE SIX OF WANDS

On the Six of Wands card, you've got this guy with a crown of victory riding through the streets. He's made it, he's won, he's succeeded. Everyone's thrilled and for the moment, it's super exciting. The thing to keep in mind, though, is that it's a six. The journey's not complete until ten—or really until the court cards—or the major arcana, if you want to be specific. So it's a victory, but it's a victory in a battle.

It still doesn't tell you anything about the war itself.

THE END OF SEPTEMBER brought our first show. I'd done two years of them already, but it was something of a revelation, the first show of senior year: we weren't just riding to ride. There was a point to all of this. To place ourselves at the top; to fight it out among all the other girls on all the other teams; to show what we could do. It was at Connecticut College, less than an hour away, but in total country. There was something familiar and sad about it, if only to me, if only if I overlooked the lushness of the landscape, the rolling hills in the background.

We'll win, I thought when I pulled that Six of Wands that morning. Annelise's clarification wasn't particularly optimistic, but when were they ever? I was starting to understand what she'd said about her own interpretations, way back when we first met. The cards weren't black or white, the way she saw them. They were stories, full of shades of gray.

Still, though. We were going to win. The cards had said so.

The team took a bus, but not us: we were our own little team of five. The trunk was packed to the top with our gear, so high Cress couldn't see out of the rearview window. But she didn't complain, just as she never complained about the driving itself. Just leaned on the horn until Lila and Andra came scrambling out of the house in the early dawn light, piling into the Range Rover where Annelise and I were already waiting. And then we drove off together into the morning in silence, the Black-Eyed Peas blaring and nobody much wanting to talk, foreheads leaning against chilled windows.

There was such a particular feel to those shows: the preparations of a beauty pageant melded with the overblown excitement of a Renaissance fair topped with the chaos that seemed particular to girls our age: braiding each others' hair frantically; swearing at too-tight boots; searching for a lost crop, hairnet, jacket. And in the ring, a series of six or seven girls on horses they'd never seen before in their lives: black-jacketed, black-booted, black-helmeted, like they could control the whole world with just a flick of their crops. Normally, I despised that kind of chaos.

But here, I loved it.

I'd missed shows while I was in Argentina. No matter how many polo matches I'd seen, no matter that I'd even been allowed to play in the very last one. As a kid, I'd loved the 4-H competitions, from the silly ones with feed-sack versions of musical chairs to the more formal ones at local fairs. When I'd first come to Yale, the idea of competing at that level—Ivy League—had made me quiver with excitement. The idea of showing everyone what I could do, without ever having to tell them. To be part of a recognized elite.

It was all I could have asked for.

Lila, as always, got us all coffees from concessions (with Cress's money? But then, she'd torn up the check. Hadn't she? Had I actually seen her do it?) and slunk off behind this barn or that one to chain-smoke until her class, which would be the last: Open, with Cress. No pressure for Lila, not usually. It was a given that Cress would win the class and get us the big points; Lila's job was to come in second, to stop any other team from being able to claim that *almost* and the lower number of points that went with it. Usually she did it; when she was particularly hungover or tired, she'd place third or fourth.

Clutch, the girls would say, hugging her afterward. *Our secret weapon.*

I was in Intermediate, where I'd been since sophomore year. I hadn't gotten enough points to place into Open; I wasn't anywhere close to Cress's level, or even Lila's. First year, I'd swept Walk-Trot-Canter so easily that I quickly placed into Novice. But Intermediate was the level of my incompetence. I'd get us a second or third, Andra usually right behind me in fourth or fifth. Genevieve, a first-year rider, rounded out our Intermediate class this year. I thought she'd do better than me, but it wasn't yet clear.

It was one of our weaker classes and I took no pleasure in leading it.

Cress and Andra climbed begrudgingly out of the car; it was bright morning by then.

"Annelise," Cress hissed over her shoulder at me, and I grabbed my bag and trudged over to the team's spot in the stands. They'd placed her in Walk-Trot-Canter last year, happy to stack the team again, but she'd pointed up to Novice so quick that she was already on the verge of pointing up again. Twice in two years; as good as what I had accomplished.

She was far better than me, though.

I didn't particularly care. I loved to watch her ride; loved to watch them all ride, loved to see the sport at its best. But it kept ringing in my head: Nine months from now, what would this all mean? It would just be something I'd done. Not a soul on Earth would care if I'd placed second or third. Not a soul would even remember.

We'd always stayed in the car and slept through the early classes, but not Cress. Not now, not this year. Annelise was her excuse, but Annelise would come halfway through the show. No, Cress wanted to show that she was the captain, to sit appraisingly in the stands, to have the girls trotting by in front of her to suck in their bellies, as they did when they passed our coach Shannon, aching for her approval. And so, while Andra—and Lila, when she returned—curled up against her enormous bag and took a nap, Cress stayed awake with watching eyes.

Walk-Trot and Walk-Trot-Canter always seemed to take annoyingly long if you weren't friends with anyone in them. I couldn't read the expression on Annelise's face as she watched the riders, or as she kept glancing back at the video camera on the tripod behind Cress.

"What's that?" she whispered to me finally.

I shook my head.

"Cress!" I called. When she looked at me, I pointed at the camera with a quizzical expression.

She made a face. *Dad,* she mouthed. Then she flipped around to look at the camera, too, as though wanting to make sure it hadn't captured her.

"Oh," I said, turning to Annelise. "It's just for Grayson."

But she had gone pale; I could see beads of perspiration beginning to form by her temples, just below her helmet.

"Grayson's going to watch?"

"Yeah, he never comes to these things—well, *you* know, you've been doing this for a while now. But I think with Cress trying to go pro, he's got a special interest—"

But then she clapped a hand over her mouth and started half hobbling, half running down the bleachers. I followed her, equally awkward, over the bags of clothing, the helmets, the crops, outside the barn and around the corner, where she began vomiting violently.

You're supposed to hold your friend's hair back. Of course I know that. But what do you do when it's already perfectly braided, in a hairnet, and under a helmet?

I set my hands on her shoulders instead. Holding her as her body heaved.

"You get nervous?" I asked when she was back upright, trembling and sweating.

"Not usually. Just the thought of—"

"Oh, it's *Grayson* that's scaring you? No way he watches anyone but Cress," I said. "Seriously. Maybe he'll watch the Open classes, but I don't think he's all that interested in the rest of us."

We went back inside and I got her a bottle of water from the team cooler and a napkin to wipe her forehead. In a few minutes, she looked almost normal. They began to announce the Walk-Trot-Canter results and she shrugged on her jacket, her gloves.

She was ready.

They called the Novice class.

Annelise, looking strange and structured and almost nineteenth-century in the formal show clothes, was on.

I grabbed her shoulders, though I had to reach up to do it.

"Do great," I said.

She smiled. She seemed to turn in on herself before competing; I noticed it again and again that fall. While some of the girls went pale and shaky, and others stomped off as though annoyed at having to compete at all, like Andra, Annelise moved to the ring like she had a wonderful secret that had been just hers for so long; and now, she was about to reveal it.

She was good at the equitation. Long, strong legs, quiet hands, anticipating her horse's every question. But she wasn't lovely to watch in the same way Cress was. Nor was she quite as ferocious and hungry, like she'd been that first day I saw her, down at the stables. She placed first, but it wasn't, I thought, a sure thing. Wasn't by any great stretch; the girl just behind her had been good, too.

But then came the fences.

Alone in the ring, just her and the horse. And I could see it in her eyes: a hard, almost angry flash of dark blue before they took off. And then they were flying, they were up and down like a jackrabbit, clearing each low fence by a good foot or more.

"She's got to be going at least—what, four feet?" Andra looked around wildly at us for confirmation. It was, I realized, her first time seeing Annelise ride.

"That's nothing," Cress said, not taking her eyes from the ring. "I've seen her do five."

"You haven't," I said. But it was more of an exclamation than a real question. "That's—fuck, that's almost *Olympic* height." Even the Open girls only jumped about three feet and a bit.

But Cress just kept on watching with a secretive smile.

Applause like I hadn't heard before. Annelise had cleared the course perfectly, in plenty of time, and was waiting now for the others to go.

She got first. Of course she won. I'd never seen anything like her.

I placed third; Andra, fifth. Genevieve got second in our class, which was right. She was better than me. By the time Cress had swept the Open classes, Lila following right behind her, it was late afternoon and we were all ready to go home.

We were all standing by the car, bags at our feet, drooping and ready, but Cress was standing twenty feet back with Shannon, gesticulating at a clipboard. Five minutes—ten. Calculating the individual scores, seeing who had done what.

And finally, Cress strode back to the car, dark Dior glasses blotting out her eyes.

"Congrats," she said as she beeped it open. "You pointed up."

The four of us looked at each other.

"Who?" Andra said finally.

"Who do you think?" Cress said, collapsing into the driver's seat. "Annelise. You're now Intermediate. You'll be alternate, Andra."

We all fell silent.

"Oh," Andra said, in as small a voice as I'd ever heard from her. And then, clearing her throat. "Okay."

13
THE KNIGHT OF SWORDS

The Knight of Swords is a man on a mission. Or, you know, a lady on one. He's got his sword of truth and he doesn't care who he has to strike down with it. Don't think you can outsmart him, either—he's quick on his feet. Well, on his horse. But his problem is that he hasn't always thought things through. You kind of just want to grab his horse by the reins and go: hey. Slow down there, Flash.

LATE-NIGHT PARTIES AND early-morning shows and classes that haunted my dreams; October mellowed into itself with gentle showers and bright leaves falling into puddles, where they'd dry and crisp up and blow away, leaving only their silhouettes behind.

Andra didn't talk to Annelise or Cress for three days. Not outright ignoring them, but slipping out of rooms when they'd appear, staying silent when they addressed the group as a whole. On the third day, Cress grabbed her by the upper arm and dragged her into the den. When they came out fifteen minutes later, Andra was talking again.

Lila, on the other hand, seemed to be riding a wild high. Everything was the *best,* the *most exciting,* the *craziest thing I ever saw.* I'd seen her like that on coke at parties a few times first and sophomore years, but I didn't think she'd started doing it during the day; I don't think Cress would have let her. But she kept buzzing around the house, so frantically feverish it felt like she'd take flight any second; and when she went off to class or practice, it was a cool relief. Like a crazed fly that had been trapped in your room for days had finally flown out the window.

Annelise, meanwhile, seemed to glow softly. She never mentioned her win or her promotion; she talked less than ever, in fact, seemed to turn in on herself. Her trips to New York had fallen to once or twice a week—though they were hard to track, as she consistently spent four or five hours a day at the stables, never telling anyone where she was going. And as she grew brighter and brighter, something in Cress seemed to be turning sharp. Now Cress was the one calling out in frustration about locking the front door, Cress the one tapping her foot in the doorway as we wrote out our rent checks and handed them over to her. Leadership was supposed to make people into better versions of themselves, wasn't it? I wasn't sure where I'd gotten that idea, but she sure disproved it that month.

And then there was me. Turning away from the chaos and the tension, pulling myself back to what mattered. To my books and my classes; to a recruitment event for Morgan Stanley, where one of the suited thirty-somethings managed to rest his hand for far too long on the small of my back before I fled the room, determined to seek out any other opportunity I could find.

But the thing about the chaos is that even if you don't come for it, eventually, it still comes for you.

"We need to talk."

Andra's voice, always a bit raspy, cut through the cozy sound of October rain pounding against my window as I did my econ reading.

"Uh, sure," I said, and she barreled in, flopping cross-legged onto Annelise's bed. Cress's power trips, Lila's check, her own demotion: the *we need to talk* list was growing longer every day. And all I wanted to do was to stay the fuck out of it.

Before Argentina, before Annelise, I would have crossed my legs, too, leaned into the drama; whatever means necessary to stay relevant to our friend group.

But I was tired now. I had my own goals. And we only had eight months of school left, one of which was winter break; couldn't everyone chill out for just that long?

Andra turned her head, rotating around the room I shared with Annelise.

"Nope, too weird in here," she said, and stood up abruptly. "Let's go."

"Andra, I'm—"

"Please."

Andra pleading. It was new.

I sighed and closed my book. "It's raining."

"Take an umbrella."

I did but she didn't, instead donning a white hooded Burberry coat that let her sulk through the streets like a reverse reaper, hands shoved in her pockets. It was midafternoon but dark as twilight, and my feet were sopping by the time she pushed me through the door of a café.

Was she paying? She should pay, right? I scanned the blackboard behind the counter. I didn't want to chance it.

"Just a coffee. A little milk."

I sighed and went to a corner table. Three of the café's walls and its ceiling were floor-to-ceiling glass, which gave a wonderful feeling of being in a greenhouse on sunny days. Now, they were steaming up from the cool rain outside, and I traced my initials in the fog, watched them fade.

Andra collapsed into the chair in front of me. All of her movements were like that. Powerful. She didn't open doors, she punched through them. She didn't hold onto her horse at the trot, she squeezed it out of him with her thighs.

"What's wrong?"

Suddenly, her near-black gaze pinned me to my chair.

"Something's weird about Annelise," she said.

Annelise and Andra were the very extremes of our group; the soft and the sharp, the silly and the serious. There was no Venn diagram in which they overlapped; they were just two circles. And now that Annelise had taken Andra's spot on the team, Andra had made up a problem that didn't exist.

"I mean, yeah. She's not the type of person we usually hang out with. But I think she's actually pretty great, once you get to know her? You seemed to think so the other day when she was reading your cards," I said.

Andra made a face. "Ugh, it's not like that. I mean, I know her type. We all have crazy aunts. It's . . ."

"What?" I said, trying and failing to mask my impatience.

Andra set her palms on the table. Her fingers were perfectly mani-
cured, black.

"I'm going to sound jealous as fuck," she said in a tone so measured it
had to be deliberate. "And yeah, it sucks that she took my spot. I wanted
to ride this year. I wanted to be part of the team, rather than just sitting
on the sidelines watching the rest of you do your thing."

"It's not like that—"

She thumped a hand against the table. "It *is* like that. But it's fine.
She's better than me. I respect that."

I believed her. She'd never been vulnerable with me before, not about
a single thing. I couldn't imagine why she'd start lying now.

"But I was talking with Bunny, my friend at Stanford?" I nodded as
though I knew who Bunny was. "And I told her about Annelise trans-
ferring here and joining the team. And *she* said she asked around about
Annelise and nobody'd ever heard of her."

I stared at her.

"Stanford's huge, Andra. Bigger than Yale, I think."

She made a face, perfect features wrinkling into monstrosity for a
split second. "Obviously. But Bunny's captain of EQ. I'd think *she'd* have
heard of her."

The team captain had a grudge against me. But I didn't want to add fuel
to Andra's fire. "Well, Annelise never actually rode at Stanford. That's
why we were able to get her into Walk-Trot-Canter last year, right? She
hadn't competed before?"

"*Rosie.* Somebody that good? Every stable for miles would know
about her."

"I dunno. Who's the best rider at Yale who's not on the team?"

"Tiffany," she said without missing a beat. The girl who fell, whom we'd
turned away. I took a scalding sip of coffee as penance for not doing more
for her. "But that's my point—we know about her. Anyways, after I talked
to Bunny, I started googling Annelise. And nothing comes up. *Nothing.*"

I rolled my eyes. "I mean, I think I have four search results to my
name, and they're all EQ shows."

"Yeah, but Rosie Macalister? You might as well be called Jane Doe.
Annelise Tattinger? I'd expect at least a *Facebook* page, for fuck's sake."

She looked down at her untouched coffee. After a second, she took off the lid and started to gulp. I watched her, fascinated; not even a wince. "I don't think she was ever even at Stanford. I'm not sure that's even her real *name.*"

I pressed my lips together.

"I know I sound crazy," she said. "But it's just weird, don't you think? Who transfers junior year? Who doesn't have a single search result, not even a single one? Who rides that well without being discovered?"

So much was whizzing through me as I listened to her questions. Questions of my own, new doubts, a curiosity darker than I'd ever felt toward Annelise.

Because, yeah. I had wondered about Annelise. Where the fuck was she going in New York, and why was she trying so hard to cover it up? It was impossible to imagine her doing something illegal, like sex work or dealing drugs. But did she actually have family money? And if she did, why was she working? Or, if it was a boy—why not just tell us?

I didn't *want* new questions added to the list, didn't want the scabs torn off of the questions I'd already answered for myself. Why hadn't Annelise ridden at Stanford? Bad blood with the EQ captain, she had said, but wouldn't Bunny have known about that? Why hadn't Annelise competed before? Some people just weren't competitive—but then seeing her at a show, that idea was laughable, and besides, she wanted to go pro. Who rides that well without being discovered? People who forego teams to ride on their own . . . but even then, EQ is a small world, and didn't Annelise grow up around her mother's horses?

None of those questions really bothered me, though. I was curious, sure. But I trusted Annelise on a bone-deep level. She had her reasons. She had her stories. They'd all come out, or not, when she felt like sharing.

The thing that bothered me? Andra.

These questions weren't hers to ask.

And I didn't have answers for her. Not for somebody who wanted to twist them against Annelise. I wasn't going to give Andra the satisfaction.

"Andra, she's nice. She hasn't done anything to us. And maybe she just grew up in a different kind of place. The West Coast is a lot bigger. And she's a hippie; does it surprise you that she's not online much? I mean,

I get being weirded out," I said, as Andra's mouth opened. "But I don't think there's anything to worry about."

The rain against the glass intensified and she looked away.

It turned out I was a pretty good liar after all. I just had to convince myself first.

"Anyway," I finished, "she'll be gone in eight months."

Andra snorted. "We all will be."

"Yeah, well. In the meantime, it's pretty likely she'll point up to Open soon, you know. That's what Cress is hoping."

After a long moment, Andra nodded.

"Yeah," she said. "I mean. It's not like she's a murderer or something."

We walked back home through the rain. I'd forgotten to pull a card that day, breaking my streak. I'd do it before bed, to understand. Maybe it would give me more information, if Annelise wouldn't.

"Does she do Equine Studies, too?" I said, as we approached the house. "Your friend Bunny."

Next to me, Andra turned her face so that I could see the incredulous expression beneath the hood.

"What kind of school has *Equine Studies*?" she asked.

14
THE WORLD (REVERSED)

The cards have different meanings when they show up upside down like this. Reversed. It shifts the meaning, twists it a hundred and eighty degrees. So normally, upright, the World's an amazing card to get. Things opening up to you, possibility and achievement and moving on to a higher plane.

Reversed, though?

You know when you're walking down a flight of stairs and you're almost at the end but you stumble and miss a step? That's the World reversed. It's like, you've missed something that's going to delay or halt your ultimate success. What drives me batty is that you don't know whether it's delayed or failed, so you just have to kind of wait and see.

Wait and see *is my least favorite kind of reading.*

W HEN WE GOT HOME that afternoon, I had a long email from my mother, detailing the foibles of the next-door twins, who'd decided to let all of the sick cats out of their cages and set them free; a note from my father, saying we should have a call soon; a full-on novel from Emily, my high school friend who went through periods of nostalgia over at the University of Illinois; and, at the very bottom of my inbox, an invitation from Columbia to come interview for the fellowship.

"Holy shit!" Cress cried when I told her that evening, grabbing her as she left for Blake's. She had the liveliest expressions when she was excited, the soft and hard parts shifting into a new face: round and wholesome. She grabbed my shoulders. "Can I dress you for it?"

"Oh my God, of course!" The relief flooded my veins. I didn't have anything like the business-casual outfit the entire internet said I should be wearing for an interview like this, and I'd been secretly hoping Cress would offer. I was closer in size to Lila or even Andra, but less comfortable asking. Anyway, I could always pin up the pants, hike up the skirt, wear a mini-dress as a knee-length. We'd work something out.

"While we're on the topic," I added. "What do you think your dad would say? What kind of advice would he give?"

She stared at me for a few seconds, her face shifting. And there they were again: her hard edges.

"I'm not some JV version of my father," she snapped. "Figure it out yourself."

She was back to normal by the time she returned in the morning. But a few days passed, then a week. *Hey! Do you have a sec to help me pick out some clothes?* and *Cress, are you busy? Because*—weren't working for me. She was always running through the house, pounding around barefoot looking for her shoes, grabbing a book on her way over to Blake's, on her way to class, on her way to the stable. And her answers were so enthusiastic: *Definitely, when I get back?* And *Of course, just not right now.*

There are only so many times you can ask.

I'd hoped that this was one of the important things that would lodge like a splinter in her brain, but on the morning of the interview, I was standing in front of my dresser in my underwear, utterly at a loss.

The World Reversed, the cards had told me that morning, and Annelise had explained. Well, yeah. At this rate, my amazing finance career was never even going to get off of the ground.

I could wear my show jacket. It was the most expensive thing in my wardrobe. But were jeans acceptable? They couldn't be. It was academia, though, not J. P. Morgan—

"Eeesh," Annelise said, halting at the door. "Everything okay?"

I clutched the top of the drawer with both hands. I didn't know why I felt so teary, so unhinged all of a sudden. "I have to go into the city for my interview—"

Her eyes widened, blazing bright. "That's today? I can go in with you!"

"For real? It's earlier than you usually go."

She shook her head. "It's not a problem. Worried about your outfit?" I laughed, high, shrill, and waved at my bra and underpants. "Uh, you could say that. Or lack thereof. Cress was going to—" But it felt unloyal to continue, even to Annelise.

Who was I kidding? Especially to Annelise.

She surveyed me. "I don't have any pants that'll fit you. But I wonder if a dress . . . what size do you wear?"

"Four."

"I have a six that might fit you," she muttered, turning to the closet. After a second, she pulled out a gray matte silk thing and held it up against me. "With your riding jacket? It'll be perfect."

That's how I ended up wearing Stella McCartney to Columbia. And going into the city with Annelise blunted the sharp edges of the world around me, making everything feel easier. More manageable. Softer.

The second she saw me gnawing my lip as I stared out the window, she handed me one of the headphones from her iPod. And so we went from New Haven to New York listening together to her songs. To Kate Bush, to Elton John, to Bright Eyes.

"Where will you be?" I asked as the train barreled toward the city. "What will you be doing?"

"I thought I'd work on my breakdancing skills down in Washington Square," she said. I stared at her blankly and she giggled. "Breathe, Rosie. I'll grab a coffee down at Angelique and get some reading done before," she said. *Before* was the end of the sentence, full stop. I grinned, about to crack a joke, but anything I could think of—sex work, escorting, drug dealing—felt too ridiculous to mention.

And that's how her job—it had to be a job, she went too regularly for it to be anything else—had remained Schrödinger's cat all semester: there and not there, both at the same time. Unmentionable, because what if it really wasn't a cat at all, but some kind of monstrous hairless thing? The closer we got to the actual city, though, the hungrier I grew to know what she did.

The transition from campus to city never stopped being a strange one. At Yale, we were princesses: not in charge, but with our own power. We weren't Bonesmen or part of any other secret society. We weren't the daughters of presidents or emirs. But we were pretty enough, rich enough, interesting enough to rise above the herd, even at Yale. Collectively, we were; if I were on my own, I'd be mixed in with the grinds; the kids in Abercrombie with the same stupid posters on their walls; the kids I'd met on my first-year hall. Not worried about hierarchies because I would have been so low on them that I wouldn't even have known they existed.

My whole time at Yale, I'd been grateful to have escaped those hoards. But I wondered, on that train ride, whether I'd have considered a life in New York City after graduation if I hadn't joined the team. Probably, I'd have taken a job at a vet clinic in New Haven, made some extra money between classes. Done an internship or two in the city if I could, spent summers learning the ropes of finance. Of who the clients were, of how you talked to them. Of where you ate lunch and whether your shoes should have round or square or pointy toes—

But I never would have known them: not Cress, not Annelise. The thought made my throat tighten.

The city revealed the differences that Yale had mostly hidden. There was a heightened reality to Manhattan for me: it was the place that everything I'd ever read had referenced; places I'd seen on TV and in movies cropped up on every corner. Rockefeller Center, Sardi's, the Met. It didn't matter that I had zero connection to them personally. They were the reference points around which it seemed all of America revolved, and it made the city seem like it was the only place that mattered.

Soon, too soon, we were at Grand Central. I could have gotten off earlier because my interview was so far uptown, but I wanted Annelise beside me for as long as possible. She popped on a pair of huge square sunglasses and for a second she looked so cool, with her cropped leather jacket and her long waving hair, that I nearly forgot that I knew her.

"You're okay getting up to 116th?" she asked. I nodded. She stood facing me for a minute, impossible to see where her eyes were through the glasses. Then she thrust her arms around me, the faint scent of honey radiating off of her. "You're gonna do great," she whispered in my ear. "Meet me at five on the platform?"

I nodded.

The crowds closed around me, and I was alone.

As it turned out, I shouldn't have worried about my outfit at all. The woman, Professor Tiggs, who called me into her cramped office was herself wearing jeans and a J.Crew sweater from a few years ago. My mother had the same one. I could have been wearing anything—but I was glad to be in Annelise's fancy dress, trendily loose around my frame, glad to be wearing a three-hundred-dollar jacket. It labeled me as a certain type of person, and I liked that I could be that person, as well as the one with the straight-A transcript sitting in front of her. It was fun to pretend I was the kind of girl who might have grown up at the Pierre, too.

Professor Tiggs's curly hair bounced around her head enthusiastically as she described the program: six months of what she called *work-study* at a financial institution, then three months of writing up my findings, with the possibility of extending the work for another few months. She asked a few questions about Argentina. When I told my friends about my time there, I'd focused more on the polo and less on the horse shit, but now was the time to focus on neither, instead extolling the *riveting lectures* from the Nobel Prize–winning economist I had, in fact, mostly not understood.

"Rosie, this was delightful. You're exactly the kind of candidate I was thinking of when I started this fellowship, and I don't mind saying, I think your chances of being in New York next year are *very* good. Do you have any questions for me before you go?"

I wet my lips. The question I wanted to ask—the only question I wanted to ask—couldn't be the first.

"Absolutely," I said. "First of all, can you give examples of some of the institutions where this year's fellows are doing their work experience?"

She smacked her forehead. "Absent-minded professor. Of course, though it really depends on the subject of their research, and this year's cohort is the first. We'd expect more opportunities to open up in subsequent years. We have one fellow down at the Fed, one at the stock exchange. There's one at Tate Associates, who have been extraordinarily accommodating, and then one at Bear Stearns." She noticed the look on my face. "But my goal for you would be a placement in a foundation linked with one of the institutions."

Tate Associates. To work for Cress's father. To watch him at work. To study him at work. It should have been an exciting moment: I could enter that world. Make it my own. Become like him so that my children could become like her.

But I had another question I needed answered first. The only real question.

"And—you mentioned a stipend?"

"Yes. We're very pleased to offer eighteen thousand dollars to our fellows. Now, if you extend your research, that will, unfortunately, be unpaid. But your access to Columbia's resources—"

I'd already stopped listening.

Eighteen thousand dollars for nine months. In New York City? I'd been extraordinarily lucky to pay less than $500 a month for a room in *New Haven.* Cursory Craigslist searches had already shown me that I'd be luckier still to find a room for more than twice that in the city, and only if I chose to live outside of Manhattan. Were fellowships taxed? I could live on a thousand a month if I got the right housing. And—

"What about health insurance?" I asked, cutting Professor Tiggs off.

She shook her head. "Not at this point, unfortunately. We're hoping to offer it at some point in the future. Of course, you would have access to all of Columbia's on-campus medical services."

"Housing?"

She looked slightly startled.

"No. Again, you wouldn't be a student, per se. It's more that the affiliation with the university would help open doors that would otherwise be closed, allowing you to—"

I couldn't do it. I couldn't make it work. Not with a $400-a-month insurance payment, not with $100 for the subway and $1,000 for rent coming out of a $2,000 check—even if it were untaxed, which I was pretty sure it wouldn't be.

And not with my student loan payments coming due.

I didn't hear anything else that she said. I must have smiled and nodded sufficiently for politeness, and the formal offer was waiting for me in my inbox when I got back home. I don't remember anything else she or

I said, because I already knew it wouldn't be relevant to any kind of life I'd actually be living.

If I'd been Cress and grown up in Greenwich, I could have commuted into the city. But then again, if I'd been Cress, I'd have had a father with a two-and-a-half-bedroom apartment at the world's most famous hotel and the money to fund me through whatever the hell I wanted to do, even if it paid exactly nothing.

Maybe she'd let me stay at her parents' house for the coming year?

But as I descended through the tunnels of Grand Central, trying to make my way to the right platform, I had to tell myself the truth: I hadn't even been able to get a blazer from her.

And this wasn't the kind of thing you could ask for.

Annelise's eyes widened as she saw me heading toward her on the platform. She grasped my wrist, the wind from the tunnel blowing her long golden hair back around her face.

"So? How did it go?"

"Just tell me, do you come here to work? Do you have, like, a job?" My tone was harsh and the words were out of my mouth before I could stop them.

She stepped back as though I'd hit her, just as the train pulled into the station.

"Kind of," she said as the doors opened.

"Is it the kind of thing I could do? In my free time?"

She slid her sunglasses back down onto her nose. It wasn't until we sat down that she'd answered me.

"No," she said.

But it *was* the kind of thing that she did. And it was the kind of thing, I was starting to suspect, that was paying for Yale.

"How can you—I'm *struggling* here," I cried. "I respected everything you wanted to keep to yourself when it didn't affect me. I didn't pry, I wasn't a bitch about it. I don't know who you are, Annelise. I don't know what kind of family you come from or why they give you some money but not enough, or why we've never heard a single thing about them, or why you think I wouldn't realize that Stanford doesn't have a fucking

Equine Studies degree, but come on!" I smacked my thigh; the sting was pleasurable. "Come on. I'm not asking you for a job. I just want to know how you do it, because I'm fucking drowning here, and I don't *know* what I don't know about how to make it in this city, and you could tell me, but you won't—"

I had started sobbing. With a little tap on my temple, Annelise guided my head onto her shoulder and let me cry, stroking my sweaty hair gently. I was sobbing, then crying; then hiccupping; then tired. As tired as I've ever been in my life.

And so then, of course, I was asleep.

And so we were silent, all the way back home.

And as we waited for a taxi in the New Haven night, she still hadn't given me a reply.

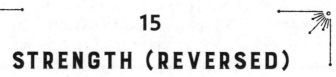

15
STRENGTH (REVERSED)

I get annoyed when Strength comes up, because it usually means you're going to have to pull through somehow. But it's still a happy card, you know, because it's all about confidence, believing in yourself, committing. Reversed? Not so great. No self-control. Hedonism. A lack of courage. I guess you could call it cowardice.

It was around mid-october that I got homesick for the very first time. Christmas seemed impossibly far away, and I never went home for Thanksgiving; it was too expensive and too long a trip for just four days. But suddenly the sight of a golden Lab on a walk was enough to make me tear up, thinking of our dog, Bailey, rolling on her back, showing me her belly, asking to be cuddled. A dead sparrow in the gutter made me actually cry; its wing was broken, it hadn't been able to pull itself back up. How easy for one of my parents to have fixed it, if they'd been there. How many motley animals I'd brought to them as a child.

But life was going on around me, as my phone insisted on reminding me. Late one morning, it buzzed insistently.

Hs minting at 4 be thr.

House meeting at four, be there. I snapped my phone closed, swallowing. Too late for any of us to be at practice, too early for any of us to be out. Except for Annelise, of course, who was staying after her new Intermediate lesson to work on one of Shannon's special courses.

But that, of course, was probably the point.

I had an hour between stats and the *meeting*, enough time for a nap, but my phone rang just as I collapsed under the covers.

"Rosie!" Mom's voice crackled through the line. For Christmas last year, Dad had gotten her a hands-free kit for the car. It was great for the efficiency of their practice, but so unromantic that we still teased him about it. It was the only time we really talked, during those long drives between patients; when she wasn't on call, she was so tired that she fell asleep around seven. "How'd the interview go?"

"Oh. It was fine."

"Just fine?"

"Kind of bad." I searched for plausible reasons. "The woman was up-tight. Snobby. New York, you know."

"Oh, shoot. Well, don't worry. There'll be a million other opportunities."

I swallowed. "I don't know, though. I mean, I don't have the . . ." *internships, work experience, life experience*: What could I say that wasn't an indictment of her, of the family's financial situation? "Time," I finished. "I don't have the time to look for them."

"Well, nobody'd be hiring for June now, anyways. It's so early."

"Look," I said. "I was wondering. What if I came home for Thanksgiving this year? I have a bit extra saved up . . ."

The line crackled.

"Hello?"

"Yeah! Yes," she said. "No, of course, sweetie. It's just—won't it take you a full day to get here and another to get back?"

"I could leave early. Cut a class or two. I could make it up easily, so many kids are out that week."

"But you know how it is, one of us has to be on call the whole time. Cows—"

"—don't know it's Thanksgiving. Yeah."

"And then we'll have people over for the game, and I know you hate football—"

"It was a stupid idea. I'll be home just a few weeks later, anyway."

"Well, why don't you think about it a bit," Mom said, and I could hear the relief in her voice. "But you're right, you'll be home for Christmas. What brought this on, though? You've never wanted to come back for Thanksgiving before."

It took me a second to respond. "I don't know. It's just—New York, and everything. I started missing home." She waited for me to continue. "It's like . . . I know I want to do finance, I know I do, but there's something in me that also wants to, like, get a farm and have some horses and get up with the sun and smell the hay and feel the earth again. Like our ancestors did . . ." I trailed off. "You know?"

"Oh, Rosie," Mom said. "Oh, honey. You've been away too long! Don't you remember what it's like for the farmers? Falling prices? Wild weather? Living according to the whims of the markets and the government? I know it must be easy to romanticize from where you are. But it's always been that way. Farming's *always* been hard, hon. And it's not the life I'd want for you."

I blinked back tears, but they started running down my cheeks anyway.

"No," I said quietly. "I know. And it's not the life I want for myself."

"Good," she said. "Hey, what about Cress? Isn't her father in finance?"

"Yeah," I said warily.

"Can't you ask her if he might have a job open for you next year? If you're so worried about getting something set up right away."

But Mom didn't get it. This wasn't an opening down at Kroger. This wasn't a job at the Amazon warehouse.

And these weren't the people I'd grown up with.

"I mean, yeah," I said. "But how do you even ask for something like that?"

AFTER WE HUNG UP, I washed my face and went downstairs. Four on the dot. But only Lila was there, cross-legged and texting on one of the sofas. Glasses and cereal bowls and used cutlery were strewn across the coffee table.

"Hey, you!" Lila chirped as she looked up from her texts. "Do you know what this is about?"

Could I actually see fear in her face, or was I imagining it? I shook my head as Andra came in. "Ask the leader."

Andra looked exhausted, circles under her eyes like bruises. "Ask the leader what?"

"What the meeting's about," Lila said.

Andra curled up on the couch next to her. "Who the fuck knows? Cress told me to text you."

"Why didn't she just text us herself?" I asked.

Andra leaned her head over the back of the sofa arm so that I could only see her chin. "She was driving back from the barn."

Thumps from the front hall, and the door banged closed. "Speak of the devil and she'll appear," Cress said, pushing sunglasses up into her hair as she strode in.

She was still in her bone-colored leggings, white shirt, and US Equestrian jacket, still in her paddock boots and half chaps. And while she was smudged with dirt and the room smelled more than a little bit of horse, she somehow managed to make it look like she'd come from a photo shoot as she crossed the room and sat in the armchair between the couches. I'd kind of thought she would sit next to me.

"You guys," Cress said, her hands massaging the lions' heads on each chair arm. "I fucking can't with this house anymore."

She bent forward and tried to pick a mug off of the coffee table. It came off after a second with a sticky *smack*.

I wondered if she was going to throw it.

"I just can't," she said. "So I called a cleaner. Twenty bucks a week each to do the common areas. Yeah?"

"Oh, thank fuck," Andra muttered. "Yes. Please, God. *Yes.*"

Lila's grin was a bit fixed. "Yeah, okay."

"I mean," I said. "You guys. It'd be so easy to keep this place clean. We wouldn't have to make a *chore wheel* or anything like that," I said, as Andra and Cress looked at each other. "But just, like, put stuff away when you're—we're—done? Clean the dishes as we use them?"

Cress bent down and ran her finger along one of the floorboards. She held it up to me, a gray line marring her perfect skin.

"I mean, yeah," I said. "If it comes to that, I'll run a broom around the living room. Or the vacuum. Do we have a vacuum?"

Three sets of eyes stared at me.

"So, like, *you'll* do the cleaning?" Lila said. "Do we pay you twenty bucks a week, then?"

"What?" I had the sudden image of being on my knees, scrubbing out the toilet, as music and laughter rose from downstairs. "No! I just mean, we could clean up after ourselves, and then if there's any slack—"

"Always going to be slack," Andra muttered.

Cress rolled her eyes, face morphing into laughter. "Rosie. You don't want to be our maid!"

"Of course not—"

"Well, *someone* has to," she said, and smacked the lions' heads before standing up. "So, twenty each? Just add it to your checks to me every month?"

I nodded.

"That's all?" Lila said in a small voice.

And Cress looked at her so strangely that for a moment, I thought: Does she know?

"Uh, yeah," Cress said. "What else would there be?"

16

THE EMPEROR

Oooh, the Emperor, he is scary. But sexy scary. Power is sexy, isn't it? Stability, security, leadership, money. Don't depend on luck, depend on hard work. Play by the rules. With the Emperor, it's always, always the rules.

I ALWAYS HAD THE VAGUE hope, when we went to Cress's house, that it would end up changing my life. A chance meeting with a shipping heir who fell immediately and madly in love with me. A Hollywood producer who saw me and just had to put my face on-screen. A horse that would take to me so strongly that Cress would immediately hand over the reins and I'd have one of my own, finally.

Normally by the beginning of November, we'd have gone to Cress's several times already and to the Tate pied-à-terre in the city at least that much. But the new intensity of her relationship with Blake, the stress of captaining the team, her new sharp edges, all of it had made the idea of visiting her parents seem like a ludicrous waste of time to Cress. So, it wasn't until her twenty-second birthday that we drove to Greenwich once again. Forty-five minutes on increasingly idyllic roads, and all I could think was: Mom was right, it could happen. Grayson Tate could offer me a job.

Unlikely, of course. But there remained a possibility: in the kitchen over breakfast, discussing life after graduation, he'd ask me what I had planned. *Something in financial analysis,* I'd say. *I have this Columbia fellowship as a backup.* And then a raised eyebrow, a grin, a golden ticket.

It could happen.

But the sight of the Greenwich house itself always made me feel ill, jealousy like an avocado pit in my stomach. And the fantasies fell away.

It wasn't an overblown, marble pillars and gold toilets sort of place, though God knows I'd have been intimidated by that, too. And it wasn't like Andra's house outside of Boston, too pretentious and self-conscious, all glass walls and mid-century-modern lines and edges that could cut you. (I didn't know what Lila's was like; she was from Main Line Philadelphia, but we never went south of Manhattan, and everyone talked like she grew up below the Mason-Dixon Line.)

It was like a dollhouse, the kind you dream of as a kid. An absolutely rambling, Arts and Crafts–inspired home with about a thousand bay windows and several wraparound porches and stained glass everywhere. Fireplaces throughout that they kept burning anytime the temperature dropped below sixty. It must have been ten thousand square feet or more, I don't know; I'm not sure I ever saw all of it. And beyond, acres and acres of land, forest, outbuildings—including stables.

It made me sad, enviously sad. And I hated myself for it.

Cress killed the motor and threw her door open into the early November evening.

"Come on! I don't want to miss Mom's drinks!" she called over her shoulder as she took off toward the front door.

Cress's mother had a few glasses of wine before bed every night—something that Cress claimed to find hilarious. At first, I assumed she must secretly be despondent that her mother was an alcoholic. But actually, no: Cress joined her for these drinks and had since sometime in high school. And it was their favorite time of day.

It seemed like such a cliché, the drunk rich woman. But Anthea never seemed to get truly drunk. And Cress did actually seem to find it funny when her mother stumbled over the line into tipsy. There was something cozy and conspiratorial about the way they cuddled up together on the dressing room love seat, more like friends than mother and daughter.

We pushed into the foyer. The house was shaped like a rising sun, the huge semicircular foyer with wings poking off of it like rays. That central space was airier than the rest of the house, thanks to the height of the ceilings soaring twenty feet above the most beautiful polished floors, the plushest green-and-gold rugs. A fireplace so tall you could stand inside it, lit with crackling flames. Window seats on either side of the door where you could just imagine curling up on a rainy day.

I mean, you could imagine it. I don't believe any of the Tates had ever actually done it.

This time, Anthea was waiting for us.

I don't think she'd ever done that before. But as I saw how Cress crushed her tiny mother into her arms, I realized this had probably been the longest she and her only daughter had ever gone without seeing each other.

And then Anthea spread her arms even wider, and Cress let go as her mother wiggled her fingers at us.

"My girls! Get in here!"

I'd met Anthea maybe ten times in my life. We'd been to the house more often, but sometimes she was in the city, sometimes traveling, and it was about fifty-fifty we'd see her. I've always thought of my parents as warm people, but Anthea's consistent effusiveness at seeing us wasn't something I could imagine them replicating. Cress had once mentioned in passing that Anthea *never got over* prep school, and the thought made me sad. She had this beautiful, gigantic house, and all she wanted was for it to be filled with other girls.

So Lila and Andra and I crowded into Anthea's tiny embrace with Cress while Annelise stood behind us. I pulled back early.

"Have you met—" I started, but Anthea had taken the cue. She set small hands on Annelise's shoulders and pushed herself onto the balls of her feet to kiss Annelise's cheeks.

"No, I haven't! You must be Annelise. I'm Anthea, it's so wonderful to meet you, dear. This one"—nodding at Cress with a big grin—"oh, wasn't she just awful last year! Keeping my college house parties from me."

"*Mom.*"

"But of course, it was really you girls," Anthea said, ticking her index finger at Lila, Andra, and me, "who were to blame. Leaving Cressy all alone! You little monsters. Come on now," she said, stepping back, "who's up for drinkies?"

Lila's hand shot high into the air. Anthea clapped her hands together.

"Oh, good. And Miss Alexandra?"

"Sorry, Anthea, I'm beat," Andra said, slinging her Louis Vuitton tote over her shoulder. "Okay if I just go up to bed?" But she was already striding toward the stairs. I frowned, checking my phone. It was just nine o'clock.

"Well, of course, dear!" Anthea called, then turned back to us with a hushed voice. "Cress, is she getting enough iron? Vegetarianism is a silent killer, you know."

"Mom, Andra's not a vegetarian." But there was laughter in Cress's voice. Supplements were Anthea's hobby.

"D3, then. I'll have Carla mix it in with her juice, she'll never know. I know that Andra can be a little," and she rolled her eyes.

"Mom, she gets enough sun! We all do. We're *riders*."

Anthea pressed her lips together.

"Well, I'll have a think on it. She's definitely missing *something*." She flipped herself around, over to Annelise and me. "And the two of you?"

"We get enough D3, too," I said, suppressing a laugh. Of course, I knew that wasn't what she was asking, but I couldn't help myself.

"No, silly. Drinks! We're doing sidecars tonight. How do you feel about your cognac?"

I glanced over at Annelise. She mouthed something—I would have thought just at me, but she was looking at Anthea the whole time.

"I'm sorry, dear, what?"

"I'd love to see the stables?" Annelise said in a near whisper, her face white.

"Oh, of course. You should have said! Maybe Rosie . . ." And Anthea twirled to me, groomed eyebrows raised. They weren't arched like Cressida's or Grayson's; instead, they were perfect 1920s-style blond lines.

"Happy to," I said.

"But drinkies tomorrow!" Anthea said, tugging at Cress's wrist until Cress, then Lila, followed her toward the stairs.

"Mom, tomorrow's the *party*," Cress was saying as they drifted away. Annelise didn't move.

"Sorry, I know she's a lot. But she's sweet, really. You just have to think of her like a puppy. A Yorkie or something. Come on, stables are this way," I said. Her silence was making me nervous.

Outside in the crisp night, Annelise stayed silent, and I looked over at her. Her face was tilted slightly, and she was taking in the whole place, not just the house lit up bright beside us. The scent of burning leaves. The violet-black sky with charcoal trees silhouetted against it. The vast expanse of it all.

And her expression was something like wonder.

Normally, being alone with Annelise felt like taking half a Xanax. I could forget the people around me at Yale, forget my classes, forget the team. The only interesting thing in the world was her crazy, swirling brain. But she was unusually rigid as we walked through the grounds. Maybe it was being in the country at night? She was from San Francisco, after all. But this wasn't real country, it was *Greenwich,* and the estate was cut through by paved paths lit up by torches.

"You never came out here last year?" I asked as we headed through the stable doors.

"We weren't that close—" And then a familiar nicker interrupted us.

"Bambi!" I cried. Cress had sent her home a few weeks ago; she was focused on Thumper, and Bambi was just *taking up space.* I think she felt guilty, seeing her discarded horse every day. The horse nuzzled us, first one and then the other. We rubbed her nose, her rippling skin; Annelise pulled a LifeSaver out of a pocket and fed it to her.

"She's so sweet. I miss seeing her around," I said, as she rested her chin on Annelise's shoulder and closed her eyes, long lashes tickling Annelise's cheek.

"I mean, we always have Thumper," Annelise said, and made a face exactly like Thumper's pissed-off expression. I laughed.

"That asshole."

"D'you know, he bit me the other day?" she said, holding up her arm. A semicircle of teeth had made an impression just below her elbow.

"Me too! A few weeks ago." I showed her my palm.

"I wouldn't even care so much if I could just *ride* him," she said.

"Now that," I said, giving Bambi a final pat on the nose, "would be something to see."

We stopped for a last look, the ten neat boxes only half filled.

"Can you imagine what it would be like to live here all the time?" I said.

"Like being a princess," Annelise said.

"Wait. Do you mean being Cress or being one of her horses?"

Annelise laughed. "Either. Both. It's just her and her parents?"

"She has an older brother, James. But he lives in London now." I'd had the sneaking suspicion that James and I would get together, the first year I'd come out here. That's what would have happened in a movie. But by the time we actually met, sophomore year, it became immediately clear that not only were we not soul mates, I hadn't even registered to him as a person. "Should we go up?"

The brief calm that had come over Annelise in the stables seemed to dissipate with every step toward the house. By the time we reached the back door, she was so taut, she was barely bending her legs as she walked.

I paused at the back door. "Are you okay?"

She laughed, short, from her throat. "Parents," she said. "Parents make me nervous."

"Oh," I said. Anthea always made me nervous, too. It didn't help that sophomore year, Cress informed me that I'd been saying her name wrong the whole time: *Anthea* instead of *Anthea*. If you ask me now, that's what you get for having an obscure ancient Greek name, but at the time, it just made me wonder what else I'd messed up that nobody'd gotten around to telling me about yet. "Well," I said. "Grayson's actually the best. It's annoying. But we won't see them again tonight. They like their guests to be a bit . . ." I searched for the word.

"Free range?" Annelise suggested.

I pulled open the back door. "Exactly."

We were in the mud room, surrounded by boots of every imaginable make and size, when I realized I didn't know where Annelise was supposed to stay.

Where put AL? I texted, afraid Cress had left her phone lying on some table in some room I'd never even heard of. But my phone buzzed a second later: Dunno ask Carla.

"Carla?" I was familiar enough with the intercom system. It still felt strange and hushed, the way the family connected with each other; in my house, we were always calling names from floors away. Total boisterous chaos. *Bailey—I mean, Rosie—shit. George!* Mom would call, habit scrambling intention as she tried to summon the chosen one.

"Is that Rosie?" The housekeeper's voice chirped pleasant through the wires.

"It is! How are you, Carla?"

"Well, come down and see me, girl."

"I will in a bit. I just need to know—where do you want Annelise?"

"Ah. Pink room. And you're in Mahogany."

"Of course. Thanks!" I turned back to Annelise, pointing to the door. "Let's go."

"Shouldn't we get our stuff from the car?"

"Somebody will have done that already."

"Carla?"

"Probably not. Carla . . . runs things, I think? There's a whole team of maids and stuff for the little tasks. And grooms for the stables. And cooks for the food. And other people, I'm sure. Carla's just the one I know."

"Weird that none of them seem to be around," she said as we crossed the foyer.

"I think," I said, "that's part of their job."

"I was kind of afraid she'd stick us in the same room," Annelise whispered.

I laughed.

"Not here. They could invite the Senate for the weekend and still have room left over for the House of Representatives."

"This house," she said, staring up at the ceiling. "Fuck."

"What's yours like?"

"Oh," she said, and looked at the fireplace. "It's fine. Yours?"

"Like ours in New Haven, but shittier."

She laughed as we started up the stairs, her face coming alive again.

"I've been missing it, though. It'd be so nice to be able to go home whenever you wanted," I said.

Annelise reached out and squeezed my wrist.

"Wherever we are, for the rest of our lives. *That's* our home," she said, and before I could figure out what she even meant, we'd reached the Pink room. She looked like she was going to vomit.

"Seriously, though. Are you okay?"

"Where's the bathroom?" she said faintly.

"There's one off your bedroom. Text me if you need anything?"

I was grateful to enter the Mahogany room like it was truly mine, to grab the forest-green cashmere throw from the foot of the bed and wrap it around my shoulders. To stare out the window at the rural night.

But my rumbling stomach wouldn't let me focus on anything else but the idea of finding food. I'd gone right from the stables to econ to the car that day, no time for lunch, and now we'd missed dinner, too.

Oh my God, just help yourself, Cress had said with an eye roll during my first visit first year, when almost a day had gone by without eating and I'd finally worked up the nerve to ask her. But what the fuck did that mean? Could I make myself a sandwich? A drink? Open a new package of turkey? A bottle of wine? What if I ate some roast chicken and it turned out to be, like, Prince Charles's roast chicken?

My own mother would have been creeped the fuck out if she'd come into the kitchen at midnight and seen one of my friends in front of our open fridge. But then, you could hear someone moving around our kitchen from anywhere in the house; the floorboards creaked like crazy. None of the floorboards creaked here.

Still, I found a back staircase to make my way down. I don't know why. There was just something so embarrassing about needing to eat.

The kitchen was dark for the night—dark except for a beam of light spilling from an open refrigerator, by far the biggest that I'd ever seen. A shadowed figure turned around:

"Rosie!" Grayson boomed.

I stumbled back against the wall, a hand to my chest. Half poking fun at my dramatic reaction, half in wonderment that I could be this startled without actually dying.

"Mr. Tate!" I said.

He waved a hand with something in it: a chicken leg. I had the sudden sensation of being in Henry VIII's court.

He's so charismatic, I'd said to Andra the first time I'd met him, parents' weekend first year, when mine hadn't been able to come and Cress had invited me out with hers. Andra's narrow eyes had narrowed further.

Is he charismatic, or does he just have a lot of hair?

"Grayson. Please." Our catechism: my formality, his casualness.

"Grayson."

"You hungry? There's part of a roast chicken and some potato salad. And I think there's a tagine in here somewhere—" He started rummaging around.

"No, no. Thanks. I—I just came down to get some water." He tossed a bottle of water to me. I caught it just in time.

"There are those EQ reflexes!" he said. "Cressy says the team's doing great this year. You Elizabeths going to bring it home for us?"

Yale students are *Elis.* I don't know why he'd turned that into *Elizabeths* for us girls. The place had been coed when he went there, after all. I never heard anybody else use that term. Only alums ever said *Elis,* anyway.

"Definitely," I said, cracking open the water and chugging. I could feel it trickling down into my empty belly, cold.

"Busy time, senior year."

"For sure."

He ripped off the remaining meat from the bone and tossed the bone into the sink with a dull thud. It was all I could do to keep from running over and pulling it out—didn't he know bones couldn't go down the disposal?

"Cressy says you're studying econ," he said, and for a second, I was ridiculously, profoundly touched: she'd talked about me to her father. "Planning on going the I-bank route after school?"

Here. The moment was here. I chugged my water so fast, my throat froze.

"I'm exploring my options," I said with a cold mouth. "I got this Columbia fellowship, but I don't know—I'd rather be out in the world, you know?"

He grinned.

"I do know. I know better than anyone. Well, if there's anything I can do to help."

I froze. My mind flipped through six, seven different possible responses. *Actually, there is—that's so nice of you to say, in fact—GET ME A JOB.*

But next thing I knew, we were plunged into an underwater darkness. The refrigerator door closed, along with my window of opportunity.

"G'night, Rosie."

Tomorrow, I reassured myself. I'd have a response tomorrow.

Mr. Tate, last night you mentioned—I was thinking about what you said in the kitchen—

I kept coming up short, though. Because what could you do with an offer like that? How could you turn it into something real?

I was so in my head that I didn't see Annelise at the top of the stairs until I almost ran smack into her. She stood still as a scared horse as I shook it off with a little giggle.

"What are you—"

"I was hungry," she said quickly.

"Oh," I said, and pointed down the back stairwell. "Kitchen's that way. Help yourself."

I WOKE UP THE NEXT morning feeling empty but whole. The path forward seemed so clear. Seven months until I could actually go out and work—but in the meantime, if *someone* were to offer me a truly exceptional opportunity, I could arrange my classes to give me a day or two per week in the city next semester. Maybe it was the thread counts on the sheets, maybe the heavy duvet, maybe the polished four-poster bed. But I felt more hopeful than I had in a long time when I woke up on Cress's birthday. Not since Argentina. Not since the summer.

I knew exactly what the day would bring. A huge breakfast buffet spread out in the dining room, to be picked at haphazardly throughout the day; riding with Cress and the girls; an afternoon of spiked hot drinks and gossip in front of the fire; and then, finally, the glittering people, all friends of her parents and the Dalton kids and probably Blake and his crew friends, too, would infiltrate the house little by little, then all at once. Champagne would appear in my hand whenever my glass went dry; tiny delicious bites would appear by the platterful in front of my nose. I would laugh at the jokes made by men my father's age and compliment the hairstyles of women a few years older than me. Cress would appear in the most beautiful dress (one I'd never seen before and would never see again), open an insane pile of presents, reacting to each one with such insincere delight it was hard to imagine that anyone believed her. Then we'd sneak away, the four—now five—of us, to Cress's room, to try some of her mother's pills and make fun of everyone we'd just met and give Cress our present.

But I'd forgotten the actual sensations. The wind-chilled cheeks I got after the ride; my face, sore from laughing as Annelise made fun of each of us in turn, imitating our riding styles. The slow defrosting of our toes in the cashmere socks Cress had lent us (I wasn't giving mine back this year) as we sat in a cozy wood-paneled room with mulled wine. The safe feeling I had as Annelise brushed out my hair and started weaving tiny braids through the top layer, twisting them around into something baroque and beautiful. And through it all, Orpheus and Eurydice, the family cocker spaniels, sniffing around our feet, curling up at our sides, nudging our heels, great soft balls of fur.

Annelise had lent me her gray dress again. I hooked in some chandelier earrings, did a smoky eye, and there: I wasn't myself anymore. I was someone better.

By the time I made it down a floor to Cress's room, the other girls were already waiting.

"You look amazing," Cress said. She was in a dark pink baby doll with shoulder-length gold earrings, the others in different versions of the same except for Annelise, who was in floor-length turquoise silk: vintage Prada, I guessed, and she confirmed, pleased at my recognition.

I felt like I belonged.

"Thanks," I said, laughing. "I feel like Cinderella. No, shit, sorry—*you're* the Cinderella, it's your birthday!"

Cress rolled her eyes, showing a dimple. "I learned a long time ago that tonight isn't about me," she said. "Come on."

To their credit, the Tates couldn't have been nicer. They always welcomed us into the mix with a touching level of attention. I think it was also to prevent us college kids from clustering together, away from the adults; I could already see Cress shooing apart Blake and the crew boys he'd brought with him out of the corner of my eye. *Mingle, mingle, you dumbasses!* Anthea was handing me around like the floating trays of food—*You've got to speak to Petey*—*have you ever met Aunt Maisie?*—*this is Georgie, she's the best tennis player you've ever seen*—and the conversations were irrelevant at best. I was in the middle of discussing the disappearance of white gloves from the debutante scene—well, hearing about it, anyway—when Cress wrapped her arm in mine and spun me around.

We ended up face-to-face with a broad-chested man, tan and dimpled as Grayson.

"Here she is! Uncle Charlie, you remember Rosie," Cress cried.

"Hi, Rosie. But come on, that's no way to say hello, Cressy girl!"

She flung herself at him for a hug without letting go of my arm. I bounced awkwardly off his side.

"And your friend here is—"

"*Rosie.*" She rolled her eyes at me. "This is my dad's best friend. You guys met before, right?" Without waiting for an answer, she spun back to him. "What'd you get for me? A boat? A puppy?"

He laughed.

"You'll have to wait and see, kiddo. Just about present time now, isn't it?"

If Cress could speak like this to one of her father's friends, why couldn't I say to Grayson: *You know, I was thinking about what you said last night, about a possible job for next year*—

In the presence of Cressida's bravado, the words felt possible. Felt likely, even.

I tried to scan the room for Grayson. But he was nowhere to be seen; then the lights went out, and an illuminated cake seemed to float from the doorway, Grayson at its side, and everyone was singing.

The cake stopped before Cress and she blew out the candles in a single breath. The lights flicked back on; a knife was already positioned for her to make the first cut. She began the ritual of sliding a slice of cake onto a plate. But instead of one fluid motion, she froze, then plucked a rectangle of paper from the plate.

"You've heard the story often enough," Grayson said. He was talking to her, ostensibly, but his Johnny Cash voice rumbled out across the entire dining room. "How I got my start, how all of this"—gesturing to the room around him—"came from one exceptional horse. And the more I thought about who I was at twenty-two, about my own entry into the real world . . . well, you're old enough for your first string of horses, kiddo," he said, and his handsome face broke into a grin. "Made the transfer this morning."

"Half a million," a man's voice murmured in my ear. With a start at the unpleasant tickling, I looked up to see Charlie standing next to me.

"For a horse?" I hadn't realized that Annelise was near—I had lost track of my friends. But her cracked voice sent me spinning back into the parallel realities we straddled. Cress was a pretty, pretty princess holding court, and here we were: her courtiers.

"A couple horses. You heard him, a *string,*" Charlie said with a low laugh and a swig of whisky.

Cress was wiping icing off of the deposit slip, laughing and teasing her father for the drama and the unnecessary mess. It was only out of the corner of my eye that I saw Annelise stumble past Lila and Andra toward the door. They looked at me, and I looked at them; it was clear neither of them was going to make a move. It was probably clear that I wasn't going to, either. Not trapped as I was beneath Charlie's heavy tanned arm, which he'd laid across my shoulders. Not while Cress's father poked her shoulder and told her to go make sure the money'd landed okay. And not while Cress trotted out of the room on her silver Jimmy Choos, off to find her computer and admire her new six-figure balance, thinking of all the horses—or the one truly perfect creature—it would buy her.

And meanwhile, Annelise was still gone.

17

THE DEVIL

Just chill, okay? I know he looks scary, but he's actually part of you. He's your shadow self. He's your obsessions and your dark desires. He's what you can't let go of, even when it hurts you. Even when it drains your attention away from everything you should be focusing on. Even when there's so much more that life is actually providing you, the Devil is your fixation on the one thing you can't have, blinding you to the banquet on offer before you.

He's about being caged by your desires.

I think about that a lot. Maybe that's the scariest thing of all.

I BACKED OUT OF THE ROOM slowly. Andra shot a glance my way; I mouthed *bathroom* and she nodded.

But Annelise wasn't in the bathroom. It was empty, though the walls were hung with important framed paperwork: a letter from Arnold Schwarzenegger, a Christmas card from George H. W. Bush, even Grayson's MBA diploma. I think the Tates thought it was funny, putting that stuff in the bathroom.

Annelise didn't know the house, and I didn't know where to begin looking. I stood, frozen beside the bathroom, for a moment; I wouldn't have found her if I hadn't heard a little sniffle from behind a curtain down the adjacent hall.

"Annelise?" I whispered, pulling the curtain aside. There, on the window seat, she sat with her knees pulled to her chest, her face scrunched and red and wet.

"Oh, thank fuck, it's you," she said.

I sat across from her, and she drew the curtains closed behind us. The little niche it made was almost completely dark, the only light coming from outside, dim and far away in the night.

"What's wrong?" I asked.

She took a long, shuddery breath.

"It's everything. It's nothing. It's just—do you know what that kind of money can do for a rider? She's going to win everything."

For the first time, I realized that their shared ambition meant they'd be competing against each other next year. Talent versus money.

Annelise was the better rider. And you have to be amazing to make it on the circuit. But you also have to have amazing horses. Annelise had the raw talent; she just needed horses, and horses were gettable. Theoretically. Cress's talent was—lesser. I didn't know if it was enough to make it. But now, she'd actually have a chance at winning. Now, she'd be able to compete for sure.

"But," I said. "Your mom? And all her horses. One of them has to be good enough—or trainable, I could help you train one—"

But her jaw was trembling again.

"I'm—I can't—"

"Are things not good between you and your mom?"

Annelise paused. "She doesn't like that I'm at Yale."

My parents hated the tuition, but they were still proud I was here. Still mentioned it to acquaintances and clients with a regularity that they should have kept in check, that they should have *known* to keep in check, having grown up in a small town. The worst thing you can do in a small town is *think you're too good for us*. Which, incidentally, might as well have been Yale's motto.

"What do you mean?"

"She thinks I should have stayed in California. Closer to her."

"But the team . . ."

Annelise gave a short laugh. "There are other equestrian teams in California, Rosie."

"But then why Yale?"

Annelise stared out into the dark. "Because any team with Cressida Tate on it had to be the best."

It felt like the first real confession I'd ever gotten from her. "But your dad, at least . . ."

She screwed up her face. "It's also—well, I never knew my dad. And seeing Grayson tonight—that looks nice."

"Shit. I'm so sorry. I didn't know your dad wasn't in the picture."

But I should have, I realized. She'd never once mentioned him, though her mother came up with fair regularity.

"Can't you find him?"

"But what if I did, and he was *amazing*? What if he was the best, and he just didn't want me? Wouldn't that be the worst thing of all?" She gnawed on her lip, looking out at the dark landscape below. "It would be the worst thing of all."

Not for me. It would have been finding him only to discover he was some kind of layabout, some do-nothing asshole whose laziness, indifference, incuriosity had prevented him not only from finding me himself, but also from finding anything meaningful to do with his life.

But she didn't need to hear that from me.

"My sister's obsessed with astrology," Annelise went on. "And she says now's not the time to look for him. That I'll just run into frustration and disappointment, that I should wait a year or two. But I think she's just afraid of losing me. Her own dad died in a car accident when she was really little. A long time before I was born."

Stars of light seemed to burst in front of my eyes.

"You have a sister?"

"Of course," she said, frowning as though I'd been the one not paying attention when she'd told me the long and storied version of her life. "Tory. She's twenty-eight, so she's always been this great mixture of sister and mother."

"Wow," I said, too stunned to say more.

A short, teary laugh. "Yeah. Anyway, tarot has always been my thing, and astrology is hers. It's all geometry and math, you know. You'd probably love it. Rules and regulations. Personally, I hate how astrology has been this tool of like . . . entrenched power . . . for so many centuries."

"But you don't find that with the cards?"

"The cards are for the people," she said. "You don't even need to be able to read to understand them. Astrologers were men serving emperors, and fortune-tellers were old ladies in huts who'd learned the practice from generations of women before them."

The image was so vivid, goosebumps popped onto my skin. I rubbed my arms.

"She's in California? Tory?"

"Yeah." Annelise's voice turned tight again. "Working with my mom."

"And the horses."

"Of course, the horses." She sounded exhausted. It scared me, that tone. I realized for the first time what Annelise had always projected that Cress didn't: faith that life would all work out, that everything would happen for the best.

But for some reason, that faith was gone.

"We should probably get back to the party," I said, trying to make it sound as much like an apology as I could. "It's just, they're going to be wondering what happened to us."

"Yeah, of course," she said shakily, turning to the curtains and pulling them apart. Blinking in the dim light of the hallway, she lay the backs of her hands against her cheeks and gave me a wobbly smile.

"One-tenth of that money," she said, almost to herself. "Do you know what I could do with just one-tenth of that money?"

It wasn't until we turned the corner and rejoined the crowd—Cressida still working her way through a pile of colorful presents, chandelier above her head making her hair gleam as she laughed, showing her even, white teeth—that I thought: wait a minute.

Annelise doesn't have access to fifty grand?

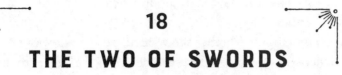

18
THE TWO OF SWORDS

You gotta wait. I'm sorry. It sucks. But it's like, you're at a crossroads and neither path is standing out to you because you just don't have enough information right now. But you have to be careful, too, because sometimes you're just avoiding making a choice and you do have all the information you need—you just don't want to admit it. Swords ask you to be really honest: with yourself and the people around you. Can you move forward? Or are you actually trapped?

I LAY IN BED THAT NIGHT unable to sleep. I hadn't had that much champagne, but my head felt like a balloon, bobbing separate from my body, attached by only a string. I couldn't shake the revelations from my conversation with Annelise, the strangeness of seeing her leveled by the excesses of Grayson Tate.

Finally, I gave up and wandered down the back stairs to the ground floor. In the mud room, I shrugged on a huge Barbour jacket I thought was probably forest green and some Hunter boots just half a size too big, and cracked open the back door.

I was flooded with security lights so fast I barely noticed the blond head snapping toward me through a cloud of smoke.

"Anthea—" I started. "Oh, sorry. Cress?"

A low laugh without any humor in it. "Fuck. I turn twenty-two and all of a sudden I'm my mom? Did I shrink a foot and a half overnight?"

"No, it was just the lights—" I went over to her on the terrace, too-big boots clunking awkwardly over the bricks. "Ugh, Cress, don't do that. You know smoking makes you sick."

She rolled her eyes and took another drag.

"My birthday."

I couldn't decide whether she wanted me to sit down next to her or not. Whether I should admit my actual intention of going to the stables. But then she kicked a neighboring chair over my way, metal skittering loud, and I sat.

In a second, the lights flicked off, and there was nothing but the low glow from the house reflected off of her hair, her skin, to illuminate her. That and the burning red of the cigarette tip.

"Do you actually like me?" she said after a long moment. She didn't turn to look my way, didn't even move. Between her fingers, the cigarette was almost all ash.

The idea that I didn't—that she'd doubt that—made me feel immeasurably sad. "Of course," I said. "Don't be stupid."

"What do you like about me?"

But I was too tired, and I didn't have the words. Besides, it was impossible to tell someone like Cress: it's the way you play with life, the way everything falls into your lap and how it makes you laugh. It's everything and it's nothing. It's a lightness I'll never have, a lightness I've never felt.

"You're fun," I said weakly. "You're so much fun."

"But what does *fun* get you?"

"What is this all about? What do you want that you don't have?"

"To live up to my father," she said drily, as if it were obvious.

Relief washed over me. This wasn't about us, our friendship. "You already have, Cress. You're at Yale. And you'll go pro. And you could always join Tate Associates if you wanted—you *know* he'd love it—"

She'd closed her eyes, though, and I stopped.

"Not something that he's already done. I want to do something that he *hasn't*."

Oh. We'd gone existential.

"You don't want to ride anymore?"

Her eyes flew open.

"Of course I do. But to beat him, I'd have to actually *go* to the Olympics. And if I give it up? Sure, I could go into business. But to beat him,

I'd have to make *ten* billion. I could go into art. But to beat him, I'd have to find even *more* Hockneys and Rosenquists and Ruschas."

"But he's your favorite person in the world," I said quietly after a long minute.

She looked at me like I'd missed something.

"Right."

"So why do you have to beat him?"

She shook her head and threw her cigarette toward the grass, activating the security lights again. I watched its arc, watched it fall. Waited for it to stop burning, stop smoking, so I could stop worrying. Before it did, Cress stood. "Night, Rosie."

"Happy birthday," I called after her. My voice sounded so weak, so thin in the night air. The door slammed behind her; and then I was alone.

It felt wrong to go visit her horses after that. I climbed back up to bed, feeling as though I'd somehow failed a test I hadn't even known I was taking.

But I'd find out what the test was soon enough.

19
THE FIVE OF SWORDS

The Five of Swords is making this star, which seems like it could be nice. Pretty. But actually, the blades are sticking out everywhere, just ready to cut you. And they can be anything: arguments, losses, your own ego pushing you ahead when you're definitely in the wrong. But sometimes the only way out is through, you know?

WE LEFT THE NEXT MORNING after breakfast. Leaving in 10 be at car, was all Cress's text said. Normally, we would have padded around the property for the rest of Sunday, making our way back to school after dinner. But Cress had driven, and it was Cress's house; Cress made the rules. All four of us were at the car by the time she got there with huge sunglasses on, jaw set.

It had started to rain, huge drops the size of hail splashing into our hair, running down our faces as we waited. But Cress just unlocked the doors without a word and slid in.

"Chasing Cars" began to blare from the speakers, but she clicked the music off as we rolled down the driveway. Everyone was hungover, everyone was waiting for Cress to say something. With that taut silence, she was either about to explode into a kind of wild fury or ignore us for the rest of the trip.

She was taking a different way back to school, a way I didn't know: through a wooded area full of hilly, hairpin turns. We don't have those where I come from. And while they would have caused me to brake until the car was barely moving, they seemed to rile her up. Each one faster than the last until I craned my neck to peer over her shoulder at the speedometer: ninety miles per hour.

"Cress—" I started. But that was all it took.

"Which one of you has been stealing from me?" she said without turning her head. Her voice was pleasant, upbeat in the false way her mother's always was.

Andra's head whipped around to the back seat: to Lila, studiously looking out the right window; to Annelise, her stare intense and forward; to me.

I don't know what my face looked like. I only know that I felt like I was choking on my pulsing heart.

"*What?*" Andra finally said.

Cress whipped the wheel to the right just in time to take the next turn.

"Stealing from me," she said, still chipper. "One of you has been cutting yourself checks. Twenty grand, so far."

I stole a look at Lila. Her mouth a little *O*, pink splotches on the top of her apple cheeks.

"Or is it all of you?" Cress said conversationally. "Are we living in a commune and I just missed the memo? Because truly, I think that the distribution of resources should be discussed"—yanking the wheel to the left just in time to miss an oncoming truck—"especially since they're *my fucking resources.*"

Silence. She pressed the air conditioning on to unfog the front windows. It was so dark outside from the rain that I don't know how she saw a thing beneath those shades.

Finally, Andra. "Not me."

Silence.

"Like I'd even need to," Andra added with a snort.

"Well, it wasn't me, either," Lila piped up. The back of my mouth watering with nausea, I turned to her. "You've known me for*ever*, Cress. You know I'd never do anything—"

"I—" I started, but Andra cut me off, turning half to the back to face us with a dark stare.

"Of course it wasn't you," she said to Lila. "We know where you came from. We know you're actually who you say you are."

Beside me, I felt Annelise's thighs tense, her breathing turn shallow.

"What the fuck does that even mean?" Cress said, and her honeyed tone was gone: all razor blades now.

"It means that Annelise didn't go to Stanford. I don't know where the fuck she came from, but it wasn't there. I don't even think her name's really Annelise."

The slightest trembling beside me. I wondered if Lila could feel it, too, on the other side of Annelise.

"She did," I said. "And it is. And what the fuck, you guys? Lila, I saw you actually taking—"

Cress's head whipped around. "You *saw* her?" Andra grabbed the wheel, steering us around the next turn.

"I saw her—" But how could I say what I'd seen without incriminating myself for not telling? To have picked Lila over Cressida? "I saw her coming out of your room."

"We're in each other's rooms all the time!" Lila cried. "Come on, that's nothing. Cress, you *know* that's nothing."

"But Annelise has her own money," I said. "Look at what she's wearing! Why the fuck would she need to take it from you?"

"Why would she need a new name?" Andra muttered, flopping back around in her seat.

"Just because she's not on Google—"

"I didn't steal your money," Annelise said, so low it was almost inaudible.

"Of course you didn't," I said. "Lila did."

"Fuck you!" Lila said, almost a shriek. "Maybe *you* took it, you're the poor one—"

"Just because I'm not rich doesn't mean I'm *poor*—"

"Li, if Rosie had stolen it, don't you think she'd have fucking *spent* some of it? Like, on a new dress so she didn't have to wear the same thing to every fucking party?" Andra, with her own brand of backhanded defense.

Lila's hands in the air. "I'm just saying. Maybe it's the long game. I don't know how these things—"

"You can check my bank accounts," Annelise said in the same quiet voice. "Really, I didn't—"

And then, without warning, the car came to a halt in the middle of the road.

"Get out," Cress said.

She was looking in the rearview mirror, but it was impossible to say which one of us she was targeting. At first, I thought it was me. But Annelise was already unhooking her seatbelt.

"Cress, you can't—" I started.

"I fucking can. Or do you want to go, too?"

I looked between them. Cress first, her pointed chin set firm. Annelise's face pale as she shook her head slightly at me.

"Oh, you want to check in with her before you decide? Your new bestie? Get the fuck out, both of you. Find your own way home."

The rain was coming down faster, harder, as I stepped shakily onto the road, Annelise behind me. I thought Cress would pop the trunk, let us get our things, but it only took a second before the Rover was out of sight, aquaplaning away.

Annelise grabbed my arm, pulling me off of the highway to the side of the road, where we took shelter under some trees. I was crying, and I think she was, too, though it was hard to tell with all of the rain on her face.

"You shouldn't have done that," she said, shaking her head. Her hair was twisting, curling up in the rain; she looked like some kind of miserable earth goddess. "Now they won't be speaking to you, either."

I wrapped my arms around myself. I'd left my coat in the car, had only the damp Lands' End cashmere sweater I'd found at Goodwill to keep me warm. "I did, you know. I really did see Lila with a check."

"I know." She pulled her phone out of the hobo bag she, thank fuck, had taken with her. "Taxi service in Greenwich?" A long pause. "Yes, hi. My friend and I had our car break down somewhere on Round Hill Road. I think we just passed the country club. Could you send a taxi? We're going to New Haven. Thanks." She flipped her phone closed and looked at me.

"I've only got about twenty bucks on me," I admitted miserably.

She rolled her eyes. In the low rainy light, she looked almost exactly like Cress. "Like I'd let you pay."

We were quiet a long time. Watching the rain fall, ricocheting off of the leaves above us. The way it patterned the stone walls alongside the road, separating the mansions from the street. Turning them from white to beige, mottling their uneven, designed perfection.

"Why'd you let them say those things?" I said finally.

"I didn't," she said. "I told them I didn't take it."

"Of course you didn't take it. That's not what I meant." A pair of headlights, coming around the bend. For a moment, I thought it was Cress. Coming back for us. But it was just our taxi, of course. "The other stuff," I said. "All of those lies."

She waited until the taxi had stopped in front of us, until I had run around to the other side.

"Because," she said, opening the door. "Some of it was true."

20

THE FIVE OF PENTACLES

This card always makes me think of that Peggy Lee song "Is That All There Is?" There are these times in life when you just wonder what the whole fucking point is. You get up, you do the same things, you see the same people, and you have the same kinds of problems over and over again. It's just a slog. But notice that the two beggars just stumbling through the snow have totally missed the fact that there's a brightly lit, welcoming church just behind them. Even now, there's hope, if you know where to look for it.

At least, that's what this version of the card shows. Some decks, the church is dark—like they were looking for sanctuary and just couldn't find it. I don't know which one's the real meaning—because the cards didn't fall down out of the sky, you know. People made them.

I go back and forth. But mostly, I choose hope.

THAT WAS ALL ANNELISE would say. At first, I thought it was just that we were in the presence of the taxi driver, because she kept sending furious glances his way every time I asked a question. But even when we were back in New Haven, alone, she just shook her head.

"I didn't lie," was all she said as we stood on the curb, facing the house. "I never lie about anything important. You know I'd never do that. Don't you?"

Her gaze seemed to cut through me. Probing for something profound, something I hoped she saw in me. A wisdom that was lacking in the rest of our friends. A level of insight that matched hers. A kindness so deep it shook her to her core.

I hadn't known I wanted to have any of those things before.

"Yeah," I said. "I do."

Annelise's weekend bag, a Tory Burch tote, had been thrown next to the front steps, left to get good and wet. My own anonymous black duffle had been left outside our room, which I guessed was a hopeful sign. But I was too full of a buzzing rage to see it that way. I was sick of trying to figure out what others were feeling, sick of how much energy I'd put into figuring out how to fix the strange vibe between us.

Sick of them all.

The other girls were either shut up in their respective rooms or had gone out. I didn't much care where they were as long as I didn't have to see them. We stayed in our room the rest of that day, Annelise reading tarot card after tarot card. Wondering, I guess, what she should do next.

I tried to take a nap, but it was useless. I was too mad. Finally, I flopped over on my side to face her. It was evening by then, dark out and raining still. The golden glow of the bedside lamps was the only light in the room.

"What are you getting?" I asked as she cleared a spread away.

"Pentacles," she said absently, laying out the cards again.

"Well, that's good, right? Abundance?" I didn't see how it applied to this situation, but she would. She must have.

"Reversed. And with swords."

She laid out another three cards.

"Well, how long are you going to read for?"

"Until," she said, "it comes out right."

"Oh no, you don't," I said, hopping to my feet. As I rolled out my neck, I could feel some of the tension of the last twelve hours releasing. "You're the one who taught me never to do that. A big reading. A Celtic cross. Make it a lesson. And then we'll put the cards away."

She looked at me, smiling as she swirled her hands over the tarot spread, mixing the carefully laid cards back together. "Yeah, get over here," she said. "But we'll read for you. Because you're right. I'm basically doing the equivalent of tugging on the universe's sleeve, and pretty soon I'm going to piss it off."

I sat cross-legged in front of her, the cards between us. She held up the deck in her long-fingered hand. I reached for it, but she moved her hand gently away.

"Hold on," she said. "Before we actually read. There's something you have to remember. I've mentioned it before, but I need to remind myself, too, sometimes. The most important part about the tarot isn't the cards you get, and it's not the spread you use."

I nodded expectantly.

"It's the question you ask," she said gently. "The question you think about while you're shuffling, the question you're demanding of the universe."

"Yeah, of course. You *did* tell me that."

"No, Rosie," and her voice was slightly harsher. "People misread the cards constantly. And that's because nobody ever asks the one right question. Not the fortune-tellers, not the querents. The question *before* the question."

"And what's that?"

She showed a dimple.

"Do you really want to know?"

"Yes," I said, rolling my eyes.

"No," she said. "That's the question before the question. *Do you really want to know?* Because if you're looking for reassurance, if you're looking for comfort—the cards can't give you that. Not any more than life itself can. They describe the truth. That's all."

She held the deck of cards toward me in both palms. An offering.

Will I get a job? What happens to our group of friends? Will I ever be able to stop worrying about money? Will my parents' practice survive long enough for them to retire comfortably? All the questions I'd had her do readings for before, all the questions I'd thrown out with only casual half belief that the cards could offer any kind of answer.

My heart tapped out the questions in my throat, faster and faster as I stared at the cards.

"Do you really want to know?" Annelise asked softly.

I swallowed.

"No," I said. "I don't think I do. Not tonight."

She nodded and began to wrap the deck up in the purple cloth.

"I didn't think so," she said. "But I owed it to you to ask."

I DON'T KNOW WHAT I expected to happen after Cress kicked us out of her car. But I had the impression that it would cost me money: that I'd wake up one day and Annelise would be gone, and I'd be on the hook for $600 a month instead of $300. Or that Cress would find a totally separate house that she'd insist we all move into, leaving Annelise alone, leaving each of us to pay two rents.

But instead, everyone just stopped talking to Annelise.

I say *just*, but it was enough. It was more than enough.

Annelise, Lila, and me in the kitchen. Annelise: "Could you hand me the honey?" And Lila squeezing it into her tea then walking out, honey bear in one hand and mug in the other.

Cressida, grabbing her half chaps from the foyer, calling out to me in the den. "I'm off to lessons. Back in a bit." Annelise, scrambling down the stairs with her duffle bag, to find the front door closing in her face.

Andra, knocking on our door. "Rosie, dinner tonight at Olea?" Annelise, studiously staring at the cards in front of her. "They only had a table for four."

It was juvenile. It was ridiculous. But it worked. Something went out of Annelise; some confidence, some bravado. The set of her shoulders, always so square, became rounded. Her eyes, always so seeing, so perceptive, seemed to have clouded. She had fallen back into herself, and it was a lonely place.

I did the best I could: I took her out for coffees, for lunches. Went for walks with her, dragged her to the British art museum. But she was gone so frequently, still, in New York doing whatever it was she did; and I had midterms to worry about, then the buildup to finals. I still had practice myself, and so did she, taxiing out to the barn alone because Cress would no longer drive her. Fifty bucks a day.

Her clothes turned somber, grays and blacks. Jeans and turtlenecks. Ordinary. The dancing had stopped; there wasn't even music in our room now.

Finally, I couldn't take it anymore. One morning before the advanced lesson, as Annelise pulled on her leggings and sports bra, I slithered down the stairs to talk to Cress.

"This is ridiculous," I said. Cress was standing in front of the kettle, waiting for it to boil for her coffee, and turned halfway toward me with an arched brow raised high. "You can't keep freezing her out like this. There's all of second semester left, and Cress, I swear to fuck, she didn't do it."

Cress turned back to the stove, blond hair swishing.

"Then who did?" she said.

I went up next to her. I was scared, but I did. The heat from the kettle rose up, blotching my face hot. "It was Lila," I said softly. "It really was."

Cress snorted. "Because you saw her coming out of my room?"

"Because I saw her with a check made out to cash, with your name on it. I didn't want to say in the car, but it was a check, Cress, it was."

"And yet you never said anything to me." Her voice was monotone, strange and dead.

"She swore she wouldn't cash it—she cried, it was so weird and awful—"

"But you never said anything to me."

I slapped a hand on the edge of the counter. "Because I know what it's like to be broke, Cress. Because I know what it's like to be desperate. And she promised—but fuck! Check their bank accounts if you want, it wouldn't be hard. You can't just believe whoever you want to believe because it's easier—"

"Can't I?" The kettle rose to a hissing scream and she picked it up, swiveling toward the French press so quickly, so close to me, that she almost caught me in the chest. "I know Lila, Rosie. I know Lila so well. We're basically the same person. And who is Annelise, anyway? Andra was right, you know. She *didn't* go to Stanford. And when I went through her wallet? I couldn't even find a driver's license." She poured the boiling water into the press, stuck the plunger on top. "Who doesn't have a driver's license?"

"Poor people!" I cried. "Jesus fucking Christ, Cress. You're the one who was friends with her first. She's trustworthy! You're the one who's going through her shit. Which, by the way, did you *find* twenty thousand dollars in there? And did you do the same to Lila? And for fuck's sake, if you're so convinced she took it, why haven't you called the police?"

She slid the plunger down hard, too early. Coffee grounds and boiling

water spewed from the top of the glass press and she swore, poured the
rest into the sink. Grabbed the bag of coffee from the counter.

"Because," she said, staring hard at the press as she poured more water into it. "I can't have my dad know that I missed twenty grand just
disappearing from my account. You don't know him. You don't know
what he'd do."

I couldn't imagine him doing anything worse than cutting her off fi-
nancially for a little while. Maybe taking back the half mil he'd given her
for her birthday. But that—looking at Cress's drawn face, the mess she'd
made on the counter in front of her—maybe that, for her, would be the
worst thing. The worst thing she could think of.

"She didn't do it, Cress," I said softly.

And Cress looked up at me with such tortured eyes that I thought
immediately of Annelise. And I almost—almost—felt sorry for her.

"Then one of my best friends did," she said, hoarse. "And *that* didn't
happen."

CRESS LEFT FOR HER LESSON, Annelise trudging along five minutes later
to go meet her taxi. I'd just been screaming into the void, incapable of
changing anything. But what else was new? At least, I consoled myself,
I'd said something. At least I hadn't let Cress intimidate me into silence.

I came back from an econ section later that day to find the house
empty—except for our room, where I could hear sobs echoing out into
the hallway. I knocked, tentatively.

"Come in?"

I opened the door and Annelise immediately burst into a fresh round
of tears. I'd never seen her like that. Never seen any of my friends like
that. I'd heard her muffled crying into the pillow at night, trying to re-
main undetected—and so I'd let her think she was. But now, face blotchy,
eyes swollen so that they'd almost disappeared, she was staring straight
at me and sobbing and there wasn't any way around it.

"I thought—you were Cress—" she said, words jittery and broken.

"Hardly," I said, and grabbed a box of tissues from my nightstand,
holding them out to her. "And I wouldn't want to be."

The falseness of the words rang between us and she gave a little laugh.

"I—don't believe you," she said, and took a deep shuddering breath, then blew her nose. "Who wouldn't want to be Cressida Tate?"

"Not the way she's acting now," I said.

Annelise swallowed, put the backs of her hands to her cheeks. "I just . . . I never had a . . . friend like her before."

"No," I said, and laughed shortly. "I don't think any of us has."

"Rosie," she said, and looked at me straight in the face. "I just want things to go back to the way they were. Can you—talk to her? I know you tried back in the car, I know you did. But in the light of day, if anyone can explain—" Her chin started to quiver and she bit her lip, hard.

I looked down at the bed. No cards out today. "I did," I said softly. "This morning. I don't think it helped much."

She tilted her head, but the mystic effect it usually gave was lost with the trembling of her red face, the screwed-up eyes. "Maybe," she said. "Maybe it did. She said hi to me at the stables."

"Well, see?" I said, and grabbed her hand, which was hot and damp. "That's something."

"Thank you," she said softly. "I wish there was something I could do for you."

It had been on my mind since she'd held the cards out to me like an offering. The question I wanted to ask. The question I had to know the answer to.

"Would you read for me?" I asked.

She paused, then brushed her damp hair off her face, stuck it behind her ears. Grabbed her cards.

"Anytime," she said. "Always."

I shuffled the cards, which were soft and pliable in my hands.

"What do I need to know right now?" I asked in a low voice. I caught her eye, and she nodded.

"It's a good question."

But the card, when I drew it, was the Tower. Number XVI; a burning building, struck by lightning. People falling out of the windows, suspended eternally in the image halfway to the ground.

You didn't need to be a sage to see that it wasn't good. And I couldn't help catching the wince on Annelise's face as she stared down at it.

"Well. The Tower's all about surprises, shit coming out of the blue. Tearing down foundations. Clearing the way for something better to come," she added with drawn brows as she saw my face. "It's a necessary shake-up. But it's . . ."

"Not good," I finished for her.

"No, nothing's not good in the tarot," she said, and there were tears in her eyes. "Like nothing's not good in life. Good and bad don't apply. It's—" Her voice broke. "It's what's necessary, that's all. It's what's true."

"And what is the card telling me is necessary now?" I said. I was almost shaking with nerves, but I'd decided I wanted to know. So here I was. And now there was no escaping it.

"Chaos," she said in a low voice. "Destruction."

All of my mixed-up, foggy readings. The questions they left standing, the pain they predicted, the unknowns floating through the air with such power that they were almost physical things. And for the first time, I thought back to the reading she'd done for Andra.

All the good things she'd told Andra she deserved. All of the jewels raining down on her from the universe: wealth and love and glory. All of the things she'd ever wanted, all of the things she could ever want.

And I started to laugh; I couldn't help it. Andra wasn't bad. She wasn't particularly good, but she wasn't particularly bad. I wasn't, either. It was just—the randomness of it, the strange distribution of luck—all of a sudden, it just struck me as hilarious. The chaos.

"What is it?" Annelise looked disturbed.

"It's just . . . it's pretty different from Andra's reading!" I said, and burst into another fit of giggles.

But Annelise wasn't laughing. Actually, her face was turning pink again, and her cheeks were wet.

"You said you wanted my interpretations. And so that's what I've always given you."

"No, I know," I said, my laughter calming. "I did. I do."

"Because there are certain people . . . you have to tell them what they want to hear," she said, so quietly I could barely make out her words. She started to sob again, but silently this time; after a second, she put her face in her hands. "This is how I make my money. This is how I'm paying for school. I do readings at a spa in the Village. I got it through this friend of my sister's—an *employer* of my sister's—she's a trainer." She swallowed. "Tory trains horses."

She stared at me, waiting for my reaction.

I nodded slowly.

"Great work if you can get it."

Annelise burst into a combination sob/laugh. "Oh yeah? Ask Grayson Tate what he thinks about that. But anyway, Spa Kitsune—"

"How much do you charge?"

She let her hands fall, but she wouldn't meet my eyes. "Two hundred for an hour. And for that kind of money . . . for that kind of money, you have to tell them that they're good people. That they deserve everything that's come their way. Nobody wants to pay for"—she gestured to the Tower card, her lip shaking.

"But Anne*lise*," I said, and she gave a little whimper. "Why would you hide that? Why would you want to hide that?" I gave a playful shake of her shoulders, but she just flopped like a rag doll under my grip. "You *earn* your money. That's amazing."

She frowned at me, face quaking beneath her drawn brows. "Because I *had* to earn it."

"Yeah," I said. "And that's important. The rest of them? They were just born with it. They didn't do a single fucking thing to get what they have."

She put her face in her hands again.

"Yeah," she said. "I know."

"Secrets corrode us," I said. "You can't keep them in like that. And you shouldn't keep them in like that. They start eating away at you like acid."

"I wanted to tell you," she said, muffled through her palms. "So many times. You were so curious, and so kind, and then so hurt and so mad. So, yeah, they corrode us, maybe." She let her hands drift down her face, and she looked me right in the eye. "But secrets can save us, too."

I pulled her into an embrace, clutching her tight.

"You're better than any of them," I whispered.

21
THE MAGICIAN (REVERSED)

This is not a guy you want at your parties. Upright, the Magician's this combination of Merlin and Santa Claus. Going around, giving gifts, making things manifest, unblocking the blocked. And the best part, of course, is that so often, the Magician is you.

But reversed? Eesh. We're talking black magic. Mental illness. The excruciating pain of entrapment. It's manipulation, and it's not being done by you: it's being done to you.

ANNELISE'S PLEA—WHAT it had taken for her to ask for help—echoed in my mind. I couldn't get it out of my head long into the night, as she cried softly into her pillow, as I pretended not to hear her once again.

I just want things to go back to the way they were.

I wanted it, too. I wanted it for her, and I wanted it for myself.

But as the night wore on, as her sobs faded out into the heavy breath of sleep, I realized that things might have changed irrevocably. Everything I'd ever believed about who my friends were at the core had been just a little bit wrong, a little bit off, like a tarot spread I wasn't yet strong enough to master. *Reversed. Misinterpreted. Full of wishful thinking.*

Even if Cress came around to see the truth about Annelise, which I didn't think she would, that still would leave Lila on the receiving end of her wrath. The dynamics of the house had changed forever, and the only thing I could think was: we've got to get out of here.

I wondered if we could get dorm rooms, Annelise and me. If we went to Housing and explained—or partly explained—the situation. Or if we could rent an apartment for just six months; there had to be somewhere on campus that hadn't been taken. No matter what it was like, how shitty it was. She had money, I had enough.

The more that I thought about it, the more sense it made that Annelise had grown up working class. Middle class, at most. She was self-sufficient in a way the others couldn't even imagine being, with just her mom and Tory there for her.

But she had me now, too. And together—well, any situation would have to be better than this quiet crying, this icy silence, this push and pull that neither one of us controlled.

It would mean giving up my friends.

It would mean turning my back on any help Grayson Tate could give me.

I tried to tuck that mean little thought aside, but it kept popping up like a gopher. Until it occurred to me: *think like they do*. Think like Lila does, like Andra.

I didn't have to actually move out. But I could threaten it. I could wave the possibility of losing another friendship under Cress's nose. And if it didn't make her love Annelise again, I bet it could make her be civil for the rest of the year. Maybe even friendly.

I resolved to do it. And immediately fell asleep.

When I woke to a bright blue November morning, Annelise's bed was already empty, and there was a boisterous murmur wafting up from the kitchen. Cress's laughter rang out, immediately recognizable. And then—

Was that Annelise?

I threw a sweater on over my pajamas and padded tentatively downstairs.

There they were in the sunny kitchen, now clean thanks to the ministrations of a Polish woman whose name I didn't know, who I never saw, who came when I was at practice on Wednesdays and cleaned up our messes for us. Annelise sitting on the counter, swinging her legs like she was happy, like nothing had ever happened. Cress cranking up the heat on the stove for her coffee, Lila and Andra smoking (chain-smoking, by the look of the ashtrays) at the table, crumbs everywhere.

"We saved you an almond croissant," Andra said, and hurled a bakery bag at my chest so fast I barely had time to catch it.

"Thanks," I said, unable to keep the daze out of my voice. I stood for a second, feet chilled against the marble floors, as Andra and Lila giggled about something, as Annelise's heels banged out a happy beat against the lower cabinets. Walking over to Annelise, I cast her a questioning look.

"It worked!" she whispered as I leaned on the counter next to her. She squeezed my shoulder as Cress looked over at us. She gave a quick glance at Annelise's hand, then caught my eye with a resigned smile. A little wink.

I'd done it. I pulled the croissant out of the bag and started to nibble, then ate in great hungry bites. I'd really done it; I'd stood up to Cress, I'd said what I'd had to say. And it had changed things. It had made a real difference in the real world.

"Why are you all up so early?" I asked.

"Oh," Cress said airily, pouring the coffee out into four mugs, then grabbing another from the counter and pouring one for me. "It's such a beautiful morning. I thought we'd go down to the stables."

"I get to ride Thumper!" Annelise blurted out. And the joy on her face—I looked quickly over at Cress, but she just gave me that same resigned smile.

She knew she'd fucked up, so she was giving what she had to give. The greatest prize, the priceless stallion.

I widened my eyes, took a sip of the scalding coffee. "Lucky!" I said.

"Some people are just lucky, aren't they?" Andra murmured, an edge of bitterness in her tone. I glanced over at her but she only raised her eyebrows.

"He's *so* pretty," Lila said. "Pretty, pretty pony."

"Yeah, but be careful, though." I held up my palm, his teeth marks now a fading white scar. "Pretty, pretty asshole, too."

Annelise laughed.

"I've ridden meaner than him."

"Besides," Cress said, her face half hidden by her mug. "If I can ride him, *she* definitely can."

There was poison in that *she*, but it passed so quickly. And if she were clinging onto some residual anger, some leftover suspicion—well, I never said Cress was perfect.

In that moment, I could have forgiven her anything.

"Are you all going?" I asked. For a moment, nobody said anything.

"Yeah. Thought we'd hack out," Andra said finally. A trail ride, through the woods behind the barn. Through the almost bare Connecticut trees in November, through the fields and estates surrounding—

"Sounds amazing," I said. "Let me grab my things."

A quick look passed between Cress and Lila.

Were they mad at *me* now?

"Shannon said four max, unless she comes too," Lila said with big apologetic eyes. "And she can't today."

I finished my coffee, put the cup in the dishwasher.

"No worries. I've got plenty of job apps to do, anyway."

"We can go out tomorrow," Annelise said to me. "If you want."

"I'd love that," I said, and grinned. "Have fun."

I HADN'T BEEN ALONE in the house since I arrived back in August, which felt like such a long time ago. I could have spread out in my pajamas in the den, the TV room, the lounge, used my gorgeous shiny laptop to pull up the job listings I'd saved, started cranking out cover letters in the desperate hope that some company would be willing to overlook my lack of internships and give me a chance. My hope was that I could start part-time, going into the city with Annelise in the spring. I was motivated as fuck. *I'm hungry,* I wanted to write on each one. *I'll do whatever the hell you want me to, and I'll do it with a smile.*

But the house was too empty. And the argument in the car just kept coming back to me. Cressida, haughty and cold. Lila, defensive and spiteful. And Annelise: so scared. *They weren't all lies,* she'd said. What had she meant?

I needed to get out of there, so it was off to the computer lab. The place where the other poor kids went—although when, I wondered on my way out the door, had I begun to think of myself as poor? Never before Yale. Back home, my family was seen as well-off, privileged: vets were considered well-meaning charlatans who'd tell you there was nothing they could do for your cow and charge you $200 for the privilege. Everybody was the hero of their own story, I guess; everybody had their own problems, needed to cast you in a certain role.

I didn't need to cast myself as the poor little match girl, starving out-side the window watching richer families at their Christmas feasts any-more. I had a computer; I had a full wardrobe of equestrian gear; I even had a designer dress, since Annelise had gifted me the Stella McCartney on our return the other day. I would soon have an Ivy League degree and a mountain of student debt. I was betwixt and between, solidly middle class.

But I was wobbling. I was right on the edge. Next year, I could end up without any job at all. Next year, I could end up hit by a car, no job and no health insurance, a hundred grand in hospital bills haunting me for the rest of my life.

Next year, I could become truly poor.

I was six months away from falling into the abyss.

So were the other kids in the computer lab. It was easy to forget that there were others like me at Yale: kids on financial aid, kids who didn't have the option of a vaguely defined *European adventure* after college, kids for whom the *equestrian circuit* was a punchline rather than a true career possibility. They were in clothes that hadn't come from any designer col-lections. They were using the school's computers, the school's printers, because they didn't have any of their own.

I wasn't alone. It should have made me feel better, but it just struck me cold with fear. There were so many of us, there couldn't possibly be a job for each one.

And these jobs, the ones I was desperate for: investing and reporting analyst, entry level. *Competitive compensation package.* Junior financial ana-lyst: $115,000 plus bonus; $120-a-month wellness stipend to *nourish your body, mind, or soul.* Market analyst: 401(k), full dental and medical, paid time off. My mouth was watering as I reread the listings, the dozen I'd saved. As I tailored my cover letter to each one, as I cut the language that reeked of desperation, as I sent my sad little short résumé (*office assistant, Macalister Veterinary Practice*—if only I didn't have the same last name as the stupid practice!) that at least boasted fluent Spanish. I didn't note that I was only fluent when it came to words having to do with horses.

Twelve applications. I'd targeted companies run or managed by Yale grads, scrolled through the alumni directory online and cross-referenced it with the Monster and Indeed listings. A $150,000 degree had to get me an interview, at least. Right? Even though I didn't have it yet. Even though half of that was covered by loans I had no idea how I'd ever pay off.

All the same, it felt good to take a step toward the future. It was November, and I was ahead of the game. I was strong, and I was smart, and I was a peacemaker; I'd be going home to a beautiful house full of laughing, cheerful friends who all, for once, were getting along.

But the house lights were off as I rounded the corner. All except the front living room, where I could see my friends lounging on the couches; they never remembered to draw the curtains when it got dark out. *But people can* see *you,* I'd said to Andra a few weeks earlier. She'd laughed. *So? Let them see.*

It was silent as I opened the door. Silent, except for a weird squeaking noise.

I stood in the doorway of the living room. Cress in the lion-faced armchair, Lila and Andra on one couch. All of them looking down. Lila crying, silent except for those occasional little squeaks.

My body suddenly wanted to convulse. To seize up into a little ball, to make itself small. To curl over gagging with the anxiety, the nausea, the fear.

"Where's Annelise?" I said.

Cress's blue gaze cut into mine.

"Annelise fell," she said.

22
THE TOWER

Okay, so imagine your life's a house. And at the moment, you've got this totally broken-down, crumbling place. It's a total freaking mess. Even if you do see how shitty it is—but especially if you don't see it—the Tower comes along and BOOM. The house is all knocked down. And there's lightning and thunder and all of this totally wild stuff happening that looks incredibly freaky, but here's the thing: once the debris clears, you have this totally fresh plot of land, made all new and fertile by the rain.

So that's something.

It's not nothing.

ONCE CRESS SPOKE, the three of them couldn't get the words out fast enough. Thumper, that dick—a tree branch in the wind—no, a garter snake—no, a hunter's gun in the distance—he was rearing, he was bucking—she never should have tried to jump that last fence, she never should have tried to ride him at all—he was only ever used to Cress riding him—

"But where *is* she?" I interrupted. And still, their words came at me like surround sound gone haywire. Her back was all weird and twisted—no, it was her legs—didn't you see her shoulder?—but she was talking when the ambulance came—it took so long, they didn't even know where we were—the countryside, the rural roads, the paths, the trees—

"Where *is* she?" I screamed.

And finally, they stopped.

"At the hospital," Lila muttered.

"Which. Hospital."

"St. Raphael," Andra said, clear and calm, as though I were the one who was unhinged.

"And you're just . . . here?"

"They wouldn't let us ride in the ambulance," Lila protested. "They said one person, max."

"There are three of you here."

She frowned at me. "But who was it supposed to be?"

"You—who *are* you?" I said, my voice wild and high. "Who are you people? She's hurt and she's got to be scared out of her fucking mind. Would you have left one of us alone in the ambulance? Would you have left me there? For fuck's sake, who even are you? She's one of *us*."

And Cress looked at me again. Really looked this time.

"No," she said. "She's not."

I RAN. IT WAS LESS than a mile, but I ran the whole way. The whole time thinking: you can't wonder what's happened. You'll find out soon enough. She's fine, she was talking. You can't wonder.

I thought, instead, of the archangel Raphael. My friend Emily had gone through an obsessively religious phase in high school, which wasn't unusual where we grew up. What was unusual was that she was Catholic; most people around there were solidly Protestant. And when she was thirteen or fourteen, she'd go into these rhapsodic monologues about the saints and archangels. Raphael was responsible for healing. He fixed things. He made them better. I didn't think Annelise believed in God, much less was a practicing Catholic. But He could still help, right?

I burst into the emergency room only to find it quiet, calm. I'd thought it would be as chaotic as *ER* or *Grey's Anatomy,* but the stillness was only interrupted by the faint regular beeps of heart monitors, the pristine smell of bleach.

"Annelise Tattinger," I gasped to the nurse at the front desk. "I have to see her."

She stared at me for a moment. My sweaty, bedraggled hair, the damp spots on my sweater. She opened her mouth—

"Please—"

"Hon, I'm so sorry. I can only release information to her immediate family—"

"I'm her sister. The girl in the equestrian accident."

A pause that was just a beat too long. Then she nodded.

"They took her in for surgery. She should be coming out soon. We have her in the ICU, in room"—she tapped something into her computer—"two-oh-three. Just up that way."

"Thank you," I called as I ran toward the elevators.

But there was no need to run. The room, when I got there, was empty; the bed, perfectly made up, waiting for her.

I stopped short, trying to catch my breath, trying to ignore the bursts of light popping in front of my eyes. Surgery. Surgery like the tonsillectomy I'd had when I was five, like the appendectomy I'd had at seventeen. Emergency surgery, but surgery nonetheless, just a little sleep and you wake up and you're better.

But how many surgeries had I seen my parents do? How many had I assisted on?

How many had ended well?

A minute. An hour. A day. Time was nothing in there, so I don't know how long it was before a passing nurse halted at the door.

"What are you doing in here?"

"I'm Annelise's sister—"

"Annelise?"

"Annelise Tattinger. She came in earlier—there was an accident with a horse—"

Her face turned from annoyed to wary.

"No," she said. "You're not."

I lost it. "Who the fuck are you to say who I am? My *sister* was here, my sister Annelise, and she had a bad accident, and I've been waiting and waiting, and I need to know what happened to her, and I can't find her—" My voice broke off into a sob.

The nurse stared at me. Then, she unclipped something from her clipboard and handed it to me.

"Is this Annelise?" she asked.

A driver's license, issued five years ago. A sixteen-year-old Annelise, smiling wide and broad at the camera. But she wasn't Annelise: she was Annie May Robinson, according to the license. Annie May Robinson, from Mendota, California.

Her birthday had been a few weeks ago. Just four days before Cress's. She'd never said.

"That's—where did you find that?" I whispered.

And the wariness was gone from the nurse's face. "In the bag with all of her horse stuff. A hidden inside pocket. It wasn't in her wallet."

"You're right, I'm not her sister," I said, looking down. "I'm her friend. Please. Is she okay?"

"Oh, sweetheart," the nurse said, and sighed. "It was her spine."

"Was?"

"Her mother's coming in tomorrow. Maybe you could leave your name and number—"

"Was?"

"I'm so sorry," the nurse said. "Your friend is dead."

23
THE CHARIOT

The Chariot is usually read as victory. But it's a victory hard won.
There isn't actually a card for easy victory in the tarot.
Everything you win, you have to fight for.
Sound familiar?

I WAS IN A TRANCE. I could only think about the task in front of me. Task and task and task. The nurse asked me to write my name and number, so I did. She told me to go home, so I started walking. I had to get into the house, so I opened the door. But then I was stuck.

Cress found me there, in the entryway. She took my arm and led me upstairs.

"Get into bed," Cress said.

"She's dead," I said, climbing in.

But Cress just pressed her lips together and left the room. Maybe she'd figured as much. Maybe she was too overwhelmed. Maybe she felt nothing at all; I don't know. In that moment, I wasn't sure how well I ever really knew her.

I'm not sure how much of her there was to know.

I stayed in bed for three days. On the morning of the third day, I woke up to a girl I didn't recognize on the other side of the room, surrounded by a cluster of open boxes.

I sat up straight. "Who the fuck are you?" I said. And then, realizing she might be related to Annelise—a friend from home, her sister—I crumpled up again. "I'm sorry," I said. "I'm so sorry."

"No, I didn't mean to—I'm work-study over at Student Services. They asked me to come over and pack up—you know." She glanced doubtfully at me. "I could come back later?"

I closed my eyes. "No," I said. "Just go ahead."

And so I went downstairs. I ate a yogurt. I lay down on the couch in the den, the one where nobody else ever went. When I went back upstairs a few hours later, there were only my things left in the room. My things, and a small package wrapped in purple silk wedged into the back corner of our shared closet.

The tarot cards.

I SLIPPED THEM UNDER my pillow. I'd give them back when Tory came. When her mother came. And when they didn't come, when a call to the Student Services office revealed that they'd had her body sent to California, that the funeral had already been held out there—I decided that the cards were mine now. I had as much a right to them as anybody, and maybe a little bit more.

There probably would have been a memorial service or a vigil if another student, a legacy who'd been at Yale all four years, hadn't died in an overdose that same week. Our inboxes were full of notes from Health Services offering *Ten Tips for Dealing with Your Grief* that included inanities such as contacting your higher power—as though you wouldn't have already—of warning us of the dangers of this and that substance, of pointing us to local therapists offering students three free sessions. But by the time I worked up the energy to call one of them, her receptionist told me that all the free sessions were taken; would I like to book a regular session at $250 an hour? I hung up.

Little by little, life returned to something resembling normal. I went to classes and remembered nothing. I took my exams and got what I assumed were pity passes from professors who must have heard something from someone; the details of death administration were always fuzzy to me, but they must have been told, because I didn't fail, and I really should have.

I quit the team. Or rather, I just stopped going.

The police did investigate Shannon, and all the corners she'd cut leaving us basically unsupervised came to light. Her insurance company had to make a big settlement, I think to Annelise's family, and then canceled her policy. I don't know if the school would have fired her if that hadn't happened, but they had to once the insurance was gone. The remaining girls were shunted to another stable thirty miles away.

I didn't want to talk anymore, so I didn't. It didn't stop the other girls from talking to me, at me. They were full of words—had they always been so full of words? It hadn't seemed like it before. But no matter how much they talked, the story was never clear. Every time, it was the same garbled nonsense. A snake or a branch or a hunter, a jump or a buck or a bolt. Nobody knew, but everyone thought they did. I thought Cress should have sent Thumper away—how could she ride him after that? But he went with them to the new stables, though he was nervier than ever and after a few tries, Cress stopped riding him.

Annelise was gone, but he stayed.

It made sense to me that she was gone. That, I understood.

What made *no* sense was that she wasn't coming back.

How often had she disappeared to New York, to the stables? But this time, she just kept not being there, and each new day without her carved just a few more centimeters out of the hole that was chipping its way outward from my core.

I stayed at the house for Thanksgiving while the other girls went to their respective families. I wanted to go home so badly that I couldn't. If I did, I knew I'd never come back. I wasn't sure my parents would even let me, looking as I did; my hair starting to twist into dreadlocks, my clothes filthy. But my parents didn't know about Annelise, and I couldn't tell them, couldn't lay that burden on them. They'd never let me out of their sight again, how could they? That month had already been filled with perfunctory texts that I was fine, couldn't talk just now, had an exam. Fine, had a show. Fine, fine, fine. Just busy.

The Sunday of Thanksgiving weekend, Cressida returned first. I knew it was her from the purr of the Range Rover in the driveway. Then the slam of the car door, the slam of the trunk; footsteps up the porch.

"Hello?" she called. "Rosie?"

I didn't answer. I was lying in bed again; lying in bed still. And I suppose I was mad at her, without any precise reason to be, without being able to explain exactly why. Because her life was going on like before. Because her life hadn't changed a bit. Because her life was exactly what she wanted it to be, all the time, and meanwhile I'd been carved up like a cow at the butcher's, cut up into all of these little parcels, and everyone expected me to get up and walk around like I was still a person.

"Rosie." Cress was at the door now, but I was facing the window and the wall. "You've got to get up."

"I don't, actually."

"Then you won't hear my news." There was such a bounce to her voice, she sounded so much like the old Cress, that I turned over. Less than a month after Annelise had died and she could sound like that; I was more fascinated than I was mad. What could I expect from Cressida, after all? I couldn't expect anything from her, and that was the truth. I couldn't believe I'd never really seen it before.

"Look," she said, and flopped down at the foot of my bed as I sat up. "I have something for you. But I can't give it to you if you're like this, okay? You have to get up. You have to take a shower. You have to be human again."

I stared at her.

"Okay," she said, smacking her hands against the bed like an exclamation mark. "I'll tell you first, then you'll do all that stuff. So. I was at home this weekend with my dad. I mean, with the whole family—well, not James, but Mom and Dad, you know."

I pushed myself back under the covers and stared up at the ceiling.

"Okay, I'll get to the point. Anyway, we were talking about next year. I'd picked out this horse—but that's not important. To this, anyway. Dad was asking about you guys, and I was saying that you—well. He thought maybe you could come work for him next year. If you wanted."

The white paint of the ceiling seemed, suddenly, too shiny; almost blinding in the daylight.

I sat up.

"What?" I said.

Cress's face seemed to get bigger with excitement: her eyebrows up, her cheeks wide.

"Yeah! And then we could be in the city together, and you wouldn't have to worry anymore. And you'd be working in finance just like you wanted—I mean, it wouldn't be finance exactly, but it would be a start. An amazing start!"

I tried to process what she was saying. "What would it be, then?"

"What?"

"If it's not finance."

"Oh! I mean, it is, but it's not. You'd be my dad's second assistant. His current one is going on maternity leave in May, he just found out. And, honestly, I don't think he'll want her back after. But those women never really want to come back to work, do they?" She barreled on, faster and faster. "So really, it's better than one of those shitty junior positions, because you'd actually get to see what he does every day. You'd meet all of these people, you'd get really good access. You know what they say, the most powerful person in any company is the boss's assistant."

I stared at her, trying to follow.

"But I don't want to be an assistant."

She bit the inside of her cheek. "See, the thing is, Rosie. He really likes you. He thinks you're great. And he loves that you were on the team—don't tell him that you quit," she added quickly. "But you don't have any experience in finance. Not even an internship. They don't know that you can *do* the money stuff, you know? But a year or two of helping him out, and showing what you know—I'm *sure* you could get moved into an analyst role."

A job. A guaranteed job. A pathway, even if it was winding, to where I'd always wanted to be.

"And it wouldn't just be Tate Associates," she said. "It'd also be the Tate Foundation. I know you love that charity stuff. And of course, his sailing and the horses—he *loves* that you can help out with the horse stuff—"

"Is there medical?" I cut her off.

She frowned. "I mean, he might ask you to make some doctor's appointments. But he's super healthy, I don't think—"

"Is there medical *insurance*, Cress."

She laughed. "I mean, I'm sure there could be. He said he'd start you—" She looked at the back of her hand. For the first time, I saw that she had notes scrawled on there. *2nd asst. baby leave. 80.* "At eighty thousand."

"Eighty *thousand?*"

I'd seen assistant jobs posted on the boards. They were lucky to make thirty a year, let alone get insurance. And a second assistant?

It was guilt, right? It was guilt that she'd brought Annelise into my life and then put her on the horse that had killed her. It had to be.

But as I looked at her—that guileless face—I thought, maybe not. Maybe it was just that she'd told her father I was sad and that I needed a job. For him, this was a drop in the bucket. A drop in the ocean.

And I'd done the office stuff before, though she didn't know it. I knew how to be an assistant. I knew I could be good at it.

It wasn't what my salary could be as an analyst. But it was here in front of me, and it was guaranteed.

I sat up, stretching my legs over the side of the bed. "That's so nice of him. Of you. Of course," I said. "Yeah. Of course."

She hugged me and it felt like before. Like nothing else had ever happened; eventually, maybe it would feel like Annelise had never been there. Like she was a dream, someone I'd made up.

Out of the corner of my eye, I looked at the deck of cards. They were still wrapped in their silk. But it felt, somehow, like they were watching me.

And so life started up again, because there was a reason for it to. I finished the semester with straight Cs, but it didn't matter; I already had a job. My parents were delighted when I told them at Christmas. My mom cried, though she said it was allergies—like she's ever been allergic to anything in her life; she's a rural *vet.* And it was easy enough, spring semester, to keep to myself. Reading in coffee shops instead of going to the stables. Taking courses I'd always been curious about taking but had never been brave enough to actually plunge into: I could now, now that my future was assured. Introduction to Biology of Terrestrial Arthropods, Biological Oceanography, Primate Diversity and Evolution, the Biology of Sharks and Their Relatives. I spent the semester thinking about animals and dreaming about home.

Nobody ever asked me to pay more in rent. I saw my friends when

I had to, and I moved my furniture so that it took up the entire room. It still felt empty. It felt emptiest at night, when I stared up at the ceiling, alone. There were so many unanswered questions. Why her family hadn't come. Why the legacy kid had been so much more valuable that everyone at Yale was basically pretending that Annelise had just evaporated.

And other, more important things, too: What had happened, exactly? And who was Annelise, exactly?

But questions, I was starting to think, were like secrets: safer kept inside.

She always was the wise one.

And gradually, Annelise did start to feel like a dream. Like a dream you have during a fever: larger than life, full of Technicolor and fireworks, brief and bright. Then gone.

I graduated in May and moved to the city two days later.

I did not get my security deposit back.

I never did hear from Annelise's mother. But I never thought to wonder why.

I wouldn't have wanted to talk to me, either.

BOOK 2

2006

24
THE THREE OF PENTACLES

Everyone's got their role to play. And maybe you always wanted to be the architect designing the cathedral, having your creation reach up there to the sky, but you're just a lowly stonemason. Except that cathedral's never going to get there without the stonemason. So they have to work together, and they have to value the work the other does. And they have to be open to learning, to honing their craft. To know what they don't know. You know?

For a time, new york was enough.

I wanted to close the parentheses on college, wanted it to be good and done, forever. And after my parents had helped me load everything into the U-Haul van they'd rented in Stamford, after we'd driven to the Brooklyn apartment, after they were gone, I sat in the empty, sun-soaked space and thought: life begins now.

But there's no such thing as a fresh start. Not really. Because I was sharing an apartment with Andra, who was coming for an internship at the *New York Post* in a few weeks, after her graduation trip to Europe. I'd looked for my own place in the months leading up to graduation. But even a studio of my own would have cost more than twenty grand a year, and I couldn't justify it. The strangers I contacted on Craigslist for apartment shares weren't willing to take a chance without meeting me first, and the crazed days of finals and graduation meant I didn't have the time to go into the city. Finally, as I waited for my pasta to boil one night in the kitchen, Cress had brought it up.

"Any luck with apartments?"

"Not yet."

"That sucks. I'd say come stay with us, but you do *not* want to deal with my mom in the morning." I would have—if it hadn't meant becoming a full-blown Tate charity case. And if it had been a real offer.

"Why don't you come live with me?" Andra's mouth was full of sushi, and I wasn't sure I'd heard her right at first. "My dad cleared out one of his rental properties in Williamsburg. There are two bedrooms."

I'd envisioned myself prancing through Manhattan to Tate Associates in pointy heels, coming from an apartment full of strangers who left me the fuck alone. What would it be like, leaving and coming back to Andra every single day?

She was mean. But she was honest. And, fuck, it'd be free.

"I mean, if you don't mind—"

"Of course not. Actually, it'd be amazing. The *Post* doesn't pay its interns anything and my dad's all about *self-sufficiency* now that I'm graduating, so you could just pay me rent. He'd never have to know."

Of course. "How much?"

She twisted up her face. "I don't know. What we pay now? Six fifty?"

We paid six hundred—well, I paid three—but I'd accepted. The place was huge, a renovated loft in a former factory, windows and hardwood everywhere; far nicer than anything I'd have been able to afford even if I had shelled out that twenty grand a year. It was a steal, honestly. And if it wasn't the fresh start I'd wanted, it was a compromise I'd been willing to make.

I knew I was far, far better off than most people. To have a huge apartment with somebody I mostly liked for a third of the market rate—to set aside money for the huge student loan payments that would soon start coming due—that was the dream.

I was good at the job, too, once I got my bearings. My first day, I'd clicked tentatively into the enormous glass-and-steel building on Fifty-Ninth and Madison in the pointy heels I'd gotten on sale at Nine West, just placeholders until I could afford something better. The security guard had sent me to the receptionist, who had sent me to the twenty-sixth floor. I hovered in front of the elevators like a racehorse at the gate.

"First day?" a guy beside me asked. I looked over at him; he was so tall, I could barely see his face.

"Yeah. How could you tell?"

He smiled. "You've got that look about you."

The twenty-sixth floor was set up like its own company, with another receptionist at a huge desk beneath silver letters on the wall: TATE ASSOCIATES, punctuated by the famous logo, the racehorse in flight. That receptionist, Dede, had me take a seat as she phoned a woman named Mary Anne.

"Miss Rosie," Mary Anne said, clicking into the lobby, looking me up and down. I took the opportunity to do the same: she was in her mid-fifties, a silver-and-black bob compact as the rest of her suited body.

When she got to my shoes, she smiled.

"Are they wrong?" I asked softly.

She waved a hand. "They'll be hidden under your desk. Come on."

The office I'd share with her was bigger than my parents' entire practice. On one end of the room, next to the door to Grayson's office, was her desk, a huge steel tank of a thing; next to it, mine. Smaller, like the children's table at Thanksgiving.

The tasks were easy enough. Answering the phones, filing, cutting checks, balancing Grayson's petty cash. Eventually, I'd be trusted enough to *liaise with clients,* which is what Mary Anne did, and *take care of the finances,* also Mary Anne's department. Since it was a hedge fund, the latter task could have meant almost anything, and I let my imagination run wild. Make trades? Research investments? Write reports that someone important might read, maybe even someone like Grayson?

But it was also hard, in its way. It was so much harder than being an analyst would have been, and it became exponentially harder once Grayson was back from a stint in the Hamptons. There was a precise routine we had to follow, from making the coffee the second we got into the office to ordering snacks from Gristedes every second Wednesday to laying out an array of menus at 11:30 A.M. sharp for him to peruse. He paid for our lunch every day, which was a nice benefit, but it was because we weren't allowed to leave the office, which was less nice. The filing system was byzantine, the contact system impossible to navigate. When a housekeeper told me that a client I was trying to connect Grayson to was in the garden, I spent five minutes looking through the fifteen phone numbers in his contact card before connecting Grayson with the gardener. He didn't find it funny.

This wasn't the kind of job Yale had trained me for. I don't think Yale thought that its students were the kind of people who would have to take this kind of job; or, at least, not for very long. And if they did, I bet they thought of it the way that Cressida did, the way that Grayson did, as a job any idiot could do.

It was not.

But I spent my weekends at the library reading books on administration. A book by a former White House assistant was particularly useful to me. I learned the investors Grayson contacted the most; I reorganized the files in a way that even Mary Anne complimented, eventually. I learned to anticipate his needs and by the end of the summer, I was a competent assistant.

And my dirty secret was that I *liked* it. I liked being useful. I liked making Grayson happy. I liked how, when I followed him into his office with the perfect cup of coffee at exactly the moment he arrived, he'd watch me set it down on his desk with a nod. I liked stocking up on the Advil and Band-Aids he required; I particularly liked laying out the Dramamine patch two hours before he'd leave for the marina. If he wasn't on the phone when I slid it over to him, he'd look up and smile.

Good girl, he'd say.

It was harder than it looked, but it took up all of my attention and most of my time, and so it was exactly what I needed. I left for work at seven and I got back to Brooklyn an hour or so after Grayson had left for the day. Sometimes at six or seven, sometimes at eight or nine. I'd shower and sleep and then I'd wake up and do it again. It was a world of paper and screens and numbers and glass and concrete and pointy heels. By August, I'd saved enough to buy Manolo Blahniks like Cressida wore, though only the cheapest kind on offer: basic black.

By the first week of that month, I could recognize all one hundred and twenty-five Tate employees, both the Association and the Foundation. I knew the names of about half of them. And I knew the faces of most of the rest of the workers in that building, floors one through twenty-one, the floors Tate didn't lease.

So when I saw a group of people about my age, six men and a woman, shifting uncomfortably in front of the elevator bank mid-month, I knew right away that they were the new group of junior associates. The woman was wearing a skirt suit with round-toed slingbacks, fake leather already scuffed at the toes.

"First day?"

Her eyes darted over to me.

"That obvious?"

I smiled. "You've got that look about you."

By then it was also all too clear to me that I'd fundamentally misunderstood the dress code of hedge funds. Googling *what to wear to a hedge fund* had ended up with me dressing dead wrong. You could peg someone's level of power in inverse proportion to how fancily they dressed. The junior analysts wore suits. Grayson wore khakis and polos and rotating pairs of his infamous sneaker collection. That summer, he was obsessed with Nike, and we saw a lot of his Zoom Kobe I's and Stash collaborations.

As his assistant—and as a woman—I couldn't pull off the same casual look. The flip-flops that Dax, Grayson's right-hand man, wore that summer were unthinkable for me. I was supposed to look hot. Not overtly sexy, but chic. Different from Mary Anne, who was older and wore a version of the same thing every day: a sleek white modal top with swishy black trousers and a piece of large, colorful jewelry. Too middle-aged for me. But soon, I got the hang of it. Wrap dresses were my friend, so, too, were fitted A-line dresses that hugged my bodice before flaring out for a ladylike skirt. Both were easily knocked off, but both were also classic. And the real thing was easily located at thrift stores in Brooklyn, where the average shopper was looking for something far edgier.

IT WAS CLEAR TO ME from the start that I occupied two New Yorks. There was the New York of Andra's apartment: the treeless Williamsburg streets full of tattooed trust-fund hipsters priced out of Manhattan and pretending that Brooklyn was a choice they'd deliberately made. The scalding-hot bodega coffee, the two-dollar corner bagel I grabbed on the way to the subway every morning. The bodies pressed around me on the L train during rush hour. So many, so close, that on my first day I thought there'd been some kind of natural disaster or maybe a terrorist attack: Why else would there be so many people all at once, and all of them so frantic?

That New York was wearing sneakers for the mile walk to the subway, slipping on my heels around the corner from work so nobody saw me as anything but office ready. It was carrying deodorant with me at all times so nobody could smell the hot, reeking summer city on me. It was bleeding blisters on my heels and chafing thighs beneath my skirt in the heat; it was suppressing my gag reflex when the garbage union went on strike and the streets filled with even more trash, something I'd never have thought possible. It was screeching brakes and screaming women and people at the end of their tethers losing their shit in public. Not once, not twice, but over and over again, every day, forever.

But then there was the other New York. And the other New York made that New York worth it.

The other New York had universal air conditioning. It smelled like the sweet bluebell air as I walked through the counters at Barney's, on my way to pick up Grayson's $7,000 messenger bags and $900 polo shirts from his personal shopper. It was the thick, plush carpeting in the Sotheby's offices as I waited for them to bring out the Hockney he'd won at auction and didn't trust to a courier. It was the reverent, unbelievable quiet inside the St. Regis as I dropped off the latest reports for a visiting investor. It was the buoyant joy of the tanned crew over at the Long Island Yacht Club when I did a two-hour round trip in a chilled, silent town car to deliver Grayson his forgotten Dramamine. It was the feel of thick, expensive paper crossing my desk: reports on sleek, beautiful racehorses, sleek, beautiful properties in Palm Beach, London, Aspen. And it was the calm respect in the voices of everyone I spoke to, from restaurant hostesses to personal assistants, when I said those magic words: *I'm calling on behalf of Grayson Tate.*

It wasn't the lush life of a Yale equestrian princess. But it wasn't the bleached-out slog of strip malls and subdivisions of southern Illinois, either.

And after all, it was what I'd wanted.

But I did miss the respect that I'd gotten as a Yale student. I don't think I'd even realized how much it had meant to me. The way the professors talked to you like you were a real person, someone of value. The way that everyone from your dentist to your parents' friends would look at you with a mixture of esteem and annoyance when they found out you were a Yalie. Nobody ever asked me where I went to school now. And when a cabbie yelled at me for only having a credit card, no cash; when a lady spilled coffee down my new Theory shirt at Starbucks and then screamed at me; when a hand snuck up my skirt in a crowded subway and I couldn't get away—it was in those moments that I wanted to scream: *I went to YALE.*

It wasn't a trait I liked in myself.

But I did understand my college friends better than ever.

I had dignity only in the second New York, and only when I mentioned Grayson Tate's name. In other words, I was living a double life. And while I didn't have to hide my real life from Grayson (how did he think I lived, exactly, on four grand a month in *this* city? Not like him, that was for sure), I didn't talk about it. I didn't complain, I didn't explain, even when his eyes drifted to the sweat ringing my collar on a late August day when the temperature had hit a hundred by nine in the morning.

BUT THOUGH YOU THINK you'll leave the past in the past, you never do. It drags along behind you, tin cans tied to rope around your ankles, clanking and clattering at the most inopportune moments. For me, the sound they made was always the same. *Annelise. Annelise. Annelise.*

Who lived like that? Who *died* like that? Who had she been, really?

I told myself I'd never know. There still wasn't anything about her online. Just one hit now, a small paragraph in a larger *Yale Daily News* article about the other kid who died that same week.

But I saw her everywhere: in every honey-blond woman on the subway. In the gaze of every perfume-ad model staring pensively off into the middle distance. In the deck of tarot cards that I kept, still, under my pillow.

I couldn't take it, the haunting. I didn't believe in ghosts, and I still don't. Not as separate, sentient, incorporeal beings. But, thanks to Annelise, I did believe in energy. And I'd also started to believe in the kinds of ghosts we make for ourselves.

So, one August morning when I'd lain awake through the night, I got up at dawn and slid the cards out of their slinky wrapper.

Annelise, I thought. What do I need to know?

The Three of Pentacles, she told me. For the first time in months, there she was: her voice, her mind, her explanations. *Everyone's got their role to play.*

I'm not going to say it was better than the diffuse hauntings. But at the very least, it was limited. It was under my control.

You get one card a day, Annelise. No more.

25
THE PAGE OF WANDS

Annelise, I asked. What am I missing right now? What do I need?

The Page of Wands, she told me. But what had she said about the Page of Wands? I closed my eyes.

The Page of Wands is your ride-or-die. They're up for anything. They may not be ready for it, but they're up for it. The real question you need to ask is whether they have their feet on the ground, because uncontrolled enthusiasm? That's just a recipe for a Molotov cocktail, ready to blow up your life.

I rolled my eyes. *Helpful. Without you around, who's that supposed to be?*

But she didn't have anything else to say.

TWO THINGS HAPPENED at the end of August: I was named a signatory on Grayson's accounts, and Andra came back from Europe. Being able to sign Grayson's checks gave me a tingle of power up and down my arms each time I did it. He trusted me. I was trustworthy. If I wanted, I could write myself checks for tens of millions of dollars. I wouldn't get very far with them—Grayson, unlike his daughter, had a whole team of bookkeepers and accountants just itching to find something like this— but I could do it.

I was finding out there were lots of things I could do. I started staying even later, because it turns out I was allowed to go through the files. I was allowed to see the history of what the fund had done, how it had grown. Grayson had made some very lucky decisions: early Apple and Netflix buys, all of the investments everyone always wished they'd had the foresight to make. But he also had some astonishingly farsighted real estate holdings: it took me forever to figure out how he'd bought so much property on the Lower East Side and the Bowery back in the seventies, when he was in his early twenties, places where nobody lived unless they had to—until recently, when they'd turned into the coolest new Manhattan addresses.

Finally, I caved and asked Mary Anne. She was Grayson's ride-or-die, had been there since the very beginning of Tate Associates. I watched her constantly, as much as she watched me. Though she never seemed to be looking directly at me, I knew it was happening. She and Grayson had their own shorthand. *Would you*—he'd start. *Already taken care of,* she'd cut him off. And I never had any idea what it was that had transpired between them.

"Mary Anne? Um. Do you know what resources Gray—Mr. Tate uses to decide on his real estate investments?"

She didn't answer. It was that *Grayson* slipup; she'd already admonished me for it several times. Despite his casual outfits, his Lacoste and Fred Perry, despite his lunchtime search for the *best hamburger in Manhattan,* he preferred this level of formality at the office. She still called him that, after all.

"It's just . . . he's made such incredible picks," I added.

As always, she didn't take her eyes off her screens.

"Mr. Tate, senior, was in real estate," she said. The disdain of it; the unspoken word *slumlord* hung between us.

So that mystery was solved: not a magic touch, but a leg up.

I studied hard, harder than I ever had at Yale. I read the reports the analysts wrote, of course. But I also read the memos from the strategists, the traders, the risk managers: I wanted to see everything that Grayson had ever seen. I wanted to know how he'd become *him.*

Slowly, I was learning. And I was learning my place, too.

I thought I was.

I saw our new associates again. I saw them all the time, running back and forth through the building, slowing to a walk whenever they saw me. Once, I even ended up alone in an elevator with the woman. She'd slumped against the railing and closed her eyes.

Yeah, you're not at Harvard anymore, are you? (In my mind, she'd gone to Harvard.) You're at the bottom of the pile, and *putting in the work* doesn't matter anymore. The only thing that matters are results.

I was so much better off than they were. I was in Grayson's office, day after day. How many of them had even met Grayson, beyond the perfunctory cocktail party we'd thrown for them their first week?

Nobody. Just me. I was the one with access.

ANDRA'S RETURN WAS a surprising delight. Two weeks in Europe had turned into two months, but it didn't seem to matter to the *Post*; in some way I didn't understand, Rupert Murdoch was friends with Andra's father, though how the Australian media magnate had become buddies with a chocolate bar heir was anybody's guess. Maybe there was a club you got inducted into once your net worth hit a billion dollars; the more I saw of Grayson's social schedule, the more I was inclined to believe it.

It wasn't just the fact that I hadn't socialized with anyone since graduation. It wasn't the fact that she took one amazed look around the empty apartment (I'd gone the summer with just my IKEA bed in my room, my open suitcase serving as my closet) and the next day when I came home from work, the place was full of velvet and glass and plants and *things*.

The real pleasure of having a roommate was that Andra was broke, too. Even though my take-home pay of just over four grand a month was even less than I'd thought it would be (there was a steep New York City tax I hadn't known about), it was definitely higher than the nothing she made. I didn't begrudge her the six-fifty a month in rent, particularly once I figured out that it was the only money she was getting. Sure, she was living in New York for free, but she was also working for free. And I didn't envy her that.

It was grating, though, when she'd complain about money. Because the thing I could never forget was that she was just playing at being poor. She wasn't poor, she was broke. And Annelise had been right: there was a difference.

But I tried not to think about Annelise beyond my daily readings.

Still, it was nice that my closest friend in the city had to refuse meet-ups at the same cocktail bars I did, the ones where drinks were fifteen bucks a pop. It was nice to have a friend who checked when the free museum days were each month so we didn't have to pay twenty dollars a ticket. Her Prada was getting out of date, and it was delicious to me.

Even more delicious was the disdain it turned out she had—had always had—for Grayson Tate.

"That is so fucking demeaning," Andra said, one of the first nights she was back. "You buy his *toilet paper?*"

Grayson didn't like the standard company-issue stuff but didn't want to spring for the triple-ply for the whole company. So, twice a month on the Gristedes order, there it was.

"I mean, someone's got to do it. And it's not forever. I do other things, too."

She rolled over on the gray velvet love seat, facing me on the sectional across from her.

"I mean, yeah," Andra said. "But why does it have to be *you?* You went to Yale, for fuck's sake."

"I'm not wiping his ass. It's work. It's fine."

"The thing about guys like Grayson Tate," she said languidly, "is that they were born on third base and think they hit a triple."

I laughed. Because she was right, but also because the fact that she knew enough about baseball to make the quote surprised me.

"And that's so different from you and your family?" I said. I'd never talked to Andra about money before. But the proximity to Grayson had given me more confidence. The sums of money crossing my desk every day—intangible as they were on the screen—were so enormous that I felt, now, like I had the right.

"Of course it is. We own the stadium. And we've always known it. If only you wanted to work in chocolate," she said with a sigh. "Man, I'd have you set up for life."

I laughed. "Only if you went with me and we could do Lucy and Ethel on the production line."

"Who?"

I shook my head. "Never mind."

She blew out her lips. "Dad would be in *heaven.* All he talks about is how you need to start at the bottom, how you need to know every part of the company to be able to run it."

"You don't want to run it?"

"What's the point? Nobody can build a better mousetrap. The company's been cranking out steady profits for, like, a hundred and fifty years. There's nothing for me to do but just kind of . . . be there."

It did sound horrible, until you thought about the money she'd get for being there.

"Speaking of just being there. I heard from Lila today," she said.

"How is she?" I'd had a few texts from Lila after graduation, but I hadn't been able to bring myself to reply to them. The last semester at Yale, we'd been polite—friendly, even. And I knew, reasonably, that I couldn't blame her more than anyone else for her part in what had happened to Annelise. Couldn't blame her more than myself.

I still didn't want to talk to her, though.

"You know. Just killing time in LA. But she finally got a job last week."

"No kidding."

"Yeah. Dad's friend is doing this DiCaprio movie—" And she was off, explaining the plot about some horribly depressed suburban family. "Anyway, she's a PA."

I sat up. "Lila's an *assistant?*"

Andra giggled. It was a strange sound on her, like a bear's laughter. "I know. Can you imagine? I feel a little bit bad for inflicting her on them." She studied her nails. "Not that bad, though. By the way, have you heard about Cress?"

"Um. Kind of." A few texts at the beginning of the summer, tapering off as fall neared. She'd been running up and down the East Coast doing the shows closer to home, then one near Chicago, one outside of San Francisco. I'd replied to her texts, perfunctorily. She'd gotten me the job, after all. What if I didn't reply and she told her father? Goodbye, job security. Goodbye, any respect I'd garnered. Goodbye, New York. "She's in Greenwich now, I think. Said she wants to spend some time with her mom?"

"No," Andra said, sitting up, too, her eyes flaring. "Not *from* Cress. *About* Cress."

I scanned my mental Rolodex for any information I'd garnered from Grayson's office. I knew she still got an allowance of ten grand a month. I knew she'd bought three horses with her half mil, all of which were currently in the country.

"Not really."

"Girl is *depressed*. She's done six shows so far this summer and came in dead last at every. Single. One."

"With those horses?" I blurted out.

Andra's eyebrows shot up.

"I mean," I said. "I know how important the rider is. Just . . . last?"

Andra held my gaze a minute, then smirked. "You know how people outside of EQ always say that the horses are the real athletes? That we're just there to hang on?"

"Sure." We hated when people said that.

"At that level? A great horse is necessary. Several great horses are necessary. But in the words of my father?" Her smirk deepened, her voice dropped. *"They're necessary. But they're not sufficient."*

"Cress, though . . ." I said. "Cress is a great athlete."

She tilted her head to the side, half pitying. "Cress is an athlete," she said. "But any guts she ever had? Man. She's definitely lost them now."

26

THE HIEROPHANT

What do I need to know for today?

The Hierophant, Annelise told me. The Hierophant scares me. He's not supposed to, but he does. I think it's because he represents institutions and power, tradition, convention. I've never done well with those. But really, don't let that influence you. He can also just mean things like group participation or the beliefs that group holds. Whenever he comes up for me, though, I always see it as a challenge to define my own beliefs, to be my own mentor, and not to push boundaries too much right now. When the Hierophant comes up and you try to push a branch of tradition out of your face, it'll come swinging right back at you and smack you right in the eyes.

I missed her voice, even as I was starting to forget what it had sounded like.

ONE NEW SECRET: THERE wasn't really enough work for two assistants at the office. At least, not all the time; when we were both needed, for big trades or investor meetings or quarterly reports, we were *really* needed. My days were interspersed with rushes of furious activity, sometimes beginning as early as five or six in the morning—as when Grayson wanted Billy Joel tickets and I sat at my phone, redialing Ticketmaster a hundred times until I finally got through. But Mary Anne took care of the important things, the high-stakes financial tasks, like putting orders through and making calls to the people who mattered.

Which left me in a strange position. In theory, a job that paid that much, with that much prestige, that required little to no work most days would have sounded like a dream. But with someone like Grayson Tate watching you—no matter how infrequently he does it—you can't be seen poking around Facebook or looking at cut-rate designer dresses from last season online. You have to be seen doing something. And besides, I wanted to do *something*. I just didn't know what I was allowed to do.

It turned out, I could do anything as long as I made it look secretarial.

Reorganizing the files gave me a good excuse to look closely at the history of the company's transactions. The equestrian legend was true: his father, Samson Tate, had bought Queen of Sheba back in 1979 for just over ten grand. And in 1981, Grayson had sold the horse—no show jumper, but a hell of a runner—for $1.1 million. The next year, he'd founded Tate Associates. And while his early investments had been good, they hadn't been all that impressive, given that they were mostly in real estate, the field that slumlord Samson had known more about than anyone. It was after Samson's death in 1989 that Grayson had really taken off. Apple at twenty-five cents a share. Nvidia the second it went public in 1999. And a block of apartment buildings on the Bowery a few years ago, just before the New Museum had announced they'd be opening in 2007. His sales had been just as impressive: he'd gotten out of Intel just before the 2000 bubble popped; it had never regained its value. And he'd dropped Blockbuster at its height, back in 2002.

Tate Associates was incredibly impressive. I had been right, back at that first Yale party of senior year; we did outperform the market. Consistently, and by a lot.

But the part of the job that made me proudest was reading the Tate Foundation files, which Grayson had started just after Cress's birth, in November 1983.

My whole life, I've thought about what it means to be an athlete, what it means to be an American. But over the past few months, I've thought a lot about what it means to be a father, too, the word-processed transcript of his announcement read. *And I know that my children will always ride. But that opportunity is sadly inaccessible to hundreds of thousands of children in this country. Among these children may be the next Olympians, the next superstars. The cost of a sport should be no barrier to entry. And so for the future of this*

sport that has given me so much, for the future of all the children in this country,
I am pleased to announce the creation of the Grayson Tate Foundation.

It gave me chills. Me. I was one of those children. Reading that statement, I felt like one of *his* children. The summer riding camps he'd set up
around the country. The 4-H clubs he'd sponsored. The travel funds for
inner-city kids to spend summers in the countryside with animals. And
beyond that, the refuges he'd set up for retired horses. Horses who could
no longer jump or race or prance in dressage competitions now spent
their golden years happily trotting around lush pastures.

The Foundation had grown since then: branching out first into college scholarships for the TF riders (which I hadn't known about—why
had nobody at the 4-H club ever told me?); later, beginning to over-
lap with the work of Tate Associates. Grayson saw factories closing,
farms being bought out, housing markets collapsing. And yes, he'd
made the right market moves, buying and selling to wring profit out
of those economic contractions. But under the Foundation, he'd also
set up retraining programs for the workers who'd lost their jobs, the
parents of his riders. He'd bought land from them at more than fair
prices, creating subdivisions with special low-income sections they
could afford. And in the meantime, the children, always the children:
after-school tutoring centers, free college test prep—you could almost
trace Cress's girlhood and adolescence by when each new program
had begun.

He was a captain of industry in every sense of the word. And I couldn't
think of anyone better to be steering the ship.

When I could force myself to, I tried to go through the accounts
for both the Foundation and the Association. I was inexperienced in ac-
counting, and besides, they didn't teach QuickBooks at Yale. I couldn't
understand, for example, why Grayson had to have a checkbook for the
Foundation in the office. But there it was, just next to the company checkbook: bound in leather, hiding the pages of stubs and blank golden checks
inside. I also couldn't understand the purpose of the checks he'd written,
either to companies or to individuals. Wouldn't the *Foundation girls*, as he
called them, pay the bills for him?

But asking Mary Anne to explain would have been too humiliating.

Surely this was the kind of thing I should already know. Eventually, I decided that he had his reasons. And, like the other assistants before me, I cut the checks he asked me to, from whichever account he specified.

One early September day, I was reading a *Wall Street Journal* clipping from 1995 that called Grayson the *savior of the rural poor* when Mary Anne cleared her throat. I looked up sharply; that was the most warning she'd ever give when she wanted something before she got harsh, and fast.

But she only said:

"Exciting plans tonight?"

Normally, no. Normally, on a day like that—when Grayson would be leaving the office around five—I'd stay until six, change into my sneakers, and grab a burrito once I was back in Williamsburg, eating it on the walk, then fall immediately into bed. There never seemed to be enough time to sleep. The fact that most people lived like this was baffling to me. How could a society function on so little sleep?

But today was different. I'd seen the blocked-off green chunk marked *Private* on Grayson's schedule from 5 P.M. onward. And I'd thought: Why not do my own charity work? I didn't have start-a-foundation money, but I could do *something*.

"Actually, yeah," I said. "I'm going down to the Animal Rescue Foundation to start training as a volunteer."

"The what foundation?" Her eyes were still fixed on the screen.

"Animal Rescue. A shelter downtown."

She gave a quick nod of her silvery bob.

Who *was* Mary Anne? I knew from the files, the files I *really* shouldn't have been reading, the ones I read when she was in meetings with Grayson, that she'd been his assistant since 1982. But there was no hiring paperwork. Finally, in an ancient folder, I discovered that she'd been his father's assistant for two years. If she'd started right out of college, back in 1979, she would have been twenty-two. Which made her about fifty.

Thirty years of helping someone else. Thirty years of facilitating someone else's projects. It was just so grim.

And yet the way she came in each morning, her red lipstick perfect and her bob swinging. The way she stared at those screens. You would have thought that *she* was Grayson Tate, for how seriously she took it all.

"I've never really liked animals," she said softly.

I looked at her, but she didn't meet my eyes.

"But that's—that's like saying you don't like *people*. How can you say that about all animals?"

She shrugged. "I'm a city girl. Bronx born and bred. Didn't grow up with them."

"Oh. I did. I guess I just—" *miss them*, I almost said. "Got inspired by the Foundation's work."

The *click-clack* of her keyboard.

"We don't do *animal shelters*. Just horses," she said finally.

A few minutes later, Grayson emerged from his office. He'd been on calls all morning, and we hadn't seen him. You could feel him behind the closed door, though. The subtle electricity crackled through me and Mary Anne. He had his sailing bag with him, which wasn't unusual. He was still sailing on lots of late afternoons, trying to catch the last of the summer.

"Oh, Rosie," Grayson said absently as he headed to the door. "We're having a little get-together tonight at the apartment for Cressy."

I hadn't even known she was back in the city. But he took my surprise for hesitation, and shrugged.

"I'm sure she'd love it if you'd come by. There'll be lots of your Yale cohort there. Blake and, um. All those guys."

"Of course," I said quickly. "Absolutely. I didn't even—" Why hadn't Andra said anything? Surely Andra would be there. She, if anyone, was one of *those guys.*

"Great," he said, swinging his bag over his shoulder and pushing the office door open. "Seven."

The door closed and I swiveled to Mary Anne.

"Is it okay if I leave early today? I'll come in early tomorrow."

Click-clack. I'd have taken it back if the idea of going to a Tate cocktail party in my blazer and work pants weren't so humiliating.

"It's just, to get home in time to change—"

"Fine."

"Everything's all set with the transfers and the call log's up to date. I'll add the later calls in—"

"I said it's fine."

It didn't sound fine, but I didn't press. It wasn't until four thirty, when I shut down my computer and slung my purse over my shoulder, that she spoke again.

"You're still not one of them, you know." She said it as though she were telling me her coffee order. And yet my heart started that old fluttering, its hummingbird beat. I *was,* though. I'd earned my place among them. Hadn't I?

I had. And the fact that she'd made me doubt that, even for a moment, burned in me.

"I went," I said coldly, "to Yale."

"Oh, honey," she said, as I started for the door. "You think that means anything now? You think anyone here cares?"

I turned back to her. "Cressida Tate is my best friend. I'm one of them."

And Mary Anne made a snorting, strangled sound. After a second, I realized she was laughing.

But she cut it off quickly and began typing again.

"If you were," she said, *click-clack,* "you never would have ended up here."

HER WORDS HAUNTED me all the way home, and I hated her for it. She couldn't be right. I hadn't done everything I'd done to be—what, a *career administrator?*

But maybe what she'd said wasn't about me.

Had *she* ever been invited to a Tate family party? I couldn't imagine it.

And yeah—in her position, I'd have been bitter, too.

Me, though? I was different. Where her career began and ended was just my stepping stone. I was on the path to something bigger, something better.

Something more.

She just couldn't stand it. That was all.

27
THE TEN OF WANDS

Sometimes you just can't take any more. The Ten of Wands is a big fucking burden. It's asking you if the responsibility and the work you've put on your shoulders are worth it or if they're something you've accepted because of some inner insecurity.

Basically, it's asking: What can you let go of? What's no longer serving you?

I WAS BACK AT THE APARTMENT by five fifteen, searching frantically for something to wear. I couldn't get any more use out of the Stella McCartney dress, not in front of this crowd. But I was too sad to give it away or sell it, which is probably what I should have done. So it just hung in my closet, no place to go anymore.

In the end, I grabbed the one cool dress I had. One that Andra had convinced me to buy on our only shopping trip to the West Village (*Ugh, it's so depressing,* she'd said at the end, *shopping without any money*): a pale blue silk dress that was so shimmery, it bordered on silver. At the top, it was held up by a halter made of white leather, laser cut in shapes that reminded me of antlers. I'd found it at a pop-up store run by some recent fashion grads. At $250, I'd hesitated, but Andra had grabbed it and haggled the designer down to $175. I hadn't felt great about that haggling.

Finding shoes to wear was harder. Mine were all practical, work-appropriate. Eventually, I crawled through Andra's closet. With two sisters, she was always urging me to borrow her things, but at six inches taller than me, there wasn't much I *could* borrow. But I found a pair of pale gray Manolos only a size too big (they must have been torture for her) and stuffed the toes with toilet paper.

It was only as I ran back out to the subway that I realized I hadn't called the Animal Rescue Foundation, and I was supposed to be there in fifteen minutes. I dialed the saved number of the volunteer coordinator, praying the whole time for her voicemail—which I got. *Last-minute work emergency, next month's training*—the words spilled easily from my mouth. I'd gotten good at the phone.

I'd been to the Pierre apartment before, but as I walked up to it that evening, September breeze grazing my skin, it felt different. For the first time, approaching the gilded marquees on the neo-Renaissance building made me feel special. Chosen. I belonged here now. I wasn't just some college friend, pretending, or some assistant skulking in the shadows.

I was a guest of Grayson Tate's.

I clicked across the black-and-white marble floors in my borrowed shoes, really feeling everything around me for the first time as *mine*. The chandelier above me, the wood-paneled front desk. The clerks behind the desk. The elevator, the huge gold panel of buttons that the operator pressed for me; even the historic gold-framed photos on the elevator walls.

This was my New York. Everything else was just pretend.

A waiter opened the Tates' door for me. In sitcoms, characters are always mistaking guests for waiters and vice versa, but trust me: it doesn't happen in real life. Not to people like the ones there. Because you could see the difference in what the waiters wore. The too-boxy cuts of their shirts, the slight polyester sheen on their pants. And even if you didn't catch the difference from their clothes, a single glance at their shoes would have done it.

I smiled and walked past him, straight into the living room with its parquet floors and tasteful chandeliers, its huge arched windows overlooking the park.

You don't *decorate* for a party like that. If such a thing had existed back in Western Plains—a welcome-back-from-three-months-on-the-show-jumping-circuit party—it would have been filled with crepe paper and balloons and at least one banner. Not here. Here, the shiny floors

the room. Surely there had to be other people I knew here, beyond the B-list riders and this fucking guy.

The one person I didn't spot was Grayson. Did he see this as a women's party? Or was he embarrassed to be giving a party in honor of an equestrian season that had been nothing more than mediocre?

Well, it wasn't like I didn't see him every day.

There was Mallory. Finally, someone I wanted to see; I hadn't talked to her after she'd graduated at the end of my first year. She'd been in the city for a few years now, working her way up the ladder at Goldman Sachs. And there, beside her, laughing, was a glossy-haired Andra. Perfect.

But all of these people must have been invited—and I hadn't. Or, I had, but only at the last minute, as an afterthought. And by Grayson, not Cressida. My heart swooped around my chest. Did she not want me there? I didn't particularly want to see her, but I didn't want to be thrown out of the group, either.

No. She'd said she'd forgotten to make calls until last night, and I believed her. Believed, too, in her asking Grayson to ask me, to save her the time.

We were fine.

All of these other young women were all just like me. Or almost like me. Because I was fancy, I was dressed up. And they were . . . well, something else. Cress, for example, was in a purple boho dress with deliberately unraveled embroidery around the neck. It was actually something Annelise would have worn, and for a moment, my throat tightened before I regained my composure.

Cool was changing. I'd noticed it already in Brooklyn, but I'd thought it was just that: Brooklyn. But all of the girls here were in strange bohemian garb. Deliberately ripped, cut off, torn. I loved it. It was like Yale and New Haven, that high-low divide. The idea that these girls could be wearing perfectly put-together Chanel outfits, but they'd chosen to wear ripped-up dresses that, okay, were still designer. It was a style I could have faked with some of my own clothes, if I'd known enough. And if I'd still had my own clothes. Everything I had now seemed to be for work. It was either gabardine wool and pointy heels or sweatpants and slippers.

Before I could excuse myself from Cress and Blake, Anthea scampered up to me, placing a cold hand on my arm. "Rosie, dear. There's a horrible issue with the Dom. Could you give the bartender a hand?"

"I don't—know anything about champagne," I said, looking at Cress as if to say, *can you believe this?* But she wouldn't meet my eye.

Anthea just stood there blinking.

"No, of course," I said. "Of course. Where is he?"

She blinked.

"In the kitchen, of course."

"Of course." I handed my half-empty glass to Cress, who stared at it as though I'd handed her a crystal figurine of a unicorn, like she couldn't figure out why I'd given it to her. And I headed to the kitchen.

I was used to seeing Carla there, up with the family from Greenwich; or, when they were in the country, one of a team of hotel maids keeping things in order for Grayson alone.

What I was not used to was seeing a muscular guy in his twenties, bent over and organizing empty bottles into crates.

"Um," I said after a second. "Hi."

He stood up, wiping his palms on the front of his polyester black pants.

"Hi," he said.

We looked at each other.

"How can I help you?" he said after a second.

"Oh—no. I'm supposed to help you. I'm the assistant?"

He scanned my dress, my shoes, and met my eyes in bafflement.

I shrugged and held out my hand.

"Rosie Macalister," I said.

"Luke Greenleaf," he said. "Let's hope you have the luck of the Irish," he said. "Are you lucky, Rosie Macalister?"

"I'm . . . I . . . don't know. *Macalister*'s Scottish; I never thought about it. Not compared to these people," I said, gesturing toward the living room.

He laughed.

"Who is?" he said. "Come on, we gotta go meet the guys from Gristedes."

I followed him out the back door of the kitchen. I hadn't ever thought about that back door before, but of course this was what it was for. The people like us. The help. After a push through a STAFF ONLY door, the hallways turned from red-carpeted with gilded sconces to linoleum-covered and industrial neon overhead.

The service elevator opened and I got in, staring at Andra's shoes. They gleamed in the fluorescent lighting. The balls of my feet were burning already, blisters forming on at least three toes. I could have been at the Animal Rescue Foundation right now. I could have been surrounded by puppies.

I could have been wearing sneakers.

We landed on the ground floor, and I followed Luke past the hotel kitchen I'd never seen, around the corner to a room full of huge crates of dirty linen. And out a door into an alley I hadn't known existed.

"What now?" I asked as Luke stopped.

He pointed up at a sign I hadn't noticed. DELIVERIES.

"Now, we wait," he said.

I fought the blush creeping up my neck.

"Of course," I said. "Sorry. Smart people are dumb."

"So you're not lucky, but you're smart?"

"Smart enough."

"Best kind of smart," he said, leaning back against a brick wall. "Too smart, I think, makes you miserable."

I prayed the truck would arrive and I would haven't to respond to whatever theory he clearly wanted to spout at me now; but it didn't.

"Why do you say that?" I asked after a long minute.

"Because being smart enough to understand the world fully, without the power to change it . . ." He shrugged. "That's hell, if you ask me."

I raised my eyebrows. "Every single person up in that apartment has the power to change it."

He smirked. A lock of light brown hair had fallen across his forehead. "But they're not *too* smart, are they?"

I giggled despite myself.

"Smart enough," I said.

He gave me a knowing look.

"Not all of them," he said.

But then a truck pulled up and two guys got out, tossing four crates at our feet. Luke slipped one of them a bill, I think a ten; and then, just as quickly as they'd pulled up, they were gone.

We stared at the crates.

"Forty-eight bottles?" I said. "You really think each person's going to drink another bottle?"

"Well, we've already been through forty-eight, and it's only"—he glanced at his watch—"eight fifteen. I'm not even sure this will be enough. So what do you think? Three and one?"

I frowned, then piled one crate on top of another.

"I'm strong," I told him as I lifted them.

He picked up the other two and we started back inside, down that same labyrinth of service halls.

"You're that strong, maybe you don't need luck," he said, pressing the elevator button. It dinged open immediately.

"What's this fixation on luck?" I heaved my crates into the elevator, my hands smarting from the imprints of the dry wood. He kept holding his, so I pressed the button.

"Luck? It's the only thing that matters. The only thing ruling our lives. Luck and desire. But even desire . . . that comes from luck, too. From how you were raised, from the things you were exposed to. I don't understand anyone who's *not* fixated on it."

"So, there's no grand plan, then?" I asked, picking my crates back up with a stifled groan as the doors opened again. "No supreme being up there saying, *you get this, you get that?*"

We walked down the hall for a few seconds before he responded. "Oh, sure there is. I just think that the supreme being's more like an infinite-sided pair of dice rather than, you know—"

"An old dude with a long white beard?"

He chuckled as he pushed open the back door.

"Exactly."

I set my crates next to the refrigerator with a sigh. "Well. There we go, I guess."

"Well, Rosie Macalister," he said, bending over one of the crates and starting to pull out dripping bottle after dripping bottle. "You'd better be getting back to the party."

I should have. I should have wanted to. But beyond the quiet calm of the kitchen, beyond the stools at the counter just calling to be sat on, to give my feet some relief—there was a little hot ember of anger at the center of me that I now couldn't ignore. Not because I'd been thrown together with Luke or even because I'd been sent to the kitchen. But at the fact that I was, first and foremost, an employee. If not to Cress, then to her family. To her world.

Which meant that Mary Anne had been right.

I grabbed a bottle, and Luke winked at me as I headed back into the living room. It was more crowded now, body heat pulsing through the room, but it hadn't occurred to anyone to crack a window. I couldn't see Mallory or Andra anywhere. Grayson had arrived and was standing in the center of a circle of people: a mixture of older and younger, athletic and fashionable.

If he'd asked me to go get the champagne, I wouldn't have been mad. At a party, after work, at 3 A.M. I worked for him, after all.

I did not work for Anthea.

Finally, I settled on Cress, who had somehow ended up alone with her champagne by the window. Staring out over the park trees in a way I'd never seen her stare at anything: into the middle distance, her gaze shallow and deep at once.

"Cress, are you okay?" I asked softly. She didn't seem to hear me, though, and I put a hand on her shoulder.

She jumped; and suddenly she was Cress again, all wide smiles.

"So, how do you like working for Daddy? Is it just the best?" she said, downing the rest of her glass and grabbing the bottle from me, gripping it between her thighs to tear the foil off. I'd actually forgotten I was holding it.

"It *is* the best. He's really great. To watch the way his mind works—" But her eyes were skittering behind me, around me, seeking the room for something I couldn't have named. "Cress. Seriously. Are you okay?"

She met my gaze with a squint.

"Oh, fuck. I'm so sorry. I've been getting these weird text messages. I don't know why they're freaking me out so much."

Over the years, she'd vaguely referenced similar incidents: a stalker when she was a teenager, a kidnapping threat. And I knew Grayson kept a security team on retainer for his personal use.

"Tell Bob," I said, naming the head of the team. "Or I can, if you want."

She made a face.

"Seriously, Cress. You can't be dealing with this stuff on your own. Bob can take care of it."

"Yeah," she said. "Of course he will."

"Or we could talk to your dad—I mean, he's right—"

"It's just so funny that you work for him!" She cut me off. "It's like, worlds colliding, right?"

As though she hadn't gotten me the job? As though it had all been one big coincidence?

"So, tell me about your summer!" I said brightly, trying to match her tone. But shit—I'd forgotten. Her summer hadn't been a victorious one. Despite the party, despite her father's pretendings.

I braced myself for stories of her losses, ready to sympathize and tell her to hold out, to hang in there. But she just rolled her eyes.

"Oh my God. I got the most amazing new horses, you *have* to meet them. Another Dutch warmblood, and this Oldenburger—"

Not a word about her performance. Not a word about the future. Just horse after horse, price tags and breeding values and fence heights.

And it occurred to me: I didn't have to be at this party.

I didn't have to stay.

But I didn't see a good way out, so I listened and nodded in all the right places. The whole time, pulling up memories of Cress as she'd been. Of her bursting into hives and laughter at the same moment, of her pulling her cheeks down to make her face a grotesquerie of itself. Of her swapping out library books over a period of hours.

Eventually, there were enough strangers around us that I could kiss her on the cheek and whisper that I had to go. I got an absent nod in response.

On burning feet, I exited through the gilded guest elevators, through the lobby. How stupid I'd been to think they were mine. And then I slipped out into the still-warm, still-bright September evening.

It only occurred to me as the train came barreling into the Fifty-Ninth Street station that I should have told her I knew how she felt. I knew what it was like: to be an impressive amateur and a mediocre professional.

It had happened to me, too.

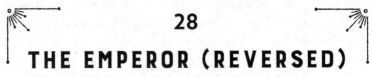

28

THE EMPEROR (REVERSED)

Annelise, what do I need to know today?
The Emperor reversed, she told me.
I don't like the look of him.
You shouldn't. Fuck this guy. He's bad news; power perverted.
He's controlling, he's domineering, he's just a total asshole. Red flag
city; run.

I COULDN'T GET HORSES out of my mind for the next few days. I hadn't thought much about riding since leaving school, and I hadn't thought seriously about it since Annelise. But now, I was googling Cressida's Oldenburger, I was watching YouTube clips of her riding. And I was staring at the stretched-out iron horse on the office wall and remembering what it felt like: to be able to fly.

So I was half dreaming—the most dangerous task of all when you're an assistant—when a tall, tan man strode toward my desk and stopped so close I had to tilt my head back to look up at him. I knew him immediately: it was that guy Charlie from Cress's birthday party.

"Charlie Roper for Grayson," he said, without even looking at me.

By that point, I knew to keep Grayson's daily schedule in my head at all times. It was only three, and he didn't have another appointment until four thirty. But it was a classic PA dilemma: he was Grayson's best friend, and so I could get in trouble either for letting him in *or* for kicking him out.

I glanced at Mary Anne, who deigned to turn from her computer just long enough to give a pointed look at the intercom between us. It was an old model, probably from the eighties. I always wondered if she'd been the one who'd insisted on keeping it or if he had. It hung under a print by one of his favorite artists, Ed Ruscha; he had so many he'd started running out of places to put them.

A PARTICULAR KIND OF HEAVEN, the print read.

"Mr. Tate, I have Charlie Roper for you."

The green light on the box lit up, and I nodded at Charlie.

"You can go on in."

"Thanks, hon."

I watched his receding back. Blue Fred Perry polo, white cable-knit sweater tossed over his shoulders, jeans just like my dad wore, a little too loose for fashion. If telekinesis were real, that little intercom would have come flying at him so fast it would have caved his skull in. *You wrapped your arm around me at Cressida's birthday. You thought I was a pretty little rich girl, but now that I'm just a secretary—assistant—I'm a nothing. I don't exist any more than this furniture does.*

I have become invisible.

Charlie came out after a few minutes, and Grayson followed. And because I was invisible, I studied them. They had the same tanned, handsome faces, the same boyish, jovial expressions. The only real difference between them was the eyes: both blue, but Charlie's were absolutely guileless, shallow. Grayson's were like telescopes when they fixed on you.

What kind of life would you have had to live, to end up with faces like theirs?

"Rosie, cut a check for Charlie, won't you?" Grayson said. He looked at his friend with raised eyebrows.

Charlie shrugged. "A hundred?"

And back to me: "A hundred should do it."

I unlocked my top drawer and pulled out the leather-bound corporate checkbook.

"Ah—the Foundation, please, Rosie."

I'd cut a few Foundation checks before. The Foundation, as far as I could tell, consisted of three women on the twenty-second floor who always tried to drag more time out of Grayson than the strict one hour a month I'd been instructed to give them. But he wrote his own Foundation checks often enough. Once when he got a letter from a little girl up in the Bronx who wanted to go to horse camp; once to one of his collectible dealers when he bought a mint-condition DiMaggio rookie card he wanted to auction off at the next gala.

I wrote it carefully, signing my name with a flourish, and waved it in the air. For the second while the ink was drying, while Charlie waited for me to hand over the money—for that one moment, I had the power.

I handed him the check, and he had the nerve to read it. Right there in front of me. Like he was checking for errors.

And then he handed Grayson the check and burst into laughter. Grayson, too, started laughing, so hard he doubled over, his hands on his thighs.

"Sorry . . . ?" I said finally.

"A hundred thousand, Rosie. A hundred *thousand*. And write it to cash," Grayson said, sliding the check I'd written for, yes, a hundred dollars to Charlie Roper, back across my desk.

I didn't put a flourish on the second check.

Thank God Grayson's four thirty was down on the twenty-third floor. Thank God he took his briefcase and jacket with him, meaning he wasn't coming back after. Meaning I wouldn't have to see him again that day.

It wasn't until the elevator dinged closed that I remembered he was heading out to Long Island to sneak in an early September sail afterward.

"Fuck," I muttered, rummaging through my desk, looking for the Dramamine. If I'd messed this up, too—the day would be completely unsalvageable.

Mary Anne looked over at me. "You gave him the pills with his lunch," she said sharply, the only words she'd spoken since the check incident.

Had I? The days were blending together. I could see them, the two little white pills on a saucer at the edge of his tray. But what had been on the tray? Was it the lobster salad he'd had today or the veal from yesterday?

"You did," she said again, softer, and bent down to the trash can between our desks. After a second, she stood up again, empty cardboard packet in hand.

I exhaled. "Oh my God. Thank you so much."

"You better thank me," she said, turning back to her screen. "Too much of that stuff can kill you."

BY THE TIME I EMERGED from the Bedford Avenue stop that evening, I'd missed a call from my mother. More accurately, I'd missed about a dozen calls from my mother. Without free time during the day, I could no longer get ahold of her between her scheduled appointments, and so we'd spoken only a handful of times since I'd started working.

She picked up on the second ring.

"Rosie-Pie."

"Mom?" My voice broke, and a passing hipster, hair swooping long over his forehead, turned to look at me.

"Kid, I've got about thirty seconds before I have to get supper on, but I can't stop thinking about you. Your last email, you just sounded . . . I dunno. How are you? Are things okay? How's work?"

"Work's good."

"Are you liking it, though? All that filing and phones and stuff?"

"I mean. Mom. You're talking about the exact same stuff I've done for you forever. Yeah, I like it. It's fine. Why are you so worried?"

"I don't know," Mom said. "I just always thought of you building something or fixing something or making something. You know—*doing* something."

I had to pull the sweaty phone away from my face for a minute and wipe it off on my skirt before I could reply. "I am doing something. I'm doing this."

"You're helping a man with a lot of money make more money," she said, and sighed. "I just wanted more for you. That's all."

"Well, you didn't want me to be a vet or a farmer, did you?" I replied sharply.

Mom sighed, half-amused, half-exasperated. "Even if I did want something else for you, don't knock vets and farmers, hon, okay? You come from a long line of farmers and healers and builders and makers. So does the whole goddamn country, if it comes to that."

"Swear jar," I said automatically.

She blew out her lips. "Like you don't hear worse every motherfucking day around all those Wall Street traders."

She never understood precisely what I did.

I laughed. "Yep. Oh yes."

"But," she said, and there was a clicking in the background: the stove turning on. "I am so glad that you'll never have to worry about money again. I am so, so glad."

"Yeah. I mean, the kind of money here—it's unbelievable. The amounts. Actually—" And I launched into the Charlie story. The story that had been so humiliating only a few hours earlier turned funny as I told Mom, as I giggled at my own naiveté.

But she wasn't laughing.

"Why is he having you cut checks to his friends from the charity accounts?"

I had been so absorbed in my own embarrassment, I hadn't thought to wonder. "I . . . I don't know. I'm sure he has his reasons."

"Yeah," Mom said shortly. "I'm sure he does, too. But you need to be careful, kid."

"I mean, I wrote a *check*. And a hundred grand is, like, one-millionth of the holdings. And Grayson was right there telling me to do it. It's fine."

"Rosie!" she interrupted sharply. "There are all sorts of laws governing how a charity can spend its money. And cutting six-figure checks to your already rich friends isn't one of them. Don't you know that?" she said, and her voice was incredulous. "Didn't you go to Yale?"

29

THE KNIGHT OF CUPS
(REVERSED)

What am I not seeing right now? I asked Annelise.

*The Knight of Cups reversed, she told me. When cups
are reversed, all the water flows out. All the good goes. Or it
gets twisted in some way. And the Knight? He's our troubadour
romantic, in love with love. Reversed, though, the Knight turns
unrealistic, turns cranky. He gets overpowered by his emotions.*

Don't we all?

Well, isn't that *the question.*

HOW HAD I NOT SEEN IT? How had I let myself become this complacent?

At work the next day, I couldn't sit still. I'd known, intellectually, that it was illegal to use foundation funds for anything other than foundation activities. Donors had made contributions, which they then wrote off on their taxes; the charity itself didn't pay any taxes, and it was, I'm pretty certain, a huge tax write-off for Grayson himself. I'd been aware of all of that in a vacuum, but I'd never applied that knowledge to my actual situation.

I'd been told what to do, and so I'd done it. Just like a good little secretary would.

The shame of that was different from not having the right shoes, or being asked to help with a champagne delivery, or even writing a hundred-dollar rather than a hundred-*thousand*-dollar check. It was a shame that burned in my chest, that radiated throughout my body. It was a shame that made me think less of myself.

Not just that I'd done it; that I'd done it without thinking. Without questioning. Without using the brain I'd just spent four years and $150,000 perfecting.

I've never been the prettiest. I've never been the best rider. I've certainly never been the richest. But I'd always had common sense.

I couldn't believe that I'd let myself lose that.

I was ashamed. But I was also mad.

I'd lost that, and what had I gotten in return? A job as a modern-day servant to a modern-day lord of the manor. You don't rise through the feudal system, that was the whole point of it.

And yet somehow, I'd thought I would. I'd wanted to believe that I'd be different.

I COULDN'T GET OUT of the office fast enough that afternoon.

At five, I rushed through the lobby doors, not even bothering to take off my heels, and they clacked at me: *Get out of your head. Get out of it. Out of it. Get out of your head.* But even as my cheeks started to flush, as I grew breathless, I couldn't seem to feel my body. How had my whole life condensed into this single thing, these thirty seconds I couldn't escape from? Was I implicated, was I not, was it a crime (of course it was a crime), how much of a crime was it, and was it my crime alone—

For a second, a familiar smell knocked me straight. Pungent, a tang, and so inextricable from this time of year that the nostalgia rose up from deep in my throat.

The carriage horses.

I hated seeing them on the corner between the Plaza and Central Park. Chosen for their docility, their unflappability in the face of the city's chaos. Rewarded by doing the same loop time after time, day after day. Where were they stabled? What were they fed? The whole group of them just made me sick, and all I could do was hurry past as fast as I could. *Don't look, don't look, don't look.*

Beyond the horses, I'd been feeling bitter about Central Park, ever since fall had begun to hit the city. It reminded me painfully of Yale: the vibrant color of the leaves, the way the wind blew them into small fiery tornadoes along the sidewalks I navigated on my way to work. From the twenty-sixth floor, the park was spread out below like a blanket I could never access, and it felt like something had been stolen from me.

It was time to take it back. Inside the park, I started wandering down a path at random, my heartbeat still high but slowing as I forced myself to stroll.

"Rosie? Rosie Macalister?"

I looked up. A tall guy, eyes I recognized. Eyes I definitely knew. From work? No, he was wearing jeans and a sweater, walking a dog. From Yale?

"It's good to see you," he said with a grin. I could see all of his teeth when he grinned, the bottom ones overlapping. How did I know him? "I was just thinking about you the other day."

"Oh yeah?" I shifted my weight from foot to foot. As long as I was moving, the shoes were fine. But now that I'd stopped, the balls of my feet were burning unbearably.

"Yeah. There was this article about the phrase *luck of the Irish* and where it originated. Turns out it was during the Gold Rush . . ." he went on, but I'd stopped listening.

Oh, *this* guy.

The bartender from the Tates' party.

I tried shifting the weight from the balls to the heels, desperate for relief, and nearly fell over.

"Are you okay?" he finally broke off.

"I'm so sorry, would you mind if I . . . ." I sank down on a nearby bench without finishing my sentence. I took my New Balance out of the tote I'd wrapped them in before stuffing them into the larger purse. "It feels like someone's been at my feet with a cheese grater."

"Vivid," Luke said with a short laugh.

I winced. But then again, if I had to wear these things, he could deal with hearing about them.

"Holy shit," he said, spotting the blisters on my bare foot in the split second before I slid my sock on. I laughed. "Okay, you're entitled to complain all you want."

I bowed my head. "Thank you very much."

The dog, meanwhile, had taken an interest in my pumps, and had worked up the nerve to give the discarded one a tiny lick.

"I'm sorry, I didn't mean—"

"Oh, that's okay." I bent down to the dog and let her sniff my hand; she started wagging her tail uncontrollably, as though we'd been best friends our whole lives but had been cruelly separated for years until this reunion. "Hi there. I'm Rosie. And you are—" But I was clutching for a tag that wasn't there. I turned to Luke. "You really shouldn't let her go around the city without a tag. And don't get me started on walking her on her collar. You need a harness, a Y-fronted one that won't *choke* her when she pulls."

Luke gave me a curious look, and I trailed off.

"Sorry," I mumbled as the dog jumped into my lap. "My parents are vets."

"No, I'm sure you're right. It's just, she's actually not mine. Her name is Bee, by the way."

"Hi, Bee!" Bee was walking in a circle over my thighs, ready to curl up and go to sleep, but she gave a brief wag of her full, feathery tail.

"She belongs to this shelter where I volunteer. The Animal Rescue Foundation?"

I stared at him, feeling like a bolt of electicity had gone straight through my body. It was too bizarre to be mere coincidence: the strings of the universe twanging, twisting, determined to bring us together.

Fate?

"That's so strange. I was supposed to go to their volunteer training session the night of the Tates' party."

He started laughing. "Wait—" he said, finally catching his breath. "I was supposed to *lead* their volunteer training session the night of the Tates' party." I met his gaze as he raised his eyebrows. "Weird, right? Were we destined to meet?"

But there was no such thing as destiny. For the first time in a long time, I could remember Annelise's voice, actually hear it. Not destiny, and no, not fate: *words have meaning*. We weren't on an inevitable path leading to an inescapable end point. There was something else at play here. Something messier than that, a pattern in the chaos.

Fortune.

"Very weird. Isn't the shelter down in the Village?"

"Yeah, it's on Christopher and Tenth. But this one can't get enough of nature, and there's not much nature down there, so I figured—"

"Uh-huh. But the volunteer coordinator I spoke with was a woman?"

"Marcy? Yeah, she gets me to lead the evening sessions. She has to be home by five on the dot because of her kid. And I've been volunteering longest, and I don't mind."

Bee stretched out, tried flipping over on my thighs to show her belly. I scratched it, overwhelmed by the specificity of her: by the tiny bumps on her wet pink-black nose; by the slight cross in her warm golden-brown eyes; by the shades of red in her hair, as dark and vivid as mine in parts, fading to white by her whiskers, in a patch on her throat.

"Does that sound good?" he asked, and I looked up quizzically. I hadn't realized he was still talking.

"A private training session on Saturday?"

Private gave me pause. But he meant well, and he clearly liked animals. And I assumed other people would be around, making me immeasurably harder to kill.

His cheeks were turning pinker by the second.

"Don't worry, I get that you—" he started.

"I'm just trying to figure out how easy it would be for you to murder me," I said with a smirk, cutting him off.

And he smiled, and it was like a twinkle, it really was: I could almost see a glimmer of light.

"Oh, it would be super hard," he said. "For sure."

"Fine. What time?"

"Whenever you want. How about two P.M.?"

I nodded.

It was the logical break in the conversation, but when he gave Bee's leash a gentle tug, and she hopped down from my lap with an apologetic wag, the sudden loneliness was almost overwhelming. My legs goose-bumped from the sudden lack of warmth.

"See you Saturday, Rosie Macalister," he said, Bee trotting after him.

I waited until they had turned the corner, then walked to the subway. Making a mental note to look up the bartenders in Grayson's Outlook and find out anything else I could about Luke, before Saturday after-noon.

Just in case.

30

THE HANGED MAN

Annelise, I asked. What am I not seeing today?

The Hanged Man, she said.

Gross.

Not gross. Just annoying. Okay, you know how I said I hate getting Strength? I for sure hate the Hanged Man more. Maybe even most. He tells you to take a break, to give in to what's happening, to let go of what you want. I know you have to, sometimes. But I never want to do it, and this guy's gonna make you.

Normally, after i changed my shoes in the mornings, I trotted right around the gray stone corner through the revolving doors, eager to get to my desk early. Eager to be the good girl. But the next day, I let myself take a minute: to press my hands to the sun-warmed stone, to feel the heat the building had absorbed flowing into me.

I don't know whether it was running into Luke or talking to my mother or writing that check. I don't know whether it was the seasons changing in ways I only spotted on my way to and from the subway each day. But I had the strangest feeling that September that there was a layer of glass between me and the world.

I wanted to feel a rabbit's wild heartbeat fluttering against my palm. I wanted juicy blades of grass between my fingers. I wanted things to be physical and present and real. Not excuses and screens and money.

Money. That's why I was in the city in the first place, wasn't it? I shoved my sneakers into my bag and headed upstairs.

There, the swooping, terrified feeling in my stomach returned. I needed to do something to fix the check I'd written, the laws I'd broken. But what?

Grayson walked in, a few minutes later, sporting that grin, the dimples, the coiffed gray hair. He was every president, every banker, every doctor I'd ever known.

I had to be able to trust a man like him. There had to be an explanation.

I was a beat late with the coffee, and he was sitting at his desk with his hands folded on top of it, waiting for me. I set it down with shaking hands. He asked me things—where was this report, did that call go through, could I get a reservation at Per Se. When he finished, I just stood there.

"What do you want, Rosie?"

"I just . . . for the accountants," I said, blinking fast. "I mean, for the Foundation team. That check the other day? For Charlie. I mean, for cash. What should I put on the stub?"

He sipped his coffee and winced. "Weak. Redo it, will you? Just put *cash*." He shoved his cup and saucer my way as he opened his inbox. "Can't Mary Anne tell you these things?"

"Of course. I'm sorry. It's just . . . isn't that going to . . . it's a hundred thousand in petty cash?"

His hard blue eyes locked on mine.

"What do you *want*, Rosie?" he said again.

Was this a test? Was he asking about my goals? "I . . . want to be an analyst?" I stammered. "Eventually, I want to start my own fund?" I tried to sound confident, but it sounded ridiculous, even to my ears.

He kept staring at me with his telescoping eyes, and finally, it clicked. He wasn't asking me about my goals and dreams.

He was asking me what I wanted to keep quiet.

I want money. I want everything. I want your life.

But I couldn't tell Grayson Tate, of all people, what I truly wanted. It had been made abundantly clear to me, the other night at the Pierre: I was no longer sure if I was even allowed to want what he had.

"Sorry, I misunderstood. Just needed to know what to put in the books!" I chirped, grabbing the cup and saucer. "Fresh coffee coming right up."

The weak brew sloshed onto the saucer, then over my hands as I made my way to the door. I'd stepped away from some cliff. Or crossed some line. Or both, or neither—there was no way to know.

"Rosie?"

I turned around.

"Yes, Mr. Tate?"

"This isn't an analyst-track job. I thought you knew that when you applied."

I stared at him. Applied?

"I—"

He swiveled back to his computer with a little snort. "Where the hell did you ever get the idea that you can get from where you are to where I am?"

31

THE HIGH PRIESTESS
(REVERSED)

What do I need to know today?

The High Priestess reversed, Annelise told me. *She's a slippery one even when she's upright, but turn her upside down? Whew. Withheld information. Secrets. Lies, but lies we tell ourselves. Reversed like this, I always imagine her hanging in the doorway between the physical and the spiritual realm. Cutting off access, separating you from your intuition.*

But I'm imagining you right now.

I could see her shaking her head slowly, almost sadly.

Imagination and intuition—they're not the same thing, Rosie. But you already know that.

A<small>ND ISN'T THAT WHAT</small> everybody in New York had been telling me, pretty much from the moment I'd arrived? You couldn't get from where I was to where Grayson was. It was impossible on every level.

But where had it come from, that bone-deep conviction that I could? From teachers who told me that *hard work will get you everywhere.* From my father, who told me *you get out of life what you put into it.* From every person who'd ever been described as *self-made.*

But I was beginning to understand. I might make money—I might make a *lot* of money. But not from this job, and not his kind of money. Not the kind of money that gave you power.

I wanted power, of course I did. I wanted to be the kind of person who could walk into a room and own it, the kind of person that others turned to.

The kind of person whose life mattered.

But now, for the first time, I let myself really wonder: What did it mean to have a life that mattered? Not the answers I'd been fed all my life. What would it mean to have a life that mattered *to me*?

For so long, I'd been putting off dating. Putting off books, movies, drinks with friends. Putting off drives to the country and walks in nature. Thinking: I can do that later. I can do that once my real life begins.

But my real life was happening now. Happening in that moment. And the next. And the next.

What if *this* was all there was? This series of moments. What if life ticked by and there was never any finish line, never any point past which I felt like I'd made it, felt like I mattered? What if it were just me, moving forward, moment by moment?

Could I be happy with that?

How?

I hadn't ever asked myself what it would take to be happy as I was; to be happy with what I already had. Perhaps it's because I was the only person who could answer that question; and because I had no idea, none at all, how to begin.

"IT'S A DATE," Andra said bluntly when I told her about my Saturday appointment at the Rescue Foundation.

"What? No. It's a private training session."

"Who takes time out of their lives for *extra* volunteer work—on a *Saturday*? No. It's a date."

I frowned.

"Do you not want it to be a date?" Still in bed, Andra looked at me with half-closed eyes. Sleepy, but because it was her, she just looked suspicious.

I didn't, but I didn't know why. Was it because Luke was a bartender? Was I really that shallow?

"Ugh," she said, seeing the confusion on my face. "Stop thinking so much and just go make out with him."

I PUT BOB DYLAN ON MY ancient iPod; he felt right for the Village. I hadn't been there since moving to the city, and I associated it so strongly with Annelise. But what I hadn't anticipated was the way his grainy voice made her come right back to life, all the quirks and specificities of her. I was halfway into the past by the time I made it down Christopher Street to the shelter.

I stopped in front of the sixties brown-bricked building. Precisely ten minutes late, as I always planned to be on social occasions. I had decided that if it were a date, Luke would be waiting for me outside. If it weren't—if it really was a *private training session*—he'd be inside, already with the animals.

He wasn't there, and for a swooping moment, my heart sank.

But wasn't this what I wanted? I shook my head, pushed through the glass doors.

"Hi," I said. "I'm Rosie Macalister. I—"

The receptionist looked up with a grin.

"Oh, great!" she said. "Luke is waiting for you. You can go on back."

As I walked down a long hallway, a familiar smell hit me: the smell of animals.

Sure, too, the smell of disinfectants and flea powders and shampoos. But beneath it all, the fur and the flesh, it was home to me. For a second just as I turned toward the sound of a low man's voice crooning something inaudible, the familiarity of it caught in my throat.

I swallowed hard and followed the voice. It led me to a big room in the back, with floor-to-ceiling kennels lining the walls. A larger version of the space my parents kept at the back of their clinic.

And there, murmuring to Bee, who pranced around his feet at her open door, was Luke. A mop in hand, a bucket beside him.

Bee ran up to me, whimpering at my feet for me to acknowledge her. I bent down and scratched under her chin. "Hey, Bee," I whispered.

"You found us," Luke said, a smile in his voice.

"I sniffed out Bee here," I said, plopping down next to her. She jumped into my lap and settled comfortably there. "Sorry, it's probably going to be hard for me to be useful with a puppy in my arms."

"Oh, she's not a puppy. She's six. Full-grown. Just small."

"No, I know, I just . . ." I blushed. "I call all dogs puppies. I don't know why."

"Well, look. It's not like I'd have you buckling down to work during training, anyway. So I'll just walk you through things, and you two can cuddle in the meantime. She probably needs that more than anything right now, anyway."

Bee gave a confirmatory sigh.

Luke showed me where to sign in, reviewed basic safety precautions that I'd been following since I could walk; walked through the cleaning supplies and how to safely lead a dog out of its kennel with another volunteer, taking it to the playroom during the actual cleaning.

It only took a few minutes, and then a weighted silence hung between us.

"So," I started. "How long have you been volunteering here?"

"Almost three years now. I love all of the animals, but Bee's my best girl. Aren't you, Bee?" He reached over to stroke her head, and she wriggled her body around in my arms to get closer to him. This close, the scent of him was strong, even under the bleach. Pine, but an earthy pine: pinecones, not pine trees.

"I think she has pinkeye," I blurted out.

Eyebrows furrowed, he bent back down.

"I mean, I'm sure there are great vets here and all. But that goop . . ."

He pulled a tissue out of his pocket and dabbed gently beneath her eyes.

"There are great vets here, yes. But not often enough. I'll see if they can call somebody in."

"Soon. It's so contagious, and it can lead to ulcerations, and . . . yeah."

"I'll definitely let them know." He smiled, then stood, and swung the door to her kennel back open. "Well, Bee? What do you think?" In response, she snuggled closer to my chest. And looking at the sparse furnishings in there—the thin bed, the water bowl—I couldn't blame her.

"How about we take her somewhere else for a little while? Didn't you say there's a playroom?"

He chewed his lip. "Why don't we take her for a walk? Bee's an old pro with the leash, as you know. And anyway"—he winked at me—"this hasn't been much of a date, has it?"

A FEW MINUTES LATER, we emerged back into the city, nylon leash in my hand. Windy beneath sunny skies, blowing my hair wildly around my head. Why hadn't I pulled it back into a ponytail? I normally would have, among animals.

"You can't just trick girls into going out with you, I hope you know," I said. I hated the sound of my voice as the words came out, the prissiness of them. This wasn't the confident, pointy-shoed girl I'd wanted to be out of college.

"I didn't mean . . . well, I thought you . . . but hey, that's fine. Just don't think of it as a date, then, if you don't want to."

In the autumn sunlight, his hair was more red than gold; for a second, I had a bird's-eye view of the three of us, a matched set of redheads. Cringe.

"I'm sorry," he said after a long moment. "I spent my teen years hopping from place to place, and I never really picked up the basics. You know. Of how to do this. Things are either way too subtle for me or way too aggressive, and I don't know how to walk that line."

I latched onto the most innocuous part of that statement. "Why did you move so often?"

"Army brat. It's not a new story."

"It is to me. I would have killed to have seen the world as a kid. Where did you live?"

And as he talked about Tokyo and Germany and San Diego, Lithuania and Virginia and Utah, his voice took on color that matched the world around us. Nostalgic and funny and bitter by turns.

"When I joined up, I thought I'd be off on some grand, terrorist-fighting mission. Dad was retired by then, Mom had resigned her post when my brother and I were little, so it felt like the mantle had fallen to me."

"But . . ."

He smiled sideways.

"Well, I couldn't be more grateful for it now, but at the time, I was pissed. I spent four years in Italy."

"Oh, poor you."

He joined in my laughter.

"Why'd you leave?"

"Well," he said. "The way I figure it, we've got one life. And at a certain point, I realized that I didn't want someone else telling me where or how to live it. That's all my life had been up to that point, you know? So I finished up my four years and got the hell out."

"Which makes you . . ."

He grimaced. "An independent thinker?"

"No, like, how old," I said, suppressing a laugh.

"Oh. Twenty-seven."

I'd never met anybody who was twenty-seven and not either obsessed with reaching the next rung in their career or ten years past caring about anything. But Luke . . . I didn't know what he was. What he wanted.

It was unnerving. But it also made me feel lighter.

"Hence the glamorous bartending?"

"Hence the glamorous bartending. Or a few days on a construction crew or painting houses or moving boxes. It lets me do the things I actually want. Tutoring uptown or reading in the park or trying out fifteen recipes to figure out the secret to the perfect mojito." He raised a shoulder. "Shit, I never talk this much about myself. What do you do? When not assisting, of course."

I couldn't think of a single thing that I did that wasn't somehow tied to Grayson Tate. A year ago, I would have said riding. But now? "Well," I said. "I guess that's why I'm here. To figure out who I am outside of work."

"Best possible reason."

Yet even here, work wouldn't let me go, and the questions I'd kept at bay while I was holding Bee began to itch at my throat. *If you found out that someone you admired did something horrible, what would you do?* But what could Luke say to that kind of question? And how could he ever understand?

Luke was about as different from Grayson as you could get.

Just then, he swooped down and picked Bee up, carrying her around a few broken patches of cement. So her paws wouldn't get hurt, so she wouldn't get a stone stuck between the pads of her feet.

Something rose up in me as I trotted after them, still gripping the leash.

Was it possible that I liked him?

I stopped short as Bee sniffed a stoop, closing my eyes momentarily. It was too hard to figure out what I was feeling while he was so close, his physical presence overwhelming with his height and his hair and his pine-iness.

"Everything okay?"

I opened my eyes.

"Amazing," I said. And it was only as I said it that it became true, the city exploding into life and color around me. I saw the brownstones, heard the leaves scrape across their stairs, felt the wind running through my fingers. "I love this time of year. Autumn and fires and forests . . ."

"Yeah," he said, low. "I do, too."

After we'd dropped Bee off, as we emerged back into that unfamiliar city of cobblestones and steel beneath bright chilled skies, he reached for my hand.

"Oh shit," he said, dropping it as I looked at him. "No. Sorry."

I laughed. His momentary panic was so different from his normal laid-back drawl.

And then I took his hand. Calloused and warm in mine.

"Do you want to get a drink?" I asked, tentatively.

"I would love to, but I have a gig bartending uptown. Rain check?"

I smiled. With anyone else, I'd have wondered if it were a polite brush-off. But I didn't with Luke. He was absolutely guileless, and it was a new experience for me; and yet I trusted him.

"Anytime."

I started to let his hand slip out of mine, but he squeezed it.

"Walk to the subway with you?"

I nodded.

We started east, walking past town houses and storefronts under a bright canopy of leaves. Maybe I could be happy in New York. Maybe it wasn't the city that was the problem. Maybe it wasn't even me. It was just—a way of thinking. A way of seeing. A new person—

"Kitsune," Luke said suddenly, with a chuckle. "Wow, I haven't thought about that in forever. Do you know the story?"

"I . . . what?" The word had a familiar ring to it, but I couldn't excavate the memory.

He pointed across the street with his free hand.

SPA KITSUNE.

Annelise.

Annelise was how I'd heard it before.

We stood there for a moment. The sign was black type on white, discreet between two windows with pale silk curtains hanging on the inside.

"Um," I said, taking a deep breath. "No, I don't think I know it."

"Kitsune is a Japanese folk character, a type of fox with supernatural powers that can turn into a human at will. Their powers get stronger as they get older. They have a bunch of tails, I think they get more as they get wiser."

I looked at him.

"Six months in Tokyo," he said, shrugging. "I was ten years old and obsessed with all things magic. Japanese folklore was my favorite because the magic always seemed possible."

I imagined Annelise as a secret many-tailed fox. It was only too easy.

"Yeah," I said, fighting to keep my voice level. "The best magic does, I guess."

I felt like I'd walked into a brick wall, all the air slammed out of me. But Luke turned and started down the street again, and it was easy enough to follow.

"Where are you headed?" he asked, as we turned the corner and the subway station appeared.

"Williamsburg." It was only as I said it that I realized it was a lie. "But it's such a beautiful day. I might just walk."

He raised his eyebrows. "To Brooklyn?"

"At least a little bit of the way. This was nice, thank you, let's definitely get that drink—" And before I'd thought it through, I leaned in and brushed my lips against his cheek.

He blinked as I pulled back, but I didn't have time to think about the zing that rang through me at the feel of his stubble against my skin, the warmth of him in the autumn air.

"See you!" I called as I turned away. Already heading back the way we'd come.

Because, of course, I had to know.

CHIMES JINGLED SOFTLY over the door as I entered. The space was trying for a vaguely Eastern aesthetic, with orchids and silk and the smell of jasmine in the air.

"Hello," a pretty blond woman said soothingly, almost in a whisper, from behind the counter. "Welcome to Spa Kitsune. Do you have an appointment?"

"I'm sorry, I don't. Do you take walk-ins?"

"That depends. What services were you looking to try this afternoon?"

"A tarot reading."

The woman made a *sorry* face that wasn't in the least sorry. "I'm afraid that our spiritualist is currently on break."

I hadn't meant to say it, but it was coming out: "Actually, I'm a friend of Annelise's. Was a friend."

The woman froze. Did she know what happened? Or in her version of the story, had Annelise just stopped showing up to work?

When she spoke again, she sounded more like a human.

"Oh my God. Her sister called to tell us, she was just the sweetest. That poor girl. I didn't even know she was a horseback rider."

We would have laughed at that. *Horseback rider.*

"I can see . . . I could just about squeeze you in with Cassandra, she should be back in five minutes. Just wait here? Don't go anywhere."

Two minutes later, she came back, followed by a woman of about sixty. The latter had that bright auburn hair that only comes from a box, candy-pink lipstick sinking into the lines of her mouth.

"You wanted the tarot reading?" she said in a smoker's voice.

I nodded, and she gestured me back down the hall with red-tipped nails.

What had appeared to be a simple shopfront was actually a labyrinth of hallways with dozens of rooms twisting off of them. I followed Cassandra down some stairs and into a vaulted basement room with cream-brick arches overhead and low-level lighting making shadows out of nothing. Low silk cushions, jade and cream, framed a large, flat marble table.

The cards were newer than Annelise's, not as supple. I couldn't see the pictures on the front, but I already felt offended by them. These were too stiff, too unfriendly.

"So what's on your mind?" Cassandra asked as she started shuffling.

"What do I need to know right now?" I said. Almost automatically.

"Want to be a little more specific, hon?"

That wasn't right.

"Um. What do I need to know about the people in my life right now?"

She laid out the first card. I hadn't even touched them. Knight of Cups reversed.

"Hmm. You're seeing someone?"

"Yes."

"Well, he's not the one for you. Now is not the time for love, actually."

You didn't get timing from the tarot. At least, Annelise hadn't, therefore I didn't. And I didn't think anyone could get it from a single card, anyway.

"Okay," I said slowly. "What's his purpose in my life, then?"

She raised a shoulder. "Company. To remind you of who you are."

She seemed proud of that last one.

"And what about my friend? What should I do about her?" *Annelise,* I thought. *Annelise, what should I do about you?*

But Cassandra didn't even shuffle again. Just set down the next card: Justice.

"Make up with her. Life's too short, sweetie."

"All right. Let me be more specific then," I said, as much ice in my voice as I could muster. "Who killed her?"

Cassandra blinked her false lashes fast. "Oh shit. I didn't . . ." But she did shuffle then, did seem to actually focus.

The Sun.

"Uh, okay. Somebody . . . like her, but not like her . . . look, hon," she said, and tossed the rest of the cards to the side. "I'll be honest, I'm in over my head here. I'm really an astrologer, I'm just filling in for the last girl while they find a replacement. Can I maybe read your chart instead?"

There was genuine anguish in her face. Under the makeup and the eyelashes, she wanted to help. But she didn't know how.

"You," I said, stumbling awkwardly to my feet, grabbing my bag, "are the worst kind of fraud. You don't know a thing about what you're selling, and you're selling it to desperate people who need answers."

She smiled, a little sad. "Honey, mostly I read to bored housewives."

"Doesn't matter. You're taking money under false pretenses. This is . . . it's fucked up," I said. "You just sit there making up . . . lies . . ." But I didn't know how to finish. I was too full: of Annelise, of Grayson, of Cressida. Of the past.

I ran up the stairs, back to the blond woman at reception. "I'm not giving that fucking con artist a cent. It's the little swindles that make the big ones possible, you know—"

Back on Christopher Street, scattered pieces of the day seemed to buzz around me, refusing to form a cohesive whole. Luke's smile. Bee's fur. Possible pinkeye. Broken cement. The Sun. Red nails and bleeding lipstick and eyes that saw nothing—

I stumbled back to the subway and onto the train, and the roar seemed to lull me into something passing for calm.

But I could still hear the voice beneath the wheels. Chugging over and over again in something close to my own voice:

It's the little swindles that make the big ones possible—
The little ones make the big ones—
The little ones.
The big.

32

THE NINE OF WANDS

*The Nine of Wands is like mile twenty-three of a marathon. No,
I've never run a marathon, I'm just saying. Ugh, can you imagine?
But it's like—you're almost there. You're so tired. Your belief in
everything that brought you this far is being tested. So are you
going to make it through even though it totally sucks? Or are you
going to walk away?*

    Sunk-cost fallacy. That's econ, right?

I HATED MONDAYS THE same way that any office drone anywhere hates them, but that week in particular, I was filled with dread. Friday's confrontation hung heavy over my head, because I was returning to the place where I'd unwittingly tried to blackmail the boss.

I didn't want to think about Grayson. But he was the center of my work life, which—as I'd established with Luke—meant he was the center of my whole life.

Mary Anne was out running errands too important to be entrusted to me when Grayson came in at eight the next morning, in the ugliest army-green sweater I'd ever seen, over khaki shorts and his Air Jordan Spiz'ikes.

Not a word, just a beeline to his office. And a slammed door.

So, Grayson hated me now. The truth was, we hated each other.

I hated him because he was getting away with breaking the rules. Because he always would get away with breaking the rules. And because I would always, always have to follow them.

I tried boiling down the facts to what I knew for sure:

A. Grayson had given Foundation money to Charlie;

B. Charlie didn't work for the Foundation, nor, to the best of my knowledge, did he contract for it or have any reason to;

C. If both of the above were true, and I was only about 98 percent sure that *B* was, then Grayson had committed fraud.

But as I ran them over and over in my mind—*A, B, C*—as I considered *what if this factor, what if that factor*—something truly terrifying hit me. Again, for the first time.

A wasn't true.

Grayson hadn't given that money to Charlie.

I had.

That, above anything, should have been the part that mattered to me. My whole future hinged on it.

I frantically woke up my computer. But I wasn't even sure what to google. *Accessory to fraud unknown complicit state of New York* didn't get me too far. All I found were statutes that meant nothing to me, journal articles from forty years ago that law professors had scanned onto academic sites, cases of accessories who'd actually *wanted* to help the main criminal.

It was slowly washing over me. Nobody in their right mind would believe that I hadn't known exactly what I was doing. As my mother had said: I went to Yale. I studied econ. I should have known.

And yet I was the girl who'd left four years of taxes unfiled. They had just seemed so overwhelming in the end, the amounts so pitiful; the IRS couldn't really care, could they?

Then again, what if they did?

I needed a lawyer. But lawyers representing white-collar criminals didn't advertise on the subway—or if they did, I wasn't interested in them. And having *criminal lawyer financial crime* in my Google search history would *definitely* make it look like I'd known what I was doing.

Could I be a whistle-blower? But who would I whistle-blow to? It was Grayson's company; going to HR was pointless. Going to the police or the FBI or even the IRS without a lawyer on retainer would be beyond stupid. Because how many checks had Grayson asked me to write out to *cash* over the past few months? A dozen. Maybe more.

It was real-life real, real in a way nothing in New York had felt since I'd moved there. The word of a billionaire against the word of an assistant. Not even. A *second* assistant.

Could I just—quit? If I left like I'd left the spa, stormed out in a blaze of righteous fury, would Grayson trust me not to say anything?

No, that wasn't the question. The question was: Did he care enough about Cressida's happiness that he'd refrain from going after me?

And then the question became something else.

Was Cressida still my friend?

I DIDN'T KNOW THE answer. And until I did, I was stuck.

So, every morning I showed up and stuck my tote bag with my sneakers in it under my desk. Every morning I turned on my computer and listened to the brief symphonic chime, watched my inbox fill up with increasingly curt requests from Grayson. I hadn't cut a check since I tried to ask about Charlie. But anytime both he and Mary Anne were out of the office, I went through the checkbooks as thoroughly as I could. The Association's checkbook was in order. It was the Foundation that was a mess. Assistants wrote the checks; *only* assistants wrote the checks. Even the ones I thought I'd seen him writing, he hadn't written—he'd asked *me* to write them, and I had. And before me, there was Tina's signature, and before her, Jenny's.

About $3 million had been written out to cash over the last two years. That's as far back as the checkbook went.

If Grayson didn't think he was doing anything wrong, why hadn't he written a single one of these checks himself?

I was in such deep shit.

At that moment, my phone buzzed, and I practically jumped to my feet. My heart beat so fast, I felt dizzy. Normally, I turned my phone off at work. But thankfully, Mary Anne was at a series of lunch meetings with Grayson downtown that day, and I was alone.

Are you ever coming back to ARF, or did I scare you away?

Luke. Luke who had been so gentle with the animals. Luke who had pulled me out of my head, if only for an hour or two. Despite everything, I was undeniably happy to hear from him.

Work's been nightmarish. But I definitely plan to—it was a great day.

But the shelter closed at eight during the week, and I was only some-times off by then, and I was too drained by the weekend to do anything except lie in bed, staring at the wall as I tried to work out what to do with my newfound knowledge about the Foundation, about the ways Grayson was skimming from his own charity. But I never let my phone be far away, as Luke rolled that initial exchange into a competition to find increasingly ridiculous animal pictures. His messages loosened my chest, lightened me.

It wasn't much. But it was better than nothing.

OCTOBER CAME AND client meetings increased, to my utter relief. More and more, Grayson pulled a suit and dress shirt and tie out of the closet where he kept them and headed out to Le Bernardin or La Grenouille for the older ones, Masa or Momofuku for the younger ones. The lunches could last two hours, but they could also last four or five. On the best days he'd also have early drinks, so he wouldn't bother coming back to the office at all in between.

I also had the utter relief of organizing the annual Tate Foundation gala to keep me occupied. I'd begun preparations that summer, hiring the party planner, finalizing the guest list, sending out the invites. But now, less than a month away, every detail had to be perfected, checked for errors, then set in stone.

I was in the middle of reviewing chair options when my cell phone buzzed.

It was a text from a number I didn't recognize, with a 779 area code.

We need to talk about Annie.

I froze. I was the only one who knew Annelise's real name.

Or at least, I thought I was.

My stomach churned as I typed back.

Who is this?

The response came blessedly fast.

Victoria Robinson.

Victoria?

Tory.

Her sister.

It buzzed through me. Here she was: one of the women I'd been waiting so long to hear from, who'd remained abstract the year before. And now, now that I had my new life, *now* she wanted to talk to me?

There could only be one reason.

She was looking for someone to blame.

Quick as I could, I turned off my phone and shoved it back into my bag. Then I shoved my bag as far under my desk as it would go. But I could practically feel the messages arriving, the phone just waiting for me to turn it back on. Eventually, I had to run over to the coat closet and stick it on a back shelf to get any work done at all.

I didn't understand why hearing from Tory made me feel so sick, so scared. I only knew that I couldn't engage with this. Not right now. There was a nauseous guilt in me, a dread of having to confront all of the ways I'd failed Annelise, of having to relive the pain of her death, over and over again, forever.

But also, I felt a kind of acceptance, a sense of inevitability. I had spent the last ten months trying to avoid the truth: nothing about Annelise, or her death, made sense. I was asking Annelise to speak to me through tarot cards. At least Tory was searching for answers in the real world. And hadn't I always known she'd come find me?

Suddenly, I remembered Cress's stricken face at her party, her comment about creepy text messages. Had Tory contacted Cress, too?

Were we being hunted?

No afternoon had ever dragged on like that afternoon did. I ordered a Jessica McClintock dress, a Carolina Herrera knockoff, to wear to the gala. I approved the wine selection the party planner had sent over. I updated the RSVP list and checked it against the accounts, and the whole time, I was thinking about my phone.

At five fifty-five, I shut everything off, grabbed my bag, and made my way outside. Breath still shallow from my sternum, I finally turned on my phone.

Just one message waited for me.

Listen. Rich bitch. I know what you did. Are you as much of a fucking coward as the rest of them?

———

Andra didn't leave for work until ten, was back in the apartment by five. "They're not even *paying* me," she said, rolling her eyes when I asked about her schedule. And there was never any chance they were going to fire her: not when Murdoch himself had gotten her the position.

So she was home when I burst through the door that evening, paging through *Vanity Fair* on the sofa.

"Fuck," she said, staring at me. "What the hell happened to you?"

"Have you been getting weird texts?" I choked out.

She frowned. "Not especially weird, no?"

I'd actually left my phone number at the hospital. But where Tory had gotten Cress's contact information, I had no idea. It made sense that Andra's would be even harder to track down.

"Is some guy being creepy?" she asked.

I shook my head, then stopped. "No," I said. "I mean, actually, yes. But not in the way you think."

Only now it occurred to me. Could I trust her with the truth about Grayson? At school, she'd been Cress's friend more than mine. But now, after living together for two months, after late-night wine and talks and being broke together—would she believe me?

"Okay, look," I said, taking the plunge. "You want a byline, right?"

She sat up straighter, tossing the magazine aside. From the floor, Nicole Kidman stared aggressively at us.

"Of course. Spill."

"Grayson has been writing these checks to his friends from the Foundation fund. For, like, hundreds of thousands of dollars. I think it's up to about three million for the past two years, that's as far back as the checkbook I have goes." Andra's spine slumped slightly. "He doesn't sign the checks himself. He gets his assistants to do it. He writes them out to cash, and—"

"Rosie," Andra said, holding up a hand. "No."

"What? Why not?"

"You're literally describing every businessman in New York. Probably in the country. It's not a story."

I frowned. "But it's from the Foundation fund. People make donations to that thinking it's going to help, like, rural kids and homeless people and single mothers, and instead it's just going to these fucking—rich guys . . ." I trailed off as she shook her head.

"It's not news. I'm sorry. It's just not."

"But he's not paying taxes on it—it's exempt—it's *fraud,* Andra!"

"It's boring. But you need another job, for sure," she said, bending down and picking the magazine up. "If someone did blow the whistle," she shuddered, "you'd be fucked. Just get the hell out of there."

"I'm the one trying to blow it!" I cried, and we looked at each other, then started laughing at the phrasing, tension fading. As our giggles died down, I closed my eyes. "Can't you do it, though? You're an amazing writer. You can make people see how fucked up it all is. And you don't even like Grayson. What's the harm in trying?"

She looked at me, pity in her face.

"I *don't* like him. But I don't want to ruin Cress's life. And anyway, like I said"—she shrugged—"it's not a story."

I looked at her, remembering Tory's text.

"Andra," I said slowly. "You've barely talked to Cress in months. Why is that?"

She stiffened, ever so slightly.

"What happened that day out on the trail?" I asked.

Her head snapped up.

"Why would you ask that now?" she asked. "What the fuck would make you ask something like that?"

We stared at each other until her gaze dropped.

"I don't know, Andra," I said, low. "What the fuck do you think would make me ask something like that now?"

"You're crazy," she muttered, opening her magazine. "The city's made you crazy. Just go to bed, okay?"

It was only eight, but I did go to my room. Got into bed and tried to sleep, tried to escape for just a few hours into oblivion.

But sleep wouldn't come, and anyway, my phone buzzed with another text from Tory just before midnight.

Guess I thought you'd be different.

Yeah, I thought. Me, too.

33

THE EIGHT OF SWORDS

*You're in a trap of your own making. You've surrounded yourself
with this cage of swords so that you can't get out—but you're
totally alone, so you can't get anyone else to get you out, either.
There's some stuff you can do, but it's all super annoyingly vague.
Like, open your mind to new ideas. What the fuck does that even
mean? The good thing here is that on this card, there's water at the
woman's feet. Water signifies intuition and insight. So she actually
has what she needs to understand her situation; she just has to
realize it and access it somehow.*

T HAT WAS ALL I HEARD from Tory. The texts stopped after that. But in
my mind, they kept coming. Message after message: accusing me, haunting me, mixing in with the Foundation stuff until there was a strange
soup of guilt sloshing around my head at all times. Everything I'd tried
to suppress about Annelise was back. I should have asked more questions
about what happened that day on the trails. I should have demanded
more from the hospital: her mother's number. Tory's.

Plus, something else was gnawing at me. If Andra were completely
innocent, she would have insisted it was an accident. But she hadn't done
that.

I'd been so oblivious. The dynamic in the house had been toxic for
weeks last fall, and the one person everyone on those trails seemed to
blame for it had ended up dead. I should have gone to the dean, the pro-
vost, the president—fuck, the police. Why had nobody gone to the police?

Did we really live in a world where you could just break your spine and that was it, that was the end of the story?

It was the end of the story because we'd all let it be.

THE YALE CLUB of New York City felt like Yale in the best possible way. High ceilings and chandeliers, leather armchairs and wooden trim. The Gothic touches, the leaded windows, the wood paneling all recalled our alma mater; and yet the sheer quality of everything spoke to the kinds of lives they expected us to be living.

Cressida was waiting for me in a corner of the bar, the sconces above her head casting a strange shadowed glow down on her.

"Rosie," she said, and there was something like relief in her voice. But I steeled myself: I couldn't let this conversation be about her.

"Look," I said, sitting across from her. "Did you know your dad's been cutting checks to his friends from the Foundation accounts?"

Bending over to sip from her straw, she raised her eyes slowly to me. Without her usual mascara, her lashes were dark blond, like a golden retriever's.

"Why the fuck would I have known that?"

"Cress, he's been doing it—for a while, at least. And he's making me sign the checks. He could go to jail. Actually, *I* could go to jail. Because if he gets caught, he could make me take the fall for it."

She rolled her eyes. "Then don't let him. And anyway, he wouldn't."

Get caught or blame me?

I tried again. "People are donating money to the fund. That's what this gala next week is for. They think it's charity."

"It *is* charity."

"It's charity for—Charlie. It's charity for Tom. It's charity for every single broke rich guy who's come through that door with an outstretched hand in the four months I've been there."

She squinted her eyes closed.

"I've always been afraid of this, you know. That they only liked him for his money."

"Cress, that is so much not the point."

Her eyes flew open. "Well, are the kids not getting their riding lessons? Are the camps not getting funded?"

"No, they're—"

"Then who gives a shit?"

"People who follow the rules! People who *have* to follow the rules!"

My voice rang out around the high-ceilinged room, and I bent forward, lowering my voice, as heads turned toward us.

"Look. He has to stop doing it. And he has to make it right."

Her phone dinged, just off to the side, and she jumped, bumping her hand into her drink.

"Fuck," she said, sudden and fierce. "What makes you think I've ever paid attention to my dad's business? And what about him makes you think that he'd ever for a single second listen to me, even if I did?"

"It's that he cares about *you*. And you care about him. This is dangerous! It's illegal! If you won't do it for me, do it for him, do it to avoid what might happen—"

Her phone dinged again.

"Mother*fucker*—"

"He's committing fraud!" I hissed, and not that quietly. But not a single head turned this time; I doubted it was the first time such a sentence had been uttered in this space. "Don't you care?"

"Do you want to know what I care about? I care that I haven't slept more than three hours at a time in months. I care that I couldn't jump a horse if the pole were flat on the ground. And I care that this fucking thing rings twenty fucking times a day with these messages from a million different numbers, but all of them coming from the same fucking—fuck!" she cried as it went off again.

"Tory?"

She looked up at me, stunned.

"She texted me, too. Just ignore her. She'll stop eventually."

Cress froze again, one hand hovering above her phone. But she wasn't laughing this time.

"You? Why would she text you?"

"Because I was Annelise's friend, too, Cress. Besides, I left my name and number at the hospital. Why wouldn't she text me?"

"Because you weren't—" She stopped suddenly.

I spoke carefully. "I wasn't what, Cressida?"

"You weren't there," she said in a little girl's whine, and put her head in her hands. "It was just a *pin*. Just a stupid pin! And I have to pay and pay for the rest of my life for a . . ." she trailed off, slid her hands down her changing face. "Stupid pin. And Thumper's totally unrideable now," she said more conversationally, though her voice was shaky.

"A pin—?" My mind was racing. "Cressida. What did you do?"

She rolled her eyes again.

"In the stirrups?"

"You're as bad as she is!" she cried, waving a hand at the phone. "Under the saddle pad, okay?"

"Under the . . ."

No snake. No jump. No branch. This was how it had always been. I just hadn't wanted to see it.

"Just, like, as hazing. Remember how they'd always send us into that neighborhood? Well, I never even did that to her! And she needed cutting down to size. You know she did. All that money—"

"She didn't—" How was I having this same argument again? A year later, after everything—new city, new people. Here we were, circling the drain, never going down it completely. "Fuck. On *Thumper*? How can you talk about torturing an animal to kill someone you were mad at like it was just nothing? That's *murder*." I pushed my chair back and it jittered across the marble floors. "You're a *murderer*."

She stared at me, gaping. "Why is everything always so dramatic with you? Animal torture? I would *never*. It was in his *saddle pad*, for fuck's sake. And he didn't even care until we started really taking the fences."

I stumbled back.

"*That's* the part that bothers you about what I said?"

She held up her hands. "I didn't touch her. If you're going to be—"

But I was already halfway across the room. I was running, even in my heels, out of the old stone building, through the crowds around Grand Central. I didn't stop until I hit the river and collapsed, gasping, onto a bench.

The way she'd said it. *Just a pin*. Like *she* was the victim. It was beyond what I'd thought anyone I knew, Grayson included, to be capable of.

Just a pin.

But why the fuck had I been so surprised?

I picked up my phone and I called Tory.

34
THE MAGICIAN

The Magician shows up in your life as a powerful person who pulls resources and solutions and—yeah, magic—out of thin air. The best part is that they have a plan. They have the talent and the intelligence and the insight and the resources to see it through. We all need a magician sometimes.

So that's the truth. I didn't meet Annelise's sister because of justice or vengeance or because of some noble quest to bring truth to light.

I met her because I was mad at the Tates, and I had nowhere to put that anger. I met her because she was foul-mouthed and aggressive, and I thought it might be nice to talk to someone with poison on the surface, right there where I could see it, for once.

Grayson was a thief and his daughter was a murderer, and I was a fucking nobody who'd bought into everything they were selling, then begged for more.

And I wanted to talk to someone who was as mad as I was.

So, no, I'm not the hero of this story. There was no hero. But that, too, was what I was finding out. In real life, stories don't actually have heroes. All they have are people.

That's all we get.

For the second time in as many days, I was at the Yale Club. It was a stupid place to meet, plenty of people who knew Cress or Grayson could have been there. But I wanted to show it to Victoria. I wanted her to see: look at what Annelise could have had. Look at what she almost *did* have.

Look at what they took from her.

But I wasn't used to going into Manhattan on the weekends, and I mistimed the trains, and by the time I emerged from the subway, sweatier than I would have liked, she'd already texted me:

???

I'd forgotten to put her name on the guest list and they were probably giving her shit. That was the other reason I'd picked the Yale Club over any random bar—the security, because I still didn't know if I could trust this woman.

"Sorry," I gasped to the man at the front desk and the dark-haired woman before him. "Sorry, sorry."

The woman turned to me. She was in her late twenties and far more elegant than I would have thought from her texts. She was wearing good, dark jeans, loafers that I thought had to be designer—the stitching was too good for them to have come from Canal Street—and a cable-knit white sweater over a pale blue polo that matched her eyes exactly.

"Rosie, I presume?" she said drily.

I nodded. "Sorry. Hi, Victoria."

"It's Tory."

I signed her in, trying to catch a closer look at her out of the corner of my eye. Just as Annelise had sometimes looked like a slightly wrong version of Cressida, Tory looked like a slightly wrong version of Annelise. I thought about the first party I'd been to with the EQ girls first year, how I'd drunkenly told a guy he looked like a smushed-up Kennedy. He'd been an actual Kennedy, though I didn't find out until later. Probably rather smushed-up, too.

Formalities completed, I gestured toward the lounge. But we'd only just sat when she pounced.

"Fuck being civilized," she said, not unpleasantly. "Why'd you take so long to call me? Or maybe the real question is why none of the others ever did?"

I looked into her eyes. Annelise's eyes, but brighter, clearer. Not a smidge of gray or gold.

"Because," I said. "They killed her. I can't prove it, you know. But they for sure killed her."

OBVIOUSLY, I'D PLANNED WHAT to say. But I didn't know how Victoria would respond. I didn't know if she'd scream or fly at me or start crying; I didn't know if she'd curse me out or break a glass or push me through one of the mezzanine windows.

I never thought she'd smile.

"I knew it," Tory whispered, leaning close, her breath warm on my face. "I fucking knew it."

A waiter appeared.

"A cosmo and a—" She looked at me expectantly.

"Whisky sour," I said, little more than a whisper.

"I fucking knew it," Tory said again, after he left, after I told her everything. There was triumph ringing through her Annelise-like face. "She was the best goddamn rider I ever saw. No way was she going to fall off some riding-school horse who saw a snake."

I shook my head. "He was Cressida Tate's horse. And he's a fucking firecracker. Nobody else had ever ridden him. It was . . . believable."

The barman came over and set our drinks in front of us. She lifted hers and took a long slug.

"If it was believable, it was because you wanted to believe it," she said flatly. "Annie never met a horse she couldn't ride. She used to help Mom *break* them, for fuck's sake."

"That's . . . that's fair," I said, before curiosity got the better of me. "Your mom breaks her own horses?"

"Mom's never had a horse of her own in her life," Tory said. "She breaks horses for her clients."

I took a deep breath. "Oh. I'd thought . . . never mind."

"You thought that the horses she was talking about were ours? I think Annie liked to pretend as much sometimes," Tory said. She smiled, almost to herself. "She was a big one for pretending."

Would it have made a difference if I'd known? If I'd said, *You have to be careful with people like our friends*? If I'd said, *The rich . . . they're different. Growing up like that makes you different.* If I'd told her the millions of ways in which that was true.

If I'd admitted it to myself. Could I have saved her?

I swallowed.

"I have just two questions for you," I said. "I mean, I have a million about . . . Annie. But about you."

Tory raised an eyebrow.

"Why," I said, "and how."

She just nodded at me.

"How'd you get Cress's number?"

"*That's* what you want to know? Easy. Horse world," she said. "Judges, riders, grooms. It wasn't hard."

"Why'd you get it?"

Tory raised a shoulder. "Annie was my sister. I loved her. I had to know what happened."

A chill ran through me. "And . . . what were you going to do with what you found out?"

She looked me straight in the eye. "Depended on what I found out."

"And now?"

She cocked her head. "I haven't decided yet," she said. "And that was, like, four questions already."

"Just one more. Why now?"

"I always meant to go talk to your coach. I couldn't picture how it had happened. Annie knew her limits, she was really practical. Except, I mean, when she wasn't." I smiled. Exactly right. "But I couldn't get the time off until this summer, and of course when I got there, Shannon told me they'd been on a trail ride. A trail ride?" she scoffed. "Maybe if she'd been working on a course of huge fences. *Maybe*." She cleared her throat, shook her head. "So, yeah. Practicalities. And Mom was in such a bad place, I didn't want to leave her alone."

"Is she better now?"

It was a minute before Tory answered. "I think she's about as better as she's going to get."

There was nothing to say to that. I took a long drink.

"Your mom's a trainer? A breeder?"

"Our mom's a groom," she said, staring at me as though challenging me to fight her on it. "She's a groom and she gave us a great life, but it wasn't the life Annie wanted. She got us a *house*. Do you know what that means, when you're making two grand a month and you've got two kids?"

"It's a miracle," I said softly.

"It wasn't a miracle," she corrected me. "It was a goddamn triumph of will."

I nodded. "I've been a groom," I said, but stopped myself. This was just what I'd done with my college friends, what I'd done with Grayson; try to find the common threads and use them to make people like me. "For, like, three months."

Tory smirked. "Try it your whole fucking life. Try it once you turn fifty. Try it with *kids.* Fuck. That's the only reason we actually learned to ride, I think. If we wanted to see her, we had to be around the horses, too."

"I thought she might be an heiress," I said finally. "Or at least super rich."

Tory nearly spit out her mouthful of cosmo. "Mom?"

I shook my head.

"Annelise. Annie."

"Oh. Well, she kind of thought she was, too. And in a way . . ." She stopped, licking her teeth. I waited for her to go on, but she shook her head.

"I know why you called me. Or I think I do," I said slowly. "I left my number for you at the hospital. But why did you go looking for Cressida first? Why Cress? Or why not Lila and Andra, too?"

"Rosie," she said, and my breath halted as I waited for the end of her sentence. "This place is creepy as fuck. Can we get out of here? Go someplace with, like, water or a tree or something?" She looked over my shoulder so sharply that I turned, too. No one was there. "Fuck," she said, almost reverently, then downed the rest of her cosmo. "I hate this city."

I TURNED US EAST. We walked silently over to the UN and the river, where we sat on a bench and stared out at Long Island City. The very same bench I'd sat on after fleeing Cressida.

It was cold. New York had turned from summer to fall in a matter of days, and yet it still seemed impossible to me that it was a place where winter could ever happen. Christmas in New York had only ever existed in movies.

What had Christmas looked like in Annelise's version of California?

Tory looked straight ahead, her hands stuffed into her jean pockets. With her blue pea coat, she could have been in a J.Crew ad.

"So, Cress," I prompted.

"Well, you know how I said that Annie thought she was an heiress?"

I nodded.

"The thing is, she *was*. Kind of."

"Wait, what?"

"My dad," Tory said finally. "My dad was some asshole teenage romance. Mom was already doing summers at the barn to pay for her lessons and he was just some jerk. He ignored every call she ever made to him after he left for college. Never even knew about me."

"I'm sorry."

She shrugged. "Doesn't matter. Wrapped his car around a tree right after his graduation from Stanford. Never had a chance to meet him. I was happier that way. Not *happy*, you know. But happier."

The wind whipped around us like another voice, chilling my ears.

"Happier than . . ."

"Happier than Annie. Annie May Tate, if she'd had her rights." Her cool gaze met mine. Annelise's gaze but with a confrontation I'd never seen in it before. A gaze like a punch to the throat.

Annelise was a Tate.

She'd been a Tate.

She was the girl a Tate would have been if they'd had to work for what they had. She was the girl a Tate would have been if they were dreamers instead of owners.

"But how? Are you sure—"

"For fuck's sake. I didn't go to Yale, but I'm not *dumb*."

"Annelise Tate," I said meditatively. "Sorry—Annie May. It's so hard to think of her as anything but Annelise."

"It's always been a joke that she had expensive tastes. Mom would tease her: *As you please, Miss Annelise Carrington Tattinger the Fourth.*"

"Tattinger," I said. "She used that, too."

"I always thought Mom said it because it sounded like Tate. Like, she didn't mean to, but she meant to."

"But—wait. She was born the same week as Cressida. And she's Cressida's sister?"

"She's *my* sister," Tory said, voice like a knife. "But yeah, Cressida's half sister. It wasn't like he was carrying the kids himself. It is possible to knock up two women—if not simultaneously, then definitely *consecutively.*"

I closed my eyes, wind fluttering my eyelashes.

"Back up," I said. "Please."

"Mom is a groom," Tory started. "But if she'd had the money for the horses, she could have ridden at the Olympics. Instead, she groomed for Team USA." She sucked her teeth for a second. "It's such a fucked-up world, you know? Like, truly fucked. You have the grooms who make next to nothing. Who work dangerous and dirty jobs twenty-four-seven, who depend on not getting hurt to keep their jobs. And then you have the rich fuckers they work for. And that's it. Those are the two kinds of horse people."

"I mean. I grew up middle class, and I rode."

She raised her eyebrows: seagull eyebrows, like Annelise's. "Yeah. But do you ride now?"

I shook my head, wind spreading my hair across my face. "Not enough time."

A head tilt. But unlike her sister's, Tory's was sarcastic. "Or money. Even with those shoes." Nodding at my Manolos. "But anyway. If you're poor and you love horses more than people, love horses more than life itself, that's what you got. It's your vocation or it's fucking nothing."

"But why *Yale,* then?" I said. "If Grayson wouldn't acknowledge her . . . wouldn't Yale be the last place she'd want to go? And Cressida the last person she'd want to be friends with?"

"It wasn't Grayson who refused to help us. It was Mom who refused his help. She was *pissed.* I was only seven, but fuck, I'd never seen her like that before, when she found out that not only was he not leaving his wife, but his wife was pregnant, too? It terrified me," she said with a dry laugh.

"But then how did Annelise find out who her father was?"

"Oh, Mom never hid it from her. Mom's got this face—she can't lie. She tries sometimes, but she starts blushing, even when it's just to us. To me. So it wasn't a secret, not even when Annie was really little. The second she started asking about her father, Mom had all of these stories ready to go. About this man named Grayson, the best rider she'd ever seen. About how they'd met and fallen in love. And he had to go off and be a rider, but he left Mom with this one gift, the best gift in the world, a wonderful daughter and a little sister for me." She rolled her eyes.

"I thought you said she can't lie."

"She can't. She believes it. Believed it. I don't know what she believes now. You don't ask Mom any question if you don't want the absolute truth."

"So Annie had enough information to track him down."

"Easily. He's an easy name to search for."

"But she didn't try to contact him?"

"She said—" Were those tears Tory was blinking back? Or were her eyes just watering in the wind? "She said that she wanted to be the best rider she could be, first. Then she'd go to meet him. But the truth? He'd offered Mom a ton of money on the condition that Annie would never contact him. Mom didn't take it, but she knew where he stood. And she kind of encouraged that magical thinking. You know, the long-lost princess riding up out of the blue. It bought her time before she had to tell Annie what Grayson was *really* like."

"But you knew."

"I'm seven years older. I heard every telephone call, every screaming match. Of course I knew."

I bit my lip.

"That must have been hard."

She shrugged. "Mom encouraged her with the stories, and I kept doing astrological readings for her and telling her *the time wasn't right,* and that held her off for a while."

"Is that how she got started with the tarot?"

"That? No, that was years earlier. She was a nervous kid. Throwing up before classes, passing out at horse shows. But then one of Mom's friends showed her how to read the tarot cards when she was, like, ten or eleven, and it just calmed her right down. The idea that she could fully understand what was happening, what to look for, the hidden influences—even if they were bad—was just really soothing to her."

I remembered that first card; remembered the Moon. "Yeah," I said. "It was."

"Anyway. She kept searching for him, watching from a distance. And when she was sixteen or so, once she found out about Cressida . . . well. Do you ever have the feeling that your real life is out there and someone else is living it?"

"All the fucking time."

"Can you imagine what that must feel like if it's actually happening? That's how it was with her and Cressida. It became an obsession for her."

"And *it* was finding a way to Yale and . . . what, making Cress into her best friend? So that Cress would take her home to the father she'd always wanted?"

A pitying smile. "Yes, Rosie."

"But why didn't she go to Yale right away, then?"

Her eyes held mine. "You think we knew how to get into a place like that? She was valedictorian. She had perfect SATs. It wasn't enough. When you're coming from what we were, that's not enough. And besides, it wasn't until you were all actually in college that she could figure out where Cressida was. Then it took her two more years of making money reading cards and taking classes at the community college, saving up for plane fare and financial aid contributions and clothes. And tuition. You wouldn't believe." Her eyes fell on my shoes again. "Well, maybe you would. But anyway. She needed those two years, she said. She needed to get special."

When I was applying to college, a pop-eyed counselor up in Chicago, whom my parents paid a hard-won $350, had spent an hour going over my applications.

"You're a good kid," she'd told me. "But you think the Ivies want to fill their classes with *good*? Honey, *good* isn't worth anything. You want to get in, you *really* want to get in? You have to be *special*. No," she said, as I opened my timid little mouth. "You have to be the *most* special. Or at least make them think you are."

For me, that had meant playing up the horse-girl aspects of my application. And if my life had been more 4-H shows and less Ralph Lauren ads to that point, who cared? It fooled the admission committee well enough. It got me there.

What would my life have been without that meeting?

"Good isn't worth anything," I said quietly.

"Yeah," Tory said, rolling her eyes. "That's what Mom always said. Being good gets you *nothing*."

"And your mom never wanted his money. He actually offered her money?"

"I heard Mom's side of it. He definitely did. But how was she supposed to guarantee that Annie'd never reach out to him? Even if she could. She didn't have the right to take that possibility away from her."

"She could have sued him for child support, even if she wouldn't take his fucked-up settlement."

"And given Annie two parents to hate? She'd never."

"So Annie did all that. Just to meet Cressida, possibly Grayson?"

"Not just to meet them. She wanted to *know* them. She was so . . . lost in her head sometimes, but she was smart about people, in her way. You think a girl from a family like the Tates is going to welcome some alleged half sister creeping out of Mendota? She had to become Cressida's best friend, then Grayson would see her riding at the shows, and after they both loved her, she'd tell them. And then he'd buy her horses and she could go on to break every record, win every show, be loved by everybody . . ." she trailed off.

But Grayson didn't even come to our shows, I wanted to say, though it was beside the point. Instead: "That was never going to happen."

Tory rolled her eyes, shook her head. "Of course not. But her first year at Yale, I'd get all these emails about how great Cress was, how they were exactly alike. How everything was coming together, and Grayson was going to come swooping in. And how he'd be my father, too, *of course he will, he'll love you.*" She cut off her saccharine voice, cleared her throat. "Anyway. After a year of not meeting him, I think she was beginning to have some doubts."

I remembered my first two months on the team, before our first visit to Greenwich. I waited at each show for Grayson to turn up, that famous face watching me ride. Being able to approach him afterward, blue ribbon in hand, and tell him that *he* was the reason I'd won. He was the reason I was there at all.

The agony of it. Those two months.

"She must have been disappointed," I said, almost a whisper. "To end up with just me."

Tory grabbed my arm. "Don't do that," she said sharply. "It's not like we talked a ton these past few years, but she emailed me about you last fall. Which should tell you something in itself. *Rosie's just like us,* she said. And no, she didn't mean *poor,*" she added with an eye roll. "She meant that you felt like family. Like home."

Suddenly, it felt like my legs would freeze in place if I didn't move. I ducked out from under Tory's grip, rose to my feet; shaking my legs out, I started pacing in front of the bench. In front of Tory, who sat, watching me.

Like home. Like family.

The vertigo of the words hit me like falling down a twisting tunnel, no bottom in sight. She'd trusted me. She'd trusted me, and I'd failed her. Every second that I'd known her. Every second since.

"Okay, but I didn't stop what happened to her. I didn't even *see* it. And her actual family, her sister—half sister—just gets to kill her? To kill her and walk away from it all while her father earns more and more money and runs more and more scams—"

"Scams?"

I explained briefly.

Tory shook her head.

"Like that kind of guy doesn't have enough already."

I stopped, my eyes watering in the wind. "They can't have enough. Enough doesn't exist for them. Not one screen, three. Not one assistant, two. Even if the second one spends half her time calculating when you're going sailing and when to time the Dramamine and how much to give so that she doesn't *poison* you—"

"Wrong fucking calculation," Tory said. "Half a chance, I'd do it myself."

We laughed, bitterly.

"So that's your job," she said.

"Is. Was, at this rate. But I don't know what comes next."

"What did you dream about before?" she asked, and it was such a startling question from the Katharine Hepburn–like figure that it took me a minute to parse. "Before you ever thought about money."

"Being a vet," I said slowly. "Like my parents. But just for horses."

She shook her head, dark waves bouncing around her square jaw. "You should do it. Get the hell away from here."

I rubbed my eyes. "You're not the first person to say so. I've thought about it. But the places I'd really want to go? We're talking, like, two hundred and seventy-five thousand dollars in debt. Even vet programs at state schools back in Illinois would run me a hundred grand."

One side of her mouth quirked.

"I know everyone thinks vets make a bundle," I said. "Trust me. They don't."

"Enough to pay back a hundred grand in ten years or so. You don't always need to be fancy, you know," she said, then snapped back against the bench. "Sorry," she said softly, running a hand through her hair. "Sorry, I used to say that to Annie all the time."

"No, you're right. I don't need to be," I said. "But the thought of going home . . . it's not Chicago, you know. It's not the fancy suburbs. It's burnt-out fields and locusts and dairy conglomerates and corn and wheat and it's all just . . . *beige*. The land is beige, the linoleum's beige, the sky is beige. And if you don't have a plan—for getting something better, for getting things back and growing again, for getting out, I think . . . your brain starts to turn beige, too."

She didn't drop my gaze. "Well, I definitely know that feeling," Tory said. "And that's true everywhere. Whether you're in LA or bumfuck Illinois or Tokyo. And borrowing three hundred's out of the question?"

"That's more money than anyone in my family has ever had at the same time," I said flatly. "That's more than my parents' house is worth. More than the house and their practice combined. But it's not just that. Yeah, I could get a loan. I just—I can't leave things like they are here. I can't just say, *Oh well, people pull this kind of shit*, and go on my merry way."

Her eyes had shifted, ever so slightly, behind me. "Certain people," she said. "A certain kind of person pulls this kind of shit."

"Exactly. I don't want to blow up the city or anything. But if I could get, like—Bergdorf's on a Friday morning."

She shook her head. "That'd just be the wives. You need, like, a whisky and cigar club on a Saturday night."

"All of them," I said with a sigh, and grinned. "Burn 'em all down."

Tory paused. "And yet you wanted to be one of them?"

Who were these sisters, who'd grown up so able to zero in on the exact right spot, the exact nerve that hurt? To know the thing that you should have known, if only you'd thought longer, reached deep enough, been just a little bit braver?

"I wanted to be safe," I said softly, shoving my frozen hands into my pockets. "I wanted to be safe, and I wanted to make everyone I love safe, and the only thing that can actually do that is having more money than you could ever possibly spend."

"And that was never going to happen," she said, echoing me.

I shook my head.

"And that's what Annelise couldn't see," I said.

She blinked furiously and cleared her throat.

"And that's who Annie was."

I began to cry, and Tory wrapped her arms, almost roughly, around me. She was warm and protected me from the wind and I wanted to find Annelise and tell her: *You had everything you needed already.*

But she hadn't. Not in the ways that had mattered to her.

"That's part of who she was," I said finally, pulling back.

Tory swallowed. "She was a dreamer, and she was brave, and she was good. And that's more than most people can ever hope to be."

What else was there to say?

Hesitantly, I picked up my purse, slung it over my shoulder.

Tory, though, didn't move.

"Why did it take you so long to call me?" she asked again.

I owed her honesty. "Because I didn't want to know," I said. "Because I'm a coward."

She got to her feet. "Well, you know now."

"We both do. Does it make you feel better?"

She thought for a minute. "It makes me feel . . . whole," she said. "It makes me feel real. Like . . . they could take my sister from me. But they couldn't take away the truth."

"They—we—almost did."

"I had to know. And now that I know . . . it's better. But it doesn't seem like enough. It won't be enough for Mom," she said, and her gaze got distant. "That's for sure."

"Would anything be?"

She just looked at me.

"What are you going to do now?" I asked.

She shook her head, wind twisting her wavy hair into ringlets for a split second. *I don't know,* I thought she was going to say.

"Don't worry about it," she said. When I didn't respond, she rolled her eyes. "I'll hang around for a bit. I've been staying with some friends out at a stable in the Hamptons for a while now, anyway. Friends, clients, employers. The lines get blurred, you know?"

"For what it's worth—which isn't much—I'm sorry. I'm so sorry I wasn't there for you. I'm sorry I didn't come through."

"But you did," she said, in what was—for her—a gentle voice. "In the end. And the end's what counts."

I bit my lip, then let it go with a shake of my head. "No. It's how we live that counts."

"Yes. And no. It's both, it's neither. It's like . . . your life? It's the evidence. And you're the verdict. You, as you are now."

I smiled despite the tightening of my throat as she turned to walk away.

"You're a lawyer?"

Half facing me, she blew out her lips. "Ugh. No. I did hair for a while. Went to beauty school, all that. But honestly, dealing with people all day is the worst. Fuck people."

"What do you do now?"

"I'm a trainer," she said, as she turned away again. "And a groom. Just like Mom."

35

THE KNIGHT OF CUPS

What do I need to know for today?

The Knight of Cups, Annelise told me. *The Knight of Cups is beautiful. He's not your average suitor. He's gallant, he's a poet, he's an artist. He doesn't have the same power as the Queen or the King, but he's more developed than the Page; he's in his prime. And because he doesn't have the same power, he doesn't have the same constraints. He can love freely, without bounds. In a way, I think he's in love with the world.*

Like you were? I asked her.

But there was no reply.

S ISTERS.

They were sisters.

Annie and Tory; Annelise and Cressida, too.

I kept going over and over their physical similarities, as though to be sure. Blond hair, blue eyes. Tall, strong. But wouldn't that be true of almost every college athlete?

Their strange, bubbling laughter. The light just behind their eyes when they'd come up with some new plan, some new revelation, some silly nothing of a joke.

Now that I knew, I couldn't believe I'd never seen it before.

I thought about the way Annelise had walked so tentatively through the Greenwich grounds, her hesitation at setting a single foot inside the hallowed halls of the manor itself. None of Cress's blithe sense of ownership, of absolute belonging.

I remembered the way that Grayson's birthday present—half a million dollars, just to buy some horses—had torn at Annelise. She was right; she could have done so much more with just a tenth of that money, and she'd never even had the chance. Because she wanted it too much, she was too hungry, and that hunger had heralded the beginning of the end.

It had made her ready to trust the thinnest of olive branches, never questioning Cress's intentions. It made her blind to things she should have seen.

It had made me blind, too.

And so Tory's revelation changed everything; and it changed nothing. Annelise had deserved the best—horses, schools, friends—just as much as Cress did; more, because she'd worked for them. Because they'd been conscious *choices* for her, goals she'd set and met. And then she had to watch them slip out of her hands because she'd chosen the wrong lies; because she was in the wrong place at the wrong time, just as Cressida and Lila and Andra had been in the right place at the right time—and always would be.

I was certain that Cress had no idea that Annelise was her half sister. She wouldn't have been able to hide it, not when she so casually confessed to murder. But did that change anything for me?

I tried to channel another of my mother's sayings.

Not my circus, not my monkeys.

But I was involved, regardless of whether I wanted to be. I was the resident stablehand at that circus. And watching the acrobats continue to soar, wild and flamboyant, as the body of one of their own lay broken on the floor below?

I couldn't get it out of my mind. The idea that beneath all of Annelise's secrets lay the core one that defined her: she was not one of them.

And yet—she almost had been.

IT ECHOED THROUGH my mind in the hushed quiet of that week. Grayson had flown off to Zurich with Mary Anne in tow for a series of meetings that were a little too mysterious for my liking, while I nailed down the final details for the gala the following Wednesday. I talked to vendors and guests and assistant after assistant after assistant. I went over the menu and the place settings so many times with the caterer that he eventually just stopped responding. Thinking the whole time how close Annelise had come to the life she'd believed she deserved. And how it didn't matter one bit.

Second place is first loser, Cress always said.

Luke's sporadic texts were the only thing that could quiet my mind. That, and thinking about animals. Every night, my dreams were full of them. The ones I'd met at the shelter, the ones my parents had treated. The guilelessness of them. Their silent communication, their wild or wandering or helpless eyes. How little they asked for; how hurt they could be. What humans could do to them. *For* them.

In the mornings, I'd wake and feel haunted, unable to shake the idea that I was in the wrong life, the wrong profession. As I dressed in the morning, I thought of the relief in a sick puppy's eyes after a shot of meloxicam. As I walked to the subway: the gratitude and love in an elderly cat's purrs as her owners held her for the last time. As I rode under the East River: the colts who had made it into the world only because human hands had intervened. As I approached the glass and steel building that housed Tate Associates: the shudder of relief a horse would give as my mother rubbed cool analgesic gel over a hot spot that had been burning for days.

How many people are lucky enough to have that? That wasn't a job. That was a vocation.

Tory was right, I *could* do it; I could go to vet school. Leave all of this, hop on a plane back home. Well. A train and a plane and a car. But then what? It'd be almost a year before I could start even my pre-vet classes. And to me, then, a year seemed like such a long time. Keep in mind that I'd only lived through twenty-two of them.

In the meantime, I'd be just another small-town girl who'd failed to get out.

Upstairs, alone at my desk, I turned back to the Foundation accounts I'd pulled up online. Time to balance the ticket sales, time to track down the last of the stragglers.

As I worked, the words of my Econ 101 professor from first year floated into my head.

The economy is a human invention. It's a human invention that we've all agreed to believe in.

It only works, he'd said, *if enough of us believe.*

And the thing was—I no longer believed.

FINALLY, THE WEEKEND arrived, and with it, a date with Luke. We were meeting in Nethermead, which sounded faintly magical, but was merely a huge meadow in the center of Prospect Park. The whole way there, I worried that I wouldn't be able to find him. The park on a sunny Saturday, no matter how chilly, had to be chaos.

It was. And as I fought my way through the joggers, the couples, the dog walkers, and the strollers, I couldn't help the sensation that she was there, hovering just over my shoulder.

Not Annelise. Tory.

But as I emerged from a wooded path into the meadow, I spotted Luke in a red and brown jacket, climbing to his feet and jogging over to me.

Just like that, I snapped back to reality.

"Hey," he said.

"Hey!"

"Okay, so." He nodded toward the open field. "I thought about taking you to the zoo, because it's not open much longer this year. But then I started to think about a picnic . . ."

"That's so much better. Zoos always depress me, anyway."

"Yeah, they are kind of depressing. So, plan B." He gestured to a plaid blanket unfolded on the grass, with an old-fashioned wicker picnic basket atop it.

"Where did you—wait, what?" I said. The basket had actual china and glass place settings strapped to it. And inside was champagne—actual champagne, not prosecco. Three crisp half baguettes and an assortment of cheeses, including a raw-milk goat's cheese that couldn't have been legal. A huge box of Ladurée macarons. "Where did you get all this?"

He laughed. "Friends in food service can get you anything."

"I think I've been hanging out with the wrong people."

He only smiled and poured us two glasses of champagne.

"And here I was, assuming you disdained luxury," I said, sipping the foam off the top of mine.

"Wait, wait—" And he held up his glass. "We need to toast."

"To luxury," I said, and we clinked glasses.

"I don't disdain luxury, by the way. I have a weakness for certain things. Good food among them."

I grinned, smearing goat cheese on a chunk of baguette. "What else?"

He thought, squinting the sun out of his eyes. "Good linens. A hot bath. Travel."

"But only to hotels with good linens and a hot bath?"

"Oh, for sure."

In the crisp autumn sun, his green eyes were almost translucent. I followed his gaze to the field around us: the crowds of people, the color and the noise. I'd been so surprised by Luke's picnic that I had barely registered any of them.

"You can almost imagine it totally empty," he said. "Three hundred years ago, there would have been sheep wandering around here." His voice sounded wistful. "Oh, by the way," he added. "You were right about Bee. Her eyes have totally cleared up with some drops."

I had been thinking, in all honesty, mostly about him.

"That's great. I can't imagine why she hasn't been adopted. She's the absolute perfect dog."

"She's six," he said. "Most people want puppies. Beyond that, she's a mutt. And she's twenty-two pounds—on the bigger side for most city people."

"She's so tiny! Where I grew up, nobody had dogs that small."

He smiled with just one corner of his mouth.

"We didn't have dogs at all."

"Not even big army dogs?"

"What's an army dog?"

"Um. Didn't they make dachshunds for the army?"

But he just shook his head.

"Too much moving. Not fair to them."

"Not fair to you."

He looked up at my words.

"Leaving friends behind everywhere, your kids' lives in service to your career . . . you're right, it wasn't."

"Is that why you don't want a career? Sorry—" I said quickly. "I mean, maybe you do. That came out wrong."

He just shook his head.

"Nah. I know what you mean, and you're right. I'm a jack-of-all-trades. And I'll probably be one forever."

"And that's really what you want?"

But the question beneath it wasn't about Luke at all. *Would I be happier if that's what I wanted? If I could allow myself to want that?*

"I mean, I've thought about it a lot. My whole life, really. Because in the army . . . I mean, fuck. Those guys, every single one of them, act like their job is to save the world, each and every day. But the whole time, they were just cogs, you know? Even the generals; everybody was a cog, and the whole purpose was just to mobilize in service of what some group of guys in Washington decided without their input." He shook his head. "Not for me."

"And bartending for rich fucks?"

"Well," he said. "A guy's got to eat. And your job . . . it doesn't give you that feeling?"

"I work for the top guy, and it's a different thing." But the words sounded false even as I said them.

A breeze rose up as he stretched his neck, as he stared out into the waves of people around us.

"Sounds like its own kind of hell if you ask me," he said lightly. Lightly, but it hit hard, my conversation with Tory suddenly roaring back. Grayson's affair and the truth about Annelise. All that I knew and all that I still didn't know.

What would it be like to live like Luke? To do a job and leave a job and never think about it again? To spend your days choosing what was important to you, what mattered, instead of having crisis after crisis dumped onto your shoulders by other people?

To realize that whatever you were living, right here, right now, *this* moment—this was already your life.

Freedom. It would feel like being free.

"Where'd you go?" he asked softly.

I shook my head.

"You're right. It *is* its own kind of hell. Because you end up going home every day, thinking: *This? This is who I'm loyal to?* All because you thought you could put in your time and become one of them," I said slowly, the idea crystallizing as truth only as I spoke, "but that's not what they have in mind for you at all. You think it's an apprenticeship, and they think it's servitude. And it's only what they think that counts."

He tilted his head, waiting for me to go on. When I didn't, he smiled softly. "Do you want to tell me about it?"

His eyes were so kind.

"It's just—" But I felt too exposed, too vulnerable. I took a deep breath, thought of Annelise. "Do you really want to know?"

He thought for a second, then he nodded.

It was the pause that won me over.

He was the perfect listener, attentive without rushing me, and he let me get through the entire story—Annelise, Grayson, Tory, Charlie, the Foundation—before he spoke.

"Wow," he said finally.

"I know. What am I supposed to do with all that?"

He made a face. "New friends? A new job?"

I rolled my eyes. "It's not that easy. I'm invested. But I'm starting to wonder . . ." I paused. "I'm starting to wonder if I've been wrong all along. That work can't save you the way I thought that it could."

"I'd be inclined to agree."

But as he bent over the picnic basket, ripping off another piece of baguette, I realized that I'd wanted more from him.

"That's it?" I said, with a short laugh. "No grand theories about love and life and what really matters?"

He grinned. "I mean, you'll have to go easy on me. It's been ages since my philosophy degree, after all."

So he'd been to college, then. I'd assumed not, when he said he'd been in the army. But hadn't so many of my recent assumptions been proven totally, horrifically wrong?

"Where'd you go? Bennington? Williams?"

"You know," he said with a laugh. "Based on that tone, I don't think I'm going to tell you."

I hadn't realized how close he'd shifted to me while talking until I had to crane my neck to look at his face. And as I did, he bent over to kiss me. Lightly, his lips grazing mine as the wind slid icy fingers through our hair. He started to pull back, questioning—and I kissed him harder.

"You make a really good argument," I said breathlessly.

He wrapped his arms around me and I let myself lean into him. The relief of having shared my secrets; the relief of letting go. We stayed there until the sun had passed behind the trees and we'd decimated the rest of the picnic basket's contents.

"It's getting cold. We should start thinking about heading back," he said in the falling dark, hesitant.

"We should." But neither of us moved. "Do you want to get dinner?"

He kissed the side of my jaw. "No," he said.

"Yeah," I said. "Me neither."

36

THE ACE OF SWORDS

The Ace of Swords is all about sudden realizations; karmic realizations, even. The jagged mountains in the background tell you that there's going to be trouble. But it's all worth it, because your mind is expanding into a new way of thinking. You have to remember, though, that the sword is double edged. Like all of them. The Ace of Swords is creation, but it's destruction, too.

LEAVING LUKE'S APARTMENT the next morning, I realized: in a few days, my worlds were about to smash right into each other. I'd hired Luke to bartend the gala back before I'd even met him, back when he was just a name on an Outlook card in Grayson's contacts. But he'd be busy serving up cocktails to rich people trying to drink back the $500 tickets they'd bought to be there, and I'd be busy—well, ensuring nothing went wrong.

But those last few days before the party were smooth enough that I was able to put Luke into the back of my head.

And on Wednesday, I threw on my knee-length strapless green silk dress, flared with crinolines, in the bathroom stall at the office, and trotted over to the Pierre ready to work.

Over the last four months—four years, really—I'd learned how to mimic the Tates' world. This year's theme was Off to the Races, an homage to both the Tate Association's origin story with Queen of Sheba and the Tate Foundation's work saving retired racehorses. I'd had the Pierre's ballroom transformed into a glittering racetrack. For myself, I'd accessorized with a single silver horseshoe necklace. A Tiffany knockoff, but you couldn't tell unless you got pretty close. And nobody was going to get that close. Even as the guests filtered in and the space began to fill, I was still on the edges: the same, but different.

Not similar enough. It was only a few minutes before someone I hadn't heard approaching hissed in my ear: "Where the fuck's the champagne?"

Mary Anne. Another champagne crisis? Waiters were circulating with mixed drinks, everything was all right there. But Paul McCartney's roadies were putting final touches on the stage, and we absolutely *had* to have the champagne out before the first song.

"*Fuck,*" I muttered, and clomped back into the staging area in the Louboutins I'd borrowed from Andra.

By the time McCartney started ten minutes later, all two hundred and fifty guests had their glasses.

Blackbird singing in the dead of night—

I was good at making other people's dreams come to life, at making the trains run on time, at putting out fire after fire after fire.

I was too good at it.

I watched Grayson throughout the first set, chatting with a group of his cronies. Nobody was actually listening to the music. They were mingling, chatting; Sir Paul McCartney drowned out by their banal discussions. A fucking *Beatle* was singing and these people were treating him like background noise. The best in the world and they were just so used to it. Nothing could ever be special enough.

Nothing could ever *be* enough.

Grayson was nodding to the group gathered around him in that way that made you feel you were the only person in the room. The mayor was speaking animatedly to him. There was also a judge, a philanthropist, a singer-songwriter from the seventies, and Dax—our sector head of global macro and Grayson's number two. Honestly, I'd performed miracles with the guest list. I'd comped the exact right people—the artists, the writers, the designers—to make the party cool. And then those people had drawn in the rich (who paid their way), who had drawn in the politicians (who weren't allowed to).

"Of course, corporate tax rates are at the top of my agenda," the mayor was saying.

"Not forgetting about capital gains," said Dax.

"But I really think that we need to be considering the role that immigration plays, as well. The lion's share of any cash business owners pay to their employees is going straight back to Nicaragua—"

A hand, soft and dry, grabbed my arm. The mayor.

"Honey," he said, handing me another glass, "could I get another drink?"

Without saying what it was. Without even saying *please*.

As I sniffed his drink (Scotch, I thought, taking pleasure in pouring from the cheapest stuff at the bar as Luke side-eyed me), as I wiped the rim, as I carried it back to him, I thought: he believes he has power. He believes the strings are connected to him. But he needs to be elected. Him and the congressmen and the senators: they all looked powerful. They always *looked* powerful. But they needed you to like them, and they needed your money, and so they were as hungry as the rest of us.

They didn't have any real power at all.

Not power like Grayson had.

Maybe Grayson wanted some laws changed. But he didn't *need* them changed. If nothing changed in this country for the rest of his life, he'd just keep hopping through the loopholes, through the path his lawyers and consultants and advisors had found for him.

And as I stood there, thinking about power, I felt a hand slide down the back of my dress. The mayor stared straight forward, straight at Grayson, and all the while his hand was crawling lower, lower.

I placed the tip of my heel on the top of his toes. No pressure yet. His fingers reached another inch down, and I pressed.

He contented himself with a little squeeze and let his hand drop.

If it had been Grayson, would I have let him?

Not anymore. But I would have, once. I would have, not that long ago.

I would have liked it, too. Not sexually. Or rather, on some level deeper than sex. Some level that affirmed I had some kind of power of my own.

A few feet away, Grayson watched the mayor's hand fall—then caught my eye and winked. As if to say, *Humor the asshole.* As if to say, *Such is the price of entry.*

By the time "Let It Be" came on, the group was good and drunk enough for me to push my way into the staging area and sit on a case of Lagavulin to wait out the rest of the party. But just as I was about to sink down and give my aching feet a break, a hand grabbed my arm.

"Rosie!" Cress cried, tugging me into her arms.

Like nothing had happened between us. Like she hadn't admitted to *murdering* Annelise less than two weeks earlier. It was all I could do to keep from pushing her away.

"Hey, Rosie," Blake, behind her, muttered.

"Oh my God, I am such a dummy, I cannot *believe* I didn't realize that you'd be here! Aren't these so fun?" She looked around us, sipping her cosmo. Her eyes were glittering; she was already drunk. Had she shown up drunk? "I always love Daddy's parties."

"Cressy," Blake said. "The keys?"

"Right." Her eyes got big, and she tapped her forehead. "So, I couldn't find parking, it's such a nightmare out there. And I *might* have double-parked the Rover over on Sixty-First," she said, making a playful grimace as she dangled a silver keychain my way. "Would you mind . . . it would be *such* a favor, you're an *angel* . . ."

I just stood there, staring at her.

"Are you fucking kidding me?" I said.

And her face snapped closed. "I mean, if you're going to be like *that*."

Blake pulled out his wallet and started rummaging through it.

A tip. He thought I wanted a tip?

"Blake, she doesn't—" But Cress was a broken Roomba, glancing back and forth between the two of us. Then she stopped, bending toward me. "I mean, *do* you?"

"New friends and a new job," a soft male voice whispered in my ear, and I startled. Luke.

"Oh, hi!" Cress said, and stuck out her hand. "I'm Cressida Tate. This is Blake Sallow. I don't think we've—"

"We have, actually," Luke said sharply. "I've been in your apartment multiple times."

Cress and Blake looked at each other, then at us, with unblinking eyes. "Luke, I think you're needed at the bar. And Cress, Blake, it was *so* good to see you. I hope you have a great time—have a go at the horseshoe toss while you're here. They're real gold, did you see? Second-place winner gets to take one home! And don't miss the gougère, it's to die for. Bernard?" I gestured at a nearby waiter carrying a tray of them and grabbed Cress's arm with both hands. "Have so much fun, you guys!"

I clacked toward the kitchen, businesslike as Mary Anne. Thank fuck it was almost dinner, and I could disappear, and everyone would assume I was helping someone else, and I could have forty-five minutes of true and utter peace as the kitchen and waitstaff scrambled around me.

"Rosie." Luke's hand landed on my back just as I reached the kitchen door. "Rosie, wait."

"Luke, I'm working. We're both working. I can't talk right now."

His eyes widened. "I just wanted to see if you were okay," he stammered. "I mean, I can't believe they were talking to you like that. I can't believe those people are your friends."

And the thing was? I couldn't believe it either. But I also couldn't hear it from him.

"You don't get to fucking judge me," I snapped.

He looked wounded, then his face hardened. "I'm just saying, think about who you're loyal to, Rosie. And whether they're worth it."

And then he turned away, and I was alone.

When no one was looking, I swung open the emergency door and emerged into the back alley. I sat there on a crate and cried until dinner was over, until I was chattering with the cold of it all. Until the prizes were given out, until the guests left for their taxis and their town cars and their double-parked Rovers.

They were gone, but I had to go back out to help clean up.

After all, it was my job.

37

THE TEN OF SWORDS

The Ten of Swords . . . nobody likes getting the Ten of Swords.
Look, I'll be straight with you. It's inevitable pain stemming from
betrayal and leading to crisis. But if you can look beyond that, the
sun's just starting to come up in the distance. It can be hard to look
beyond that, though. Almost nobody does.

YOU DID NICE WORK ON the gala," Grayson said to me the next day, as he tossed his suit jacket onto my desk. As though he were giving me a gift.

I'd spent most of the morning texting Luke apologies under my desk and could only breathe when he finally wrote back a few hours later. Sorry, just seeing these now, was on a job site all morning. No biggie, it was a tense night.

"That's my job," I said. I tried for a bright smile, but it just came out flat. Almost accusatory.

We stared at each other. And then he smirked, mean.

"So, you *do* realize that you have a job."

I froze.

"What?"

"Your outfit," he said, looking down at my dress. It was a basic fit-and-flare silhouette but low-cut, with chunky hardware in the form of zippers and buckles. I had bought it on a whim at a boutique on Bedford Avenue. It was the first piece of clothing I'd owned since moving to New York that actually felt like me. "Office wear from now on, Rosie. And a Dramamine? I'll be going to the marina over lunch."

He held out his hand and I slid a patch into it. It was almost November;

the marinas were mostly closed for pleasure sailing. But it was a bright day in the fifties and if you were Grayson Tate, nothing was ever closed to you. Not really.

Coward. Coward, coward, coward. In that moment, the refrain in my head was so loud that I could think of only one way to shut it up. I stood and followed him into his office.

"Actually, Grayson, there's not going to be a *now on.* I'm quitting, effective immediately."

He stared at me. His eyes weren't mysterious anymore, they weren't all-seeing, they weren't telescopes. They were just hard and mean.

"You're not giving notice?"

I glanced at the clock on the wall. "I can give you five more minutes."

"After everything I've done for you," he muttered with a shake of his head, turning to his computer. "Mary Anne—" And it was only then that I noticed she was standing in the doorway.

"Everything you've done?" I said. "Like implicating me in tax fraud? Like assuming I'd take the fall for your handouts to your friends?"

He laughed, loud and short. "And just who the fuck are you?"

"Who the fuck are *you?*"

He looked at me with a mixture of pity and disgust, as though I were an amnesiac recently out of a coma.

"I'm Grayson Tate," he said. "And you're just some idiot with ambitions so far beyond her capabilities, she doesn't even know what she doesn't know."

It was my biggest fear, confirmed by the person I'd once dreamed of becoming. Even though it was no longer my goal, those words still drove some poison blade through me: the idea that I'd been fooling myself.

How *much* I'd been fooling myself.

"You're such a fucking hick, hon. A check for a hundred grand makes you nervous! Not even nervous—it's beyond what you're capable of imagining. The money—it means too much to you." He shook his head like it was a shame, like it was just too bad. "You have no sense of *play.* That's the only thing you need in this field to make it, you know. Well." He paused. "I guess that's the problem, isn't it? You *don't know.*"

Who would you have to be, to see money—*other people's* money—as something to play with?

He was right. That was never going to be me. It could never have been me.

"Besides," he continued. "You have a startling lack of understanding of the business. You don't go from being a secretary to being an analyst. For fuck's sake, haven't you watched what goes on around here at all? We hire those guys after their first few years at the best I-banks. We don't hire admin girls who haven't had so much as an internship. What world do you think you're living in?"

I glanced at Mary Anne. She stared straight ahead, but splotches of pink had appeared on her cheeks. It was the most emotion I'd ever seen from her.

I found my voice, turned it to steel. "I'm living in a world where guys like you get away with anything they fucking want."

"Is this about the Foundation again? For Christ's sake, it's *my* foundation! I'll use the money how I want—it's *my. Money.*"

But it wasn't about the Foundation, or not just about the Foundation. Not anymore. Not since I'd met Tory. Since I'd learned the truth.

"Fuck your foundation. This is about your daughter."

He stood abruptly, pointing a finger at me. "Don't you *dare* bring Cressida into this."

"Your other daughter," and I swear my lip curled as I said it.

His hand fell.

"Annie?" he said, almost a whisper.

"Annie."

He collapsed into his chair. "You know Annie?" he said.

"I *knew* Annie. Actually, you knew her, too. Only you knew her as Annelise."

I could see him searching. But how much had he noticed us? Who were we to him, really?

"It would have been her birthday this week," I said. "Did you know that? Or could you just not be bothered to remember? Four days before Cressida's. You sure were busy back in 1983. She would have been twenty-three. But she's never going to be twenty-three, because your little princess, your *other* daughter, killed her."

With that, I turned to gather my things, for what I knew would be the last time.

But before I'd even made it out the door, a crystal award flew by my head and smashed against the wall.

"What does that mean?" he cried.

"Why don't you ask Cressida? Let's just put it this way," I said, glancing down at the pile of shattered glass at my feet. "I think she may have inherited your temper."

It took everything I had to keep breathing as I walked measuredly to gather my things, grinding the crystal shards into the carpet. But before I could make my dignified departure, Grayson pushed past me, holding the filthy yellow canvas bag he kept his sailing stuff in. The elevator came right away for him, so I stood at my desk, waiting for him to disappear. I wasn't going to be trapped with him for twenty-six floors, that was for certain.

As I waited, I focused on my breath. It hadn't been what I wanted. But it had made him react. That was something.

And yet, his words rang in my ears.

Maybe I didn't know how to play with money—but I knew how to play.

One text to Tory out in the Hamptons. That's all it took.

Guess who's on his way to the marina?

Just one tiny pin.

And then I was gone.

38

JUDGMENT

Judgment sounds super scary, but it's actually about reaching a higher stage. The real question is: Are you ready? The call's coming for you, but are you ready to step up and embrace your highest good—even if it's not what you thought you wanted? And yeah, you'll get what you get based on the universe's judgment of your actions to date. But that opens up paths to the most awesome stuff. Rebirth, really. And absolution.

I WAS STEPPING OFF THE subway in Brooklyn when I realized: I'd left my cell phone at the office.

I wasn't going back to the twenty-sixth floor. *Left my phone on my desk,* I emailed Mary Anne once I was back in my apartment. *Could you please leave it at reception?*

The next day, I let myself sleep in past noon, and then it was once more unto the breach. Just in and out; I didn't plan to leave the lobby. But I had to wait through about twenty calls coming into the switchboard before Dede at reception had a second for me.

"Mary Anne should have left it," I said, as though that would make the phone ding into existence in front of me.

"All I know," Dede said, picking up another call, placing it on hold without a single word to the caller, "is that you're supposed to go up to HR." She held up her hands as multiple lines jangled.

"Did the market crash or something? What the fuck is—"

But she had already returned her gaze to the ringing phones. "Tate Associates."

I hadn't been to HR, on the twenty-fourth floor, since my first day at the company when I'd gone in for what the bland, nameless woman had called my *paperwork fiesta*. It had been a sedate, calmly gray space, with a mass of cubicles separating the women (only women worked there), with a single office at the far end for their boss, a man named Louis with a hapless grin whom I'd only met a handful of times.

But when the elevators opened, the place was thrumming with activity. All the women seemed to be talking at once, their voices lifting into a high, monotone buzz.

I stood looking at the room for a minute, but nobody stopped to help me. Finally, I walked over to the cubicle of the woman who had printed out my paperwork that first day. A nameplate on her desk, I saw with relief: Laura. That was her.

She was talking on the phone in low tones, but covered the speaker with one hand as I approached.

"Hey, Laura. I just came to get my—"

"Mary Anne's in the office," she said, nodding her frizzy ash-blond head in the direction of Louis's door.

"I don't need—" But she'd already swiveled her chair around, returned to her call.

I knocked on the door, waiting for Louis's reply.

"Come in." It was Mary Anne's voice, but calmer than I'd ever heard it.

She was sitting behind a desk, the office completely empty save for a double-screened computer.

"What—"

"Have a seat," she said.

What was she doing here? I just wanted my phone, then I never wanted to see this place again. But I made my way tentatively to one of the two chairs in front of her desk.

"Look," she said, and her chair swiveled to me with a lightness I'd never seen from her on the twenty-sixth floor. "I know today's a little overwhelming for all of us. But I wanted to make sure—"

"Wait," I said. "Why is it overwhelming? What happened?"

"Oh," she said. "Oh. You haven't seen the news, have you?"

I frowned.

She took a deep breath. "Grayson died in a sailing accident yesterday afternoon. The board had an emergency session and named Dax his interim replacement this morning."

We stared at each other. Her face wore a mask of dignified regret, but I thought that maybe 1 percent of her looked pleased, and I liked that.

"What . . . happened?"

And a flicker of something, almost like amusement? But no, it couldn't have been.

"It was strange, actually. The coast guard spotted the unmanned boat late yesterday and started a search and recovery. He wasn't far from shore, but his head was . . . there was a substantial injury. They think the boom must have knocked him overboard. And he'd been sailing all his life, you'd think . . ." She shook her head. "Just one of those things, I guess. One of those sad things."

I grasped the arms of my chair, and she tilted her head.

"The seasickness?" I said weakly. "Maybe he wasn't feeling well and so . . . there was . . . that?"

She tilted her head, her eyes fixed on mine. "I'm sure the police will sort everything out."

I swallowed. "And Dax put you . . ."

"Well, he has Liza to help him, you know. And HR has been a mess for years. So Louis got slid over to take Dax's role, in global macro, and"— her shoulders lifted—"here I am."

Through her glasses, she held my gaze, as if daring me to challenge her.

But I understood the board's calculation completely. You don't want to lose someone with institutional knowledge like that.

You can't *afford* to lose someone who knows where all the bodies are buried.

"Okay," I said. "And you're—what, taking the time on your first day to chat with me?"

She pressed her lips together, and her throat bobbed. Something was rippling through her, but it was an emotion I didn't recognize, couldn't read.

"I wanted to see you again," she said tightly. "Because I wanted to say that I respected what you said to Grayson. About the Foundation. You were the first assistant to do it, and it took cleverness and bravado and—just guts—to call it out." I stared at her. "That's all."

I was too stunned to say anything except the first thing that came to mind. "If you knew what was going on, though . . . why didn't *you* do it? Why were you so loyal to him all these years?"

Her face slammed shut, and she was the Mary Anne I knew once again.

"We can't all afford to choose our virtues," she said, clipped. "And loyalty is what I could afford."

I wanted to snap back something clever, something devastating.

But I had nothing.

Just the image of Cress at the foot of my bed, this same time last year. Offering me the hellscape of a job I'd just quit.

As if reading my mind, Mary Anne's face softened.

"I remember when Cressida was born," she said. "And Grayson had taken the week off work. But it was Grayson, and so he only made it until Wednesday before he was back in the office. He was already here by the time I got in at eight. I was mortified." She gave me a small smile. "He called me in a few minutes later. I was nervous he'd be angry with me, that he'd think I'd been slacking off because he was supposed to be out. But damned if he wasn't sitting there with the baby on his lap, bottle of formula in hand."

Cress as a baby was almost impossible to imagine. Especially without thinking of her counterpart, six days old and a country away.

"And he looked up at me"—and Mary Anne's voice was tight again—"and his eyes were huge. You know those eyes. But they were just huge, and . . . wondering. And he said, I'll never forget this, he said, *Isn't it amazing? This person. She's a person, and we don't even know who yet. She could grow up to be a deep-sea diver or a mountain climber or an explorer or an astronaut, and we get to watch it all happen. Can you even believe it?*"

Her eyes were watery behind her glasses, and I couldn't watch the quiet tears fall down her face, I just couldn't. I looked away.

"Even a mountain lion," I said after a second, "protects its young."

She laughed, short and abrupt through her tears.

"Well, that may be the case. But how many dream about their futures?"

I was frozen into silence. Crook, philanderer, asshole. Champion, genius, father. How are you supposed to weigh up someone's life?

But wasn't that what Luke had been telling me all along? I didn't need to be judge and jury. I shouldn't have to be.

It wasn't for me to say.

I nodded and stood. "Do you have my phone?"

She reached into her pocket and slid it across the desk to me.

"And what is next for Rosie Macalister?"

"I was thinking of going back to school," I said. "Vet school."

"Vet school!" she said, breaking into a surprised laugh. "Hedge-fund assistant to veterinarian. That's one career path I haven't heard before, and trust me: I've seen a lot of résumés."

"Of course not," I said. "You want to know why?"

Her face was full of benign tolerance.

"Sure."

I opened the door.

"Because nobody owns a vet," I said.

I TRIED TORY on the way to the elevators. I tried her in the lobby. I tried her on the way to the Fifty-Ninth Street station, then on the way back from the Bedford Avenue station, then about twenty times from the empty apartment before Andra came home. I had six frantic voicemails from Lila, twelve missed calls from Cress. Nothing from Andra.

She walked in with a serene smile plastered across her face.

"Oh my God," I said, setting my phone down, trying to instill some kind of grief, or at least surprise, in my voice. "You didn't hear—"

"That Grayson Tate's dead? Of course I did. I work for the *Post*, Rosie."

I stared at her.

"Look," she said, and swung her purse down onto the coffee table. "I know I sound like a fucking psychopath. So I'm going to say this to you once and just once. I'm not going to answer any questions about it, and if you ever tell anyone, I will ruin you. Our first year, Grayson and I—"

I held up my hands.

"Andra," I said. "I don't want to know."

She held my gaze a long moment, then gave a quick nod and picked her bag up. "Fair enough," she said, starting toward the hall. "Anyway. Some people are just lucky until they're not. I don't know about you, but I'm not planning to attend that funeral."

On the couch, my phone dinged.

Some people are just lucky until they're not.

I'd finally found words for the one question that had been hanging between us.

He'd been sailing all his life. You'd think . . .

She was the best goddamn rider I ever saw.

"Andra," I called after her. "Annelise and the pin. How much of that was you?"

Her face hardened.

"I told you before," she said. "You're crazy if you think I had anything to do with that."

The reminder bell on my phone dinged. But I just looked at her.

"All I said to Cress—*all* I said—was that everyone else on the team got hazed but Annelise," she said. "That was *it*."

Nausea rose in me as she turned and disappeared down the hallway.

I swallowed, reminding myself to breathe as I picked up my phone.

A single photo message, sent from a number I didn't recognize. It took forever to download, but eventually I was able to open it and see: blue water stretching out to the horizon, lapping waves frozen forever in their undulations.

I called the number. I called Tory. I alternated them another thirty times that night, but Tory didn't pick up once. Neither phone even rang.

I kept trying a thousand times over the next year, but neither of them ever rang again.

And she might not have been like her sister in most things, but they could have been twins in one significant way.

Just like Annelise, Tory became a ghost.

39
THE TEN OF PENTACLES
(REVERSED)

Everybody wants something. And the way that we go after those things determines who we are. Ten of Pentacles, when it's reversed, is all about the traps we get ourselves into. About what we've let define ourselves and our self-worth; about how we've forced ourselves into certain roles because of the compromises we thought we had to make.

I DECIDED TO STAY UNTIL Thanksgiving to wrap up loose ends. But most of all, to come home with a plan.

It turned out that my biology obsession during my final months at Yale had paid off. I was only missing a year's worth of pre-vet credits, which I could start that spring at the local community college. In the meantime, I'd earn my keep doing my parents' admin. There was a job at the local Kroger, too, that I applied for; something about bagging groceries for a few months sounded more soothing than I could have previously imagined.

I'd be busy. But then, I've always been busy.

I've been lucky that way.

Despite her earlier horror at imagining me as a vet, Mom was elated that I was leaving New York; Dad was calmly accepting. Andra was pissed until she realized her father, proud of her newly emergent *work ethic,* had changed the terms of her trust and she'd have access to it on her twenty-third birthday, that coming January. Then she turned gently stoic.

I cleaned out my closet, making piles of what to sell and what to keep. Except for those goddamned shoes; I walked out of the apartment in my New Balance, Manolos in hand, and dropped them in the nearest trash can. Ten minutes later I realized that it was a stupidly cinematic gesture; they'd be worth at least two hundred on the resale market.

But by the time I went back downstairs, they were already gone.

Everywhere, loose ends were being woven into the tapestry of my life. But I couldn't leave just yet.

I APPLIED TO ADOPT Bee and was approved. That was the good part. But I had to say goodbye to Luke, which was much harder.

We met at a Park Slope café on the corner of two brownstone streets on my last Thursday afternoon in the city. His suggestion, near the construction site where he'd been working. I hadn't been to Park Slope since coming to the city; now, I probably never would again. It was so much more polished than the other parts of Brooklyn I'd seen. The smug married forty-somethings to our falling-apart-at-the-seams twenties. I was both relieved and sad that I'd never age into it. What would that life have been like?

He was waiting outside for me when I arrived. We kissed, my heart dropping in preemptive guilt, and ordered lattes at the counter. And then we sat outside on the sidewalk together.

"I'm leaving the city," I said without preamble. "There's a whole story, but basically, I realized you were right. I need a new job, and new friends, and I'm not going to find them here. It's time for me to go."

"Well, you should do whatever you think is right," he said, after a long, painful silence. "It's not like we're married or anything."

And of course it wasn't until he said it that I even imagined it: what it would be like to be married to him. Not the wedding day—weddings always sounded like hell to me. But everything that came afterward: how he would sleep hot and I'd always be cold; him so cavalier about his next paycheck and me always worried about the next unexpected bill to pop into my inbox; about the trips to meet each other's families and the family we'd make ourselves.

Not a wedding but a marriage.

I saw it, and I lost it, both at the same time.

"No," I said slowly. "We're not married."

I knew he was hurt, otherwise he wouldn't have said it. I knew, too, that it was ridiculous to even consider doing long-distance; we'd been on two dates and slept together once.

So he was hurt, and I was hurt, and there wasn't any solution for us except to be hurt together, in that moment, however long it lasted.

We made civil small talk until the light started to fade, sitting in our too-thin jackets in the cold and the dark, drinking the dregs of coffee we were pretending still tasted good. Finally, it was time for him to go to a bartending job.

"Well." He stood, his height still catching me by surprise—and already he was turning into a story I was telling myself, already he belonged to the past. "Goodbye, Rosie Macalister." He crouched down to the dog's height. "Goodbye, Bee."

It was only in those last two words that I heard the tightness in his voice. Only as he straightened that I saw tears in his eyes.

And the urgency rose in me and I wanted to say something, anything, that would fix what I'd just done. *If you could—if we could—maybe, possibly, probably—could I love you?*

But he was already walking away.

WITH MY HELP, Tory had punished Grayson. And while I wasn't entirely proud of my role in the events of that fall, I felt more at peace than I had since Annelise's death. The waves of guilt grew farther and farther apart; eventually, I knew, they'd leave me altogether.

But the question that haunted me: What was Tory going to do to Cress?

Cress, the match and the candle. The horse girl and the heiress. The goofball and the murderer. My best friend and someone I'd never truly known.

Should I warn her or deliver her? Tell her to get out of the city for a bit, or find Tory somehow and whisper *aspirin allergy?*

But days passed, and then weeks. And then I was leaving for Thanksgiving, leaving for good, and I settled on: to say goodbye.

In the weeks since Grayson's death, the tabloids had made a banquet of the Tates. First it was "Investigations into Billionaire's Mysterious Death." Once they brought witnesses into it, "Too Tough at the Top? Tate in a 'Funk' Before Death, Say Sailors," with its implications of suicide, started to fuel the rumor mill. Nobody outside the inner circle knew the details of his death yet, otherwise it might have strained credulity—how do you bash in your *own* head? But when someone in the coronor's office inevitably leaked the grisly truth, it became "Murder at Sea? Police Suspect Foul Play," which tightened my chest. I was only able to breathe again when that turned to "Staff Say Tate Sailed Solo," confirming he'd been alone. Confirming that there were no unknown fingerprints on the boat, no signs of struggle.

It all tapered out anyway, after the autopsy, as they discovered the unusually high levels of Dramamine in his system. Grayson was wearing a patch *and* had taken a few pills; there was an empty box of the stuff on the passenger seat of his car, and it can make you loopy; it sure can make you loopy. "Hedge Fund King's Accidental Overdose Led to Fatal Fall" didn't last as long as the earlier, more lurid headlines, but it was where they finally petered out.

I never even got pulled in for questioning.

And then the papers turned to Cress. Not the *Post,* at first—but eventually, even Murdoch couldn't help but admit that she was making news. Her father's fraud wouldn't have been news, but Cress's exit from a town car sans underwear definitely was.

There were pictures of her on the page of every celebrity blog: snorting blow with some rock star I'd never heard of; stumbling down the street, one arm around Lindsay Lohan, a half-empty tequila bottle in the other; vomiting into the gutter as Paris Hilton held her hair.

She wasn't picking up my calls, and I didn't know why. Because of grief? Because she was too busy with her new friends? Because Grayson had confronted her with my accusation that day, somewhere between the office and the marina? Each scenario would require different handling—a text, a personal visit, radio silence.

Finally, I pulled the rip cord.

Leaving NYC next week, moving back home. Lunch?

And there she was.

Friday 1pm Bergdorf.

There was no question mark. She knew I'd come when called. And I would. One last time.

That morning, I went to a new hairdresser in the Village who specialized in curly hair. It was amazing to see that my frizz could be defined, could be turned into ringlets. That it had always been beautiful, if only I hadn't spent so long trying to make it into something else.

I showed up in the dress I'd worn the day Grayson died. Cress was wearing a black cashmere turtleneck dress, stark against the pale blue and gold restaurant. Vintage, her mother's or her grandmother's, from the pilling below the arms. No makeup except for last night's smudged under her eyes.

"You look good," she said. "More like yourself."

"You, too," I said. But it was rote.

She snorted.

"I was thinking of shaving one side of my head," I said.

"Going full hipster? You've been in Brooklyn too long. Wouldn't suit you. Besides, the curls would just cover it up, and you'd lose the sharp edge. Nah," she said, pulling one of my ringlets out straight toward her and letting it boing back up. "That's the Rosie hair. Always should be."

We drank for a minute in silence.

"You weren't at the funeral," she said dully. "Neither was Andra."

"No," I said. I meant to leave it there, but she looked at me with those dark-shadowed eyes. "The crowds . . ." I said.

"Oh. Yeah. I can't remember if I told Mom to, you know. Put you guys on the list."

I nodded.

"I'm sorry," she said, squinting at me, fighting back tears.

I couldn't bring myself to tell her I hadn't even tried to go. There was still something in me that loved her so much, but there was also something in me that never could again.

"How are the horses?" I asked.

She tossed back her hair, wiping her eyes so quickly it might never have happened.

"Fuck if I know," she said, taking another drink. "Bambi's upstate, Thumper's out in Cali. The rest I sold to some sheikh."

"Are you . . . getting a new string?" I wouldn't have blamed her, after the season she'd had.

She rolled her eyes, setting her champagne flute down with a wobble. "I'm getting a new *life*. I'm no good as a rider, Rosie. But I bet you knew that all along."

"You're a wonderful rider," I said.

"No," she said, and it wasn't until she held her finger up at me, trembling slightly, that I realized just how drunk she was. She was trying to stare at it instead of me, but couldn't seem to fix her eyes on the single point. "No. I'm a rich rider. And there's a world of fucking difference."

"This is a difficult time," I said helplessly as she picked up the dripping bottle from the bucket. "You're not seeing things clearly. Think back to Yale. Think about all the wins you had. For fuck's sake. You were good, Cress. You *are* good."

"I'm a good *amateur*," she said, pouring her glass until it nearly overflowed on the table, leaving me the dregs. "And I was a good amateur with the best horses in the world. You know what that makes me as a professional? Mediocre. At best."

I thought of her puppyish prancing. Her match-like fire.

"No," I said. "Cress. Just—no."

"Yes, Rosie. Just yes," she said, mimicking my tone. "Fuck! Without Dad's money, I never would have even made the Yale team in the first place. I never would have even gotten into Yale in the first place if he hadn't gone there, if he hadn't made me into some kind of a rider. And I think I've always known that. And I also know Annelise didn't take my money," she cried, holding her hands out, one with a dripping flute, the other with the empty bottle. "It was obviously Lila! And even if she did take my money, fuck—Annelise was my dirty little secret of a sister, she'd have fucking deserved it, who the fuck—"

"It *was* Lila," I said, sharply. "But how did you know . . ." I stopped. Because, of course, I wasn't supposed to know that Annelise was her sister, either.

Cress gestured at the waiter for another bottle, which came unnaturally quickly. "Annelise. Now, *she* got Daddy's talent. Can you imagine her on one of my horses? Not Thumper," she added quickly. And so, of course, the only thing I could think about was Annelise on Thumper. Of her wild grace as the pin dug deeper and deeper into his beautiful downy flesh—

She caught the expression on my face.

"See? By comparison, I'm mediocre," Cress said. "Not even. And morally?" She blew out her lips, sticking her thumb down.

"I mean. You can't do anything about that now. But you could try to make things right with the people who are left."

"Oh, *fuck* you," she said, but there was no fire in it.

"You don't have to go to the police or anything, but you could—"

And she looked at me with such contempt, it was almost senior year again.

"Well, for fuck's sake, Cressida. That could have been you. Switch two little eggs around, four days apart, and Annelise *would* have been you. There are worse things than what you've been left with, you know. And self-pity isn't your look."

We stared at each other.

"So what am I supposed to do?"

"I don't know, Cress, it's your goddamn life," I said. "Reach out to Annelise's mom and sister. Who could have been *your* sister, by the way, so incredibly easily."

"That girl Tory?"

"Yeah," I said, my heart starting an uneven, thunderous purr in my throat.

"She'd been texting me for, like, months and months. Saying that Annelise was my sister, too. And I told her to go fuck herself."

She seemed to have forgotten that Tory had texted me as well. Small blessings.

"But what was I supposed to do? Shit like that—I mean, not *that*, exactly, but shit like it—my dad gets it. Got it. All the fucking time. But then his will came out and a whole bunch of money ends up going to her *estate*, of all things."

I startled. "Annelise was . . . named in the will?"

"No, it just listed a bunch of stuff that went to Mom and a bunch of stuff for the Foundation and then just: *The remainder of my assets to be divided evenly among my children or their estates, should they predecease me.* And the lawyer had a copy of her birth certificate, so it's all divided up *three* ways now instead of *two*, and she's not even here to *get* it—the estate of Annie May fucking Robinson gets it. Andra was *right*, you know."

Among my children or their estates.

Had Grayson tried to redeem himself in the end? Or was it just legalese, a simple provision for future offspring he and Anthea might have had?

Could I ever know?

"She was *right*," Cress repeated fervently.

"Sorry. Who was right about what?"

"Andra. Her name was never Annelise."

"Yeah," I said. "I know."

But it had been. Once.

Cress stared into her champagne.

"I just . . . I don't know what to do anymore," she said. "I always did what Dad wanted and everything turned out okay. But even with him backing me up, I wasn't that good. What am I supposed to do without him? Fuck. Sometimes I wish I *had* been born Annelise."

I stared at her.

"Cress, Annelise died. You killed her."

She stared back, dead-eyed.

"But at least I would have been something. On my own. Without . . ." she trailed off. "How did it even *happen*?" And she squinted her eyes closed. "He was the perfect sailor. The perfect everything. *Watch the boom, out of the way of the boom.* All the time, he said it. And then just a little too much medicine and it all goes down the drain? *Watch the boom.* He took such good care of us—" And her voice broke, and she stopped.

And it clicked.

Even if Tory was gone for good, she had already done her damage to Cressida.

It was the same thing that had been done to Annelise. To Tory herself.

She'd made her father disappear.

"Cress, you can literally do whatever the fuck you want. Breed race-horses. Get a job at Tate. Start a charity. I don't know. I've never not wanted something, so I can't relate. I'm sure that deep down, you could find something to care about."

"What do you want?" she asked, and she seemed genuinely curious.

I inhaled. "I'm going to take the pre-reqs to go to vet school."

She cocked her head. "But where are you going to get the money for that?" And for a moment, I was absurdly, profoundly touched that she'd even think of such a thing.

"Scholarships. Loans. It's not ideal. I mean, it'll run me, like, three hundred grand if I go somewhere great like Cornell. But maybe I don't need great, you know? Illinois would be, like, a third of that."

She looked at me with haunted, sagging eyes.

"So few people are good enough. At anything. If you can do *great,* you should always do great."

Spoken by a woman whose shoe collection alone would cover a year at any school in the world, and then some.

The thing is, I don't know what kind of life I would have wanted for Cressida, if I'd been able to design it myself. A grunt job? Nobody deserved that. A Kubla Khan pleasure dome of an existence, jetting off around the world to visit the Chanel boutiques in every major city? Nobody deserved that, either. The best you could hope for someone like her was that she'd find her talent and make the most of it, share her vocation with the world. Barring that—well, maybe Anthea didn't have it so wrong, after all. Give away as much as you could, as elaborately as you could. Change something. Or, at the very least, *do* something.

I could not believe that I pitied her.

But I did.

And I also never wanted to see her again.

WE LEFT WITHOUT even eating lunch, though I think the three bottles of champagne and 25 percent tip Cress left had appeased the waiter somewhat. If I hadn't been at least a little tipsy, I never would have al-lowed her to drag me to look at the bags. I remembered all too well what a fucking bummer it was, standing in the background while your rich friends shopped.

I watched her feel up, try on, play with about six different bags before I hit my limit. I just turned and started toward the escalator.

"Cress, I'm out."

And for the first time in my life, I heard Cress's feet running after me. Heels on marble floors, trying to catch up.

We exited into the chill November afternoon, Cress with such relief on her face after the escalator that I really think she'd been about to vomit. I was so busy plotting the logistics of getting home without an excessive good-bye that I didn't even hear the alarm that sounded when we stepped outside, or notice the security guy come up to us.

"Miss," he said to Cressida. "May I look inside your bag, please?"

She tried to stare up at him but had a hard time holding his gaze.

"You most certainly may *not*," she said, imitating his tone.

"Miss, I'm afraid I'm going to have to insist—"

"Do you even know?" she cried, waving her purse. "Do you even know who my father is? He's Grayson Tate. *Grayson Tate*. He has more money than everyone you've ever met all put together, and I swear to fuck, if I wanted one of the janky little bags in your janky little store, all I'd have to do is pull out this"—she rummaged around the purse, I assume for her Amex Black, but didn't find it—"and I could buy every single one of them."

The guard looked at me. Helpless.

I shrugged.

"She really is rich," I said.

Cress gestured at me, eyebrows raised. "See?"

"I'm sorry," I said softly. "It's just, her father just died, and we had a little too much at lunch—but really, she could buy anything in the store. She wouldn't have to steal."

His eyes went back and forth between us.

Finally, he gave a sharp nod and went back inside.

Cressida grabbed my arm and yanked me across the street, faster and faster until we were standing at the doorway to the Pierre.

She held out the quilted gray purse to me. Its silver chain dangled between us, swinging and jingling like church bells.

"Cress, *what*."

She flared her eyes. "Open it!" she said.

Inside, there was nothing but a price tag: $4800.

I stared at her.

"Oops!" she cried, and burst into giggles.

"You didn't."

"I didn't on *purpose*." Her eyes were huge now. She pulled an Asprey wallet out of her jacket pocket and wagged it at me. "I just forgot that I didn't bring a purse. I didn't even remember until I opened up the bag to look for my card, and by then, well. I mean, what was I going to do?"

Apologize. Hand it over. Get fingerprinted. Confess to everything?

"Well, you were definitely wrong about one thing," I said. "You have a major talent. It's just for shoplifting, that's all."

And her face cracked into a smile. A Cress smile, an old-days smile.

She held out the bag to me.

"Want it?"

We should have taken it back. I still lived in a society of rules, and Cress should have been living in one, and in no way, in no world, was that bag rightfully ours.

Not according to the rules.

But for fuck's sake.

It was Bergdorf Goodman.

It was Cressida Tate.

Having the bag or not having the bag made absolutely zero difference to either one of them.

"Sure," I said, slipping it over my shoulder. It was heavier than it looked, the leather butter soft against my hands.

Nobody who held that bag would have given it back.

It was the first—and last—present Cressida Tate ever gave me.

Maybe.

BECAUSE THE NEXT DAY, my final day in New York, I withdrew a hundred bucks from an ATM before picking up my rental car. And there, on the receipt, was my outstanding balance:

$279,850.

I ran inside the bank to check with a teller. Went back home and pulled it up on my computer, one of the last things I still had to pack. But it was there. Free and clear. A transfer from some jumbled letter-and-number-named corporation for $275,000.

Was Cress starting her philanthropic streak? Was I her first official charity case?

Did I want to be?

But the Tates had gotten me this far and back again; and I wasn't too proud to take it. Pride is such a fallible compass, after all.

Or, it slowly dawned on me, as Bee and I pulled onto the West Side Highway, as I was about to leave New York behind for good, it might have been someone else. It could have been Tory. But the sequence of events that would have had to happen—Annelise's estate receiving the inheritance and their mother, I assumed, getting it; then giving all of that money to her elder daughter, the daughter unrelated to the man himself; the daughter deciding to send a chunk of it to a cowardly stranger she'd once spent two hours on a park bench with . . .

Occam's razor. It didn't add up.

It had to be Cressida. Thirty seconds on her computer—or one call to her money manager—and it'd have been done. After all, someone at Tate still had my banking information—it was only a few weeks ago that my final paycheck had been deposited.

The simple solution is always the most likely.

Honestly, though? That didn't totally add up either. But it was New York, and nothing had ever added up there for me. Value, worth, quality, merit: they were imaginary concepts. Belief systems, as my lauded professor had said all those years ago at Yale. Belief systems that we've grown up with, that we've studied, that are now indelibly in our blood and nerves and a million electric impulses zinging through our fallible brains.

I no longer wanted to believe.

But a part of me, a very small part, still did.

So there it is: the real reason I left New York.

Epilogue
THE WHEEL OF FORTUNE

The Wheel of Fortune tells you that huge, karmic changes are happening. They can be good or bad, amazing or painful; they can be anything, because the Wheel of Fortune is destiny itself. If things are up, they'll eventually turn down. Things are backward, they'll eventually move forward again. And this card tells you when it's happening, but it leaves the interpretation up to you. You know, all the cards do, really. In one way or another.

They can't tell you everything will be perfect forever or that this is going to ruin your life, because that's just not how things work. Fortune sounds like a wonderful thing, but that's just because we've told ourselves fairy tales about it for so long. Fortune is nothing more and nothing less than the idea that there are some things in our lives—so much more than we'd like to believe—that are out of our control, no matter how hard we try.

And that's why you have to ask. You absolutely have to ask, but almost nobody ever does. Because they don't really want the answer.

That's not what the women down at the spa want. They want comfort, they want security, they want to know that the only changes that will ever come their way will be changes for the better. As though life could be just this crescendo to total bliss. As though it's like that for anyone.

Except you do want that. I can tell. And so, clear your mind. Make the mindscape horizontal, not vertical. Embrace any possible outcome, as long as it is the highest possible truth, for the highest possible good.

But, before you ask your question, you have to do it. You have to ask yourself.

Do you really want to know?

T HAT'S ALL. THAT'S ALMOST all. I don't like telling the rest, because what people became makes me sad.

We all went off the deep end in different ways. Yes, including me.

At least, that's what the other girls must have thought.

Lila lasted a few months in her PA job before quitting in what was allegedly a dramatic blowup. There were rumors that she was dating Leo himself, though nobody who told me that had ever heard it firsthand. Then she started acting, which she had a bit more luck with. Some bit parts on big shows, supporting roles in some independent movies. Andra told me that she'd gotten heavily into Scientology for a time, but this gradually got replaced by crystals and jade rollers and an *evangelical belief in wellness*, whatever that meant. She married a director of a big sci-fi show when she was twenty-eight and started a blog right after their first baby. She posted a few times a year and mostly used it to complain about their nanny. I use the past tense because she hasn't updated it since 2016. But I still check it every now and again.

Andra did well at the *Post*. She was hungry in a way I don't think any-one expected her to be. I certainly didn't. Her biggest break was when she pretended to be a Realtor and broke into Bernie Madoff's apartment, though she was caught before she found anything of use. It still made a great story. But journalism was no longer a career the way it was when we were growing up, and she was laid off in 2010. She followed the *Post* with a stint at Gawker, then Jezebel, then BuzzFeed. When her father died a few years ago, she joined the board of the Cooper Foundation; within a couple of months, she was chairwoman. I still hear from her from time to time, mostly when she wants to do something animal-related with their money. I don't know if she loves her life or hates it. With Andra, I never could tell.

I never heard from, or about, Tory again. But that made sense. How many famous grooms can you name?

And Cress. She spent a few years training abroad, after her father died, trying her hand at various disciplines: dressage in France, cross-country in England. I even heard she tried polo for a while in Argentina, but neither Ana nor Miguel ever ran into her. She finally married Blake in 2015. After

Columbia, he'd nepotismed his way into a consulting job, but since suc-
ceeding in that career actually takes talent, had failed to progress beyond
entry level. He then tried to run for some city position—comptroller, I
think—and lost in a landslide. He ended up working for a lobbying firm
somewhere downtown. Nothing like hiring a congressman's son to en-
sure your cause gets at least one vote.

I followed Tate Associates after the financial crash. They lost about
half the value of their holdings, which means that Cress likely did, too.
But there's a point at which that stops meaning anything. It's not like
she'd had $50,000 and lost $25,000. Half of a billion is still a fuck ton of
money.

I actually heard more about her horses than I did about her. Thumper
made it to the 2008 and 2012 Olympics. But in 2016, he fell over a water
jump and had to be put down. I felt like I owed it to him—to both of
them, to all of them—to keep watching as the vets came onto the screen,
but NBC cut to commercial.

I didn't see Cressida again for a long time. Andra told me that she and
Blake had moved into the Pierre apartment, that they'd had a daughter
and a son (what else would Cress have had but one of each, one of everything?). Still, I couldn't fathom how she spent her time. So many hours in
a day, so many days in a life: What was she doing?

I didn't know. I was upstate at Cornell, first for my pre-vet require-
ments and then for vet school; then I worked as a locum in the Hudson
Valley while I saved enough to set up my own practice. The smart thing
would have been to go home and join my parents with the ultimate goal
of taking over for them, but I couldn't do it. Couldn't face the rest of my
life back there. Anyway, Mom and Dad eventually sold the house—they
tried to sell the practice, too, but they couldn't have given it away—and
joined a small animal group in the western suburbs of Chicago. They're
doing okay, though I don't think they'll ever be able to fully retire. With
the little I'd managed to save, I bought a heavily mortgaged rural Victorian house with a wraparound porch in an area with only one seventy-
five-year-old vet for a hundred miles.

And then, as Annelise would say, my fortune took another twist: because there was Luke.

I ran into him at, of all things, a veterinary conference; of all places, in Illinois. But we had been like that from the beginning: if not fated, if not destined—then still tied together, somehow. As he'd have put it that night we first met, lucky. He was giving a presentation on a training program they'd started at the Animal Rescue Foundation, where he was working full-time. His specialty was dog training, which didn't surprise me; I'd just finished my DVM, which surprised him even less. He was still in the city, I was in the Hudson Valley. It took us all of two months of long-distance dating before he grim-facedly told me that he just couldn't do it anymore and I grim-facedly agreed.

I spent twelve hours sobbing into an ancient Bee's fur before I heard the strangest noise, and looked out the window to see him rolling an enormous suitcase down my gravel drive.

We were married the next spring.

Don't get me wrong. It's not always easy living with someone whose life goal is *curiosity* and whose occupation is *trying things* and *occasionally training dogs*. Sometimes, those early days in the city with him feel really fucking far away. And he still hates taking care of what he calls the *unfortunate necessities of living in twenty-first-century America*. His credit score nearly gave me a panic attack when I finally saw it.

But at the core, of course, are the deeper things. The slight hitch in his breath when I get back into bed after a late-night house call; his warm body wrapping around mine. There's never knowing how his wild plans will turn out; the joy in his still, quiet delight.

It's lush and green where we are. Most of my calls are small animals, but there's a fair number of horses. I ride when I can, though I haven't in some time, and I'm away too much to keep my own horses, even if I could afford them.

People avoided doctors as much as they could during the pandemic; vets suddenly seemed like a total luxury, dog trainers an absurd dream. We missed one mortgage payment, then two. And eventually, I was forced to make an appointment at the bank to talk about remortgaging the property last January. After five years, we—well, I (combining finances never appealed to me)—had some equity in the place, so it shouldn't have been a problem. But on the train into the city, where my branch was (I'd never transferred it after setting my accounts up there, that first year after college—why bother, when everything was online?), I couldn't shake that sick, stomach-sinking feeling I'd had back in college when I had to ask one of my friends to borrow a jacket, a purse, *twenty bucks until next Friday.*

IT WAS A WINDY mid-January day and I was waiting for my appointment, wandering around the Upper East Side, when I saw it: our college bathroom, perfectly recreated in the windows of La Perla. For a moment, my brain revolted against the bohemian grunge, so uncanny in the neighborhood's strange Stepfordness. I stood there staring at the display, like a child searching a pair of magazine pictures, trying to spot the differences.

On closer inspection, it was grunge lite, a sterilized iteration of the real thing. On closer inspection, it was our bathroom, minus the mildew on the shower curtain and the hair in the drain from five girls. But the tub, with its clawed feet on checkered tile—that was the same, minus the rust. The mirror, lit up around the edges like in an ingenue's dressing room—that was the same, minus the two bulbs that had burnt out midyear, which nobody had ever been motivated enough to replace. The lingerie hanging over the ceramic lip of the tub, strewn haphazardly over the edge of the door. That was exactly the same.

On closer inspection, it was uncanny.

Seeing those tiny, lace-trimmed thongs hanging in the bathroom to dry—all those years later, that same sense of astonishment swept over me like a riptide. As a twenty-two-year-old, I couldn't believe that people wore *lingerie* every day. Girls I knew wore lingerie *every day.* Not on a date, not to a job interview, but to class, to the library.

Underneath their clothes, they were princesses.

Trust me: that knowledge can change a person.

I hesitated to go in. I mean, I was on my way to grovel at the bank; I didn't have three hundred bucks to spend on a La Perla bra. My one and only *business casual* outfit wasn't good enough to shop here. Who isn't afraid of having their own personal *Pretty Woman* moment? The salesgirls would be sure to recognize my polyblend pants as Brooks Brothers from three seasons ago, by way of T.J. Maxx.

But then a middle-aged woman—a nobody, like me—wearing this huge duffle coat and tourist-approved L.L.Bean snow boots, walked right in.

If she could enter, so could I.

The heavy glass door was held open by a suited guard, and a rush of warm, perfumed air hit me, melting the frost of the city from my skin.

I approached a rack with lace bras on tiny hangers. The tags twisted and turned like a baby's mobile in the crosscurrents from the heating: $215, $260, $300.

And that was when I heard it.

"Rosie?"

Her voice like wind chimes, her voice like the wind itself.

But that window display had primed me. You don't see your college bathroom and then run into your college roommate in *the same store*. It just doesn't happen.

Synchronicity, Annelise whispered in my mind.

And it especially doesn't happen on a day when I was already thinking about Annelise.

But I whipped around, and there she was. The Empress.

Her mermaid hair, gold waves halfway down her back. The kind of hair you never see on women in their late thirties outside of Instagram, because who has the time? Wearing a white bouclé coat, Chanel's logo delicately engraved on its buttons. Forget Chanel; I've never even owned a *white* coat. Diamonds, I thought, in her ears, though all I could see was the twinkle of them in the lights. And the heels—I knew they'd have red soles even without seeing them, because it was her. It was Cressida Tate.

"Cress?" I said.

Her midnight-blue eyes widened. And then she was rushing across the store, as only Cress could rush, all long limbs and coltish grace even though we were too old for it now, we were too old and it wasn't fair.

She kissed my cheek, enveloping me in her familiar scent.

She smelled like orange blossoms. She smelled like spring. She no longer smelled like horses.

"How *are* you?" she asked, grabbing my arm in hers, shepherding me toward the door. We ended up there at the same moment as my fellow tourist, all three of us pushing through together; then, at the blaring of an alarm, the woman in the puffy coat stepped back just as we stepped forward.

She looked at the security guard, a tall Black guy in a suit, her eyes wide and guilty. Cress rolled her own eyes as the man took out a wand, scanning the poor lady, and pulled me by the crook of my arm until the New York winter rose up around us again, stinging our faces.

"Wait!" I cried, as she yanked me forward. I'd forgotten how tall she was; I felt like a Yorkie, trotting at her heels. But she didn't stop until we were around the corner.

Breathless, she stood there grinning at me, as a crow landed and clung to a bough just behind her.

"So, you're in the city now?" she said. "Where are you living? I can't believe you didn't call, Rosie—"

I held up my hands, my gaze catching on my ragged fingers. I work with my hands, and it shows. I yanked them back down. "No, I'm only in from upstate for a few hours! I would have . . ."

But she let me cut myself off without any help, without any reassurances. Without completing my sentence herself, the way she would have done, before senior year. Before everything changed.

"Don't worry about it. It's nice to see you, Rosie. After all these years."

My mouth was so dry in the cold; I was beginning to pulse sweat through my shirt, I could feel it.

"Cress," I said, and the thin arctic air carried my weak voice with ease. "I never did thank you—"

She flinched.

"The money," I said, searching her face, catching a tiny twitch of the muscles beneath her eyes. "Really, Cress. It got me this whole new life—"

She shook her head and her hair was alive in the wind; transforming her from a mermaid to a Medusa, covered in a mass of writhing snakes.

"Money?" she said, like she was repeating a word in a foreign language she'd never have considered studying. Farsi, maybe. Swahili.

"When I was leaving New York. The money you sent . . ."

"Oh my God. You think I sent you *money*?"

"Didn't you?"

"Why would I have sent you *money*?" she said, with a quick, sharp laugh. And then she reanimated, shoving her bag up her shoulder, sliding her hands in her pockets. "Well, it was good to see you, Rosie."

She turned to go.

And as she did, something pale and pink fluttered out of the folds of her ivory jacket. It floated to the ground with all the weight of a leaf.

For a moment, we were frozen in time. Her cheeks colored, her throat bobbed—I'm not sure if I bent down so that the thing wouldn't blow away or so that I wouldn't have to look at her anymore.

A pair of silk bikini briefs, security tag still attached.

By the time I stood up, though, she had already turned to leave.

"Cress!" I called. *$185.* "Cress, you dropped something—"

"No." She didn't look back, but her voice floated over the traffic. "I didn't."

And so I stood on the corner of Seventy-Eighth and Fifth, and I twisted the pristine silk through my ugly fingers, and I wondered how I could have gotten it all so wrong.

And there she was again.

Annelise.

Nobody ever asks the one right question. Not the fortune-tellers, not the querents.

But this time, too, I could hear my own voice: laughing, still not fully believing. Fourteen years younger.

Oh yeah? And what's that?

I watched Cressida's pale back getting smaller and smaller. After a moment, she wasn't there at all.

In my memory, Annelise smiles slyly.

Do you really want to know?

THAT WAS THE LAST TIME I saw Cress. That night, I rode the train back upstate with my new mortgage paperwork tucked firmly in my canvas tote, my breath coming easier and slower with each mile from Manhattan. The sun had set spectacularly, fading the scenery outside to black until all I could see out the window was my own reflection.

I arrived home, my dogs Benji and Henry crowding around me, begging for attention, to find a series of increasingly panicked messages from Michelle, a farmer who did some breeding on the side. Her mare Molly was going into foal early, could I come? Could I please come? She thought the foal was backward—or maybe it was breech—and I threw on my sweats and got in the car, dogs in the back. Molly was the sweetest thing, wide-eyed and cuddly, and Michelle'd been wanting to breed her for ages. The thought of the dystocia wiped everything from my mind but possibilities: Had I come back in time? Would I be strong enough to get the foal deeper into the uterus? Could I save them both? Could I save even one of them? And if not, could we get them to the nearest operating theater for a C-section before it was too late?

I was in time. But when I reached inside Molly, I couldn't feel a thing. It wasn't until I hit the cervix and felt a tail that I knew for sure: backward.

It took all of Michelle's farm workers to help hoist the hindquarters so I could reposition the foal. Pushing it deeper in, shifting the hind legs over the pelvis. I was gasping, panting for my life by the time two little legs and a tiny nose protruded. A filly—but not breathing.

In the corner where the dogs lay, watching the spectacle, Benji whimpered.

Hands shaking from the effort I'd just made, I grabbed some clean straw from a bale and rubbed it gently on the inside of her nostril. A second—then she twitched, coughing and sneezing.

Alive.

Heart rate, lungs, blood sample, bone check, colostrum check. Molly was in a state of calm ecstasy, nuzzling and licking the little girl delightedly from her position on the ground. We waited for the foal to stand, waited for her to start nursing. The scent of blood and fluids and sweat and hay and shit thick in the air; our breath visible in front of our faces. And that tiny baby horse. Those wobbly legs, those big eyes.

Without me, without the work I'd done, both Molly and her baby would have been dead. For a second in the barn, I could see the life in them, like steadily burning flames.

This, I thought as I went back to the car, as dawn cracked over the trees. Flesh and fur and bone, instinct and effort and love. This was what life was about. Not the cut of a skirt or the quality of some boots or some invented numbers on a screen. This, right here: my dogs panting in my ears, the cold air rushing around us from the windows I left open so they could stick their noses outside, and Luke waiting for all of us back home. This, back there: a mare and a foal, yanked unwilling into the world and now learning what it was all about with each second. Delicate and tender and loved.

Back home, I collapsed into bed beside my husband, filthy and exhausted. And whole.

Don't you dare glamorize veterinary work. In the years I was away from home, I was more guilty of that than anybody. The wide-eyed animals, their fluffy fur and soft mewls? They're a story we've all agreed to tell ourselves about what this job actually is. I mean, they're not imaginary—but they're not the work. It's not about cuddling puppies and kittens. Mostly, it's about watching them suffer. Mostly, it's about trying to fix their pain. Mostly, it's dirty and scary and hard.

When you're lucky, you can do it. Many days, you can't.

The fight, though? It's the only thing that has value in this world. That much I know.

I finally know it for sure.

But then again, I've been lucky.

Have you?

ACKNOWLEDGMENTS

As per usual, this book came about through my magpie-like tendency to gather settings, activities, and objects from my life and recast them into a new story. However, that doesn't mean that any parts of it reflect my own experiences in any literal sense. So, to begin with: I had the absolute privilege of being part of the Equestrian team at Brown, and my first thanks have to go to them. They were nothing in the *slightest* like the team described here. My time on EQ was filled with hard-working, dedicated riders who truly loved both the sport and the animals, and who supported me in every possible way. There were too many wonderful people to name here, just a few of whom are the fabulous Kim (no surprise!); Grace and Courtney; our wonderful team mom, Marcia; and our absolutely superb coach, Michaela, who is the hardest-working person I've ever met and the polar opposite of the negligent Shannon in every single way. I am so grateful for all of the wonderful memories, both in the barn and outside of it.

I wrote this book during a very hard year, and it never would have been finished without my amazing sister. Thank you so much, Liana Kapelke-Dale, for coming to Paris and taking over logistics of daily life so that I could finish this! You are a wonder and I will forever be so grateful that you are in my world.

Thank you so much to Nafkote Tamirat and Nina-Marie Gardner, two wonderful Yale alums who helped me pierce through my own college-tour dream image/*Gilmore Girls*–inspired reverie to get the details of that school down more accurately. Any changes that deviate from reality have been made for artistic effect and are entirely on me.

I am incredibly grateful for the keen editorial eye of Sarah Cantin, who shepherded this book from outline to final draft with her characteristic grace and genius, with the help of the great Drue VanDuker. I can't thank the people at St. Martin's Press enough for their hard work and passion in making this book come to life. I am once again so lucky to have Katie Bassel in publicity to help *The Fortune Seller* find its audience, as well as the amazing talents of Amelia Beckerman, Brant Janeway, and Austin Adams in marketing. Meanwhile, Sue Walsh's design and Ervin Serrano's cover so beautifully encapsulate my vision of the book. Sara Thwaite brought such skills to the copyedit—skills I lack myself and am incredibly grateful for! My deep gratitude, as well, to managing editor Lizz Blaise, production editor Ross Plotkin, and production manager Adriana Coada.

A million thanks to Sarah Phair, whose unparalleled combination of intelligence and support is matched by her charm and wit. It is so rare to find a literary soul mate, and I am so very glad you are one of mine!

Thank you, now and always, to DWG for providing such a wonderful and warm literary community: Albert Alla, Peter-Adrian Altini, Amanda Dennis, Nina-Marie Gardner, Heather Hartley, Rafael Herrero, Matt Jones, Corrine LaBalme, Samuel Leader, Fedia Lennon, Spencer Matheson, Reine Arcache Melvin, Dina Nayeri, Chris Newens, Helen Cusack O'Keefe, Tasha Ong, Alberto Rigettini, Jonathan Schiffman, and Nafkote Tamirat. To have such great writers who are also great critics and great people in my life? A true honor.

Many thanks to Daniel Goldin at the Boswell Book Company in Milwaukee, Pamela Klinger-Horn of Valley Books in Minnesota, and Iasmina of Bill & Rosa's Book Room in Paris, for their incredible support of my writing and the amazing events they've thrown to help share it. And thank you so much to the phenomenal writers Julia Fine, Avery Carpenter Forrey, Jillian Medoff, and Genevieve Wheeler for their early support of this book in particular.

A million thanks to my family: Steve Kapelke, Kathleen Dale, Liana Kapelke-Dale (again and always!), Jessi LeClair, Dave LeClair, Alden and Alex LeClair, Phil Kapelke, Joan Cushing, Paul Cushing, Tom and Kevin

Cushing. Huge thanks to Athena Arbes, Charles Coustille, Sarah Dosmann (and all the Dosmanns!), Frances Leach, Ben Veater-Fuchs, and Genevieve Wheeler (again!) for their incredible support. And, as always, all the gratitude and love in the world for Jess, who has been at my side since the beginning.